P9-EAO-457

LUCY & MICKEY

LUCY &
MICKEY

RED JORDAN AROBATEAU

Lucy & Mickey
Copyright © 1991, 1995 by Red Jordan Arobateau
All Rights Reserved

No part of this book may be reproduced, stored in a retrieval system,
or transmitted in any form, by any means, including mechanical,
electronic, photocopying, recording or otherwise, without prior
written permission of the publishers.

First HARD CANDY Edition 1995

First Printing July 1995

ISBN 1-56333-311-2

Cover Photograph © 1995 Robert Chouraqui

Cover Design by Dayna Navaro

Manufactured in the United States of America
Published by Masquerade Books, Inc.
801 Second Avenue
New York, N.Y. 10017

"There's a place for us.
A time and place for us.
Hold my hand and we're halfway there.
Hold my hand and I'll take you there.
Some how, some day, somewhere!"

—S. Sondheim
West Side Story

CHAPTER ONE

The way Lucy and Mickey met was at a freakshow.

It was Chicago, Illinois at the turn of the decade, 1959. Mickey was 18. She stood on the windy corner of Clark & Division streets. Dressed like a man. Short. White skin. Black thick wavy hair. Handsome.

No jobs had worked out, and money was bad. Wondered when the tears would come off from under her eyelids. Wished she could shed the skeleton of hunger, peel it up off her lips and eyes and tear it out of her soul permanent. Hunger made her stomach flat. Patted her belly—"it's flat, like a man's." Stood out there like a match waiting to be struck.

She really didn't know where to go at this point. Rent in her small room was paid for less than a day & still no promise of legitimate work.

Because she was young & desperate was why she was panhandling & looking. Been to 30 places to apply for work. Didn't know what to do. Couldn't get a job dressed so masculine in this age of the fifties; & so gay. She couldn't get a job with no prior job experience & a jail record. Mickey was desperate.

A car sails by & she thinks she hears a voice. Female. Looks up; a minute later, here comes this car again—blue & white with big fins, and it pulls up, just up the street ahead of her and a voice calls out: "HONEY, COME HERE! I WANNA TALK TO YOU!" A female voice. Mickey turns to look; a woman in the backseat beckons from the car, then sticks her whole head and upper torso out the window and waves frantically at her.

The actual intersection of Clark & Division at the time was a notorious hustling corner, a fact documented in police reports. Mickey had been traveling down streets thru what would become Old Town, to Clark Street, a general vicinity which is a semi-gay, semi-hustling, semi-artist area. Mickey looks enough like a man—a small one—nobody messes with her. Problem is, she is small; some can read her—in the language of her sisters, the Drag Queens, that is to see thru the drag & male persona to the biological female underneath. Mickey never was sure if she was passing or not. And this is the problem why she can't get a job—in addition to being unskilled.

And suddenly there's this long white & blue car, fins in back, smooth metal skin, expanse of chrome that goes on for miles from front to back.

Mickey is drawn to the car by the sight of this woman hanging out of its window, waving. There was two big men in the front seat and some unidentifiable people in back as well.

So Mickey walked toward them, within a scene of sparse green foliage, trees dotting the curb, montage against the cement; buildings of huge steel & concrete—metal cubes and geometric shapes in the distance & decrepit tenement flats here with nightclubs below; all mingling into a blur.

The woman was big, full bodied in satin showgirl clothes; red mouth, big hair—beehived & teased up bouffant from many hours at a beauty parlor—image of a prostitute; white milk-colored skin, with a few lines of age.

"Honey, my name's Lenore! You're a butch broad, ain't yuh? How would you like to come with us? We're having a party! There's money in it for you.... Us, me and this girl here—" And the hooker gestured at a redhead woman nestling back into the interior of the car.

"Go with you?" Mickey asked. "All of you?" Looking up at the men in the front seat, and then back at Lenore, and there was yet another man, old, in the backseat.

"YEAH, ME!" Hooker said wearily. "Me, and them and her. Us!" Mickey just looked at her.

"I'm OK! I know Lill down at the 409 Club. Where the butch broads hang out—you know!" Impatient voice rising. "I know you kids from the 409—that's where all you gals hang out, ain't it?" Mickey's cool white face, close, stared back at her.

"I'm OK! I know Lill! I'm up at the Twilight always! I know all the guys and gals up there—all the *gays*." Hooker said the word uncomfortably. She spoke in despair, red mouth mouthing appeals to the butch.

Now the Twilight was a transvestite show club catering to johns. Prostitution. Quasi-gay bar of the very dirty sort.

"Lill! You know Lill, don't you? Ask her, she knows I'm OK—we do this all the time. She gets butch broads for me.... The guys like to see that."

"Tell her we're OK joes." One spoke, gruff, from the front seat.

Looking inside into the back seat there was an old man, wrinkled, hat on his head, shirt, no jacket, & beyond him, a redhead female, cute, sunk back into the upholstery.

Lenore was in her 40s, very straight and the redhead woman, straight, considerably younger, 22 or so.

For just an instant, the redhead woman opened her eyes, looks across the old man who's sitting; past the hooker who's jumping up and down, animated—casts a long look at Mickey. Then she slips back down into her dreaminess.

Hooker with ample bust, wiglike blond hair, or was it hair, sprayed & garish.

"Honey, listen, come here." She drew Mickey closer with a beckoning finger; "It's a party see, listen! All you have to do...is let this girl here... Or me, give you some head. Just for the boys here, you know. You'll get paid $20."

"Hell, no!" Mickey snarled, backing away from the window.

"They won't touch you!" Lenore says. "It's just a *show*—a party! It's *me* they want. *I'm* taking care of business—just you and her give 'em a good show." And her mouth twists peevishly.

"I ain't droppin' my drawers." Her boxer shorts & T-shirt under man trousers & a shirt—in defiance of the Vice Code of that day, for which she could be arrested. Hard muscles flex in her arms as she jitters on the pavement & Lenore sticks her whole upper torso out the car window again, hand grabbing at Mickey, waving a green $5 bill; she's insistent.

"Jeeze Honey! Here's $5—take it! Just to show I'm seri-ous! It's from me. You'll get the rest the minute we get up there! I'll pay you myself—$20 *more;* it'll be over in a few minutes! YOU DON'T HAVE TO DO NOTHING I'M TELLING YOU! You can just pretend to do it!" she whispers in low tone.

The butch had the $5 in her shirt pocket. Rolled up shirt-sleeves. She looked at Lenore. A man in the front turned back and looked directly at her; he had black hair, swarthy; big face. Huge shoulders visible over the seat. Mickey turned and looked into the john's eyes only a second. Dull, lustful & in them was like looking into the pit of hell. The burning hell of her desperation for money & the john's ability to pay.

And the beefy john looked at her, his eyes seeing her not as a human being, but an object. A freak.

"You don't have to *do* nothing. You're lucky," the hooker whispered. "Watcha complaining about!"

The butch was pulling away. "Honey, wait a minute!" Lenore grabbed Mickey's shirtsleeve, and her touch felt good. "Honey, look, *we'll* take care of *them.*" Pointing at herself and the redhead who is slouched up in the corner; and Mickey looks at this other straight woman.

Day whizzed by on Clark & Division. Blue clouds in white heavens. And the attention from this hooker—leaving her perfumed scent on Mickey's arm....

"Don't she want to make some money?" a gruff voice inquired.

The hooker was exasperated. Had the car door open and wouldn't let go of the butch's hand. "HONEY!" And the $5 bill is sticking out of Mickey's shirt pocket, Lenore shoves it down deeper with sharp red fingernails.

Squeezes Mickey's hand, & turns to the redhead in tore-ador pants and a blouse and high-heel sandals. "TALK to her, Lucy!" Whore nudges the redhead in the ribs. "Tell her it's gonna be OK!"

"Trust us," says a man in front.

And Mickey's handing the five back, and Lenore's frantic. "It's no funny business! Nobody's gonna touch you but her! LUCY! Tell her how good you're gonna make her feel!"

Old man in the back, with the hat on, just sat there like he was dead. And Mickey looked inside the cool interior of the car again, and the redhead looked sweet.

"*SHE'S GONNA DO IT TO YUH, BABY! THE WAY YOU LIKE IT! SHE'S GONNA MAKE YUH FEEL GREAT!* She sucks butch broads off all the time, don't yuh, Lucy!" Lenore winked at the woman. The redhead didn't say nothing.

"Girlie, we ain't gonna do nothing to you but watch." A man says in front. "Ask Lenore, we been doing this show thing for years. Ain't we Al! Ha ha." He laughed.

"NOT THAT MANY YEARS!" The whore snapped back. They would put no more lines of age on her than were necessary.

Mickey was suspicious. Torn between caution, and desperately needing to earn money. And desire to follow the women.

"Get in the car, will yuh?" Man looks around. "There's a lot of heat out here."

Tired, Lenore ran down the scene again. Like a machine she'd said it so many times already. "You'll forget we're even there, she's gonna suck you off so good. If you want to do anything else to her, it'll be even better, and you get *paid* for it!" And the hookers pulling her by the lapels of her shirt.

Now in the sex act, Mickey was supposed to let this redhead woman pull down her trousers and suck her cunt—or pretend to suck. Simulate this if they can get away with it. The woman has to take off her clothes and show her tits & dance for the johns & then Mickey stands above the woman getting oral sex, and moaning and hollering like there was no tomorrow.

Mickey refuses to take off her shirt anywhere. She has a binder on underneath to flatten her bust so she looks masculine. Says she ain't gonna take none of it off. Plus she wasn't going to cum for a bunch of stupid fucks.

"Then just pretend to!" the woman whispers in her ear with perfumed breath. "Lucy don't even have to touch you if you do it right!

"Holler and fake like yer doing it!" Lenore says.

"Just pretend to!"

Mickey dances on the curb in men's shoes. "I'm not doin' nothing! I'm not touching nobody! I'm not taking off my clothes!"

"Well, just drop your drawers around your knees for her—" Jabs at the redhead. "That's the show—you and her. Just stand there & let her do what you girls do and holler. Make a lot of noise like yer enjoying it!"

The whore runs her fingers thru Mickey's wavy black hair. Touch thrills the butch. Sun shines down. The $5 bill is sticking in her shirt pocket where Lenore's manicured fingers have put it back.

Mickey thinks about the $20. She's hungry & her stomach hurts—rumbling. Feels the whore's fingers run thru her black hair & she sees these two females and they look good just to be next to...her keen eyes observing.

Also, to go along with it meant anger, involvement. 'All I have to do is let them stare at me—a fucking freak dressed like a man getting sucked off. With all these men it's dangerous.' But Lenore seemed to be in control.

Now this hooker looks so straight, she scares Mickey—even the bold & brave Mickey, who's been in jail and had sex with B-girls in New York, Jersey City, Miami, but not yet in Chi-town.

Now, secretly, Lenore herself didn't want to fake any sex scene with no woman. Didn't like dykes, couldn't stand Lill, and if one got too close to her, she'd slap her. By now, figured she'd get the redhead to do the dirty cuntlapping work.

"We won't bite," one john says in a deep voice. "Al here, he's harmless." Indicating the old man in back who sat, hat on his head. "All Al can do is suck it anyway.... Girlie, come on, be a sport, will youse?"

"She's gonna fuck her for free & the broad's complaining?" Other man said in a bass voice. Thick hairy arm over the backseat. "She don't have to do nuthin' but get a nut."

"Come on, girlie! Be a sport, get in!" And his hair was shaved so close in back of his head; showed white flesh wrinkled in rolls, dots of black hair whiskers; bullneck. Gruff baritone voice.

3 men in the car. 2 big guys in front; one in back, old.

Hot & stuffy. 6 feet across the interior space of the car. Mickey's eyes narrowed. "Who else is gonna be there?"

"Just us! Just us who you see here. 3 guys and 3 gals.... Whoops...I mean butch."

"Well, hell." Mickey ducked her head back out, into the sun.

Hands with hair on their fingers grip the wheel. Barrel chests, big heads; haircuts; tan skin from driving around in the sun all day.... Or maybe they had enough money to have gone around the world, both in bed and across the globe.

Traffic is whizzing by them, heat—the police. Going after some violator; blue lights flash & siren wails. Guys turn their heads to watch the police. "Let's go. Let's get out of the street. This ain't cool."

"The police have pictures of me! They're riding around with 'em on their dashboard!" Lenore whispered in frantic exasperation. "I ain't suppose to be out in the streets working! If the Vice goes by, it's good-bye, Lenore! Back to Cook County Jail! *Mickey! Darlin'*—that's yer name, *Mickey?* At least get in the back here, right next to me, so we can talk!" And she pats the seat next to her satined rump.

Man in front, his voice so deep it cracks & fluctuates bass to deeper bass, resonant from his chest; flexes his hairy arms. "She's a cold fish, too." Referring to the redhead. "Don't she talk?"

"DON'T WORRY ABOUT HER!" Hooker yells.

And all the butch's attention shot back to the buxom Lenore: large, curvaceous...whose touch she still felt...who had run her red-nailed fingers, brief, thru Mickey's hair.

Out in the sun, Mickey took one last look into the interior of the car. The women looked so good, she just wanted to be with them, even at the risk of having these men around. And because she needed money.

'They're her tricks...all I'm for is a show....'

And Mickey's tempted, thinks: 'This redhead is cute. It's her who's gonna go down on me, put her lips on me.... That's already set.... She can't say no. The problem is, in front of those dumb fucks.'

"JUST GET IN! For chrissake!" The whore tugs Mickey's arm.

So she got in.

And Mickey looks back and forth between her and the redhead, their red-painted toes in open-toed shoes; smells their perfume; and they're the first females she's been near since she arrived in this city & the woman said $20 more, and Mickey had had nothing to eat that day nor the day before but a can of corned-beef hash stolen off a supermarket shelf & the women looked so good to be near, so she had put one foot in the door & had climbed in; and the whore's smiling proudly like a fisherwoman reeling in a catch; pats the seat beside her & the butch sits down.

Now, just a moment before, Mickey'd been out there, dull, just looking at the street, wondering what to do next.

You could say she was drunk & went with them, but it wouldn't be true. Sober as a judge. Hadn't ate, much less afford a bottle.

The car bounces along Clark Street headed north, full of people; dips low. Bounces thru the hot, sunny day, buoyed up as if air were under the big fins in back, and the wheels were out of alignment, imperceptibly going side to side; fast.

Cigarette smoke flew out the window & radio played. & the hooker completely ignored the butch now, was glued to the front seat with the 2 johns, laughing in a low conversation. And the old man and these 2 other females in back say nothing. The old man said nothing because time had castrated him. And, underneath it all, both the women were afraid.

Summer day, bright & sunny. Summer day for the beach with suntan oil, sunshades & swimming; in a mass of pink people getting tan at Lake Michigan; with hot dogs & mustard, and Coca-Cola. But instead, they were on their way to turn a trick. For people who live in the underworld, or are forced to exist on its fringe, delving in illegality of sex trade, gambling, drugs & petty hustles, must work round the clock when opportunity knocks; like robots. Industrial workers, sex workers, freaks & madwomen of mid-century Amerika.

Mickey sat back, sunglasses on now, mouth pursed in a

tight line. Redhead curled into herself, legs in toreador pants, crossed.

A middle-age potbellied man spoke, gruff. "Get some life into these gals, will yuh? They act like they're going to a funeral."

Now Mickey was faint with hunger, & Lucy was high on drink she'd had before in that bar where she'd met Lenore.

"Get 'em a bottle, something. Stop in this store here!" Hooker said in a low voice. Then she turned to look at the butch beside her, and then the redhead, brightened her tone, & said, too loud, "We're stopping to get some cigarettes & a pint of scotch. Yuh gals want anything else?"

Hunger gnawed at Mickey's stomach. "Yeah, a candy bar." Came a growl from her solemn white face. She'd already taken the $5 bill and put it in her wallet.

When the guy came back with a bag, Lenore took it & handed the candy bar to Mickey, who wolfed it down.

Car sails off, air under big fins.

Now in front they were talking about old times. Lenore's squealing; the whore likes an audience, she was an exhibition-ist. She can't wait to brag about herself to her whore girlfriends. And Mickey thinks: 'I don't want nobody touching me....'

Brazen whore in big starched-out hair & red lipstick twists off the top of the scotch bottle. Words fly out of her mouth. "Whew, it's hot!" Fans herself with the empty bag. Two men up front make a short laugh, say something nasty; and the whore reaches over the seat and slaps his shoulder playfully. "That's not what I meant! It's a hot *day!*" Now secretly Lenore was very grateful for this freakshow that was about to transpire because she would be making easy money, quite a bit; & she and the two johns up front discuss what they are going to do, and Lenore turns to the old man, slaps his leg. "Wake up honey!" Old man just nods his head under his hat. Then Lenore elbows Mickey, and jabs the redhead. "Look alive, girlie!"

CHAPTER TWO

The building rose up, steel, chrome, into the sky; in a nice part of town.

Waited for the elevator in the lobby; 6 of them—a funny combination of different worlds overlapping for a brief & specific purpose. They went up.

A medium-size rental apartment belonging to one of the cronies; he took out the keys.

The whore was haughty.

"Now, this is a nice apartment," the whore said as the door opened. "And I'm a nice girl."

"It's John's. His wife's out of town." Man said gruffly, closing the door behind them.

"How long she been gone?"

The beefy man looked down at his wristwatch. The hooker burst out laughing until water came to her eyes.

"He can't do without." Other man says. "He gets it every night." Butch walked in beside them, short, tired; she heard this and was mad because she hadn't got a woman to lay for all the time she'd been in this new city.

Thick black hair, wavy thick little arms, white; scars of acne on her cheeks, dried. Dark eyebrows.

Mickey was the only lesbian among them. She looked around the spacious living room, finds an armchair, and sinks back into it, far out of the way.

& Mickey glowers, angry about life. So edge of her feelings is dull—like she don't care. Waiting for the whole trick to end, and she'd go. And then, out of one recessed corner of consciousness, unsuspecting, thru half-lowered gaze of her narrowed eyes came this person Lucy across the carpeted floor. Nondescript walls of the apartment provided a backdrop. Toreador pants, short halter top blouse, belly showing; on sandals that once had been gold & which elevated her to a height taller, picks up the bottle pours herself a drink; slow. 'She's straight. She probably hates gays too.' And Mickey knew, according to the script, she would soon be naked.

Now, the redhead slumped in the other armchair 10 feet across the room away from everybody. Tired, but knew she had to dance; prolonging the moment, having got a glass & took another drink.

And all Mickey's attention shot back at her, and the buxom hooker, curvaceous. Ignoring the johns. Large woman in her wig-hair who ran around enjoying making money, playacting, entertaining the tricks & setting the stage.

20' by 25' room. Pictures. Bedroom to one side.

Redhead girl surprised everybody, because it was sensual, as she removed her clothes, slow; naked from the waist up, big breasts, plays with herself, touches her nipples, eyes half-closed, full of drink, off in a separate world. Red lipstick. Begins to dance, holds up her tits to show everybody, turns around and pulls down her toreadors, dances around in satin panties; red hair sticks out, wobbles a bit; a little drunk; does a miscellaneous step of her own, then strips off her panties, spreads her legs bends over and wiggles her naked ass; then turns, sits on the carpet, opens her thighs and pulls back folds of her pussylips, shows cunt, snaps her legs shut, gets back up, sways to the music; and Mickey feels a slow excitement flood her body.

And Mickey sits there, pretending to be one of the johns herself, watching Lucy dance.

Then Lucy was back in her chair, naked, looking up at the ceiling; in any direction but at somebody.

Mickey drops her eyes to the floor, so she sees the hooker walk back and forth in open-back shoes showing her rounded heels & shapely ankles; toes with polish chipped.

Hooker had made them give their money right away.

Lenore had two tens and a five rolled up, hands it to Mickey. Mickey puts it all in the wallet in her back pocket, & sits back again, appraising the room like taking a long cold drink, tries to steel her nerves to get ready for this. T-shirt shows under her shirt at the neck. Had had her sleeves rolled up because of the hot Chicago climate, showing the little balled-up muscles of her arms; but inside here it is air conditioned, so she rolls them back down.

Lenore has the role of stage director. She came up to Mickey & gave her a limited amount of attention, saying; "Remember, talk nasty, call her a slut. Tell her, 'Suck me, slut!'—anything nasty! Tell her, 'Suck my juicy pussy, nasty bitch!' Now remember!" Lenore hisses. "Make it look good, it'll be easier for *me!* Get 'em ready so I can get it over with fast!" Then switched away, over to the redhead to coach her in her part.

Now, heavily lidded eyes began to focus on the woman. Earlier, the butch had not paid her too much attention, assuming Lucy to be a stupid man-liking whore. It had become apparent she was barely interacting with the tricks at all.

So Mickey saw Lucy, bored, distant sitting in a chair far away from the rest; not interested in the goings-on whatsoever.

Whore is very animated; it is all her show. "I arranged the whole thing." She boasts. "I found *her.*" Jabbed with a red fingernail. "Then I found *her.* Have another drink, Lucy! I never drink on the job myself." Lucy extended her glass out by a naked white arm. Mickey's drink sat on the coffee table, untouched. Later, when Lenore is putting some music on, back turned; the redhead takes Mickey's drink, too, & collapses back in the armchair, naked, full-figure. A sleepy expression flickers on her face; then it goes blank.

And the hooker comes out of the bedroom & music plays; and says to the johns, "I'm always good to my customers, see what I got you!"

A john moves the coffee table back. Men & Lenore sit on two sofas across the room, and Lucy kneels down in the middle of the carpet; legs, white, hunched under her, tits jugging; hair, red wisps; smiles at the butch, her mouth opens faintly, says, "Come on." And beckons.

And Mickey slowly gets up and walks over to this woman kneeling on the floor; & music grinds; hooker has got her hands on the first john, Mickey stands in her shirt and trousers, feels the woman's hands, gentle, tug her belt, pull down her zipper, feels hot flashes of desire; sees this woman's face, so sweet gazing up, looking at her; feels her trousers come down around her legs, she stands in boxer shorts.

A voice laughs, baritone: "See that? Same as you wear! Is it a man or a broad?" "Check their ID next time. Ha-ha!" And the redhead has got her face up in Mickey's sex.

"TAKE 'em *ALL* OFF!" Lenore coaches from the sidelines, "That'a girl!" And Mickey feels woman's hands on her, gentle, moving; so long denied—that touch; breath out of her mouth hot, near her sex; and now, in this setting she can feel little of it, frozen in emotion. And the music grinds; window shades down, air-conditioned air settles on the floor with stale cigarette smoke. Lucy's got Mickey's shorts down to her knees, her red hair brushing into black pubic hair, naked, Lucy's arm's tugging the shorts & pants down to her ankles; bare white ass in the living room light. "That's it, take 'em all the way off." Then gentle hands push away curly black hairs of her mound and the butch feels the woman's tongue searching her sex, licking her cunt, mouth grinding up into the pussy-folds, sucking her & heat grows, her guts tense, intake of air. Mickey's breathing quickens, the woman licks her, warm hands going behind Mickey's ass, to pull her cunt into her face, sees the redhead working in her crotch. And the tricks are making noises; out of the corner of her eye sees Lenore trying to make one john's dick stiff, noises in the background, music; here, in intensity, focus of Lucy's mouth in her cunt; and Mickey's dark wavy hair on which sweat from the day has dried, is starting to warm again, yet tho she feels it in her sex, she feels nothing.

The pain in her belly is gone because of the candy bar, & way off in the outer realm of consciousness she is wondering will she ever get a job in Chicago. And Mickey tells herself, 'Lenore's doing the dirty part of this, not me.' Trying to block the scene from her mind & Lucy's face right up in the wispy black pubic hair of Mickey's cunt, licking steadily, circular, her tongue, & sucking, drawing out her clit, so involuntary the butch draws in her breath with a groan. Tongue licks over and over, inside her wetness.

Boxer shorts—men's underwear & trousers in a heap at

her feet; tricks grunt in the background & this was a real freakshow with a real woman-man. Lucy's hands run over Mickey's ass, naked for all to see. "Spread your legs a little for me, baby." Lucy's gentle voice floats up from where she kneels between Mickey's legs, warm soft, a woman; seldom has the butch had loving this good, and she looks down, Lucy looks into her eyes with a look of compassion on her face for the butch, which Mickey don't realize at the time. So Mickey takes a step out, spreading her legs wide & tries to steel herself as the woman's tongue goes probing her cunt, and lips press up against her hot pulse, throbbing and she don't want to feel it, don't want to be moved, to give it all up in front of an audience—who's laughing, masturbating, fascinated, and climaxing with her; wants to stay cold, hard inside.

The hooker is fascinated. Sits a moment, arm around the john, hand on his dick by his open fly; thinks about Lucy: 'She's pretty good at it; wonder if she's one herself.'

"FUCK HER! FUCK HER! HA-HA! Two broads fucking each other," the other trick says. He's unzipped his pants.

"Come on for me, honey." Hooker voice floats across the room. 'Who's she talking to?' the butch wonders vaguely. Her sex feels hot. Lips to cuntlips. Lucy's sucking mouth trying to draw the cum out of her, & Mickey wants to be unmoved. Stone. To feel nothing. In fact, part of her feels cold. Her white face, cheeks with acne, closed expression, wavy black hair butch style slicked back behind the ears, stays tough. Now she looks down at the woman & begins to thrust her hips perfunctorily.

"Squeeze those big tits, baby." John says.

Lenore is seated majestically on the sofa in her huge wig, jacking the trick's dick up and down, to get it ready & watches Lucy and thinks, 'Nothing would bring me to my knees for another broad, nothing. But it's what the tricks want to see, so I'm lucky I found Lucy in that bar.' Pumps the limp trick with her hand, watches Lucy lick Mickey's cunt in hideous fascination & thinks: 'Jesus Christ! Is that Lucy a lezzie? I told her just to playact, but she's got her lips all over it! I told her just to pretend to suck it, not get her whole mouth up in it.' Lenore couldn't stand the idea. 'And the one who's supposed to be a goddamn lezzie, she ain't hollered or nothing. Maybe she ain't a real lezzie at all, just an impostor. Honestly, what I have to go thru with these dizzy dames!' And mentally consults her watch. 'Now I got to go thru these 3 damn tricks.' Decides the first john has seen enough. Her hourglass figure gets up, straightens out her satin dress, & takes john along. "Come on in the bedroom when you're ready, boys, and don't take too long!"

Casts a look back at the women; fairly hollers: "NOW LOOK ALIVE! PUT SOME SPICE IN IT!"

Lucy stops working the butch to show off her tits to the audience. Scrunches down on the floor by Mickey's feet, spreads her thighs to show cunt, cups her tits in her hands. Her tits are big and good. And Mickey's thighs quiver standing right over this, her sex has started to melt, and thinks: 'Oh, God, I want to fuck this woman. I want to cum so bad.' Lucy touches her again, warm hands reaching up around her legs to her ass; giving her the touch of a woman so long craved, warm, going back to work—drawing her ass in so Mickey's cunt goes back into her mouth thru curly black hairs, into her sweet face. Mickey sees Lucy's tits big, nipples hard at attention, and the white strap marks on her shoulders where her bra had been, tanned thru her blouse by the sun.

Deep voices and sounds behind her; Mickey blots it all out. Concentrates. She wants this woman, to fall down on the floor and hold her, and kiss her, and roll with her, embracing & licking & loving. Cumming together. Now they are divided from each other. Tho cunt is fused to lips; emotionally, they can't touch. Mickey looks down at this redhead woman on her knees frenching; licking her pussy, feels her so good & her hips thrust forward to meet Lucy's mouth.

The old man still sits there with his hat on; wrinkled, weather-beaten face. Lenore makes sounds from the adjoining bedroom.

Shadows move around the room; music plays, soft; and Mickey looks down as Lucy sucks her, wonders; 'Would she really do this for me if we were alone & she wasn't getting

paid? I wonder how old she is—she ain't much older than me.
I wonder whose woman she is. Is she married?'

Mickey now hung in space for a moment. Only Lucy's
arms, strong, held her; Lucy feels her shake and rises up; holds
Mickey tightly; fits body to body, like she's afraid the butch is
going to lose her balance, trip over her trousers still around
one ankle; & runs her hand behind the back of Mickey's neck,
just holding, in an act of compassion.

The last trick has his dick out, it's half-erect; he's masturbating a short distance away. Mickey's eyes in a tight line, jaw
grim; in the back of her sight could see it—and the redhead
woman slid back down her body, kneels before her, pushes her
sweet face into the butch's wet cunt and sticky pussyhair and
begins turning her body a degree higher up the screw of
orgasm. Lucy didn't seem bothered by the scene transpiring
around them. Expression on her face was out-of-this-world,
dreamy, from all that alcohol.

Mickey had just stood there, not touching the woman
anywhere else but her cock; hands with square fingernails
hanging at her side; just let her sex be taken by Lucy.

Suddenly, it's all too much for Mickey. Music grinding &
bass voices laugh & can't help her sex melting, flowing; &
hunger not far off in her flat stomach; so Mickey starts shaking. White flesh, cold, nerves trembling. 'Why did I come
here?' Knew because she needed money & the girls looked so
good—the way she liked them—& she's been without female
companionship so long, and the redhead stops, tips her head
up looks into the butch's eyes. "Don't be afraid," she whispers. "I'm OK." Mickey answers in a flat voice, not her usual
voice. Then Lucy bends her head back to her work. And it's
gonna cum, real soon, Fiery hot plateau of ecstasy has been
reached.

Now hooker Lenore has told Mickey she was supposed to
be doing it—or pretending to really slam it into the redhead
woman's mouth. But Mickey's standing there. Makes a few
thrusts of her hips. Not trying to see how long she can go;
just holds back inside. But feels her body warm up, hot, near
bursting, cunt swollen; discharge & Lucy's spit wets her

thighs; & tries to hold it back, in front of an audience she don't want. Gazes down at the woman frenching her with cold eyes. The rubbery licking feeling of Lucy's tongue. In the back of her mind, the butch thinks, 'She's rubbing her lipstick off on me; my cunt's in her mouth; I wish she was mine. I got $25. Pay my room rent for a week and buy $15 worth of food.' Music grinds.

Redhead sits back on her haunches; takes a breath, looks up at Mickey quizzically. 'Why is she holding back?' A while had passed. The 2nd trick had disappeared into the bedroom.

Mickey had seen enough of square big men in suits and ties & perspiration rings under their armpits watching simulated sex acts & spend the money, amid bar girls back on the East Coast; whores patting their wigs, & now here is one wearing her lipstick off on Mickey's clit & grunts and noises from the other room, of the tricks while she's getting frenched, and Mickey's stomach turning. Mickey's bitter. Pit of her stomach clenched; thrust her hips to Lucy weakly a couple of times. 'As much as I want a woman, I can barely cum now.'

Do all Lucy was doing, and the physical response had to happen. Felt orgasm rise up thru her frozen body, no longer minded if she didn't want it, couldn't stop it; sex pulsing, Lucy's tongue licking fast, hard over her clit, lips sucking it.

Like a solid begins to turn to liquid, Mickey was being moved. Hands that had dangled listlessly at her side came up to rest on the woman's head. Then fingers clenched into the sprayed red hair; naked, pale, her body bent over; muscular lithe frame surrendered. Suddenly Mickey felt her body jerk, giving herself up; giving up her cum into this woman's hot mouth, & to the caresses of her hands, the aroma of her perfume, the feelings. Mickey doubled over, a look clutched her face, moaning, twisting her hips around and around and around, thrusting involuntarily to orgasm.

Lucy kept her mouth pressed to Mickey's sex awhile. Then looked up at her. Eyes still closed; fingers had loosened their clutch on her head. Lucy gave Mickey a little hug.

And the show was over.

The Scene was done. Thread of a situation pulled out of the fabric of The Life.

"Man, that's it!" Mickey snarled. Pulled her trousers back up & looked at Lucy while tucking in her shirt & zipping up her fly. Lucy went hunting for the bottle. Mickey felt dead inside, shell-shocked. Rhythm of sex still rocked her, yet her feelings dead. Absolutely dead. She felt like slapping somebody.

The last john, limp, fly open, plays with himself to get ready for the hooker and not waste his money; & Mickey felt like half a butch. In fact, barely human, & music grinding on & on & she had ground her cunt into the woman's face like she was supposed to—and moaned, instead of hollered. Had felt the redhead's hot lips and tongue in her cunt do their job. Knows intellectually, 'She did it good—how come I'm mad about enjoying myself?' And a john grunts from the background & the hooker's in the other room making noise and the impossibility of the situation clenched its fist into her guts and twisted.

She'd cum. Her job was done. Had $25 & was frozen inside. Good part was still feeling the heat of the woman's mouth on her sex traveling with her in time & space after the act. Lucy had a drink; she had wiped her mouth with a tissue from her purse—that's all. 'She didn't go in the toilet to vomit or nothing. My cunt's all over her mouth and my juice is down her throat & it ain't bothered her a bit. Jesus... I wonder if she's a little bit gay.'

Redhead slipped one arm into her brassiere, put a big tit into the cup & Mickey's sunk back into the armchair.

And in the bedroom Lenore works, thinks: 'Jesus Christ! One more after this one. I wish those dizzy dames out there would give me a hand.' But don't want to spare any more money.

And music has stopped. Air conditioner hums.

Mickey sits back in the armchair. 'I earned enough money in this stupid fucking hour than I would in two days.' At her level of poverty, she could survive another week.

Room surrounded them, beige, plain; plastic pictures on the walls. Fell silent.

Mickey thought. 'Hmmm...she don't seem to be in a hurry to run off into the bedroom.... She won't make any more cash that way... Well, maybe they're not supposed to be her tricks; maybe Lenore's keeping all the money herself.'

But Lucy was happy for her $20 & wasn't doing anything else.

Inside the bedroom, Lenore, hard eyed, stone faced thinks: 'One more after this one...' Hoped dimly, somehow, by magic the other woman—the other real woman, that is—would come do something for these men, & she'd still get to collect all the cash herself.

So, that's how Mickey and Lucy met, at a freak party in which they were the star attraction.

Mickey should have left by now, but because of looking at the redhead, she continued to sit in the chair. Lucy's tits wobbling back and forth as she put them in the bra had begun to turn Mickey on inside. Emotionally. Made her stomach churn. Her sex was warm, throbbed still. Satisfied. It was confusing. And Mickey wanted to know: 'What kind of woman is she?' Who had sucked her off so well. 'Has she got a pimp? Or a husband somewhere? Will she really do to me what she got paid to? Put her lips up in my sex for free if I asked her to again? Hold me tight around my hips with her sweet arms & accept my love?'

Thinking, and blocking out grunts and noises coming from the bedroom: 'Wouldn't that be a switch, stealing one of their women...' Thinking: 'Will she?'

Lucy slipped on tiny panties made of silk or something. Mickey was all dressed, wondered; 'How can I get to her? What should I say? Is she waiting for Lenore, to go somewhere with her?' And Mickey sets her face; cheeks of acne scars, chin in her hand, sits back in the chair with a scowl, observing.

Door opens a moment. A man comes out, motions to the old man in the hat still seated on the sofa, and goes down the corridor to the bathroom.

He just sits there, shakes his head, "No." Lenore runs out,

got her slip back on; "COME ON, AL WHAT'S THE MATTER! YUH'LL HAVE FUN! LEAVE IT TO LEN-ORE!" Practically drags the man inside.

Now Mickey sees Lucy is dressed & would have been out of there, & down the elevator & gone with her cash inside her wallet long ago, but wants to see what the woman is going to do.

"I'm leaving. How about you?" Lucy looks at Mickey, shy.

Suddenly, something strange happens, after this so-called party; now Mickey had come alive. Felt her sex throb, remembered the hot lips. The burning heat under her pants. Felt like an adventure was going to happen, a second orgasm to cum. She started to come alive after the brutality she had just witnessed—the rape of her emotions.

CHAPTER THREE

Out of the air-conditioned apartment into hot Chicago evening; temperature way up in the 90s, no breeze from the lake; now was the time to make her wants known.

Not barely wanting to talk about where they'd been—the redhead woman's face in the butch's cunt, and what had happened—for it was strictly business; and now they could act like acquaintances, or partners in crime.

Butch not wanting to talk about where they'd been, but wanting to know Lucy more—not wanting to miss one of those moments of a lifetime.

So whatever direction Lucy turned to go, Mickey would follow.

And they walked down Clark Street, conscious of passersby eyes on them.

Mickey in men's black lace-up shoes, male trousers & shirt; at the stoplight impatiently tapped toes of tiny size on the curb.

Her keen features held in a hard mask. To most, appeared to be a boy. To others, a strange man. Still fewer read her as a female in drag. Each reaction could be different from the next.

"I was looking at you, too. How could I miss you, dressed like you do?" Lucy reached out and fingered the lapel of the jacket thrown over Mickey's shoulder.

Mickey, a stone butch, strange thing she did: when she went out in public and it was daylight, where she could be seen, she takes this boy's size suitcoat off & swung it over her back, carried on the crook of one finger. But at night, or indoors, safe from glares of eyes, those straights & squares & police, she put it on. Straight lines down, no hips, many pockets, wide lapels & massive shoulder pads. A tie, and she was in stone drag.

Bold.

Shadows descending & soon this jacket would be on. Defiantly, Mickey snarled, saying something about how she couldn't dress up completely like a man in public. Swaggered, walking along with a cigarette behind one ear.

Mickey was the gentleman, walked on the outside, if they crossed a street and got turned about with Lucy walking near the curb, Mickey would switch over to walk on the street side protectively.

So, during the conversation, finds out Lucy lives near the gay clubs, in a trashbin hotel room & she was on her way there now to pay money on her rent, same as Mickey would, & then get high.

Caucasian couples of middle-straight Amerika welled by them, and lower-class types, too; still in a better part of town. Someone jostled Mickey's arm. "Excuse me, sir."

The redhead & the butch looked at each other, Lucy's face cracked a big grin. "Be glad. You don't have to be so embarrassed."

"It's not that…if they really think I'm a sir. It's when they realize I'm not a sir, but they're still calling me 'sir'—that's the bad part. And my voice is too high to answer them."

In those days of 1959, it was illegal to wear complete drag—male or female impersonation. Liable to get arrested. Could escape this if you had on 3 articles of female clothes, & she had none of it. So Mickey had the tie stuffed in her jacket pocket. "I wear it at night."

"Yeah." Mickey replied, shooting Lucy a glance to figure out how personal she meant this. Lucy had this dreamy look, sailing forward over the hot Chicago streets.

The Hawk city. Across from Lake Michigan.

Modern buildings, huge, glass & concrete, a grand scope of architecture. And old ones, layer after layer of brick stacked on brick. Pigeons swirled in the eaves.

The 18-year-old butch had a lean and hungry look, passions that drove her out into the night.

Felt her sex in her pants; a burning sensation—heat exuding into all the other extremities of her body leaving a red glow.

"I came out here early in 1957—January. With Billy and some other people. They went on to California. When I got here, there's people I know, Duke, Freddy, the whole gang of bums who use to hang out in Greenwich Village. Everybody's out here, I says."

'Wonder if Billy's a woman or a man.'

"How old were you when you first struck out across country?"

"For the first time? 15 years old."

"What brings you here?"

"Better things."

"Have you ever been west before?"

"No further than St. Louis."

Chi-town, New York, Frisco. Headline major cities. Capitols of the U.S.—Gaytowns. Hustler rows. Neon. Beginning of the end.

It was to fulfill a fitful shadow moving at midnight till dawn, approaching along the clear black star-glistening highway toward 1960 that she had first begun her journey, now barely an embryonic dream. Past towns of middle Amerika deep in countryside sleep—that mentally she'd escaped.

That morning the butch awoke from naps—not a complete night's sleep. Many days in this new city, fears arose direct out of her unconscious. Fears of being alone in a new town; she held them down like one checks nausea, buckled nightmares under.

"So you're a long way from home aren't you, to be so young."

"I'm not that young!"

Yes, and oftentimes she felt it. Waking...so far away...in the bleak Chicago morning in a rooming house farther north; she could taste fear. 'Suppose I just fall apart.' Walls start to close in, and especially awaking, after sleep has stripped bare her consciousness, and she has no resistance to fight back. Walls closing in, no security, 'no people I can hold onto who'll understand me.' Just blank walls in this suddenly hot, stifling climate. 'Fear comes again and again, and I fight it.'

Saw Lucy for a second under the street lamp: 'What would it be like to romance her?'

Looked up and down length of her pretty body in cool appraisal. Woman's round tits, shoulders, hips, thighs crammed into the toreador pants; & bare heels and toes sticking out of a pair of glittering high heels.

Recalled the sensation less than an hour passed, of pressing her sex into the woman's mouth; now yearned to hold her body fiercely & to be held in return. To take her as she'd learned to take a woman from loves gone by...

Envisioned her again & again; Lucy, naked; red hair & fingernails & toenails polished and made up; an imitation gold chain on her left ankle—a slave bracelet; baring her weight up on high heels now by a lamppost which had just gone on, marking the division of day tonight, going on down North Clark Street.

It was a shame what she had to go thru to get a woman. Nights sitting up in the Twilight Club; that Syndicate hustling joint. Cruising daytime streets in the Loop, while job hunting, actually approaching straight women: 'I want to meet some nice straight woman who's not tainted by the Gay Life. We'd be just like a man and a woman and live a happy life together. That's what I want.'

Felt heat stir in her guts, where it hadn't been for a long while; deadened by life in this mad world.

'I get this close to a woman, finally, and it has to be this way. Have sex with her—then the feelings come for her, too.... I want more.'

A little girl age 5 or so, strong limbed, blonde, pink skin, skipped onto the bus with her mother, waving good-bye at someone in the street. The kid looked boyish, like Mickey had been. Maybe this 5 year old would be one—the wave of the future. Whose colorful lesbians could one day walk the streets of Amerika; one day, when repression against gays would subside. Walk, even hold hands together. Girl-girl. Boy-boy. Out in the sunlight instead of dingy bars at midnight under cover of darkness. Free to attend its universities—in drag—if they so desired. To work its jobs. Instead of alone, & poor & denied employment; relegated to the midnight hour. Kids whose love dared not speak its name, assembling in toilets and taverns and special street corners of the USA and the world.

Or be like a far-removed species—extinct.

Two decades later, when these same Amerikan streets would be populated with an army of dykes and fags just like her. In any dress code they chose. Weird hairdos, orange, pink, or bald. Arm in arm, living normal gay lives.

But lesbians of those days had no idea of where the future was going. It was still Before Stonewall. Under her heavy-lidded eyes, Mickey observes; wonders; 'What is she? Straight? —or Bi? She can't be too straight.'

Feet walked down blocks, past stoplights. Now a few ramshackle tenements began, with more & more dives, taverns on their ground floor, on Chicago's Near North Side, decaying, descending into a pit.

Too much to hope for—to cum in her open embrace; for her arms to open, inviting Mickey into her heart, to cum into her.

'She keeps walking with me. She's not trying to get away. Wonder if she has a girlfriend?'

Planned what she'd do: 'Finger-fuck her first. Some dykes, that's all they know how to do. I'll get on top and get between her legs and ride her, and take off all my clothes.' Wouldn't be like some of those dykes she knew who ride their women thigh between thigh interlocked—with their clothes still on. Trousers & man shirts—too embarrassed of their bodies. 'I'll strip down & give her a thrill. I'll eat her out as good as she ate me.'

The two walked past all the assholes, freaks, geeks & Seekers; they were headed toward skid row.

'Maybe she'll let me french kiss her.' Mickey would get Lucy to invite her up to her hotel room, and they'd sit together on the sofa—if it had one—and the rest would be unbearably good. Flash of images: the redhead would let Mickey remove her clothes, & naked, go all the way & do everything for each other mutually.

Mickey wore her love—that dared not speak its name—out on her sleeve. A butch sailor. A tattoo for all the world to see. They knew who she was & how she wanted to have her woman—but only by Lucy's actions or verbalization could somebody tell. So Mickey had to guess. And the short black-haired butch observed that this lady was paying a lot of attention to her in her silent way, with eyes on her all the time like a fish undersea.

The bell-tower clock chimed 7:00 P.M.

Night's falling shadow across a jagged line of building tops.

It would be a shame to part, never knowing what she could have had.

Mickey spoke to Lucy in sign language. Walked close, brushing against her light as a feather, walking with a slight swagger, to keep her attention; arched back on her feet when they stopped at a light. Front of her chest flattened down by the binder; patted her stomach, looked down deep into Lucy's eyes and wouldn't let go.

The baby butch was in a low niche. Was like quite a few dykes; living out their lives, trying not to be discovered as female; this "passing" regulating their job level to the more menial. Those few females who passed entirely as men, doing heavy lifting—warehouse, factory; in low-income jobs or places where there was less chance at being discovered.

Mickey'd had a job as stockboy, which lasted until they discovered & promptly fired her. Then one wrapping packages. Then zilch. Nothing.

Cautious & tough, Mickey swaggered when she felt right. Had money in her pocket. Shirt turned up at the collar; pack of cigarettes stuck in her rolled-up sleeve.

Too many incidents in cities past; teenage males circling in cars, angry, drunk, snarling insults and hollering at the cute women among their gay group; and they'd get the shit beaten out of them, if she didn't look enough like a man and could pass.

So it was freer at night, no one to recognize her as a female in the streets; all the stares. Yet more dangerous too when gangs harassed them out in front of the gay bar.

And Mickey knew she was going to ask Lucy for what she wanted…thinking: 'Will she?' If she'd receive her—if she'd want her as hard as she'd acted at the freakshow; or just reject her. 'Oh! That's ugly! I just did it for the money! Didn't you know! Are you kidding? I don't go that way! I've got an old man! I just have to earn a living, that's all!'

So Mickey had cum, back at the trick pad. But she wanted to do it again. Wanted to taste Lucy's cunt, too. To suck her vagina & straight-fuck it—on top, and with fingers work her cunt juice out & make her flop about on a mattress in joy, and then lay in her arms like a whimpering child.

And wanted to get to know her.

So, as she walked beside Lucy, Mickey is thinking it's sort of a sweet revenge against those tricks. And alternately vacillating between assuming Lucy's straight as a rail, and maybe, at the other end of the blue-green night-light spectrum, is a party girl who's dipped her toe in the gay waters more than once.

As the street full of people floods down alongside them.

Sweat under armpits; desire shot a short bolt thru her stomach; her mild state of arousal ebbed, then flowed as they rubbed elbows, walking together.

Both the same height. A summer evening…in the genre of nightlife.

State Street. Rush Street. Erie. The territories of the Cities of the Plain.

Rush Street—they entered it now, with its hustling chicks and same old dames.

Chapter Four

Carnal carousel. Rush Street taverns & nightclubs & regular restaurants & bistros, and coffeehouses & beatnik joints.

Now, ordinarily, Lucy the redhead would have put the change from the $20 in her brassiere, and gone off somewhere & digest it all with a bottle of bourbon—the sexual encounter would pass slowly out of her memory—flooding over the lip of conscious with the amber liquid until The Scene was gone. She had committed the cavities of her vagina, her mouth, and her soul to other Scenes past. And it wasn't pleasant.

Neon street lamps made silver lizards scurry in the brick crevices; garbage cans sitting lopsided began to appear here & there, as they trod, descending toward Lucy's hotel.

'Everybody's scum. Me.' Mickey counted them: 'The dumb fucks... Maybe the hooker let herself go if any of them lasted long enough or did anything right. But not Lucy. I can make her cum. I could make her be my girl.'

After sex, Mickey's gayness had taken on a new dimension—instead of being simply a cardboard cutout image in hat & trousers & men's shoes; a profile character flitting thru the days and nights; this sex act was what her lesbianness was all about. The real deal. Her masculine sex drive returning.

Fantasies turn in the butch's head. 'Hold her by the shoulders and kiss her all over her naked body, little wet kisses from her neck down one side, then up the other; down to her toes & back up again, I'll go 'round the world, sucking her and licking her.'

Mickey remembers now—thru the weeks of poverty and no food, and tossing in her broken-down bed, in fear, sweating—remembers back to a better time when she got to love all the women. Sliding her hands down their breasts, taking her time & for free.

It had been so long since she'd even thought about sex & now, here it was back again.

'Another B-girl. Straight or bi? Will she give me a chance

with her? When we get to her hotel, is she gonna say her boyfriend is upstairs in the room? Or is it gonna be "come on up with me, baby, and ride, Sally ride"?'

Wanted a second orgasm from Lucy, after experiencing the dynamite impact of the first. Her pants were wet from before, now juice flowed from the 18-year-old's cunt; cream in her boxer shorts & down her legs. Mouth in a line. 'Why not? I should get what I want! I want this woman here beside me! And damn these squares and fuckin' freakin' straight assholes! They prevent me from getting a job, and they try to arrest us in the streets & at the club! Damn them! Nobody's gonna get between me and the love of a lady, even if I have to wait another month or a year!'

Rush Street. Green, blue, yellow; of solicitors & entrepreneurs.

Lucy has thoughts, too—saw a touch of mystery and danger in this young woman who she knew to be a lesbian butch. And kindness, too. She had felt her tremble with fear back at the trick pad. Had read the uncertainty in her young eyes. And now, been a half-hour walking side by side. 'You can never tell about a person. It's deeper than her hard butch clothes & that sexy swagger, but she has a warmth in her.'

Rush Street. Establishments full of girls; Mickey's eyes feasted on the neon come-on as they descended. Girls, but girls performing for men in establishments run by men. Whether it was a strip show, B-girls at a tavern, or a house of prostitution, Mickey wasn't one of the ladies, and was not welcome.

Big beefy men, their big fat wallets, $750 watches and diamond pinkie rings. She thought they had access to women more than she did, but what Mickey didn't realize was that they acquired the outward attention only. They buy time & service by the minute, but Mickey could have it for free. What the butch had was the key that could access a woman's inner soul—they wanted to come to her & lie with her & be with her because this butch was what she was—a female lover of women—& stay with her until society tore them apart.

So Mickey decided before she got too personal, first she'd brag herself up to Lucy.

"At least I've never had to pay for it—at no time in my life! I'm better than those tricks and their fat fuckin' wallets! Women *like* me." Mickey said simply.

The redhead shot her a glance, smiled. "Do they?"

"Yes." Butch Mickey said.

And the redhead looked back down. "Never paid?"

"The women I've had was on my own merits. I'm a real lady lover." She bragged. Making her small 5'2" size seem giantlike in prowess & in a sense of adventure.

Mickey gestured at the pink, blue & yellow neon billboard advertising GIRLS!

"I'm not that bad off because I've had plenty of these women & they give me plenty of time. Time to do what I need to, and time for them, so they *always* get satisfaction." Mickey climbed out of her own loneliness just for a little while, as she bragged & strutted.

"I know what to do. I know all the moves."

And was not like the old gray hulks of dykes, eyelids closed, fate sealed, folded over the bar at some back-street hustling tavern, holding a beer bottle with feeble hands, 40, 50 years old. Passing a ten-dollar bill to some dizzy bisexual girl to lay down for them nude in a room upstairs. Lined faces, guts falling over x pants like creatures from outer-space with no woman in sight.

Brave & bold Mickey had frequented these establishments. Now the drinking-age limit in the bars in both NY and Chicago was 18, which they later raised to 21, same as the guys.

So B-girls had let Mickey love them, and strippers; even totally hard-hearted whores.

And these carnal thoughts returned, after two months here in Chi-town & on the road, so long without money not even horny, had felt her sex dry up inside her like a pea. Now it was coming back; in lightning bolts to the hot pit of her groin.

Blows society shell-shocked her psyche & then she internalized, along the battlefield of life, so she'd become frigid. Greeted the world with an emotionless stare.

In the secret midnight hour, in the past, had done it herself; with furtive creaks of the bed, nervous that people in the adjoining rooms would hear. Recently, had been too beat to beat her own meat.

It'd been a long time between women. For this interval, she had forgot the full depth & meaning of her sexuality. What it meant that this pint-size butch was a lady lover. Had been so preoccupied with dealing in society; face set hard to face the faces that she met, the mainstream squares that scorned her; their church—their politics—going from that point into full-fledged aggression; bullies challenging her & her kind in the streets; the blows, & jeers; her pulling out her knife in self-defense; this hell from the straight human race; all the way back uptown to the landlady in her hotel reminding "rent's due"—which means survival. If she could just find some kind of job & be allowed to work—as an open dyke. This is what it had meant for so long, to be a lady lover.

'Getting what all the men have all ready,' she thought angrily.

Problem was, Mickey didn't fully realize that conditions had not been set up for her from the beginning—but set up against her.

Neon party lights, pink and blown up big across the urban sky.

Trade. Tricks of the trade. Strippers in pasties & G-strings. She had touched under those scanty clothes into the hot wet cunt of the real thing.

At her young age, Mickey had had the finest women. "Some men pay $15 just to look at those girls; ain't nuthin' I ain't seen myself—after the show. And the $100-a-night hookers? Ha. I've had my share and not a dime in my pocket." These girls went off on a date 20 minutes, then stayed with the butch the other 23 hours of the day—for her sake & the hot loving she gave & because she had a cunt like theirs. "They lay down with me, even tho I ain't 6' tall and 200 pounds of muscle and a wallet full of cash. Even tho I'm nothing."

The redhead listened, feet slip slopping in her backless

shoes as they strolled down Rush Street at an even gait. Mickey bragged, strutted and eyed Lucy to see the effect of her words. "I ain't never had to pay for it in my life. The girls want me for who I am." She looked down at her sex; damp in the crotch of her pants; patted her flat belly to give Lucy the idea. "And what I do to them, I have a way of touching women, and loving them." Wanting to show how she held their bodies next to hers, fingers in them, working the cum out of them. "And some of them, because I'm a woman, too. I been known to lie down myself."

For an instant, an all-wise knowing crossed her eyes. "In this way I'm superior."

The two stood at a traffic light. Hitching her trousers up, shirtsleeves rolled up; a runt; yet, above it all, she was superior.

For Mickey, in the past it was easy to get women. Learned the Love Arts in reform school; then later adding to her knowledge on the streets of New York. Because of her good looks and her toughness, was a fine catch to many party girls.

And had none since arriving here—these problems of survival had been so great. A month of pounding the pavements in her gym shoes looking for work as a female, or in hard-drag men's attire & boy's-size lace-up shoes, trying to pass. Not even thinking about sex, dried up in an emotional way. Fainthearted and full of fear. Not even once had she masturbated.

Under neon lights & silver moon rays was a hamburger stand; its neon sign blinking FASTFOOD. Aromas drift to her nostrils. Hunger had begun to grind in her guts—the candy bar digested long ago. Mickey decided to stop for food. They got up to the window to order; suddenly a bigger man cut in front of Mickey, who stepped back, bitterly aware of her inferior size. Huge man 6'7", 300 pounds stood in front of her, practically hid Mickey from the sight of the white-uniformed waitress at the counter behind the glass. He placed his order in a gruff voice. Her anger of stepping aside for giant men bigger then she was digested in turmoil in the familiar acid pangs of hunger. Another big dumb man strode up front, opened his wallet to pay & there was a sheaf of green bills.

Lucy was pretty, and one of the men looks at her, his eyes traveling up and down. "What's your name?" he asked the redhead, flirtatiously.

"SHE'S WITH ME!" Mickey shouts back, risking her life. "DON'T BOTHER US!"

"She's pretty," says the man, staring at them both.

"Come on." Lucy takes Mickey's arm firmly. "Lets go."

But the other man has the food & they both turn to go sit down at a picnic table in the lot.

Mickey bought herself a $2 hamburger. It had everything.

Even had to eat after everybody else was served. They hated her as a lesbian.

Embittered. Angry. Is how she felt. So it was lucky she didn't have a gun or she would be back in jail doing time for manslaughter. It was because of her inferiority.

Slapped her $5 down with a sneer, took the burger & moved off, in a swagger.

Saw them at the picnic table out in the lot; big huge arms & legs, white men, 2 of them crowding up the table; they ate tons of food—many deluxe hamburgers & french fries and milk-shakes, like huge bovine pasture animals.

"Let's walk." Lucy urges. So they don't stay, but walk, munching.

And couples arm in arm—straight, parade past under the star-filled night; while she and Lucy just walk side by side—but they don't know each other well yet—(other than the redhead has had the butch's clit & furry cunt in her mouth) these white men & their ladies going into posh restaurants & nice night-clubs with their money and the respect they got.

Heard herself tell Lucy: "I got a new rule for living. Look the motherfuckers straight in the eye." With backbone & guts she squashed her soul back upright again. It had been tipped like the mast on a sailboat on the high seas.

"It's all a rat race." Lucy murmured. She wasn't eating. Had declined the invitation, wasn't hungry. "You see where other people are getting ahead and getting more, and with some girls they get and get more and more just to show off. To prove they can. It's a rat race."

Mickey watched her talk, mouth tugging at meat & hamburger buns with catsup. Her orgasm with Lucy justified all of it. The men challenging her, the fear.

"I don't choose to step into the rat race." Lucy looked at Mickey quietly and confided. "I'm not a cold-blooded hustler. I don't do that all the time. I just earn enough to survive, that's it."

A stage in the towers of power.

"I guess the only answer is to outbutch the next butch." Mickey was talking; bantamweight strut, cocky confidence having flooded into her being along with the sugar adrenaline of good food.

Fire in her loins. She tossed the grease & catsuped waxed paper in the gutter as she strode. Warm air came up thru a subway vent with a WHOOSH.

Rush Street; nightclub row. Gaudy strip of taverns; now they left it, turned down Division—where they'd met just a few hours ago.

By then, Mickey noticed a sexual magnetism between them. Same as when the woman was on the floor at her feet looking up, into her eyes. And wondered if Lucy felt it, too, or would she block it out like so many straight women did.

A club with curtain over the entrance; Lucy wheels to a stop on her high heeled pumps, turns, and goes in there. Mickey follows. They peek inside.

Some people set up at the bar looking not like they are drunk, but like they are dead.

Dank interior, cool. Jukebox croons Mafia tunes.

Gruff old man wheels around in his stool near the front; steel blue eyes flash at them. "We don't allow your type in here."

"They let anything in here," says somebody.

Lucy exits with Mickey. Who thinks, face in a frown, 'Are they talking about her because she's cute & kind of wild like; because she's a party girl, or me 'cause I'm a dyke?'

Going back thru the curtain of the entrance a gentleman steps aside for them. "Excuse me, sir," he says politely to Mickey.

As they go off down the street Lucy looks up at Mickey under the moon & stars; and wind from the lake ruffling their hair. A little smile plays on her red lips. "*Sir*. Lucky you." Lucy repeats with a laugh.

"They always do that!" Mickey is chagrined. "What the hell! I never know if I'm passing or not." Thinking privately: 'Lucy knows what sex I am, out of all these friggin' people in all these crappy places in this godforsaken city—she knows, because I can smell my cunt still on her breath—under the alcohol.'

"And then," she confided a butch-secret, "I hate to say anything back to 'em, 'cause they'll hear how high my voice is, and then they'll really suspect."

Traversed the meat-rack streets. Now gay men appeared in abundance, heading home into their territory, of sorts.

"I got enough to put on my kitchenette for a week. It's $11.50. I'll buy a sack of potatoes & some meat & borrow a pot from the lady that runs the place. Everybody borrows her stuff.

"I been to 30 different places, but I ain't got no job experience, and being new in town don't help none. And I wear pants & tennis shoes, and they know I'm a girl and that's a joke, they won't hire me. I go in drag. I can't get a job 'cause I got no job record. I got some jobs back east as a man, and they found out and fired me. In one place the broad looks up and down at me, from my legs up to my face & back a couple times and says, 'Not bad!' But I didn't get the job."

"It's just a fuckin' rat race, Mickey," Lucy said in a soothing tone. "Don't take it serious. Get on welfare. That's what I did. I have an income. It pays for almost everything—but fun."

Step step on time, under the moon's rind.

'I'll have to do it to her as a man.' Mickey thought, having fantasies, thumbs hooked under her belt buckle. 'Get on top of her and stud her good—Get all my fingers in her, suck her tits and keep going strong.'

"It's a shame when a femme has to make love to a butch." Mickey said. "Yuh know, when the butch gets the lady home, then rolls over on her back and expects the lady to do everything."

"Maybe some ladies would like to do a few things, too." Lucy smiles.

People have been coming and going in the street all around them, & in the places they've been ever since they met that summer day. They take a risk, cut into a bar with hardly any people in it and go straight back to the toilet. Lucy goes in the stall to piss. Then she's out, and both of them are standing in front of the mirror, Mickey hoping no dames come in, to shriek when they see this man in the ladies' john. Lucy is fussing in the mirror with eyebrow pencil: "OHHHH! I haven't done my eyes!" And Mickey, fussing even more than Lucy, combs her black wavy hair back behind her ears, changes different facial expressions, her reflection ducking in the glass, bending at the knees, tries to get her appearance straight—as a man, and pass so as not to be harassed on the street. Makes several grimacing expressions. Lucy picks at the stray red wisps of her beehive hair. No dames have come in, and so suddenly they are alone.

Mickey reaches out and puts her hands firm on Lucy's waist. Redhead looks up in the mirror at Mickey behind her; smiles slow & shy, mouth in a line; & doesn't move.

The butch bends down, puts her lips on that white neck; and flicks her tongue across Lucy's skin, over and over, suggestively, for just a second. Then pulls away, inhaling the scent of Lucy's perfume.

"You done me. I want to do you." Says it simply.

"I want to." Lucy replies in a soft voice. "That would be OK."

Back outside they slowed their gait; in spirit could almost see they walked practically hand in hand.

Mickey had eaten the hamburger; strength had flooded back into her. First good food she'd had in days—had been alone on the edge of survival and almost fallen over into the abyss. Was 18 and having trouble making it in the world; and then the world says, 'We want you to meet Lucy.'

The city of Chicago has many huge churches, Cathedrals, built on a small scale to those in Europe. The one near Lucy's hotel was complete with stained-glass windows, gothic spires, a towering steeple. A huge marble entrance.

It was like a landmark, pointing their direction home.

Lucy turns down Clark Street; her eyes wink as she watches Mickey, who follows.

When Mickey met Lucy, the redhead was not turning tricks, but would simply be with men as drinking buddies, and some sort of took care of her at times.

Lucy was not a bona fide lesbian. She hung out occasionally in gay bars, and in wino establishments simultaneously. Was independent & very poor in fact, from not hustling much. Gay life itself was new to Lucy, tho she had experienced the love of a female at 12, had done this because she was easy & not uptight like other girls; went with a youthful lesbian dyke near her age, 13, in a foster care facility.

Oddly, in gay bars, the woman didn't feel as free...to get drunk out of her mind. It was due to personal head trips.... She felt eyes upon her. Because the straight bars she frequented were so low class, there was no judgment there. No gossiping about style and clothes. Just pursuit of mad drink. Dope shot. The blown-out veins in arms, tattooed hands shaking, holding a substitute glass of piss-colored beer; veins sunken so low beneath the skin that a junkie couldn't find them anymore.

She'd do her drinking there, for these straight bars were cesspools; alkies too far gone to want her body for her sex as much as in a regular place.

As they turned down the block of lower Clark, going toward winoland, the street darkened from the glitz of Division & Rush with its party goers, well lit with a lot of advertisements that blink off and on.

Mickey was suspicious. "Sure you're not coming home to some old man?"

"I told you I deal solitary. I'm solitary. Don't have a man—or a lady either." Added this, shyly. "I'm not personal with nobody. Nobody means nothing to me."

"Me neither."

Now, Mickey knew a lot of hustling women would take on a dyke for a while as a lover behind closed doors, but seldom as their man. They'd leave her when the going got rough. They scorn the butch—so many couldn't keep them because they had no job. A real lesbian had real reservations about cross-over ladies from the straight world; but for a lot of dykes, that's all that was available out in public where you could get to them.

Imagine how she loved a woman, her clit going up and down on the woman's cunt; whose legs are spread, held back for her; Mickey's ass going around and around; their cunts glued together, feeling so good. Got it in the right place to please them both. Then moving fast, pumping till they hit the orgasmic plateau and took off with fireworks.

As they had walked down the kaleidoscoping streets, turning day into night, space between them had always remained no greater than a single body width. Also, a new element had evolved. Sensuality began to envelope them together under the vast bell jar of night above, enclosing them together— sensuosity left over from the sex act they'd shared; so they already knew each other.

The soft tone of Lucy's voice, so relaxed, supercalm, like the rub of fingers over her nerves. Soothing; & mutually, the redhead Lucy drew strength from the lesbian butch Mickey strutting at her side.

'Why should she want me when she can have a man?' the butch thought.

Her motive was to make love to Lucy in earnest. 'She must need a woman like I do. Maybe I can win her to be my girl-friend.'

Two transvestites walk past. Can tell they're in drag, but only on close scrutiny, & that, only to the naked eye. Some-thing about their hips: bigger, not totally abrupt straight up and down as a male. Also, there is something about their vibes, not as bold, large gestures; a quality of restraint. And as if they were masking something.

Breasts tied down, trousers, men's lace-up shoes, suit coats

& open collar shirts. Hair slicked back behind their ears. One blond hair, one brown, in short ducktails. Both were tall, about 5'9" or 5'10"; that height helped give them a masculine impression.

LaSalle Street bus zoomed up across the bridge over the Chicago River in the distance. The deserted-by-night area polka-dotted by some esoteric beatnik coffeehouses and artist lofts. The two headed straight down Clark, that teems with alkies, rummies; crowded both night and day in a seething river, a torrent of humanity.

Fire in her loins. Men's black lace-up shoes hit hard soles on the pavement. By now, Mickey had watched & appreciated Lucy in every degree and had noticed she had a tinted complexion; a cast to her skin. Not completely white. Her mouth wider than European, her cheekbones high. A quality different about her facial structure.

"What nationality are you?"

"I'm half Sioux Indian."

"Oh. I thought you might be…something."

"And you?"

"Italian."

Now Mickey had left New York City to escape the confines of her family. Actually, they were going to kill her. She had run off to the safety of the streets because there was practically a contract out on her by the hands of her own mother.

Each of her brothers was instructed if he should see her in public, to beat her as much as possible, short of killing her—and this restraint only so they wouldn't go to jail for manslaughter.

Her future was an embarrassment to the family. Her lesbian lust a loss of face. Her stern mother was practically insane with the thought, for it reflected on her own womanhood and how she must have raised her daughter. Their family could have no respect from other families with Mickey in drag running around town sleeping with women.

No relatives would help her. Many blamed it on drugs.

Her school friends looked the other way and wouldn't speak to her.

"My daughter's dead. I don't have a daughter." Mrs. Leonardi lied.

Mickey didn't use pills & was very much alive, and thus needed a helping hand. Was behind on rent, no food & no fun—in New York. This, compounded by the need for love driving her, the need for real emotional contact, the passion for sexual intimacy... So, she'd lived in the street, finally; sleeping in fitful catnaps in doorways, and going home to bed with women & had a few jobs that didn't last, and stole money, and met some girls that hustled, knelt between their thighs and sucked their pussies, and went to Miami, Florida as a kept butch; hoarded a little money, and when that fell thru, left for Chi-town, to seek legitimate work.

Hag face of an old crone broke her reverie. Suddenly this ancient being popped up, crooked, shouting gibberish; marking the first outpost at the edges of the slum beginning—her gnarled hand palm up soliciting coins.

Neighborhood changed now—fast. Gone were the rich restaurants, ample menus; with real grass & trees in front & luxuriant booths and spotless chrome inside, scrubbed clean daily by a squad of assistant cooks in chefs' white hats. Large blinking ads that by night flashed; FAMILY DINNERS. Places women of their sort were not allowed in. Lucy who often wore a red bandanna to tie her falling-apart red hair, was suspect. And of course Mickey—they'd be stopped and refused entrance at the door.

They'd left the tall expanse of high-rise buildings.

The rich, and their Money Funds and Working Assets.

A breeze caught Lucy's blouse, and it fluttered.

A motorcycle roared down the street, a big metal horse with a death spirit; iron, blazing headlights. A gay man, tall, burly, bearded, in a black leather vest and chaps & cap; black gloves. Nobody around to point an accusing finger. Down here nobody cares. None of these goons and witches who couldn't afford nearly such a nice bike.

Passed the Rawhide Bar; a men's gaybar, its door open, so they could see in. Big, stocky white men, huge as bears with barrel chests, hairy; attired in the subculture high fashion of leather jackets, chaps, & boots with silver chains. Caps studded with silver. Strips of leather dotted with silver; harnesses crisscrossing their backs; muscular and sweating; glittering with metal fastenings. One-half block down from Division Street on Clark. Summer night. The open door showed so many of them, so bold. "They must pay the police a lot to get away with all that." A lot of big motorcycles parked in front at a diagonal slant. This bar allowed no females.

Amazing to see so many gay men—200 or so, and most of them older than her fag friends.

They allowed no women—not like the colorful girl/boy bars of their vicinity. The ones the Vice cops perpetually raided & closed down. It put out a tremendous amount of juice; that's why it never got busted. And never closed more than a day or two around election time, when precinct politicians vowed to clean up the neighborhood.

200 gay Daddies and their slaves. Chains hung from ceiling to floorboards. Drinks in their hands. Standing around, eyes on what was in each other's pants.

Handcuffs on their belts. Whips on the wall. Floggings were the meat of their conversation.

It was a dark place, strange. "These men are up to serious business. Sadomasochism." Mickey told Lucy as they went past.

1959, when Mickey was lost in infatuation, amidst a sea of drink & not having to feel anything else but the buzz of a hangover, had then squared up in Greenwich Village, New York. It had been beer, wine, bourbon & ale. Green ale. Gin. Reefer, too. Anything. Just moving thru this crazy set; scuttling over the silent floor of seas like a crab—just, upon occasion, reaching its arms up, out of the buzzing ocean of alcohol in her brain, to grab at a pretty girl, while passing each other down there at the bottom—Someone she wanted very much—Or something, like an apartment which she had & shared with a girl briefly; or a car, which she'd never yet obtained, except stealing one. Some more butch clothes; yes. Men's shoes. Facing the embarrassment of trying them on in the boys' department. Or…a dream passing.

Neon lit. Suddenly an ugly snaggle-toothed face hung in space before them like the ghost of yesteryear past, & then they were gone on by. Mickey was secretly glad she'd stopped the disillusion of drink. Then thought, how ironic: 'It was another lady who picked up both of us, separately in different places. Ha.' And remembered riding thru the better part of town in the white big-finned 1955 car, smoke whipping out of rolled-down windows. Hooker. In skintight satin dress. Butch. In male attire. Female. Sunken back on the upholstery, with no stated sexual preference. And they'd had some fun.

And questioned Lucy about this, and Lucy explained, "Yes. I've done it before." Meaning The Show. And yes, she could have frenched one of the tricks and got her red-lipsticked mouth ejaculated into a second time for extra money, but had declined.

First had cum Mickey; cunt in her mouth. And Mickey held back her words; and was mad, watching the redhead's tits bob, moving beside her down Clark Street; mad that she'd done it before with another butch; wet pubic hair & pussy in her lips. And mad about the men. "I didn't want to. Especially not after having you." Lucy looked at Mickey.

And Mickey's emotions were brought to a boil by the moon.

Looked at the half-Indian woman sideways, and wanted her bad. Hadn't cum prior, in 2 months. Partially the reason was her Catholic upbringing; didn't think it was right to do it alone. Like it was a waste. Under turned-out light bulb, window shade drawn. On a lonely Sunday. Sexual tension all bottled up inside her—so that only when drunk could she abandon herself to solitary self-pleasuring. Feel her clit with her fingers and gasp; pinch her own tits with her other hand. So the long sex starvation alleviated briefly. Sex had come back to the red-blooded dyke. Her 5'2" frame tingled with erotic tension, stretched between her arms & legs like a child's jumping jack, springing; from east to west, north to south; & then Lucy's telling her how she wanted to keep Mickey's scent in her mouth, her juice, and nobody else's; so Mickey's fingers grew cold at the tips in shock & then red-hot, and her eyes burned. Especially since food had given her a boost; and had new moral support with the $22 filling her wallet; jammed her fingertips down into the lining of her trouser pocket. Making her deliriously happy mouth into a hard focused line—so as not to betray any emotion.

'Maybe I'll throw it all away. Forget everything else! Treat Lucy. Buy her something she wants. A present. And spend the night. All night with Lucy. And love her 3 or 4 times. 6 times. I have gone 6 times before. Lay together, proper, in a bed, in private.' Do to each other things that are illegal in 26 states of the United States of Amerikkka.

'Then I can't keep my room. I'll go back to the Clark Theatre and sleep all night in the balcony for 25¢.'

Had spent many nights there with nowhere to go when first arriving, to save the little money she had.

And caught herself blurting it out, something to that effect to Lucy, who replied, "I've exchanged my love for presents from a woman. It wouldn't be a trick. I'd give her all night, not just 10 minutes or a half-hour. I give 'em ten minutes—tricks. If they can't make it in 10, too bad. If they take 8 minutes to get their pants down, too bad. That leaves 'em 2 minutes and 3 seconds to get it on. But I always give a woman the night. Women are the nicest to me... I knew a girl, she said one-fourth of her book was women. I don't know where she found them, or if she was lying, and just wished it was true because women are the best lovers. They're the freest. They take their time. I wish I could have plenty of women. They wouldn't be tricks to me. Anyway, you don't have to buy me a present... *Mickey.*" Lucy finished, and her mouth smiled big; in a closed line, her liquid eyes watching.

'She's going for $10.' Mickey was mad. Thought about the $20 and how long it would keep Lucy off the streets.

"But I'm not very experienced with women. I'm not a prostitute either, really... I just do it sometimes for money to stretch between my welfare checks. If you're Indian, they give you welfare—no questions asked. They think it's all you're good for. I don't find too many women. I don't know too much about...*butches.*"

Rage cooled at the sound of Lucy's voice & what she was saying.

Power—she wanted it. Power over life. Over how she lived & who she slept with.

Moon floated in the night, clouds in the sky covered it in shadow, to emerge, silver, beaming.

Mickey's carnal desire.

Pats one hand on her flat belly. Felt heat glow between her legs & knew she could go again.

Felt like a stud horse in heat, she wanted to fuck so bad. To get on top of Lucy and plow her.

Mickey flexed her muscles, jaw jutted out. 130 lbs. solid. Dark trousers, dark hair, dark shoes, white shirt, collar turned up; down of black hair covering her arms & legs—hidden under clothes, for only a lover to touch and to know.

Now, looking down from the skyline; the jagged monoliths of downtown—the Loop—& high-rise luxury suites by the lake. Skyscrapers of steel and metal and glass. Bold geometric shapes—built in mathematic precision.

Two figures, a redhead in toreador pants, blouse & sweater and sandals. And a tough butch, small, rolling down her sleeves. Like ants here below. Whose souls were of infinite more value than those skyscrapers in the distance. And immeasurable on the scales of life in the *Book of Changes*.

Put on her mannish jacket at last; become even more a visible lesbian to eyes who could read.

'Now I've been to this, your city of Chicago, and had a girl suck me off. So now I yearn to press my body full of her, and have all of her—to know her pussy intimately with my fingers & tongue & press my clit there; and suck her tits. And enter her mouth with my tongue and feel her tongue searching my mouth; and to squeeze her entire body in my arms.'

How she longed to fuck a woman's cunt with her fingers & taste pussyjuice on her lips, have it on her breath. Press her nose to Lucy's hair and smell her perfume like she had back in the toilet of the bar; this time to linger in her hair for eternity. To know every inch of Lucy's body and find out what pleased her. To work her fingers around and around in a circle up in her cunt & hear her groan, and feel Lucy tug her hair, and cum good. Feel her tighten inside. And if they positioned themselves right, to ride Lucy's cunt with her cunt, clits rub wet and smooth up and down against each other and give them both an orgasm at the same time. Then, after a nap, maybe she'd let Lucy ride her thigh; femmes like to get on a butch; it gives them a thrill. And to love each other orally.

The vision faded back to the streets where they were.

A character came walking stone-headed like a zombie, one leg straight, not bending at the knee, feet shuffling, eyes glued ahead stumbling & mumbling.

"LESTER!"

"Ohhhh, Lucy!" He dribbled spit from the mouth. "Duke & Freddy are up at the 409 Club. Freddy's gone, man; he's gone out of it."

Hallucinating, the out-of-action thief grabs and hugs Lucy. Blue tattoos stitch up patches of his white skin. Covered with inky blue serpents & roses. In a huge sunburst of affection that winos have for their compatriots, he produced a half-empty pint of gin. Both had a swig, Mickey declined. Watched the two talk their hot alcoholic wind saying little to each other but churning up their forces from alcohol. Then he was on his way—to nowhere along the time zone of drink, to make the world pass by thru whiskey eyes & tell bourbon lies. Mickey gawked at this denizen of lower Clark Street. As an ignorant country fool gazes up at tall buildings in a foreign city, so she stared in disbelief, shaking her head as Lucy gesticulated "See you back at the Bomber Club."

CHAPTER FIVE

Life in the barracks of these streets—an area circumscribed by Clark, Erie, the Chicago River, Rush Street, that formed the nucleus of skid row—the heart of wino town with the troops that Lucy knew.

"When we get to my place, come up and we can smoke a joint." Lucy tells Mickey.

This ain't what the butch had in mind.

So they had got down to the mouth of lower Clark Street, where the dregs spill up—the rummy bums, the troops of drunken Indians; whites—hillbillies with bib overalls lounging on doorstoops chewing a broom straw, unemployed, cold blue eyes gazing at nothing. Drink in a half-pint in the rear pocket, up from Kentucky; the Appalachians; & no jobs. And the Indians had lost their teepees; pursue now a warrior ghost across the cities of the plane.

This area was a degree below gay playground turf. Drink was the common denominator, so lower Clark Street held a little bit of all persuasions.

Two fairies flit by. Weren't many visible dykes like herself… Never are. Mickey walked the beaches, haunted El train stations & libraries. Like them tonight, just a few gay women were visible in this territory.

People wore poor broken-down shoes. Population of poverty increased dramatically.

Here on skid row, no one judged her harshly—too full of their own problems. Winos stumble by bleary-eyed; not casting looks of criticism—but staring at eternity before them thru an alcohol-funneled prism.

So, as soon as she entered this neighborhood, Mickey felt more comfortable dressed in drag.

Lucy turned into a wino bar to talk to some rum-bummies she knew.

'Aw…' Mickey thinks. 'She's gonna go in this dump & fuck off and forget about me.' The bantam butch spits onto the curb. 'I might as well go home and get drunk.'

Inside the club, the hillbillies were out; both men & ladies, like roaches crawling everywhere. Some Native Americans— Indians, weathered red-brown faces, wrapped in tribal blankets against the wall. Lucy peers in & don't see who she's looking for, ducks back out. The twosome hits the pavement again. This ducking into taverns is the shape of things to come.

At the Hasty Tasty on the corner, Lucy waves in the plate-glass window; seems to know people there also. It's a big hustling corner. "I know girls who turn dates out of there." Lucy brags.

Tattoo parlors and pawnshops.

Human throng with its fetishes, sex hang-ups, drink/drug needs & memories which haunt them still. They had entered this particular precinct noted in police files.

Cops flashing badges under fluorescent lights of the restaurant. Lucy's secret thoughts, as she pats a wisp of red hair back in place: 'I'm glad we turned that trick easy. Had to do nothing except love this butch broad, and I liked it. Don't have to be out here struggling, running the risk & going to jail & getting diseases. Mickey is clean. She is a clean person.' Sees the Vice cops, and feels the fear inside her. "See them guys with all the rings & watches & jewelry and expensive suits? They're cops, but they go into undercover work because that's where they can make all the extra money—from payoffs."

People who have lost their fortunes & they are here.

An old couple descends the open stairwell of a broken-down hotel. Very poor. The ancient woman is bent over in the spine, so her face is perpetually focused down at the sidewalk; helped along by the old man.

"There's a place in New York used to be called Hell's Kitchen." Mickey says.

"I seen it. It's rough."

A bum walks by, feet stuck in run-over shoes, so he walks on their worn leather sides. Another bum scurries by, trousers held together by safety pins.

The what-happened-to-them? people. Old grizzly face. Denims turned gray, no longer blue. Do a slow shuffle.

"Skid row ain't as big as the Bowery." Brimming full of thousands of alcoholics it made Clark Street look like a wino kindergarten.

As if somebody had pulled back the lid of hell to see all the creatures in torture; faces contorted by red flames, which grimace and twist; bizarre; who strike odd poses, whose lives had somehow wound up down here in the gutter.

A living mental institution.

Psychos, and drug-induced nuts who pop amphetamines for candy. And a gray-blue strain makes a stratus thru this—the sane-but-poor Appalachian presence in their too-often-washed denims. Women in gray dresses washed out too many times so all color fades out. They had worn the same clothes every day. It was all they had—on their backs. Yet a lot of the Southern hillbillies had their noses up in the air. Thinking they were better because they were simply poor and not mentally damaged. They were the Lords & Ladies of Clark Street.

Bomber 29 Club. Lucy pushes open the barroom door. See them. They had come to life—alcohol set fire to their spirits & they were spinning in motion; gaunt, raw boned skeletons. An evening full of characters in compost. Freddy, Duke, all the Clark Street troops.

Ghouls—on closer inspection, they were dead people. Just shells who stumble on and on—their dreams having flown.

The moment the door swung open, the troops, defensive in their barricade, turned around. A few hailed Lucy—then went back to their bottle.

The pretty Indian woman was right at home. Her hunger for drink would be fed here at the trough. Lucy's sexy round derriere sat on a bar stool—no sooner did she squat there, immediately is surrounded by a hag & a crone, one big white man, 2 smaller drunks, & a full-blooded Indian with a blanket over his shoulders standing behind her silent like a warrior of the invisible plains.

"Chief." Lucy spoke to her half-brother-in-spirit. "How's it going tonight?"

"Bad news." He muttered.

"It's the same, huh, Chief?"

He mumbled again.

Drunks were dancing as dancing bears, toothless; alcoholic fire forked out of their mouths.

The urban heat settled in here, and cold beer flowed. Lucy had a mug & Mickey at her side, foot up on a rung of the ladies' bar stool, drank the same. Her paying for them both. 'Hell, liquor's cheap down here.' Noticed that as she counted out her change & put it back in the wallet.

Alkies and Hobo Queens, drunk mental cases, robotlike, gone mad on doctors' drugs, stayed mad on the firewater.

"DUKE TRIED TO CLIMB UP ON THE BAR AND DANCE!"

"Everybody wants to be a star." Lucy says flatly, upper lip mustachioed with beer foam.

"Any fights?"

A few short fights, & by looks of the rough customers, there would gladly be more.

TWANG! TWANG! TWANG! The "Yellow Rose of Texas" floats out from a poor stage in back. Gravelly voiced cowboy with a southern twang, accompanied by a hillbilly on a washboard. He & his guitar twang together.

Suddenly Mickey looks back & sees danger.

"YOU BETTER COME HERE!"

"NO!" Lucy replies, arching her eyebrows peevishly.

A big white man looms over them; "WHEN YOU SEE ME, GODDAMMIT, SAY SOMETHING!" James hollered. "DOES IT COST YOU ANYTHING TO SAY *HELLO!* TO AN OLD FRIEND?" He yells icily, in a bellow, deep, from out of his bull chest.

Mickey felt herself lose ground inside, to fear. 'I might have to fight this big sonofabitch.' Her pale hand snaked into her pants pocket, cracked open her knife, ready to pull it out.

"*SHIT!*" He finishes and turns and goes back down the bar where he was, throwing his meaty leg over a bar stool, sits down, picks up a beer mug and downs it in a gulp.

Nearby a hag with no teeth from no dental care & a few of life's blows to knock them out, discusses Lucy. "Yuh see that redhead & that tall man with that big beer belly, that big man—they was having trouble. She's a bisexual. She can't keep her scenes straight. Here she comes in tonight with a butch. That's a woman she's with, a lezzie. And her man—or her ex-man, depending on who you talk to—hangs out here, and she knows he does. He's mad—look at him. He's gonna pick a fight with some guy & there's gonna be blood all over the floor. Blood all over, and the police will be crawling all over, too; heh, heh, heh!" The crone savors the idea. "James is mad. The butch, she's goin' for a knife I'll bet, or a razor. Look at her. What's she got her hand on down in her pocket, sweetie? Not money, I'll bet. She's jealous over that woman. Jealous. She got her eyes trained on Lucy hard. Lucy brought another butch in here a while back, and the lezzie left her— just left her at the bar drunk. They're all chippying on each other and Lucy don't care. She just wants to get drunk. I should know, I bought her enough drinks."

Mickey leaned, elbow on the bar, other hand clenched inside her pocket around the knife handle; foot up on the rail. Stood by Lucy, who blithely tipped up a second beer. Mickey saw the faces of Lucy's people. They were a population who entirely lined the benches against the wall and made few & steady sorties up to the bar for drink. 'She's one-half of what they are. It's a mess what alcohol did to this race.' Cracked red-brown cheeks from being in the sun day after day with dead time on their hands. Long oily black hair that hadn't been washed for years. 'Lucy's not one of them.' The butch thought, defensive.

B-29 Club. Hillbillies bellowed at each other; the guitar twangs. Indians silent back in their place, mute, make a few grunts & then a knuckled brown fist would fly out and blood spurts from somebody's nose. Squaw faces seated on the long bench that runs the length of the wall; coats from the Salvation Army pulled around their shoulders, and shawls, & ragged, filthy blankets. Sparks of fire from the firewater oozes out of cracks around their eyes and mouth. Faces scrunched up in silent pain. Deadened pain. Long black hair, missing teeth, brown-red skin—smooth skin. They never laughed. CRACK! A brave strikes his squaw backhand across her cheek right below her deadened eyes. And the hillbillies holler in a hellish din.

Gang of blue-jeaned men scream at each other thru gin— continuing the Great Hillbilly Debate which shall never die— whether to go back home to Kentucky or stay up here in this cold-blooded Yankee town and try to find work that don't exist.

"BLOODY MARY." And Lucy bangs her empty beer mug on the counter. Had escalated her drink to the more potent vodka—the alkies' choice.

Did she drink this Bloody Mary because it was the color of her dyed red hair? Or because tomato juice has nourishment? Or because vodka is the strongest-proof alcohol she could get? Native Americans staggered around in back drunk on mere beer. Genetically, Lucy could drink along with a purebred white. Irish, German, anything. Alcohol didn't drive her completely crazy. Would sit, emotionless like an underseas fish; mascara rubbing off, her curvaceous body in toreadors & low-cut blouse holding its slender dignity on a barroom stool.

Somewhere jasmine bloomed a sweet stinky smell. In some distant epoch, the buffalo roamed. But all together here was a mishmash of personalities; & nothing left of nature; confined within the bare walls of a box-shaped bar.

Bums in clothes that stink shuffle by.

Lucy is completely high. Teeth smile. Eyes half-closed emit laser sparks when she bats her lashes. Feels real good. The incessant gloom which rolls back begrudging and gives up its golden lining—and lets her live a brief moment; as it has to do when she gets high & everybody is welcome. Hags come up and squeeze her around the waist and sip a drink out of her glass; men stop and babble incoherently at her; she's friendly with everyone. Slow metabolism of her body comes alive; & leaves Mickey from time to time to go around the tavern plucking people on their sleeve to talk, recounting some mystery of her life to one and all.

Mickey watches, draws into herself, nurses still, her first beer. Powered by a high place—a very high and black place inside her soul—a great force whirling, winding out of the core of her being, a spirit funnels up like a tornado.

Butch Mickey abandons the safety of her bar stool, strides thru the crowd; click of her shoes over the worn bloodstained floor. Grabs Lucy tenderly, but firmly; and as a tugboat guides a big ship, guides her back to port, their place marked by the drinks. Here Mickey comes on with everything she has. Every word whispered, touching her gently—briefly—so no one has a chance to notice. And finally the redhead turns her face to listen to and be swept up by Mickey, ignoring the old cronies & rum-bums & toothless hags.

Mickey wanted a home—as clean, peaceful, pretty, and safe as could exist.

Her life, with her women had been a struggle to work toward this. To join hands with a woman on this earth place and begin to share their lives.

Mickey was a powerhouse, pouring out her guts and spilling her soul. And Lucy is caught up by the conversation, & personal attention, and by Mickey's dark eyes boring right into her—seeing her, a thing the alkies can't do. And so the redhead did a thing she seldom did—was really moved. Let herself be touched by another human being. and responded. Tugged shyly on Mickey's jacket with her nail-polished fingers. "Oh, honey. I want to be with you. OK. I guess we can leave. I was just having fun. Don't be mad at me! Don't leave me, Mickey! *Please don't leave me!*"

"I'll buy you some Chianti, and we can take it to your place."

"In the nice bottle wrapped in straw. It's romantic."

A stoneface Indian, head held up in pride, silent lips wearing no smile glided beside Lucy, stopped, stiff, stood, beckoning the bartender for another firewater, using no words, just grunts, and sign language. The black-haired butch saw the two of them in profile. That's when she noticed the resemblance in Lucy's part-Indian face. And Mickey realized: 'I'm gonna have to hold on to her tight, or she's gonna slip away and find her way back down to this gutter night after night.'

A member of the alkie troops sports everybody on his pension check: "ANOTHER DRINK FOR MY FRIENDS!" Peels greenbacks off a wad. Old cronies & strangers alike lift their glasses in a salute.

The guitar man comes back on, pours golden notes into the dismal bar; simultaneous as the rush of 99 proof hits Lucy from her new drink.

But she has not forgot Mickey. Soon pale white arms are flung around the butch & a slobbering kiss on the cheek, as she tries to fight Lucy and seat her ladylike back on top of the stool & not get them harassed by the straights; amid the twang of steel guitars. Lucy sees nothing but Mickey now.

They are leaving. Old bums stumble thru the cavernous bar, worn out, they drink up their social security; buy a few eats, pay room rent & drop dead. Some, retired from jobs with big pension checks, are comparatively rich. Sport others to free drinks; not mean or cheap that way, under the red-blue light bulbs & honky-tonk music grinding out day into night into day into night. The two lesbian lovers spill with the music thru the empty doorway amid aromas of sour milk spilt from garbage cans and a cry of "ANOTHER DRINK FOR MY FRIENDS! SET 'EM ALL UP!"

Night. Starpoint whirls firecrackers spiral in the black sky.

Back in the interior of the tavern, the hag confides in a crony: "She's got bad habits, that girl. I've seen her hand sneak out and clip money from the bar—many a time. She has a quiet face, but she's the devil. She's pretty, so she gets away with it. Just wait a few years and look at her then. Lucy clips money off the bar, & everybody knows it." Her toothless face smiles & snaps shut. "She better be careful." The crony mutters to the hag, in a warning.

Cribs made of sticks. Tenement flats of yesteryear subdivided into rooms that house a greatly multiplied number of people from their original design.

Music of taverns rises, floats to the sky.

Some old dame is out begging under starlight.

Ruffians shuffle thru it—seen from above are dots. Billboards illuminated by lights are colorful spots. At the windows, people gaze out. Between the middle of the block & the newspaper stand on the corner might be 500 people, counting all the dwellers loitering around behind the torn yellow shades half naked in their slips and underpants.

Past restaurants with pickle smells & hamburger & fries on the grill wafting out in the night air.

Beer smells stale, stank of decades of spilt drinks from a tavern. They walked into the night; occasionally their hands would bump against each other.

"There's so much goddamn trouble in these honky-tonks. Worse than the gay bars. Somebody always getting slapped or knocked down, and bleeds. Blood splats all over."

They passed the wine experts, who abbreviated their lives. Alkies, who dedicated their life to the cause of Jack Daniel's.

Disheveled vessels, stumbling, upholding life's banner of a huge vacant need.

Mickey touched Lucy's hand. They were together, weaving amid the dangerous & mad.

"Gotham Police Force." The redhead mutters, half-drunk. Sees the police ride by, scoping, but not at them. "Yesterday I was walking from the El station at North Avenue, back home, and I had on a pair of shorts because of the sun. And a fucking police van follows me all the way back up North Avenue and don't stop tailing me till almost at Clark."

"If you are my Lady, you'd never turn a trick again. I swear it." Mickey fixes her with a gaze.

What had started as trade was become a Love Story.

CHAPTER SIX

Buildings of the East, like the tenement hotels of the Tenderloin, New York, Chicago, Baltimore, remind one of each other. Tall, drab, full of gaping dusty windows and fire escapes zigzagging up.

The midday heat of real summer in hot Mid Amerika daze continues on into the night, bursting from the searing pavements. Laundry washed in suds in bathtubs hangs out on grillworks of the fire escapes to dry, and people sleep there to find relief. All nationalities being of the same race—poor. Chattering, wild.

Bag ladies scurry, busy, under tons of paranoia, along the pavement that she must share with Lucy & Mickey who drift by hand in hand. Hag clutches her garbage sacks defensively, and mutters to herself.

Social security recipients still sit in the Hasty Tasty restaurant window, reading a newspaper—at 2:00 A.M.

"WHEN I CLOSE MY EYES THE WORLD SEEMS SO MUCH BIGGER IN DARKNESS." Mickey told Lucy as she bumps along beside her.

"Open your eyes, dumbbell!" Lucy is still drunk, walking

in open-back pump shoes that take on towering heights.

Floor after floor of desolate buildings; some shades are pulled down, others ripped open, by a derelict's claw hands. If these buildings had a soul, it would be one forever about to cry.

Street faces. A madman persecuting himself relentlessly as if in an evil spell. And Mickey tells Lucy: "I used to pick my acne and get open sores and I was anxious about this, and worried that I wasn't improving myself. Now I see most of my worries are in my head—and the fact that I don't have a job." Glanced in a window they passed, yellow-lit, of a brick hotel, wondering, 'Is this her place? Are we there yet?'

People of the street carry a weariness. Immediately Mickey notices that Lucy has a weary relaxed air, as if she don't give a damn. Mickey on the surface has adopted this attitude, but down deep inside, secretly, she does give a damn. Wants to make life work for herself somehow, some way, no matter if it is against all odds. Inside of her there is something so precious that she is afraid for it, and doesn't know how to handle it, and blocks it up mostly, behind her face, unfeeling like a wall, her stance, mean, like a gangster; yet secretly does not want this flame, this alive, growing thing to die. Like a match waiting to be struck, out here in The Life.

And Lucy's attitude is not the same as the drunks—who fight the same fights over and over; she sees there is a place beyond it—maybe a hereditary memory of the tepees of the plains—not wanting to get stuck in the rat race; sits & drinks & walks thru this dead land of alkies cold frozen fear, yet in her mind knows of a place beyond; beyond all the madness…while the troops' assumption is—they live by this code—that there is nothing else. Because it's invisible, this flame, this green growing thing. And it's a nasty life with nothing else. The calendar grinds on over mathematical space of days—without a spirited sight of someplace far greater.

"Freddy offered me some scag—heroin—back at the B-29 Club." Lucy looks at Mickey shyly, her red hair wisps flying from her head. "He knows some broads who chippy with scag & any kind of drug you want. I said no, because I'm going to be with you tonight."

"I'm glad, Lucy!" The butch grabs her in a bear hug, as their feet walk rapidly, tussling together.

Before, Lucy would have been in a hurry to pop pills, or ingest anything else offered to her so she'd know everything would be OK, in her low self-esteem. Now, her mind was preoccupied by this new person at her side.

"You don't use drugs?"

"No. They kill people. I want to stay alive. I stopped drinking, too—mostly. When I was younger, I stayed drunk."

So, they walk, busily talking between themselves about what they've done in each other's absence—all the years before they met. And have an argument—brief, about stopping in another bar: "Just for a quick minute!"

"NO!" Firmly.

They walk thru the pattern of blocks. Vast cranes loom in the night where the city is demolishing a building.

Redhead clutches her decorative sweater to her. "Brrr…it's cooling off."

Wind blows its fingers thru their hair. Rattles her teeth. "It's as cold as a witch's tit on the dark side of the moon."

Cars exhaust, shifting gears, fly by. Party goers headed to the 5:00 A.M. license clubs on Broadway.

A pigeon feather flew out of the eaves of a building's cranny, floats down onto the scene. And Mickey would never forget that place—the hotel that Lucy now pointed out to her; or the night, and how they met…in love…

So she lived here, on skid row where everybody's old, wrinkled, and wears old clothes; or young and drunk, or crazy, or mean and unemployed.

Alkies take different forms—a nameless showgirl once billed as Boom-Boom now has no fame, no longer a star, bare legs still in short costumes; wrapped up in a drab coat for protection drinks her guts out at a skid row bar, losing her teeth, till her face becomes plain.

West Erie. 600 block. Fleabag hotel. The Bristol.

Mickey didn't know Lucy yet, but already didn't want to see her become like that aged showgirl the redhead had pointed out back in the tavern. In the yellow pool of light gathered at the hotel entrance, they stopped; the butch looked around her; then at the woman, imagined what it would be like when again she'd come out of her clothes, naked; wondered how Lucy'd wind up...living like she did, being what she was...a pretty girl, too shy to earn big money, too low to climb up out of the skids; just teetering on a bar stool until the hand of fate would give her a shove in one direction or the other. And caught like Mickey herself, in a web of poverty and chaos.

The hotel housed a tavern below, in its bowels; lights blinked off & on. Buildings & hotels 4 to 5 stories created a solid wall down the street; elevated, rooms faced other rooms across the span of the street, clothes draped over fire escapes drying in the night air. Cement, and thousands of windows, TV aerials, chimneys and the black sky above.

"So you like it, living down here? With all these chumps and tricksters?" Mickey says, sarcastic. "My room rent's the same as yours, almost, and my area is nicer."

"Every club I go to is here."

And all the fine art of this world, born thru pain; Van Gogh paintings worth millions of dollars which thieves steal from the Louvre & people go wild and crazy over collecting the genius, the art—it's as hard to get as to reach up and take a star out of heaven; this genius smothered down on skid row. The flame is doused. 'You'll never be good for anything.' Mrs. Leonardi had told her daughter. And Mickey was struggling to keep her flame, her genius or whatever that inner quality of people—and not be like these derelicts, not even old, who sit on the ash cans mumbling to themselves. To not disintegrate.

See a pile of rags, with feet stuck out and wonder—is that a human being under there? Didn't want it to be her epitaph: HERE LIES MICKEY—THE LIVING DEAD.

So, the two turned, headed into the doorway, past ghouls and paranoid troops and bullies and black marketeers selling heroin, and drooling idiots who use.

In the entrance of Lucy's hotel, that contained them, on the doorstep; having gained semi-privacy; Mickey briefly cups the woman's shoulders in her strong hands. "I'm gonna make it so good for you."

They trip up the stairs, jog by the ruined faces who mumble in descent.

At the second story, down a tattered-carpet hall; behind every door—death, or mutters, screams, or raving going on and on and on upon an even keel thru eternity....

In Lucy's building the first floor of the residence starts on the 3rd story. At the first turn of the staircase, on the landing, was a man talking to himself; at the second landing a wino spitting up bloody vomit stinking wine. At the third, a hag curses at them. Peeling plaster walls, utilities don't work. Pipes bust in the walls in winter. Toilets jam.

Come to a battered door with a number affixed. Lucy has a key on a big plastic tag; opens it, they walk in, the door shuts behind. A room to themselves. At last they were alone.

At once Mickey saw she had a front room. No heat. Red lights shot off/on; and music's rhythm thru the ceiling from the tavern below. Rumbling. Bar stools overturn in a fight that breaks out every few hours or so. Chaos, muted by layers of floors, issuing up from the cavernous bar below—as if from hell; realm of the perpetual drinkers, sending a message to remind the butch that security seemed just out of her reach.

This room 10 by 12. Sink; porcelain yellowed by dripping water. Transient. Where a parade of whores both male and female had done blowjobs over time; and pigeons swish their wings in the eves, who have been with us since civilization dawned, evolving along beside humankind.

Mickey feels fire in her sex; can't keep her eyes or hands off Lucy, who brushes off the amorous butch, for she has to go around her room doing stuff first.

And Mickey goes to the window; by the radiator, opens a torn shade, puts her hands on the filthy window ledge, leans, looks down into the street below. 'It's a dangerous world out there. Dangerous to the heart.' Private thoughts. For she has seen the cronies Lucy has, how they influence the redhead.

Those hags and bums with their bags of pills and connection to drugs. Swimming in their unending sea of drink.

And knows from experience that the world tries to crowd in thru insidious ways and underhanded means when it's not wanted; and shuns you and leaves you insanely lonely, cold and blue when you need it the most.

CHAPTER SEVEN

Mickey pushes Lucy down on the bed, french-kisses deep into her mouth; pets her tits; eager to take her like a man; to prove her prowess as a lesbian butch; to put her fingers in Lucy's hole right away & try to make her holler and climax. After, to use her by riding; her furry black-haired cunt pressed down in Lucy's cunt.

Lucy's femmy shoes clatter to the floor, thrown off over the edge of the bed. The butch peels off the woman's sweater, opens her blouse & smells the perfume.

Lucy looks so fine, in flickering illumination from the tavern sign. White skin tan above the neck, hands and face from being in the sun. Removes her bra, and out bounce large breasts with rosy nipples as a secret treasure coming out of her brassiere. Lush, full tits.

"Oh, baby!" Mickey caressed her square hands on Lucy's shoulders, then breathlessly cupped each large tit. Stomach pressed to the warmth of Lucy's curvaceous back. Hips rounding outward. "I love you." Mickey breathes fast & short. Squeezes hard the nipples on her breasts.

"Mickey!" Lucy moans.

Turns around to face the woman and unzips her toreador pants. Body heat & aroma spill out from her white thighs that are seldom in the sun. Pubic hair, brown wisps & fragrance of wet delights. Mickey slides Lucy's panties, satin, down over her legs; and woman aroma hits her nostrils. She pets & hugs and watches, and is so glad they're alone, in a room streaked by neon from street lamps, and a wall flickering from the advertisement like a heartbeat. 'I know she's mine, mine for the taking.' And Mickey would take her well.

'Wonder if she'll take off her shirt? Butch dykes do it different.' Lucy's blunt nose, solemn expression on seeing Mickey still fully clothed, watching her in such appreciation. 'What a butch she is. Wow. Will she ask to see me again after this is over? So many others have just left me. Maybe she has a woman already & just ain't telling.'

Mickey appreciates Lucy's beauty, touching her, as she sat, stripped down out of her clothes; and then came out of her trousers and shirt. Now, the butch—it was no doubt what she was—a woman with a woman's body. A dyke who wanted females, and who took on the man's role.

Lucy saw the Ace bandage wrapped around Mickey's chest. The butch was embarrassed as she unwound it; but Mickey wanted to go all the way with her ladies and let them experience her full body; and not hide herself in rough clothes like a lot of diesel dykes.

Mickey's own breasts fell out, large, white, firm. Pink nipples stood up hard, because she was so aroused. The redhead marveled, asked shyly, "Can I touch you too?"

"Yeah, I don't care." Mickey replied, gruff. Pulling down her boxer shorts to show the black fur of her mound. "But don't tell nobody."

And thinking secretly—as this Lady's persona was not written bold in a statement like her own: 'Is Lucy bi? Or could she go gay and be my girl? It's for sure her love is good and hot towards a woman.'

Blue boxer shorts were off on a pile of her clothes on the floor & the bed creaked under them. Mickey felt thrills of desire as she caressed Lucy and felt the woman's hands loving her tits, too, fingers twisting the nipples gently; felt her cunt about to break forth in a climax of lusty power.

Rode her for a moment, Lucy's thighs clutched hers, felt her sex hot and damp against Mickey's thigh.

Mickey sucked each ripe breast, then slid down Lucy's belly, parted the moist pubic hair and tongue-licked into her wet cuntlips. Fingers working with her tits. Lucy moaned, lay back wiggling. And Mickey was in her with two fingers pounding up to the last knuckle. Felt her legs go rubbery, hips thrust upward involuntary. And the butch felt lust grow between her thighs.

Her full lips on Lucy's. Pushed her tongue round and round; so thirsty, probed deep into her mouth, tasted her breath; hands pet feverishly. 'Ohhhh she's got to let me go all the way.' And, as an answer, slowly Lucy's tongue responds.

Lucy waits as Mickey pets her. Hand between her thighs. "Oh, baby. Sweet, sweet baby. Mickey's baby." Ran red-nailed fingers thru the black butch hair; as Mickey slid fingers over her wet clit. And she opened up so easy, moaned; and held one of Mickey's hands on her tit. Mickey's tongue searched into her mouth, and her fingers entered her wet chamber.

Came together for all the carnal, sensual and erotic reasons. Juices flow. Sex so hot the blood ran cold in her veins. Loved Lucy's bust; ran her fingertips over warm skin of her curvaceous hips. Mickey wanted to quench that fire in her loins in the worst way.

10 by 12 room, half of its space taken up by a bed. Tall ceilings with dust & a rusty sink—this didn't matter. A woman lay under her to be taken. Scent drifts from her armpits and cunt; breathed into Mickey's narrow nostrils. A woman who wants her—waits. Free, easy. Who gives Mickey the control —sex power pulsating between her legs for a few minutes of joy snatched from the universe. Tonight, gave Mickey the control. A hot one-night stand? How long would they make it last?

Kisses up and down the length of Lucy's body, licks two fingers, covers them with spit and slow, pushes her middle finger down thru the pubic hair into the wet folds of Lucy's pussy and goes into her hole, deep, while sucking a tit, and moves her finger around inside; comes out, then goes in with two fingers, and begins pounding away on her. Beside the bed, thru the shades, red lights from the tavern advertisement blink off and on spattering the green walls.

"You don't have to keep on doing that Mickey. That's enough." Lucy pants. "Lick me awhile, please—just for a minute."

White, naked, Mickey leans over Lucy a moment, her wavy

black hair tousled. "Why didn't you go in there with Lenore and make some more money?" Asks, because she wants to hear it again.

Lucy lays in the sheets, hands holding her lover's face. "Because I wanted to keep the taste of you in my mouth. I wanted you to go with me—I could see you were a butch, and I want a woman, and I hoped I could be with you, but I wasn't sure if you wanted to be with me. I didn't know if you had a woman somewhere. I wanted to keep your taste in my mouth—in case you left. You're the first woman I've had in so long."

A thrill shot thru Mickey, head to toe. She moved down to be between Lucy's thighs, hands caress warm flesh, tongue licks, burrows thru the fur of her mound, into the juicy pink lips, hands spread them; then as she sucks caresses up to Lucy's tits, squeezing hard, and the redhead exhales sharply: "OHHHHHH... Baby... Ohhhhh... God..." Noises in rhythm to what the butch does to her.

Mickey clutches Lucy to her; their tousled heads together; red & black on the bed. The butch felt she was bursting with cum.

Lucy stroked Mickey's hard little muscles, raised her hips; Mickey, determined, shoved a pillow under her ass to tip her hips up so she could ride her.

After the bigger people pushed ahead of her, and society pushed her under the rug and out of the way; society got what they wanted first; now it was her turn. A Lady in bed, encircled by naked arms. Touch white breasts, her hand strokes their fullness. A sweet, deep kiss. To ride her wet cunt, lick it, love it.

For a moment, fingers traced a line down Lucy's stomach to her thighs, to her crotch, as she continued to sweep in waves of lust, long, swirling.

The bigger carnivores had left the scene. The world had gone by—the shops and factories that didn't want to hire her. Restaurants and bars that didn't want to serve her—after they all did what they wanted to for themselves, and closed up shop and said 'ho hum,' and left—now, at last it was Mickey's turn.

She had stolen a piece out of this insane world with its trade & freaks—now it was Mickey's time. Behind a pulled-down tattered shade in Lucy's hotel room that looked out over rooftops of a mean city; felt sex lust rise between her legs, up thru the core of her body. Hot glow of desire suffusing thru her chest and arms, a hot rush making her catch her breath; anticipation, expectation bending over the woman in the bed, a master of this love.

Got between her legs and jammed her wet sex against Lucy's cunt. Saw the expression on Lucy's face as she thrust her hips round and round; clutching Lucy, kissing her, and groaning. The butch's cock was hot!

Her toes dug into the sheets. Bed creaked under the weight of their bodies. Bed, ancient, dipped in the middle, held them.

Cunts pressed together; the axes of their beings spun. Mickey's hips ground, driving her clit, bearing down, & Lucy receiving her; they were as one body.

Mickey stops, raises up, licks her fingers, rubs spit on their cunts to make them slide together along with their cuntjuice, and her ass is going around and up and down between Lucy's thighs. "WOW." Dull thuds of the bed, exuberant; pounded her loins. Lucy feels it too, runs her fingers over Mickey's strong back.

Lucy gave herself so well; clutches Mickey's slippery wet back & moves her hips, so the butch knows she's striving for an orgasm herself.

"OHHHH! IT'S SO GOOD!" Hot and hard, firmly slapping her sex, pubic hair mixing, release was coming…. Gave it to her hot and hard.

Lucy wiggled, moved her hips up and down, rubbing her cunt in Mickey's, in fast motion.

Manicured hand on the back of Mickey's neck—felt it grow even hotter; the butch's back was beaded with sweat as she labored, grunting to a climax.

Finest thing, when Lucy's cunt hungered for Mickey, moving herself, hungry as well, working under her. Mickey was tired of being so restricted, so angry, so afraid, so poor.

This was the answer to it all!

Prickling heat fused up from the center of her back, spread across her shoulders, making her neck tingle. White-hot bolts of fire shot up out of her clit. She worked, pumping her hips, moving her sex, red hot in Lucy's juicy pussy. And the bed against the wall went; SLAM SLAM SLAM!

At last she was cumming to power!

Wanted to fuck to tell their message of love. White bodies congress under the stars.

Pounding her, flat belly slapped hot against Lucy's, her shoulders were raised up above Lucy, propped up on her hands, like doing a push-up. Now she stopped, lay down on her breathing hard, hot lust zoomed up from her groin. Questioned Lucy, panting: "Want me to go down on you and get you hotter so we can cum together?"

Perfumed, painted, warm... Juice of their bodies, discharge and sweat rubbed together; between their legs.

Pungent female smell. Raised up on her hands on the mattress, toes clutched into the sheets, raised up above her. The woman's hot, smooth thighs spread for her, her butt on the pillow. Rested above her a moment, still panting; to prolong the moment of ecstasy.

Now focused down on the girl beneath her with full sexual intensity, her hips driving like a piston. The bed jiggles, her clit rubs; ecstasy rolls in waves, the letting go inside; cumming of herself.

Her whole body is on fire, jerks, a sobbing motion, between Lucy's legs spread, muscles tight in sexual anticipation, her toes dig into the bed.

The redhead Lucy bottom receiving her love.

Lucy arches up under Mickey, groans, feels Lucy's red fingernails dig into her freckled white shoulders.

Wanted Lucy to cum with her. Went down on her again. Slides down her bare legs, kissing & licking. "Ever done it like that?"

"Yes."

"Can you cum?"

"I think so."

Mickey wants to make sure, so she gets her hotter, licking her cunt, sucking Lucy's clit. Raises her head up for breath a moment; "Tell me when to stop and come back up." So they can have a mutual orgasm.

Mouth on her pussy, stimulating with tongue and lips. 'Hope I can make her cum with me.'

After a time of oral love, mounted her again, looked down at Lucy while moving her cunt around in Lucy's pussy; tall in the saddle, holding back the reins; wanting Lucy to cum.

Thrust her hips, driving her cunt up and down, Lucy moves her hips fast, moans, fingers dig into Mickey. Hot juices flow, burst forth.

They work to a hot finish. Faces flush; cunts fused together, hot cuntlips full, making better contact.

Holding herself raised up on her hands, between the woman's legs spread out on both sides, ten painted toes twinkling in the air; humping her hips fast, pounding Lucy's cunt; moving and enjoying the pleasure as she came a long time. Kept screwing and cumming.

Lay on Lucy's warm body, in her embrace; in a while rolled off because Mickey knew she was heavy.

Sweaty. Lay on her side; held each other, felt the rise and fall of one another's breath.

Could cum a third time!

Gathered her into her arms.

So she got on top and began humping once again.

Lucy and Mickey's bare meat coupling together.

And her toes dug into the bed, clutch for support, to get traction, as her hips kept thrusting, her sex powerfully hot.

She gave it up so sweet. She gave it up so good.

"I WANT TO GIVE YOU MY LOVE! UH UH UH!"

Cum corkscrew unwound out of her body from a deep core.

Chest rose and fell from the passion they'd just shared, with release of her cum.

Her sweat dripping off her flesh, dried in the tepid air of the hotel room.

After these orgasms, they clung in each other's arms.

After, Mickey held Lucy. Her hot cunt, her warm tits; just being close.

"I'll show you a way you can cum with fingers inside you; a woman taught me."

Lucy smiled.

"Can you cum with me just being inside of you?"

"Very rarely."

Used butch fingers inside her. Tight sphincter muscles pushed open; two fingers glide in; Mickey felt her lush, full pussy; savored Lucy's scent. The redhead moaned with urgency as she felt fingers moving inside; then Mickey slid down the femme's damp thighs to put her other hand in her pussylips and pressed on her clit to stimulate it, too. And knew by the hard jerking reaction that Lucy would cum again soon.

Her vaginal cavity was big, wet; felt the rippling movement of her inside walls; the hard piston thrust of her fingers got a reaction from Lucy, who murmured.

She was glad, oh so glad. Deep thrusting tongue, mouth, fingers; Lucy's sexhole, hot and good. Other hand rubbing up and down over her swollen clit.

Drove her fingers in and out while stimulating her hard, swollen clit until her pussy began to clench in a vaginal orgasm.

Thrust into her hard.

Her red-hot sexhole; down into the core of her being, beginning to cum.

One, then 2 fingers stroked down into Lucy's wet chamber.

Immediately the redhead spread her thighs wider, mouth opened, let herself go.

The butch comes out and rams 3 fingers back into her hole; while running her tongue up and down her slit in her cuntlips over and over her clit; held her, breathing hard.

The femme rolls her hips, up in the air, back arched, straining; a deep vaginal tightening.

Orgasmed quickly on her hand.

'Wow, she came quick. Didn't even get to go down on her again.'

"Ohhh."

It had been a long time cumming for Lucy, too.

Sex with Mickey was fine.

To Lucy, one of the most exciting events of living was sex with another woman. Her own passionate heat, and Mickey's adept style of loving her body, building the fire in her, one thrill crashing into the wave of the next. Mickey's tongue licking up and down her clit; lust crashing over her body in hot, ecstatic waves like the sea upon the shore.

Now, as once again the red hot butch got on, between her legs and rubbed her sex down into her cunt as she lay there, thighs spread, pinned to the bed; an ecstasy she could not have imagined built to explosion. Her back arched off the bed; moaning, cries, hands tightened on Mickey's strong, sweaty back in orgasm.

Mickey, pale white flesh, humps; their stomachs slap together, abandon to pleasure of this butch woman, felt her hips thrust up, with each thrust rubs clit to clit and builds the fire higher, till her hips thrust involuntarily, to completion.

Her hands wrapped shyly around the back of her lover's head, fingering the ducktail hairdo.

Mickey felt her whole body go hot all over; such a long time before this evening since she had that feeling.

Mickey finished. Lay on top of her panting. After a while passed, thoughts of the future, of being left alone once more drifted thru her mind. 'Oh, if she'd just put it in her mouth once more. 'Cause I may never see her again, nor have this opportunity….' "Lucy!"

"Yes baby?"

"Honey, put it in your mouth once more please!"

Fourth time the butch came, she wanted her cock in the redhead's mouth.

Demands it. "French me like you did back there!"

They got up from the bed; Lucy kneels on the floor and Mickey stands over her.

Lucy smiles dreamily, her hands slowly reach up around Mickey's ass. "I'll suck you any time of day or night, *Mickey*." She looked up and said this, then bent back to her work in earnest.

Mickey's cunt, still throbbing, went into Lucy's wet open mouth.

Red heartbeat of the advertisement, as a pulse smears the walls.

Mickey stands over Lucy for the second time in that 12-hour interval. Redhead took the butch's cunt in her mouth again. Familiar now, but here in private they loved so much finer. It felt so good to Mickey, it stirred her soul; and she really wanted Lucy to be her girl.

She serviced her.

Her cock went back and forth in her mouth, in little jabs, red-hot.

And soon let go; she felt warmth build up, she felt her sex, strong, virile. "Oh, it's good, baby! It's so damn good!" Was letting it go.

Hips thrust wildly, giving up her cum.

Finished.

Bed creaked as the two lovers tumbled into it; held each other fierce. Red smeared the walls off and on in blinks.

In a sudden burst of emotion—from her heart—the butch kissed Lucy all over her neck, her shoulders. "Thank you, baby, thank you."

CHAPTER EIGHT

Mickey was surprised; Lucy's room wasn't half-bad—considering the dilapidated condition of the building.

Gradually, as red lights blinked off & on from the sign of the tavern, and neon street lamps; it became visible.

Accustomed to the dimness, blinking, black hair tousled, the butch could see what the reason was. The half-breed Indian woman had done little things: hand-sewn curtains hung on the wall as decorations; wooden fruit cartons painted, used as shelves—that fixed up the place.

Bed where Lucy lay was old & lopsided permanently from weights of hundreds of occupants over the years.

FURNISHED ROOMS WITH OR WITHOUT BOARD $7.50 PER MONTH. A sign practically faded by time off the brick side of the building—from the 1940's. HOT WATER.

A luxury feature for those post-depression days seldom existed here now. So the decline of the neighborhood here on skid row, from the status quo to subhuman. A painted sign from antiquity. No hot water. Lack of heat in winter. And full of the firewater the tenants were insulated from feeling.

A pipe in the plaster-peeling wall made a dying rattle. It was the worst place, but far better than being in the street. Mickey stood under a naked gold light bulb that hung from an electrical wire.

Now, this dwelling was very sparse of items. The redhead traveled light. Few clothes, very few household goods; 2 sheets, 2 or 3 towels. 3 plates. A battered old black-&-white TV.

On the table a hot plate. Stack of canned goods.

The 10-by-12 foot room had a broken-down bureau & chair plus the bed of their night of lesbian love.

Just a place for an alcoholic to flop down in.

Little details in this great moment that surrounded Mickey. She saw the box of cereal, the food cans on the table. It was Lucy. Lucy's home! Lucy's embrace around her!

Like the match, her flame had been struck!

White; tousled wisps of red hair in which roots of brown had begun to show thru, full tits, wide hips, Lucy sprawled on the bed. Her vagina hurt; feeling it was not pain, but just feeling inside her cunt where Mickey had used it with her fingers, hard.

Mickey saw that Lucy had nice teeth, smiling. 'She ain't like these bums down here on lower Clark Street. Lucy is nice looking, she still has her teeth. Her place is fixed up. She ain't drunk now.'

Mickey stood, naked, a statue in the room; bare feet on a disintegrating carpet, brown, threadbare.

Catholic, she envisioned God as a darkness. A great power to whom all missing animals and peoples souls are bound back up; & are comforted & reunited in heaven when they somehow get lost on earth.

'Thank you for your kindness,' she wanted to say to God.

Had felt the lust drain out of her body, received into the body of a woman—Lucy; and her loneliness too, relieved.

'That Lucy's the silent type.' Mickey observes.

Yellow-lit room. Cracks in the walls and sounds of derelicts beyond.

"When we first met, I guessed your nationality was Spanish."

"Italian. And you're a—"

"Sioux Indian. Half."

"What's the other half?"

"I didn't have a father."

"Then my guess is as good as yours."

She knew the Native Americans down on Clark Street, wrapped up in their blankets & their drink.

Mickey shrugged off the unpleasant memory.

Was at the window, looking thru the curtain Lucy had made by hand and hung over the antique shade, sliced & torn & dusty which she hadn't bothered to remove. 'She knows the art of kissing. So receptive to me as a female lover. No matter if she likes men or not, she is the type I can safely pursue, because she needs a woman. I feel that. Maybe because I'm a butch I can be both for her, the man & the woman.'

Mickey's handsome face peered out the window. Across the street, a brick building with dusty windows & tattered shades just like this.

She saw outside these human prison walls, the pigeons.

Clumsy bodies, tiny heads on top of the huge bottom—the rest of their body. Red feet. Stupid-brained pigeons.

What a magnificent gift they have! When their wings spread, borne up by a current of wind, & they hover, airborne!

Transformation is instantaneous—like a wink of bright sun when they take flight! Bare wingspan, grace. Then they descend lightly, red toes touching cement ledges just an arm's reach from where the butch stood now.

Stared out into space just a moment. Red light blinked off and on.

'Pigeons, in jail how I watched them fly.'

And just a breath away, back inside the darker interior, was love.

Neither one of them had a timepiece. Lucy wore a gold dial on a band as a feminine decoration. It didn't work. So she'd have to get up with the sun like her Native forebears; guessing what time it was; and go sit out in front of the Welfare office & wait till it opened. Every 6 months to be re-evaluated by her case worker. Other than this, the days and nights of her life were free.

Tub down the hall didn't work & had capped-off pipes which was illegal. The building had 175 violations of public health. Tenants who were sober enough to think, lived in fear the city would shut the place down and demolish it, so nobody complained. Lucy didn't take full baths. Just washed her privates and underarms in the sink. 'She'll be glad to take a bath at my place.' It was a public bathroom, too, but the landlady made sure it was kept nice. 'I could move her in my place. Then she'd really be my woman.'

Lucy's place was a combo of garbage can & intense artistry. Scavenged pieces nailed together & odd fabrics sewed inventively. TV in shaky black-&-white images showed her favorite program: Desi yelling at Lucy about one of her wild harebrained schemes with Ethel Mertz.

Mickey struts, a peacock in the tiny room. Very satisfied. Tired & her body totally relaxed. And her stomach hungry. Ravenous in starvation.

Lucy saw Mickey; all wrapped up in a neat little package. All the working parts; fingers, toes, tongue, clit. This 18-year-old who'd pleasured her—made her orgasm internally.

Mickey gazed down at the pretty redhead. Lucy revealed no emotions, not a trace. But she'd open her mouth in a wide smile & laugh sometimes so that a sparkle lit her eyes. Then the laughter would die; just her eyes retaining their sparkle.

White body came to the bed; it creaked under her weight. In these close quarters, Mickey could smell Lucy's womanly scent. It was so good & languid; her red-nailed fingers caressed the butch's arm. Lucy's warm arms waited to hold her.

"I'll keep it up for you, baby." Mickey came between her legs that parted, came into her warm arms. "For you it's up all the time." Mickey came to her, a butchlesbian, red-hot, sex on fire!

Lunged between Lucy's thighs, her fingers twisted under damp cunthairs, her tongue probed Lucy's. Stroked the wet meat of her cunt; and she moaned, gripping Mickey's back as she entered her.

Lucy & Mickey in a red heart, breaking all the rules on earth.

Went into her again and again; fingers strong, careful, firm, insisting, inside the woman's lush cunt.

They loved again till they were tired.

Just 2 days ago, the lesbian butch had been alone —severely so. Walked, down the curve of Lake Michigan; where blue water crashes on white rocks at the beach. Warm Chicago streets, gummy tar asphalt melting; the march, staccato, of high-heeled secretaries; the punctuating noise of traffic; honks; gasoline fumes; fled this as she went thru the graffiti-decorated underpass that opened up at its other end into the city's edge; a scenario of clouds; water & open space.

Beyond waves & sky lies the mathematical precision of astronomy. The stars. Neptune & its frozen moon Triton.

And the fixed misery of her days had melted into opportunity, as if within an astrological change. So this woman, that Mickey now held in her arms, had come to pass.

'People get hot; then they grow cold. Like a weather vane, they turn one face of acceptance to you; then become cool, civil, then, finally, they pass by without speaking.

'Now, this Lucy,' Mickey thought. 'What is she like…after last night & now….is she a B-girl, a full-fledged prostie, or just a petty hustler, or what?

'Will she want to see me again? Is she playing games? Fooling her & me, & some other person she's already going with? The way she gave herself to me last night… Either she's a nymphomaniac, or it's been a long, long time since someone's loved her, just like she said.'

Red light blinks. Pigeons coo under the eaves.

After; after hours.

Time when the carnal gives way to higher feelings that were struggling within her.

Lucy was restless. Her addiction for the street, her addiction for the night, for The Life didn't die easy—not even with the young butch's professional touch.

A hint of memory of scag and its golden feeling that made non-feeling thru her web of veins. The blinking light of the bar downstairs & its cowboy honky-tonk beat. Fizz club; a bar a cut above the others—it all set up the mechanism of longing, to revolve in a giant carousel in her mind's eye—the yen for drug oblivion, yet wanting to enjoy her young lover some more. Longing; remembering how the Fizz opens up in back with a stage and country-western glitter. And Indians there, too, long, greasy black hair, black as Mickey's.

Big pool table right under the bandstand, as if it was a spectator sport, or part of the entertainment; and Lucy wanted to be there, to be a part of life, floating along like a silver fish in the stream.

Now, Lucy had never righteously been hooked up with another female.

In youth, foster-care facility, she had had a girl's love. At freakshow parties for tricks with butches, or femmes, them halfhearted, too drugged to feel the tricks they would turn later. And here & there laying up with some man fantasizing another woman. Lucy'd thought about it, this question of lesbianism; couldn't escape it—it was part of her. & she had James, a one-nighter who had become a slight friend. And one old dyke down at the prostie hustling gaybar Shrimpie's under the El tracks who paid her regularly to get naked & who just fondled her, and kissed her mouth, and stared & did little else; not like Mickey who'd taken her like a man, like a woman, like a lesbian, up in her cunt; all three personas twining throughout the sensuality of her whole being.

So, here it was, laying naked, pale skin in arms, a tuft of pubic hair, a cunt, tits, a replica of her own... And yes, Lucy had to think about it, seriously.

Same old window shades; dirt of decades, torn holes & a crone that owned a room next door muttering faintly; peering out as you passed by in the hall; dead & still living, in her 80s.

Time, passing...

'God, if we could only stay here.' Mickey oozed in the circle of warmth. In this low, humble yellow kitchenless room. The outside world seemed so much now; saw the handwriting on the wall that spelled trouble—Lucy tipping off downstairs on tarnished, glittery high-heel pumps to go back there with her drunken buddies on lower Clark street.

'I wonder what I got to fear most? The men she has, the tricks, the drink, or the drugs she craves?'

Or was it something in the interior soul and mind that must first be worked out & changed into a state of peace.

Then they stared into each other's eyes, and knew this was going to be a long relationship.

"I was so glad you came. Afraid you wouldn't." Shy, Lucy spoke.

Mickey laughed, tossed her black hair. "Why wouldn't I cum? It's the only thing I can do best." And turned to look down at Lucy. "Besides make love to you."

"My Jane can't come. She paid my room rent last week. I've been with dykes before who couldn't." Lucy lay back on the pillow, reflecting. "She's so possessive. When I go in Shrimpie's she comes up & sits next to me & bothers me all night. Wants to know every move I make." Lucy saw the old woman, breathing over her face, her wrinkled hands loving her breasts & her thighs, but no more. And her kisses, false teeth slipping, bad breath; small pressure of her lips on her own lips; tongue darting into Lucy's mouth, quick, lizardlike, just to withdraw; then she'd gaze, heart beating tired inside a man shirt, bleary eyes full of pain.

"Don't pay your rent, move in with me! We could save $11!" And the teenage butch bubbles with excitement at this suggestion.

And so that's how they would come to live together. So much faster than two rich people.

Red lights blink off & on, marking time. Time to tell the truth. Time for Remembrance of Things Past.

"One foster home, they tried to psychoanalyze me." Lucy

stuttered the word a little. "So I got my mind set for that. Got that game mastered—just when I got my act right, got all the answers they wanted to hear memorized—then they put me in another home, one with a whole new angle. That's the one where I got molested."

"What did he do?"

"Played with my tits. That's how it started. Finally he raped me. I kept trying to stop it, and told the lady—his wife—who ran the damn thing. We were just there for them to collect money from the State; they didn't care about us. And got us to do work, hard labor around there all for their benefit, too. He kept on and kept on. I just gave up. 'You kids are really bad, you show no appreciation.' The old bitch would tell us that. And her husband is fucking me and he was doing it to other girls. Fucking me like a grown woman, & she's treating me like a little child. They punished me for this; they punished me for that." Lucy's dreamy eyes wide, mouth in a solemn line like she was seeing it again. Mickey's arm around her, firm hand on her, helped bring out the memory because it was making a circle of security even in this godforsaken skid-row palace. "He was a child molester—don't that take the cake?"

"It happens to everybody." Mickey said. "Don't worry, you're not alone. And now, you've got me!"

"I could never do anything right! I did everything wrong!" Lucy went on, spilling out words as she seldom had before. Worry on her face, the first emotion she'd shown—as she saw into her past.

Saw his blond hair, tan face, wrinkled, of middle age; nose like a clown a different color than the rest of his skin; in his eyes a demented look. All over her with his hands, his body, his dick. Outside in the night streets of lower Clark, in an area filled with some of the saddest people in the world; the clutter of the old, the poor, those in mismatched colors, broken-down shoes—was it they, too, were cast outside humanity by these same hands? These foreign lusts? Turned out by someone long ago in this way? When they were still children? Or some other way—it was different for everybody on lower

Clark—these ghosts of the past. The standard of excellence was Richard's Wild Irish Rose wine. Expectation was enough drug left in the syringe when it came your turn, passed thru scab-covered hands of the junkie circle. The poor, starving from an insult of a thief of the past.

"Lucy! I'm sick of these men always bullying us! I'm angry!" As a gay, as a woman. "Everywhere I look, I see it! Closing in on us!"

"The wife was worse." The redhead shrugged, nonchalantly. "She could have stopped him. But she didn't want to lose the foster-care home—it was her livelihood. The bitch!" Lucy added with a spark of venom.

Two forms, entwined, in the middle where the bed dipped. Red light streaks the room then is gone.

It's 5:00 A.M. Downstairs patrons file out into the cool Chicago morning.

Lucy's resistance was broken. It had begun in childhood in foster care; a still-young child reaching for love—for emotional food, not like the bowl of gruel in *Oliver Twist,* but of the spirit of people. She was open, trusting, and reached out and was slapped down. She went down. Every time Lucy came back up, somebody knocked her down again.

"They don't kill you all at once; it can take 20 years sometimes. They don't kill by cutting your throat & stealing your watch & wallet."

Lucy was very feminine. Her eyes lost their twinkle now, and emotion faded back. Her fighting spirit had come back less and less.

Just sometimes, in the tavern after too many vodkas, under the party lights, her blood brought to a boil, in an irrational burst of anger she'd swing at somebody with a fake-ring glittering fist; then turn around weaving on the bar stool and look, and no one was there. Just the ghost of Christmas past.

Mickey lays back on the pillow hands folded behind her head. 'It takes so long to find a femme woman, the kind I like & we'll go in the gay club and all these other butches eyeing her.... Try to take her away from me....' It takes so long to find a femme woman, & society was going to force them apart.

At the bottom of the bed was the boxer shorts, blue and white striped that the butch had leapt out of in her zeal to mate with her Lucy, & had not put back on; her T-shirt, and the blanket.

Lucy sighed. Wide mouth in a line, lips tight. Eyes gazed into space. Lucy had cum more times this night than she had in a lifetime, so it seemed.

So Lucy was 23, half Sioux Indian. And Mickey Leonardi, alias Nicki Varner. Both had lived in New York.

"Yeah. I was the one who was Sherry's butch. She was my girl. Yeah, the pretty one, always the center of attraction. That's what broke us up."

"Gosh, then I've probably seen you down there!"

They marveled at the wonder of the world.

"So yuh was in New York, then Miami, too, same as me!"

"All the hustlers go to Miami in winter."

"We ran in different circles, so we must have missed each other by days!"

Lucy turned to Mickey, "I was straight, Mickey! That's why you didn't see me. I wasn't with the gay kids in Miami, or New York, either."

Mickey was silent.

Finally she spoke. "It's hot and humid and sticky. People wear bright clothes. When I left Miami and came up here to Chicago, everything looks so drab. Everybody wears brown. Brown shoes. There's a lot more rich colors down there. And everything's bigger there—tropical trees and plants. A lot of palm trees everywhere.... I hear they have them in California, too...a lot of avocado trees, too, and mango trees."

"Miami is mostly a city like any other city, like Chicago, or New York." Lucy sniffed sarcastically. "Just an ugly city. A lot of Cuban stores. No Indians, just Cubans and rich Jews. It's a city. I can be in any city and don't see a difference. That's why I like living down here in this place. To get away from the rat race."

"Florida is too hot because it's hot all year around.

Constantly, even in winter. People aren't as motivated because it's too hot. The temperature is too evenly hot."

"It limits your wardrobe. I couldn't wear my boots in Florida. Or even a sweater! It's hard for a girl to dress up."

Two made small talk. But in back of Mickey's mind were memories about her past as well.

They were both castaways. Both spent time in facilities run by the State. Foster care & prison.

It was like a dream sequence; Mickey told it to Lucy in a sleepy voice. "We're going to do *laundry*." Mother says, with this acid tone she has. And we understand that we all better do our laundry or die—at her hands.

"Yes, she'd hit us, and pinch us, and use objects to hit us. Break things. She'd just throw something at you, she'd be so mad. And lock us up in our rooms. And always make us go without food. 'No dinner for you!' That was her favorite. Because she saved money this way, and also as well to punish us. This way it was a double bonus to her and double hell to us, & so this is how I've learned to do without food in my life."

Mrs. Leonardi was a stick, not really a woman. But a stick. Shock of black hair turning gray. A dry stick. Her non-body flat as a board. Hysterical mouth always painted red. Hands flew around waving red fingernail polish, screaming at everybody. All she needed was a broomstick. She wasn't real because she had no heart or soul. Was a machine somehow wound up & alive mechanically. She was borderline nuts. Insane. Had given birth to 3 sons & Mickey out of her washboard body. She'd examine each detail of their house with eager eyeballs to find mistakes—something the children had done or not done. And gave her daughter no love at all. In fact, hated her daughter & gave more credit to her sons.

Mickey's mother tho bereft of heartfelt emotions had an overabundance of brains. Had her whole family and neighborhood convinced she was a Catholic saint, and had once been elected Mother of the Year—in 1948. Praised her sons highly & so, tho abused, they'd do anything she asked.

And Mickey, too, was traveling light. One barroom out of

New York, another girl in bed. Trying to start her life again.

Dawn streaked the window.

As a butch lesbian, Mickey had learned she wanted the best women. Ones that danced dirty and talked nasty—to make her cum hard. Had learned this. It wasn't butches like herself, tho they were gay; but ladies like Lucy who stimulated her the most!

Vision of a woman under her, legs spread at both sides of her torso; hands caressing her back as she fucked; were enough to send cold chills up her spine and ice & fire to her crotch.

Mickey had assembled a man's wardrobe at home, plus stuff from the thrift stores. Strap her breasts down & gone out in the world, being an adult.

As she became more man-styled; more of her inner persona reflecting with fire outward; more gazing at sweet women; she knew one ambition was to have mastery over sex. That and a job, and a happy home. Sex. Which is what she totally wanted & craved above all—sex in her control. Women, obedient to her desire that burned long & strong. And Mickey would give her life to protect that woman, and their home. Knew she would not be whole without these embraces, this fragrance that only a female has.

And again, one circle farther from the inner core of a hard-core lesbian butch—lay the snares of the world. Its billboards, TV; cinema with which its straight people engulfed her. As gays were nowhere. And had yet to be publicly empowered.

"Girls come home with me all the time. How I get them is a technique. Older butches told me what to say at first. I learned the rest myself."

Lucy's eyes sparkled with mirth. "Tell me what you say!"

"Well...." Mickey grins wickedly and turns over, holds Lucy in her arms pressing her back on the bed, kisses her neck, then whispers in her ear, "You ain't just a plaything to me, you're the real thing. I could have any woman in this place, but I chose you. Because you're so beautiful. And you're nice inside." And Mickey took Lucy's hand and kissed it.

"That's very nice."

"And you have to be kind. Kindness works." Mickey said. "I never slap my women around. I hope I never will."

Mickey remembered New York & how she'd learned to play the game. There was an old hooker—over 30—half the gay kids in the Village knew her or had seen her. Over a period of several years, she had 3 girls she'd taken in off the street with nowhere to go. Had taught them the prostitute game. A girl would run off, she'd get another. So they rented a house in Jersey City and worked out of there. And the hooker had seen this little lesbian Mickey who was 15 then, and handsome & liked the way she moved, and danced & knew she could please her girls. First time Mickey had taken off her pants and got on top of the old hooker, who taught her what to do to a woman, and what to do for herself. And Mickey loved it.

So, when they'd been brutalized by tricks, by the same boring faces, by the days, and the worries; young Mickey, by her hands, by her tongue, by her thighs, in her love had restored them to being whole women once more. In a circle dance of musical beds shared, a screwing motion of their bodies in love in the back room of the house of prostitution in Jersey City, run by a Madame who time and life had made gay.

"I was born gay. I'm a prenatal lesbian."

"Pre-what?"

"I was gay before I was born. Some people become gay in life. Some of us are born this way."

"You're lucky you know what you are. Not everybody can decide."

"The world makes women hard. I try to melt them down, so they can be…at peace. It's the chippies who held me in their arms who taught me how to love—because they need it so bad. They taught me to give myself in bed, really give! I hug them tight! I rub their feet what's tired from standing out on the street corner all night. And rub their sore muscles. I can lick their cunt all night & use my fingers till they cum because it takes them so long to climax; it's the work they do, the emotions they fight back; they can't give themselves in a sex act to every stranger they meet, so it gets bottled up inside. I suck it out of them. I fuck it out of them. I find a way. The prosties, they took me to their bosom, when all the good girls couldn't. When all the middle-class girls had to get back on the subway and go back to Long Island and their happy homes with their rich parents; it was the bad girls who spread their legs for me and took my cum. I would have starved waiting outside for the world to stop and give me a good girl."

Mickey had felt weak about herself, powerless. Life was very big at 15. Going around and around and she not getting a piece of it; and was desperate to get a woman to receive her lust. Desperate to live!

She was afraid about today and fearful about tomorrow.

When Mickey got old and would look back in time at the things she'd done with her life, she'd realize this period of time wasn't as healthy as others—years of living in the street, of not working, of drinking from the lips of many girls, but not one to call her own. the uncertainty; and she was young, learning how to get her hearts desire. To go against a society of frowning gray rules in order to be who she was. The vital secret was to keep trying, & she did.

'I came to this your town of Chicago in the year of 19-and-59.

'The mayor was an Irish politician who hated gays—but the Vice was on the take, so we could party for a little while.'

The natural progression of alcoholism ends up on skid row. The natural progression of living on skid row is death. The sequence of drug time, bottled wine is a sadomasochistic death.

'I had fought off the demon drink, and so come to the Windy City clean.'

Two days past, Mickey had stood, jet-black hair pushed back behind her ears like a boy. Man's shirt and trousers; gazing down the white rocks was the blue-green water, under a blue sky. Wind whips along the lakefront, tosses her short hair, ruffles her shirt like fingers of a spirit courtesan.

First way, the very first that Mickey'd learned about girls was as a baby butch.

Jailbait.

Mickey hadn't been superbad, just had run away over and over to go live her life as a gay, down in Greenwich Village.

So Mrs. Leonardi literally went wild, and had the police pick her up and had her put in reform school; which Mickey escaped, so when the police caught up with her—having been betrayed by the anti-gay parents of a girlfriend she was romancing & staying with—chasing her over the rooftops of Manhattan, Mickey wound up in a locked facility for minor girls.

Reformatory is a big, big place. Buildings that are prisons. Wards & dormitories of captive girls. With its own medical clinic. Cottages where the basic curriculum of school is taught without its unfortunate inhabitants ever having to go out into the free world. A wall around it. The women guards were big fat hillbillies all weighing 250 pounds apiece—minimum. The women guards tried to get pussy from the young girls. They were brutal, and there was hostility between girls and guards.

Mickey wanted comfort in the night—being still young enough to cling to a Teddy Bear. But when she went to the toilet, there was a matron right behind her, jamming her big white hand up between Mickey's legs. And they liked her because she was young and gay & thus one of them, although Mickey didn't see it that way.

One particular guard who the baby butch didn't like at all was constantly on her tail. Stern face appeared, in guard uniform—a dress with a deputy's star pinned to it, white socks and brogan shoes—in the kitchen, thumbs of her big hands hooked in her belt: "*Mickey*...if you're not gonna make no action in here, you're not gonna *get* no action." And the word got around to stay away from this baby dyke Mickey. Nobody would loan her cigarettes; nobody would let her take a magazine into her room.

And Mickey had found a little girl, age 12, who met her perfect fantasy. A sweet blonde with youthful curves, lipstick, & who did her fingernails, and the girl let Mickey care for her and put her arm around her—at the same time as the 45-year-old guard was trying to get in Mickey's underpants.

The prison work was slave labor. It's very costly to maintain an institution, so having the prisoners do the work is a big savings. They were paid 10¢ an hour. Enough for a pack of cigarettes, which costs an exorbitant 75¢ in lockup. Candy bars were 50¢, which on the outside would have been a quarter.

So, the girls bought these little items with the money they earned from jail work, or if they were lucky enough to have someone on the outside sending them money. And if anybody gave a girl a cigarette, or loaned her a magazine, this was a favor; and the basis of business transactions without money, one exchanged for sexual favors and other considerations.

Mickey was a food handler; then she mopped floors after dinner.

In jail Mickey did push-ups and leg raises. Hand grips, and rose up and down on her toes to make her calves strong and big with muscle.

Soon muscles grew in her arms and thighs and back. Small muscles; enough that little femmes would be enamored of her.

So Mickey had turned 13 years old, and the guards go around poke each other in the ribs, and slap each other's ass: "How'd yuh like to get in that ones pants?" Or, "I just knocked off a piece of that sweet little pussy in the shower room" and etc., about some misfortunate girl. And this particular guard had warned them: "Hands off Mickey, that little butch in ward E. I'm taking her."

Guards are the enemy. Big & fat, hillbillies who wear bobby socks. Dumb & have low IQs, and get paid just a minimum wage which dehumanizes them even more. Some are nice to the girls, and kind, but these are few—these are the ones who have somebody backing them up in life, too. The hard ones are the guards who are struggling to survive in life on minimum wage, and don't have a woman, or need more woman than they've got.

To break the monotony they look at the girls as sport. And use sex to vindicate themselves.

So this guard, Lou, wore her heart on her sleeve for Mickey, who was 13. She was 45.

The bathroom wall spoke: "MICKEY WAS HERE! SHE LEFT HER NAME TO CARRY ON TO THOSE WHO KNOW HER VERY WELL, THOSE WHO DON'T CAN GO TO HELL!"

Mickey left her mark in the hearts and minds of girls as well.

A few of them would carry her memory as they grew up and got married and went to live in different cities, and raised families; would remember that the first gentle touch of love they'd known was from another female.

The guards did girls favors. A particular matron would miscount the pills and give them to a girl if she let the guard finger-fuck her. And if the girl made it good to the matron, shit, who knows where all those pills went to!

The first approach the matron made on Mickey, the woman caught up with her in the kitchen where the baby butch was washing dishes. She wore elbow-length black rubber gloves and a large gray cook's apron. Lou was big, 5'8" weighing 290 lbs. As Mickey bent over to get more racks to put up on the sink for the dishes, the matron stuck her hand between Mickey's legs and grabbed her whole cunt. The teen knew better than to turn around and hit her, so she just fought her off with the rack, pushing it between them, until Lou walked away in disgust.

The green-uniformed guard wasn't too friendly after that; in fact, she was mean.

So there were all these plots going on daily. Some of the older girls nearing 18—legal emancipation—could not be held any longer and were ready to be transferred out. One girl was a murderer and was playing a butch role with another girl; and she'd trade beds every now and then with the girl's roommate. They were on open-ward privilege because they'd been sentenced & had proven themselves capable of handling responsibility—if you want to call folding sheets in the laundry "capable." This was the petty level they were reduced to. So girls on open-ward privilege would go into each other's cells and fuck. And the matron would come in the cell and pull the cover back to see who was in the bed together that night—being lecherous & a voyeur.

Reformatory was a big, cold place with a wall trapping them inside. Only guards came and went; girls had to stay. Lesbian feelings were here. Straight girls could be swayed by a strong butch. And that's why most of the matrons came to work here in the first place; most of these women guards tried to get cunt. And it was the pastime of their days.

In an institution, all the girls dress in the same gray dresses, sleep in identical beds under identical blankets, enclosed in green walls and ceilings & screens over the windows so they can't escape. So, to choose not to play the game results in death—total death from boredom.

If a matron wanted to fuck an inmate, they'd go into a cell, or the shower room. They always kept the shower rooms locked. Or take her into the medical room, which was locked. The matrons had outlets & held the keys. The prisoners had nothing.

Mickey saw the goings-on around her day to day like an endless chain of cigarettes.

Older butch girls swaggered around, sleeves of their uniforms rolled up, collars turned up in back; & played men to the other girls—straight girls who gave in to these butches because it was better for them to be protected.

Soon Mickey saw it. Older butches had open ward privilege because they'd proved they were trustworthy, and because they'd earned favors from a guard. They could go into any girl's cell and fuck. So the butch girls were fucking, and the matrons were fucking.

Oddly, the matrons weren't jealous of the butches fucking the other girl prisoners, because a stud butch kept the girls quiet. They had their stud on their mind for better or worse, and thus got into less trouble or conflicts with each other. Their stud would straighten them out with good hot loving.

Mickey soon learned to go along with the program.

She favored the guard Lou, with talk, and by allowing her big hand to stroke her wet cunt outside her panties from time to time.

Mickey started her lesbian life there, very young, and didn't know what she was doing. Soon she had this little girl,

12, just a few months younger than she was. And Lou had given her open-ward privilege in exchange for feels between Mickey's hot legs. And Mickey and the girl held hands. The girl just let Mickey kiss her and hold her. Just soft little kisses with tender lips on the face, and on her lips, too. Mickey didn't know how to french-kiss and was trying to learn, but the girl kept pushing her away because she was straight. She let the butch put her arm around her and feel under her dress, but then she'd snap her thighs closed and wiggle away, and the resistance she put up was tiring. Finally Mickey settled for putting her arm around her and trying to take care of her.

Now, in the past, men had tried to force Mickey to have sex against her will. They'd tried to fuck her & she'd fought and run. But this matron was approaching in a different way.

The favors. Then trying to take payment for it out of her ass.

In the back of her mind, as she tossed & turned on her cot, felt that it was her own fault. But truth was, it was a way of life to Lou, who had done it with others before & would again, with others after.

So it was a good setup for them. If a matron eyed a newcomer—a particular girl she wanted to fuck, they'd take them off into the shower-room section, which they always kept locked. Another place was the medical room, which was locked on account of the drugs. In there was an examination table and also cots. Many girls laid up on the table with their legs spread, to allow a matron to insert her fingers in them with a good view of what they were having, not like standing up against the wall in the shower room; or put their heads between her legs & suck her pussy. The matrons had to hide this action—but they had these locked places to do it, and ways to cover what they were doing.

Evenings Mickey sat in her 5x8 cell. A metal slab on which was a mattress and blankets & sheets and a flat hard pillow. A sink and toilet. A tiny desk. There was room for nothing else. Lights were on 24 hours nonstop, just dimmed at 9:00 P.M. Mickey smoked cigarettes back then. The guards gave the girls a deck of cards—if they were nice. So at first, Mickey couldn't get shit out of the guards—not like the more advanced prisoners. Then she saw. Eat a little bit of pussy, or let your pussy be eaten, and then you got these certain things. Cards, cigarettes, magazines, freedom to walk openly on the wards. Go play around in the laundry room with one of the big, burly matrons and she'd do things for a girl. The better the sex got for her, the more she'd do. Light work duty. Food, dope, alcohol. Ensure her ability to get to a little girl her own age and be with her all night. Everything but the key to the front gate.

Mickey began to see the truth & it scared the hell out of her, because the matrons had total power over her life.

When she was on the outside, a free teenager, Mickey had taken the daughter of friends of the family to the beach at Rockaway, and there on the sand spoke to her about love, and touched her hair, and talked about what a beautiful thing an orgasm is—tho she'd never had one yet.

An anonymous friend told her mother of this interlude, which she'd heard of secondhand thru gossip. Mickey's mother went completely hysterical & it got worse from that point. Had police come by their house in a squad car and arrest her own daughter. Lied & claimed Mickey was stealing things from the house & selling them to buy drugs. That she was unmanageable and needed to be incarcerated for her own good. And the mother testified to these lies in a courthouse hearing in which her daughter wasn't allowed to be present and give any kind of defense—because she was underage. Her red mouth twisting with lies in frozen hysteria. Her black hair and features a duplicate of Mickey's own. Her own mother sentencing her child to live out the remainder of her minor years in lockup.

So Mickey lay in the shadows serving year 1 of a period of 5 that she'd be in and out of reformatories because of her troubled home life.

Mickey lay back under a green blanket, pale skin beaded with sweat in the stifling prison air. Black hair stuck damply to her face. She wanted to feel a girl's pussy under her fingertips —just as she touched her own every night since she was a child.

So here she was in a tiny cell that an animal shouldn't even

be in, because her own mother testified that she was a dangerous psychopath—because she was gay.

Now, nobody had showed her sex like they teach the
alphabet. Had taught herself all alone; to unlock that world,
one of the greatest of all, at her own fingertips.

Mickey, not full grown in height, bent over the mop and a
pail of water; she had to swab all the damn floors to hell and
back. Soapy water all over the floors. Mad that she was in jail
mopping public halls. Around the curve to the laundry room,
back to the dining area.

And had come to bed at lights-out, tonight, as all nights,
her square nail fingertips probed under her curly black pubic
hair, white fingers touched her clit, then moved up and down
& around, felt herself grow wet, and her legs relax. A small
female, little breasts still growing out, not yet full; had just
begun her periods—only had 8 periods in her life. She was not
yet a woman, no longer a girl.

Felt a vague excitement in her body, a longing deeper than
ever before. Maybe it was the conditions under which she
was—confinement, and fear, that allowed her to just give up to
the feelings. And especially at night, wanting…rubbing her
sex…. Nothing had ever happened before. No climax. When
the matron touched her & tried to enter her, it was painful,
and she'd fought her off, squirming away but still not hauling
off and slugging her because she wanted the favors, and definitely didn't want to be punished by solitary confinement. And
after all day of boredom spiced with intrigue of her romances
with the girls her age, her hand between her pussylips, moving
wet; in the past had alleviated the despair somewhat…. On the
cot, laying on her side, noticed the feeling was more intense
than ever, hot & strong, so lay on her back and kept up the
motion, rubbing this one spot, just rubbed, and not thinking
about anything in particular, & suddenly, a new sensation
made her gasp. Her head started to shoot thru the stars; the
most beautiful feeling she'd ever known cumming over her
kept on & on rolling over her, higher, complete. Finished.

Mickey had taken a giant step. Had, by her own hand, for
the first time, cum.

Mickey did her work detail; Lou the matron went by, eyed her and grunted hello, uncertain how far she'd get with this tough baby butch.

And the baby butch went around crying inside half the time. And masturbating; petting her girl; spicing up life with intrigues over cigarettes and how to get into girl's rooms, and magazines & extra food, the other half of the time.

Mickey parted her thighs when Lou caught up with her in the kitchen, let the big hillbilly stroke her pussy—over her panties, until it got swollen and wet, and Lou's panting, big eyes bugged in her flabby face. Then Mickey pushes her away, and Lou is obedient.

"I want a pack of cigarettes and to borrow the scissors from the laundry room."

She had to beg for this favor, but got it, and cut her hair short, butch style, because it had started to grow out. Made herself as butch as she could look—collar turned up perpetually, sleeves rolled up showing her muscles, with a cigarette pack in one, and hair pushed back severe, behind her ears. Swaggered when she walked.

Mickey had now 3 different little girlfriends she saw, with the help of Lou, who turned over the key to their cells at night. Mickey's toughness had caught these girls' eyes, but still none of them had gone all the way nor allowed Mickey to touch them freely all over their bodies, to stroke their small tits and young cunts and bring them up to those same firecracker explosions in starlight heights she'd just discovered.

So that's why she cried inside.... Felt she was losing everything anyway. Her life behind bars until the State let her go. Wanting to be close, inside a girl, inside a girl's love; but the girls were keeping her out. And wanting to lay over them just like a scene from a movie with the man over the woman, who lay back in the splendor of the grass; in sizzling movie ads that had aroused her since age 11; and now she was coming of age to be that man, loving that woman, if a girl would just melt to her caress and let her in.

So she did time behind windows with iron screens bolted into the walls so they couldn't get out.

The girls were always giggling, laughing at the guards, and fighting among themselves. It was hard to keep them in line. It was a tug of war, matrons vs. girls. The girls did things like insult the cook if they didn't like the food that day, and say nasty things about how wide the guard's ass was, just loud enough for them to hear; or ask each other was a certain guard pregnant, because her stomach was so fat—just to aggravate. So, although the guards were grown women, they'd do little things to get back at the girls, like lock down and lights off at 7 instead of 9. Shitty stuff. And they traded shit back and forth.

And all this was secluded. No one can see what's going on behind those walls.

"I'm good to my pets, Mickey." Guard Lou spoke.

Green walls surrounded them, 8 by 5 foot space. They were alone. Lights buzzed in the ceiling and din of jailed females hollering & banging things just down the hall.

"I could *take* it from you, Mickey." Lou said. A smile played over her lips. "And nobody would believe you if you told them." Mickey faced her. The guard was two heads taller, 190 pounds heavier. Lou continued in her slow, deliberate tone. "But I never *take* anything that's not offered to me. You're lucky, *Mickey*. Not every girl here is so lucky."

Now this huge guard Lou was a good goddamn hillbilly from Kentucky; earned $1.50 an hour, which was minimum wage in 1954. Every pack of cigarettes she bought her pet cost dearly to her budget, every piece of special candy or magazine. Lou lumbered out, wearing a cynical smile on her face in a tight little line.

CHAPTER NINE

Mickey had her older girl, Patty, in her arms, jammed her up in the toilet area against the wall, felt up under her skirt. Girl shivered, clutched onto Mickey's strong back thru the cloth of the uniform. Mickey wanted to stick her fingers in her so bad; this girl would let her—other butches had—fumbled, pulled her panties down over her thighs, groped hastily, then found her hole and her finger pushed in; felt cunt inside for the first time; then jiggled it going in and out, in and out. Then Mickey pushed her finger deep, in to the last knuckles. The girl gasped, clawed her back.

Then she wanted to go down and put her mouth there, too.

The girl saw the need, yearning in baby butch Mickey's face.

The girl only let her for a few seconds, then stopped. It was over. And Mickey's pushing her back against the wall, fighting to get her fingers back in that warm, lush place; but the girl is finished, she don't want it no more. And Mickey goes on thru the days heavily into fantasy. Into wishing. Dreaming. Mickey wants a girl to want her, and give in, and let her try & experiment all the love ways.

Now each girls' compartment was called a room, but, was in reality a cell to which they were confined.

Mickey had Patty awhile, petting, breathing heavy; a few minutes of her cunt, then being pushed away; it's how Patty did it with everybody.

Then she had turned 16 and was transferred out.

Cold wind of December blew. Gray walls. Pigeons flew free, circled outside.

Mickey had turned 13; nobody had come to visit. As far as her mother was concerned, her daughter was dead.

Had turned 13 inside the reformatory & had had her first menstrual period there; blood on her panties.

And after Patty had left, she'd worked on another little girl who was 12.

Barbara let Mickey fondle her tits, reach under her uniform and feel the nipples on her naked nearly flat child's chest, and kiss her face. Then one day melts and lets the baby butch kiss her full on the lips.

They are in the girl's room; when comes a click sound of a guard approaching. Mickey pulls away hurriedly. Door opened, and Mickey froze. There was Lou looking at them. Huge body filling the doorway, thumbs looped thru her belt. Lou knew what they were doing and just grinned. Lou knew this was Mickey's girl and said, "OK, kids, just wanted to see who was in here and *what* was going on." And shut the door. She didn't interfere.

Mickey goes back to romance. They never have time or peace.

Then as she lays back on the bed loving her girlfriend, damp young bodies thru the cloth of their dresses, the matron sticks her big head in again.

"GO FUCK YOURSELF YOU JEALOUS BITCH!" Mickey hollers. Lou just laughs and shuts the door again.

"Nosy bitch! She just wants to watch me with you."

An hour ticked by, and the big guard didn't come back.

Mickey and her romances were OK with Lou, And the stout woman had tough glares for any other guards—adults her own age who might be eyeing Mickey. And secretly got wet in her cunt, dripping wet, to see the butch touch her little girlfriend's tits—they were so cute; she wouldn't interfere for the world.

So, with open-door privileges, Mickey could work on her little girls. Next time she got to see Barbara, the 12-year-old let Mickey fondle her under her uniform right away. Kissed her and pushed her down on the bed, but there met resistance. Barbara held her off. "Please, please, please!" Mickey begged, while the girl was fighting. "Please let me kiss you down there! Please!"

"Let me go! No! No!"

And pets her and kisses her, and finally the girl relaxes and lets Mickey do it for a minute. Puts her mouth down there, and tastes pussy for the first full time in her 13 years. Puts her tongue in the wet lips and tastes, licks, smashing her face around in it, sucking, licking; & when Barbara pushes her head away, gets on top and rubs her swollen clit on Barbara's thigh, humping wildly, passionately, until she feels her sex lose control & she's cumming, cumming with Barbara squirming around under her; lets out a gasp and it was finished.

Mickey was proud of herself. After that she felt years older. Felt she was becoming an adult.

Proud. The smell on her fingers from the girl's cunt. A

precious scent. Held it to her nose over and over all that night & each time ecstasy would flood over her; & chills shot down her spine, and her legs trembled remembering being on Barbara while she squirmed and cumming—for the first time with someone else.

Mickey swaggered around juvenile lockup, thumbs hooked in her belt.

Guard Lou's attraction to Mickey must come to a resolution.

Lumbers into Mickey's room, brings her cigarettes a candy bar. Yellow lights had dimmed as it was after 9. Mickey looks up suspicious; short cropped wavy black hair sweaty against her skin, from heat in the close confines.

A little sneer spread over Lou's lips, her eyes squinted, appraising Mickey. "Dick and dope. That's all they think about...young girls. Especially in *incarceration*. Some young girls, you look good to them, Mickey. There's no dick here in lockup, and you're the closest thing around. You should be thankful for your good fortune. You've had your share of the girls. Every night you get some kind of action. Some girl's door is open to you. Young love. It's so *sweet!*"

A big fake diamond ring glistened on her puffy white pinkie finger. Lou played with the pack of cigarettes. "Now, Mickey, you're smart, you don't use drugs. And you give your girls dick—of a sort; you're on your way to success. It keeps them in line. They're too busy thinking, 'Oh, hum... Mickey... Should I let her? Maybe I should let her?... No I won't let her...oh, hum...' And it keeps them out of trouble and out of *my* hair, as we both know. And aren't you lucky that *someone* thinks enough of you to let you wander the halls freely at night and do what you want? By the way, here's the cigarettes. Now, come on and deliver your part of the deal—let me play with you, don't put up a fight! Stop making faces and just relax and enjoy me a minute!—I bet you tell your little girls the same thing!"

So from time to time in the shower after the other girls left, nude, skin red from rubbing dry with their towels; shaking their wet hair leaving drops of water; wrapping the small towels around them, filing out; the baby butch would stay behind and let the guard come up to her, and drop the towel so Lou could paw her, and rub her fat fingers into the pussy-folds of her cunt, & stroke her thighs; and fought back silently and emotionally by being stiff as a board and cold; but felt the thrill of excitement rush thru her despite her subterfuge every time Lou did this, and the shower is running to mask their sounds, and steam fills the place; it's a tile trap; and feels her thick white hands pawing her young newly forming breasts—the feeling was superb; but attached to the person doing it who was hateful. And after, Mickey would pull the towel around her and go to the lockers and get her clothes, hating the guard and the institution and feeling an erotic libido, and not knowing whether she was cumming or going crazy.

So, finally it had to happen. They're in Mickey's cell. Lou sits on the bed right beside the young butch. Breathing heavy from lumbering her big body down the halls at top speed, and sexual tension seethes on her fat face; the wry smile flits on her lips; her hair, very short stuck to her head in wetness, just like her uniform with big sweat stains spreading on the chest and in back. "I just want to bring you out." Mickey heard the ominous words.

"You're so nice.... Your clean little cunt, with no disease..." Lou smiles. "Not like those *big* girls on the outside. Like half of these girls are gonna be after they're out of here."

"I told you I'd think about it."

And Lou raises up off the bed with a grunt and strides to the door, like matrons walk, fast in their dresses and oxford shoes. Slams the door in a terse response, locks it, because she's tired of the game; and lumbers off down the corridor.

Yellow lights dim. 4 walls. Noise of girls talking, moaning in sleep, coughing, crying. Noises that never cease.

Door opens and Lou's back once more. A smile on her lecherous lips.

"What do you want!" Mickey snarls.

"*Mickey,* I just want you to know something."

"WHAT!"

"The *trouble* I go to ensure your open-door privilege. When I left Tuesday—which is my Friday—I *forgot* to tell the duty guard on this ward about your privileges of open door. So I had to turn around and drive all the way back here to tell her in person—there's certain things we just can't say over the phone, you never know who's listening—which left me an hour less on my 2 days off—just for *your* sake."

Mickey grimaced.

"Well, doesn't that deserve a thank you?"

Mickey mutters.

"I can't *hear* you, Mickey. Say it louder...."

"Thanks."

Lou smiles. Her eyes gleam. Fat folds of her belly ripple with a sharp intake of air, under the green uniform. And goes out. The door remains unlocked.

So Mickey had these games and worries to contend with.

The only punishment Lou used was to withhold favors. She wasn't the type to injure her pets. Just stare coldly, a pack of cigarettes in her hand which a girl might desperately want, and take the pack and stuff it back in the pocket of her uniform over an ample breast. Some guards would go up to a girl standing alone and grab her and feel her up rough, and the kid would have to fight them off. Mickey knew from hearing the others talk about the sadistic guards. Some were brutish and very jealous & wanted to keep their pets under lock & key. So, as the nights & days ground on in the 24-hour yellow light; Mickey begrudgingly had to admit this prison guard was better than some, and better than any man who had tried to rape her on the outside when she was a runaway in the streets; better in fact, than her own brothers who had been trying to make her, too, in her unhappy home.

Nights, walking down the hall, silent, turns into Ellie's room; with cigarettes and a magazine. Mickey gives her the present and sits right down next to her on the mattress on its metal slab; and Ellie accepts. And they're touching right away, & Mickey not having to slide over by inches, and work her way over to Ellie; they embrace immediately. Runs her hands over the cloth of Ellie's uniform. Light bulb stares down at them under its grid, dim. It's 10 P.M. Sound of other doors being shut, and this one and hers still unlocked because Mickey is a guard's pet.

"Can I come back?"

"I guess so." Ellie replies.

Went back to her room, lies down, stares up at the ceiling all night. Baby Mickey wakes up in a sweat, tosses & turns on her narrow cot; dreams about touching that girl's lips, holding her, feeling her soft breasts again, thinking about that pleasure, that unbelievable pleasure that Ellie allows her—to taste her pussy, to go down and lick; and penetrate with her fingers that mysterious place seldom touched before. And to lay on top of her, wiggling her ass, to rub her clit against the smooth flesh of Ellie's thigh until she came. Came to her little girl-friend, came in her embrace.

One day the girl prisoners caught a girl who was snitching. 5 girls, rougher, older; they jammed the snitch up in the bathroom & one had been on housekeeping duty earlier so the gang had access to mops and toilet paper; they wet the toilet paper in a wad and shoved big wads in her mouth so she couldn't scream, and they rammed the pole of a mop handle up the girl's vagina, so far it broke her inside. The girl fainted dead away.

When she managed to drag herself back to the open area, blood was flowing down her legs; hemorrhaging & they had to take her out of the facility by ambulance to the City Hospital and sew her vagina back up.

Mickey, like the rest, heard the horror story thru the grapevine from those girls who had eyewitnessed her crawling in a trail of her own blood thru the corridor. The baby butch thought about her own insides. Her female parts seemed vulnerable, a weakness. She had barely investigated her own cunt at that early teen age, but already knew it was somehow causing her a lot of problems.

"You see what happened to that girl, *Mickey*...ain't it terrible, the things that go on?" Lou was sanctimonious; a false smile flits on her lips. Fat white fingers tap, tap, tap on the green blanket covering the bed between them. Mickey is scrunched up at the other end, leaning against the cold brick wall. Stares at her. Lou, in turn, appraises Mickey from under heavy-lidded eyes, studying her to see the effect of her words. "A *broom* handle, or a *plunger* whatever it was!... It could happen to *you*, you know, Mickey.... It could happen to any girl."

Yellow light, the tiny cell. The matron and the girl, weight shifting on a bed.

"Mickey all I want to do is to bring you out... Let me get to it before somebody else does."

Which meant that Lou wanted to take her virginity.

The baby butch glared. Said nothing. And the horrible thing about it, was, of all the rotten people on earth, Lou had treated her the most fair.

Like a wild bird's wings—her heart beating to be free, the butch died behind the bars of boredom, and mean spirits of other teenage girls & the warped adult guards was molding her into an old person instead of a 13-year-old kid.

Brutal. To not have an escape. No one on the outside knew she was alive, except her family. And what her mother wanted to do—or get her brothers to do to her—had made it worse to be at home than being in the streets.

Lou had moved her big bulk off the bed, which sighs in relief, its flattened mattress popping back out to its original width. Stands up. Hooks her thumbs in her belt, rattling the ring of keys. "If you're not gonna give it up, Mickey, you ain't gonna get nothing more. Period. All these favors don't just fall out of the sky—I have to pay for them myself. Think about it."

After this, cigarettes stop. Special food stops. Nothing. The cell door is locked day & night & Mickey wants to kick its iron plates in with her foot in gym shoes; but there is absolutely nothing she can do about it. And up in the day room she sees her little Ellie smoking and her demure mouth reddened by lipstick still eating candy she's brought her in the past, and she wants to know why Mickey didn't come visit her last night—she was waiting—and the butch nearly goes mad, feels bitter and enraged; and knows that to remain Ellie's man she has to have the open-door privilege so she can go down the hall to her room in the evening.

The matron wore bib overalls & big buck shoes. Dark hair slicked back behind her ears. Hips so wide and tits so big anybody could see she wasn't a man, but looks like a huge man with a figure. She was leaving for her weekend and leaving her pet locked up for the duration.

Hostility in the reformatory could be cut with a knife. Girl against girl. Girl against guard. Some guards against other guards. And all guards united in full fury against the State Investigators who swoop down periodically to stage an inquiry about the conditions inside. They come with slates & pencils and notepads, and look at everything twice a month in one fateful month—then not again for 3 years.

It was probably why more wrongdoing didn't go on. Why more pets weren't taken advantage of. Because it was possible, just a slim chance, that matrons could be caught molesting their young inmates, or other harassments. And none of them wanted to risk their jobs. Big matrons working for minimum wage who dare not lose their income. Or risk being incarcerated themselves.

After she made her last approach to Mickey, Lou ignored her. Her bulging figure, massive arms and legs crammed in a uniform dress swaggering by making a dirty look; a small butch being eyed by an even bigger one. And didn't like her at all after that, period.

Stood wide-legged, thumbs hooked in her belt and discussed this difficult case with a guard she trusted. Jangled her keys, she growled; "I've never raped a girl. Never." Matron Lou scowled. "I have principles. These other guards, they get 'em drugs & alcohol from the outside, and of course the dizzy girls get high out of their minds & don't know what they're doing, and the guards will do anything to them. My pets, they just come to me. Some, like *her*—take a while." Lou grinned. "I get 'em anything they want—and I'm all they got."

She liked her girls young. 12. 13. As long as their bodies were beginning to be womanly. And she had an adult woman at home waiting for her. And this woman she'd met while working as a janitor in a high school. The woman had been 16 then, Lou 35, and they'd been together 9 years. Lou craved young meat. That was it. Maybe to recapture her lost youth. But she had been doing it for years. Didn't take much to satisfy her. Some girls did nothing but allow her to penetrate them. They didn't even have to go down; she had a woman at home for every desire. It was simply that her woman was not a child anymore, like when they'd met. Lou wanted to fondle tits; grunting, her pig eyes narrowed to slits, & touch young pussy-with lingering strokes. She didn't just go up and grab them like the cruder matrons. She tried to be halfway nice. And it was an awful place, and she was their only friend. So, after a while, girls would let her stick her fingers in them. And when her thick, fat fingers came out with thin watery red blood on them, that was the crowning joy—when she had a virgin.

So, under yellow lights, a huge matron grunts, dress hiked up over her big thighs, laying half on top of naked Mickey who's on her back on the cot. A female stench—like fish—floods the cell. Lou's bull neck is beaded with sweat, her short cropped hair wet, sticks to her head; she's humping. Runs her fat hands over the baby butch, over her tits & and the ripple of the ribs visible on her still-slim body, and caresses her shoulders and thighs & squeezes her as she rides her wet hairy cunt against Mickey's thigh; sort of side by side and not completely on top or she'd crush her to death; grunts, humps, breath coming harsh, fast, and has an orgasm.

So now Mickey has open-door privileges—thanks to the guard.

Came to Ellie's room.

Light shone down in the 5 by 8 cell. Mickey struts in, collar of her prison dress turned up, sleeves rolled up to show biceps—with a pack of cigarettes stuck in one. "I brought you some smokes." They light one up; casting shadows close together on the brick wall.

"So how are you?"

"OK."

Mickey puts her small hand on Ellie's. "Did you miss me?"

Ellie shrugs like she doesn't know.

It's very silent between them. Seated inches apart on the cot. Clamor and commotion from the cells outside. Mickey raises Ellie's hand to her lips and kisses it without saying another word. Reaches around her waist in an embrace & the girl doesn't say anything, either.

Hand with close-cut fingernails reaches up to touch Ellie's small tits thru her dress. The nipples harden with excitement. And her chest pounds with intake of air. Both girls hearts are beating faster. Ellie didn't make Mickey stop. Fondling her, feels the hard nipples stand out under her dress. Ellie's fingers clutch her shoulder. Mickey fully embraces her with the smoldering desire of long lost love. Ellie sighs.

Tenderly she puts her lips to the girl's lips; they touch like that for a long time, pressing her lips fully against the girls closed lips. Then begins to push her tongue against them, pushing to gain entrance, while continuing to pet her tits. Mickey feels Ellie's mouth part, teeth open. Her tongue met no resistance, pushed into that soft cavity, and Ellie's tongue came to meet hers, too; hesitant, touching tongues inside each other's warm mouths, seeking, sucking each other's tongues.

A thrill so great, they were exploding.

In unexpected pleasure, the girl's hands touched her, stroked her muscular arms; and arousal shot up Mickey's back so that her fine body hair stood on end. Ellie was responding to her lovemaking, and this was the greatest feeling on earth.

Mickey pushed up Ellie's prison dress. Her hand went under it; her lips drew away from Ellie's, wet with saliva and she bent, head going under the dress to kiss her thighs, then licked the soft, hot flesh up to her fur; carefully moved the pubic hair aside and licked inside her cuntlips & sucked with her mouth and tasted it, smelled it, and loved it. Then gingerly inserted one finger. As it went in, Ellie gasped: "OH, MICKEY! OH!" Her hands reached down & grabbed clumps of hair on Mickey's head in passion, while the baby butch's finger is going into her wet chamber & licking her cunt, too, at the same time, breathing wildly. Then Ellie clamps her knees shut and pushes Mickey away. And the golden moment is over.

Mickey lay in solitude back in her own cell. Thought over the lovemaking scene again, again and again; while bringing herself to arousal & climax.

Mickey was young and totally insecure about herself. She needed a guide, a friend—not a demon in a green prison uniform.

Fat matron sashayed her big hips down the halls, a glint in her eye with a purpose; keys jangling, star-shaped badge pinned to the green cloth of her uniform; proud as a huge peacock. For she had claimed Mickey as her own for sure. The other guards weren't jealous, they had their pets, too.

And Mickey hadn't had to do nothing to her, just lay there.

Matron always came up, gave Mickey a playful slap—just a tap—on the side of her face, stunning her, making her cheek red; and laugh a coarse, hard laugh. Wary in the beginning, defensive, Mickey had blocked the slap, or ducked. Then she got used to it. Steeled herself and gazed hard, right back at Lou as the slap was delivered. Light, very light, just a sting. More symbolic—of domination—than a slap to rattle the teeth in her jaw. And then stuck her own young hand out to receive her cigarettes and candy and magazines. After a while Ellie suggested Mickey should show the guard some special attention and maybe she'd get more than that—cash maybe. And then Mickey could share it with her.

"Play with her, Mickey! Play with her like you do with me! Do it to her—what you do to me and I bet she'll do anything you want! Maybe she'll let us out and we can go to a picture show in town! We can buy some nice clothes!"

Mickey had no home. She'd never again crawl back to her mother's to get more abuse, so that left only the wide world open to her, and what it had to offer. She began to rely more on Lou, like a buddy she hated but trusted somewhat.

Older girls getting ready to ship out of prison talked about getting jobs, or collecting welfare as soon as they turned 18. And Mickey trembled in fear, nights alone in her cell, thinking about what she would do when she was put out on the streets again. Hating the prison; yet it was the only security she had.

Now, the guards really liked their own private jail world because on the outside they weren't the boss of anything. But here they were kings. The big, burly women had the keys to the food, cigarettes, and cells swinging on their belts. They wore the uniform of power and were invested the star of authority.

The matron keeps working on her, working on her a little bit at a time, like water wears away rock; and bribes Mickey with alcohol and pills from the dispensary, which the butch uses in turn on Ellie to make her more responsive to her love. And gives her special food and magazines.

After a while Mickey says to herself: 'Aw, what the hell, she can go ahead.' Part because she wants the food, part because it will be a worry off her mind—there are worse things that can happen—and then she'd get this virginity thing over with, and see what it was like. Because Ellie wasn't ever going to touch her there, not in a million years, because she wasn't gay; so there was no point saving it.

Guard sat on the mattress, leaned back against the brick wall of the cell, quite at home. Mickey at the other end, wary, and weary.

Lou's lips twisted in grotesque displeasure. Eyes too bright. Stared at Mickey in her gray dress with sleeves rolled up; a butch in a dress which they were forced to wear—like herself, a guard in a dress, and white bobby sox and oxford shoes. Nothing like the mannish attire she'd don after her shift was over & she was free to go. The bed creaked with her weight as she shifted around to stare at the baby butch. "You have your choice, *Mickey*." Lingering on the name, savoring it; and reached over and ran her fingers down the middle of the butch girl's gray dress to come to stop right on her crotch. And poked it. "Give up your little cherry to me & get *all* the privileges. Candy, cigarettes, open-door privileges, even *money*. Money, Mickey. Maybe you can *buy* a piece of your little girlfriend, since she's so reluctant. My spies tell me your luck isn't very good. She won't let you go very far with her.

With open-door privileges and *money,* you can go see any girl in here who's not spoken for, and a lot of them aren't. Ellie's just 12 years old. Try some of the 15-year-olds and you'll have success, I guarantee. And all I ask is for you to give it up to me. *Now,* soon, and anytime after that. And you'll get *paid* each time. Now, think about that. You're a sweet little butch; you deserve a sweet little girl. You'll get her if you have money, and stop concentrating on that child Ellie, and try one of the older girls who know their cunt from their ass. Give it up, or just sit on it—save it for that worthless little girlfriend. *Ha,* what a joke! If you don't, it means we're finished. No more cigarettes, no more open door, no *money.* And go back to your work detail mopping after dinner. I won't cause you any problems, it'll just be like we never knew each other. So, see, I'm a nice person. Nicer than most. *Mickey,* make your choice. You got all night to think about it. *Here....*" Lou reached in her pocket; there was a pack of cigarettes already open, but none missing. Matches stuck in one side in front under the cellophane, and a $5 bill stuck in the other side in back. Then, grunting, raised her bulk off the bed, lumbered out, her wide ass cleared the doorway, and the metal door stayed open.

Mickey lay in the twilight, smoking. 'I can buy Ellie the heart-shaped valentine box of chocolates....' Grim, set her expression to be tough. But also, hated to admit, that what Lou did to her felt good, very good—when she could feel anything thru the hate & rebellion. 'If only Ellie would touch me there! If she'd just do the same things! And want to feel me, and love me too!' But Ellie was only 12 years old, not 45.

So, that would have been the finest way, but it wasn't to happen.

CHAPTER TEN

"I asked you for it, I'm not taking it. You said yes. It's not like some of these other guards.

"It's nothing like with those little girlfriends of yours, I really want you, Mickey.

"I'm not taking my clothes off, Mickey... I know you'll appreciate *that*.

"You might *like* it, Mickey. Think of that!"

With a firm hand, the matron pushed Mickey down on her back.

"Ohhh, baby...ohhh, Mickey! Your titties are so sweet, your cunt is so hot! Oh, little baby! Your body is so sweet! Oh Mickey, it's you! It's you, my little baby!"

Both their breathing quickened, fast, rapid heartbeats. The matron bent over Mickey's slender body to kiss the baby butch full and deep in the mouth, tasting her breath for the first time; huge body pressed up tight against her.

Laying back in the matron's arms was comfortable, in a way, because she was big and padded with fat, and very strong, & Mickey tried to relax, as Lou had told her to do.

She could feel the matron's heart go THUMP THUMP thru the green cotton uniform, like a big bass drum.

Matron's big hand moved up on the inside of Mickey's thigh till her fingertips touched the lips of her vagina & worked into its folds; rubbed over and over her clit. Mickey moaned. Wetness dripped under the stroke of the matron's fingers, until her clit was swollen, and Mickey's hot little body was ready for her. Lou wet her fingers in her mouth with spit; eyes bright with lust, a crooked smile on her face and breathing sharply thru her flared nostrils she bent over the baby butch, kissed her face, and began to push her index and middle fingers in. Mickey held the stout matron around her shoulders bulging in green cloth, breathless, gasped; her grip tightened. The push of her fingers was slow & hard. Pressure in Mickey's little cunt built up; the matron pushed harder; "AHHHHOOOWW!!" Mickey gasped. Her flesh was fever hot. Pain shot thru her sex. Held the matron's arms fiercely. Sweat ran down her. Held on for dear life, and Lou clutched her so tight, pushing her fingers in; the pain shot out of Mickey's cunt through her whole body as the fingers went in up to the last knuckle and the matron was in her.

And it was over.

Lou pulled her fingers out slowly, and there was blood.

Thin, watery, red; on her fingers. Afterward Mickey held on to Lou with her eyes closed, until her heart pounding slowed, steadied. The matron put her fingers up to her lips tasted the blood, then wet her fingers with spit for lubrication and went down into the wet curly black pubic hair of the young teen's body, searching out her hole again.

Blood, a little, in thin streaks down Mickey's thighs from her popped cherry. The baby butch stifled a cry as the matron entered her again. There was noise in the cells down the corridor; a din, as yells ricochet off green walls. The 24-hour light beat down on the two females. Mickey's body arched to the deep thrust of Lou's fingers which took on a rhythmic beat. "You're mine tonight, Mickey," Lou gasped. "You're mine tonight, Mickey!" Lou gasped. "You're mine! Every inch of your body belongs to me, and I'm taking you!"

At each deep thrust, Mickey made a sound: "Uh, uh, uh!" Feeling it—thru the pain a growing excitement. Felt the thrusting fingers make a wide circle in the tight ring of the entrance of her cunt, while filling her up inside. The matron pounded in her and did something else with her thumb as well—so it went around and around on Mickey's clit, which made the enjoyment so great it was almost unbearable; and she opened her knees wide, her body relaxed, gave itself from down deep, opening for Lou in an intense excitement. She was going to cum from the steady pressure on her clit and pounding exerted in her cunt.

Matron Lou had taken her virginity. Juices dripped down Mickey's thighs, onto the coarse green blanket, from her own cunt, the older woman's spit, and thin, watery blood of her broken hymen.

After this interlude, Mickey hated the matron and didn't want to have anything to do with her at all. Just held her hand out for the favors; and when Lou came to give her sex again, accepted it, while ignoring her; head of short cropped hair turned away; expression cold, while the matron grunted over her, fingers pounding inside, working around and around, and in & out of her pussy, then got on her, with her dress hiked up, one fat leg on either side of Mickey's thigh hairy cunt pressed down on her, and rode to an orgasm. And thankfully never asked Mickey to give her oral sex.

"If it wasn't me, it would have been somebody else—who would have really stuck it to you—and cheated you of your privileges as well." Baby-blue eyes wide with fake innocence set in her fat face.

The matron might come by in the hall, and Mickey would glare at her coldly, pass by saying nothing. And the money kept coming, and the cigarettes, & also extra food.

Finally Mickey just gave up, dropped all her barriers and let Lou do what she wanted to, any time she wanted.

The butch had done what she had to do.

Ellie wasn't acting any better. Lou kept telling her to go see one of the older girls, but Mickey was a lover, and in love.

Now Mickey had no work detail. No work at all, and had more candy bars and cigarettes and magazines & privileges than the girls who did work.

Sat up in her room all day with the door unlocked so she could wander around.

The matron was making it too easy for her. Young Mickey was giving up & not learning to be a man—the image she wanted to be. Neglected the schoolwork they were assigned. Didn't work & read magazines & watched TV all day. And let the bulldyke fuck her & was not able to fuck some little girl—this gnawed away at her self-esteem. For this sex favor, she got in return everything it was possible to get in lockup. But she lost the power of saying she got it by herself. And this power was desperately important to Mickey. Freedom would come from it. And adulthood.

Light bulb shone down on the figure on the bed.

'The little bitch won't let me fuck her, and I let Lou fuck me so I could buy her the valentine-shaped box of chocolates. Ellie won't put her mouth on my cunt; she won't let me be a man with her. I'm just nothing! A nobody! I gave that fucking matron Lou my cherry. It would have been so much better with Ellie, her little fingers inside me and me gazing into her smoky eyes! But the bitch didn't want me!' Mickey's face squinted shut, fighting back sorrow.

So again she was abandoned by the ones she loved, & brutalized by strangers. And of the two, missing the love & desire of her little girl was worse.

Mickey beat her fist against the gray-green concrete wall of her cell. 'I've got to get a girl! But I don't have nothing of my own! No money, but what Lou gives me! I can't even get out of this goddamn cell to see a girl, but because of the privilege Lou gives me, & I have to fuck her for that! No keys to turn to get us out of here! I hate myself!' Her butch face twisted in rage and self-loathing. "I hate myself!" Bangs her fists against the walls until blood oozes out of the broken skin.

So days continue unbearably until she'd be released back to the streets.

Alternately hating the matron and accepting her begrudgingly, for Lou was the only one paying her any attention.

Wanted to kill the matron, but had nobody else to befriend her.

And the big burly guard went around bragging to her buddy guards about how she'd popped another cherry on ward E, and the 13-year-old was embarrassed about the insides of her pussy being broadcast all over the place. And felt lower than dirt. Hated Ellie, too, and all the other little girls who were probably straight. And even after Lou got what she came after, the matron didn't desert her, coming back for more of Mickey and continued to give her open-door privileges so the butch could prowl around the jail and get another little girl from among the inmates.

'I'll never go down on Lou. *Never*. If she pulls me by my hair—if she can even get a grip on it, it's so short—and forces me down between her stinky legs, I'll bite her!' Once, in an act of almost-friendship, Mickey spoke honestly to Matron Lou—words which she meant only to explain a fact as one does to a close companion, but which secretly hurt Lou more than anything else Mickey could have done: "I can't go down *there* and suck you, Lou, like I do a girlfriend, because I don't love you. That I reserve for some woman I love! You understand that! Even tho I desperately love to lick a girl's cunt, and you *are* a female, you're not the type of female I like!

Lou, you're too mannish. Too tough, and so much bigger than me that I hate you!"

Mickey had seen too much blood. Saw her soul seep out from under the locked iron doors & bolted windows which held her. Saw her own blood. Her popped cherry. Blood of menstruation marking the crossover from girl to woman. Busted knuckles & smashed face—from life's blood spilled down the corridors as girls fought with each other, tearing hair, gouging each other's eyes. And Mickey turned 14. Drops of blood wrung from her heart being twisted and tugged. Pain as she banged her fists on the cement wall till they swelled up & the joints of her fingers didn't work right. The world watched her die. And didn't do anything to stop it. Her blood; her pain; her parents; the guards—the world walked right on by, stepping over her without saying a word; in a great unplanned sadism; a constant unchanging sadism; and the only person who approached her with an interest inside the locked ward of Mickey's loneliness was the big bulldyke who slipped fingers & tongue inside her pussy and straddled her thigh, cumming on her night after night.

'I got to get a virgin! I got to get a little girl who'll let me love her in every single way! If only I could have got it from Ellie!' Visualized her golden hair, her soft lips, small tits, sweet preteen body which she had seen naked now dozens of times. 'If it had just been her loved me enough to desire me; instead of that big ugly bulldyke.' Black hair mussed; head on a flat pillow, Mickey felt very hard and old.

So for weeks, every day here comes Lou, breathing hard, forcing Mickey down on the bed, or up against the tile wall of the shower room, sticking her fingers up inside her pussyhole; she feeling herself melt & ooze in sexuality and get more & more excited with each thrust, and cum; and submit to it because it felt good, and because of the favors, and because of being trapped in a cage; and Matron Lou would rub up against Mickey and make herself cum that way. And after, pulling up her panties & pulling down her dress, and setting her face stubbornly to look mean as she could; after, Mickey would be enraged.

'I've got to get a girl weaker than me, somebody my own age.'

"YOU FUCKING CHILD MOLESTER!" Mickey snarled.

The fat dyke's eyes squinted as she looks down at the baby dyke; unconsciously, her thick ring-decked hands turn into fists. "To think of all the *cigarettes* I let you have! The *magazines!*" Lou spoke calmly. "The special food—all at my own expense. I earn very little, only minimum wage. And *this* is how you repay my kindness!"

"YOU NEVER GOT ME HALF THE STUFF YOU PROMISED! YOU TOLD ME YOU'D GET ME A DIAMOND RING FOR ELLIE SO WE COULD GET MARRIED, YOU LYING FAT SONOFABITCH!"

"There are uh…certain pleasures you never delivered either, *Mickey.*"

"I TOLD YOU I'D NEVER DO THAT, MOTHERFUCKER! I'M SAVING THAT FOR SOMEONE I LOVE! YOU FUCKING CHILD MOLESTER! SOMEBODY NEEDS TO LOCK *YOU* UP I'LL NEVER DO THAT TO YOU! *NEVER!*"

The dyke stood, huge as an armored tank, in her green uniform. "*Mickey, you yourself* have preyed upon every little 12-year-old on the E wing. Several have dropped their panties for you. In part, because of *my* cigarettes, and *my* magazines!" And in latent anger, her big hand swatted out across space to tap Mickey on the cheek as she had done constantly during this period of months of their knowing each other. Small pig eyes glaring, double-chinned face grinning a hateful smile; TAP, on the baby butch's cheek.

P O W! Mickey swung back. *W H A M!* Mickey punched at Lou. The matron was fast, skidding back in her bobby sox & brogans; but one blow caught the side of her ear; the other grazed off her arm upheld in defense, jabbing harmlessly into air.

Lou charged in. Grabbed the teenager by her dress front, pulled it up in her fists, shoved her into the concrete wall. There the matron stood, with an amazing calm, holding

Mickey. Eyes narrowed into slits, harsh breath labored out of her flared nostrils; sweat stains spread over the cloth of her uniform as her chest rose and fell. "No, you won't make me lose control, you little bitch." Jerked Mickey up and dropped her back down on the bed. A slow smile spread over her flaccid lips. "Well, *yes, Mickey.* I started to punch you out, but then something made me remember how you gave up your virginity to me so sweetly, so I'll forget everything you've said or done."

"YOU BASTARD! TO THINK I LET YOU INTO MY LIFE!"

Lou's full face was trembling, but made herself stay perfectly calm, and merely shouldered her big bulk back out of the cell, slammed the iron door. The last thing Mickey heard was the sound of the key—turning.

"FUCK YOU!"

So Mickey was on her own, and the months stretched into another year. She hadn't known how deep her pain was, or her disgust; but after this it started coming out like a coiled snake; in her snarling, in her meanness, in fights with other guards, and girls.

Followed the savvy matron's advice—started talking to older girls, and it worked. Got a 16-year-old who let Mickey roll around on top of her naked and cum triumphantly.

And finally the glorious moment when a girl she really wanted put her mouth on the baby butch sucked her off for the first time.

Amid clanging noises outside her cell, of inmates in hell; and the memory of her mother trying to kill her, and her former little 12-year-old girlfriends who weren't woman enough to overlook the fact she was a girl and not a boy, and wouldn't love her all the way; and the matrons bullying them in the corridors; thru this, they made love. Experienced a real lover's warm fingers inside her, hesitant; in lush fullness and sexuality; moaning and clutching in a fierce embrace a girl she really loved, a girl near her own age that she could be butch too.

Every time they could steal away and find a bed & lay down, they fucked; until the girl got transferred out.

And Mickey would walk around with tears frozen inside, in a veil of crying which stopped just beyond the mask of her handsome hard face—until she'd be able to win the affection of another girl.

Cigarettes were gone, so Mickey quit smoking. And was chagrined. The guard Lou had a new turnout, 2 years younger than Mickey; age 13 again, a girl-woman; & she was starting it all over again. The butch felt insulted and relieved, and weird that she was no longer desired. Which didn't make sense because she'd always hated it.

Mickey had experienced fear, hunger, humiliation, anger and a sense of total worthlessness. Her teenage exuberance was locked in an iron cage. Had the key turned in her face. Secretly she feared she had no power over her own life.

Men had tried to take sex from her against her will. She'd given herself to an older, more powerful woman who wanted to fuck her, as a means of protecting herself against what lay in the future, and for money. And none of it was her fault.

She'd had five little girls her own age in the reformatory—in progressing intensity—& it was sweet. They'd responded to her lovemaking. She had made choices the best she knew how.

When she was released to her parents custody at 14, Mickey didn't ever want to hear that iron door click locked behind her again. Was deathly afraid of the turnkey.

But after a fight, Mickey ran away from home again; met a madam in Jersey City & made love with her girls; then got a real job by lying about her age; then met a showgirl, Lisa, and went on the Strippers Burlesque circuit tour thru to St. Louis, back thru Ohio, Pennsylvania, NYC, was picked up by the police as a runaway at the home of a lesbian teenager she met in the Village & sent back to the reformatory to stay until she turned 18.

Then suddenly it was over. Sentence snapped shut. The statute of limitations closed on Mickey's case. She was out! In a breath of fresh air; didn't care where life would take her. Freedom! To go thru the streets, walk walk in a straight line and not have to go around, doubling back thru endless repeats of the same corridors like a rat in a maze. To have a choice of what food to eat. To wear clothes that pleased her. Tennis shoes on the pavement; running with the exuberance of a girl-woman-butch. Released back into the city.

Wild hot summer of 1959.

This is the story of Mickey, her triumphs and her tears.

She faced the streets, the highways of the world ahead.

Seemed just a minute ago she was 13, losing her cherry; now 18. A woman.

A butch turned out.

CHAPTER ELEVEN

So Mickey backs out of this window of memory, & here she lays with a woman of 23. Lucy. A redhead.

Turned to her; the bed creaks its ancient springs; props up on one elbow to cast her eyes over the sleeping woman. Of course, jail was light-years ago. A span of infinite time between puberty & young adulthood. A maelstrom of 5 years on & off, in & out of lockup that dragged on longer than 50 years. The butch knew a lot more about women now. And touching Lucy's face for a moment, remembered their cum had been great.

"You have a nice day sir." The fag smiled at Mickey, tilting his head cutely, to one side and flipping his wrist.

"Freakin' fags flirting with men." Mickey says as they walk away.

"Sir Mickey." Lucy smiles & puts her arm thru Mickey's arm.

Windy City.

Redhead and butch with wavy black hair went under the blue day sky, on the prowl for groceries & to see about Mickey's room, farther uptown.

"Excuse me, *miss*," a man says in a vituperative tone.

"I hate when they call me 'Miss,'" Mickey growls.

A big crane hung at the 14 story of a building that shot up into the sky. The black-haired butch looked up—POW! Sun, blazing, hits her in the eye; she squints.

Downtown Loop. Huge buildings of concrete and glass and steel. Two days ago Mickey had been here looking for work; sad, angry, and disgusted. Now, with Lucy at her side, femmy & sweet, and money in their pockets the butch danced over the windswept plaza.

Glass fronts three stories high, then steel up into the clouds. Modern day replicas of the castle fortresses of medieval times. The bosses & rulers of these palaces frowned on gays; and their shopkeepers & receptionists thought she was a joke and they would never hire her. Far as the eye could see, these castles—skyscrapers march in a totalitarian army. 'We paid Lucy's rent for two weeks at the price of a single night in one of these hotels.' The huge buildings created a natural wind tunnel that blew them along; the redhead had a scarf over her hair which fluttered & nearly came off. Wind from the lake. Newspaper blew, and leaves from the sparse trees planted here and there growing out of circles cut in the cement sidewalks in a geometric design. And the Loop was littered with human wrecks. Bag women shuffled, heads bowed thru the alleys. Mickey was afraid of these discards of society. They made her uneasy. Her young life was just beginning at 18. What were the things not to do, so she wouldn't end up like them?

Machinery, drab mustard color splattered with mud, sat on lots of building sites. Jackhammers riveted through the day's sounds. Honks of traffic. A hidden machinery—a vast huge God in blackness had hung in eternity, driving forth the opportunities of her life, the chances, pitfalls & daggers alike. Aim was, to tiptoe around the pitfalls & to seize a cog of this wheel when the time was right & score a victory.

Mickey had scored Lucy.

Had experienced the tender thrust of Lucy's cunt beneath hers; the oral love, the kissing & emotion-filled eyes—the butch rode the merry go round & grabbed the brass ring!

Lucy had been in the business world a little. "I worked in offices $1^{1/2}$ years. For what they paid, I make enough on welfare and have my time to myself."

"It's easy for you, dressed as a femme."

They walked around downtown, in the Loop. Lucy went to Carson Pirie Scott & bought the cheapest thing there—nail polish.

The butch's roaming eye was attracted to none but the redhead at her side.

'Do it to her, experience her cunt and her delicious tongue. Ohhhh.' Nervous, Mickey jammed fists into her trouser pockets. It was too good to be true! A dream become reality! 'Her thighs… Ohhhh… Her scent… Ahhh… To use her sweet sex over and over… Ahhhh… Just as long as I make her cum…. She's mine now; I'm like her husband.'

Mickey got some clothes, men's discards, at a thrift shop on the fringe between lower Clark & the Loop. "It's so embarrassing going in the men's department at Sears. It's much easier at the bargain stores; it's not as formal."

In their wanderings the two women go out where the Outer Drive curves along Lake Michigan—where a bitter Mickey had wanted to jump in—just days past.

Salty fish smell, like the biggest woman of the universe. Mother of us all. Of life.

They stand on the rocks together & look down. Surface is calm; after the incoming tide and before the outgoing. Surface is flat; silver eyelets sparkle on each tiny pyramid shape crest of waves that last but a moment, then blend into the whole.

Clumps of seaweed. Sand packed yellow-gray under foot gives way with a crunch, yet is firm beneath them.

Mickey didn't have her swagger now; they just talked.

Legs ran, jumped! She poised on a precarious pinnacle.

Huge rocks tumble down into the water. Mickey leaps from rock to rock. Lucy's face lights up in mirth, narrow lips smile wide, eyes accented by makeup twinkle.

Pungent smell of fish. Wind.

Everywhere is blowing wind.

Then the lovers hug; the wind blows around them.

Lesbians, entwined, kissing deep & stroking each other in a profession of commitment.

Arm and arm they walked now, back up on the cement's winding turns that match the winding Outer Drive. Mickey tells Lucy: "They'll think of a way to reorganize society into a love society. No more lonely teenage butches like I was. No more lies. And nobody can open their lips unless they are making a conversation to help people & not snitching on people, or gossiping behind their back or doing something that will wind up killing the person."

"Sometimes, well...it's like I'm living in a dream.... I have a bottle of Richard's Wild Irish Rose...." Lucy confided. "And I just sit up in my window... I wait at the window, and look out—it's like a living TV set, watching the street from my window and drinking wine. But, I'm afraid of it...because...I need to be with people, Mickey!" Her face spun about, looking up, filled with rare emotion. "I don't just want to die...live and kind of die each day...fading away... I need to be in the middle of life and live! That's why I go to the clubs every night...to live!"

Bell chimes from the cathedral tolled a sad song.

"On the pool tables of Chicago and New York City, I learned a lesson. Shoot the balls you have. Take what you have in front of you. In a cafeteria in the Loop, I learned another one. Take what you want for what it is, instead of reading the price list. You'll find out the price. I wish I could do this with people. I'm not free enough."

"I'm self-conscious. Except when I'm drunk, or high."

Mickey grinned wickedly; dark eyes twinkled. "What's your price, Lucy?"

Lucy bit her lip and shoved Mickey, tinkling laughter. "Beat your meat, sir? Beat your meat, Sir Mickey?"

The two wrestled for footholds on the sand in a shoving match.

"I bet I owe you hundreds by now!"

"Yes! You do, Mickey! I've let you have my body for—"

"Three days!"

"Yes, so you owe me $300—you'll have to make it up in trade!"

The two walked. Then, when people came from the opposite way, dropped their hands and just walked close, sides brushing each other's side.

When they passed under the viaduct and got back to the city streets, they could feel the hostility of society once more—not washed away by the water and waves.

A male's eyes met Mickey's, scorching. Dully, she felt the hatred. The memories of lost nights when she'd cruised looking for women, alone...familiar to her, come back over, like a cap back over her soul.... Now she had a woman at her side, and the single people were glaring at her, envious. Mickey had forgotten her pain overnight. Lucy was beside her, close, warm. Together they could withstand straight people's hate & the ego wars of men. The butch felt a pang of joy, the so-longed-for freshness of this morning.

"When I was young, I loved people. I got hate letters from my mother in jail; it was a knife stuck in my heart. I fantasized her letters to be this way instead: 'Oh, daughter, I want you home so badly, I'm so worried about you.' And fantasized a dream mother, who had been the mother of one of my school friends. Then she stopped writing and I didn't have to flush the real letters down the toilet. I came out here in a whirlwind. In a hurry. I went into each department store, all the employment agencies. Then went back to the streets and just turned in every shop and restaurant, everywhere! People's faces...their eyes...they're so cold...I walked, and walked. I got madder and madder. My mind is getting stiff & uptight and mean. I'm taking this game of life too serious, and I hurt every night. It hurts. Even the butch game; I take it too seriously. I just want to be with you and love you, Lucy. Lucy, you're good for me! Took her by the shoulders and held her in her arms.

And passersby saw a he-she in drag embracing a woman who looked poor & a little drunk, or like a gypsy; and they frowned and cast judgment.

"Mickey, you're only 18. That's kind of young... A lot of 18-year-olds are still living at home; that's what makes life so rough, being on your own.

"No, it's not young. Depending on how you look at it. Anyway, I've got to live now! I might not get old. I might be dead in a few years!"

Now, On-The-Road is when you travel from one state to the next; the roads between towns. In-The-Streets—that's when you get to the city of your choice & hang out.

There are always these special streets in The Life of a gay; for one who is Out of the Closet & practicing—or trying their best to find that special someone. Even those closeted gays who seldom venture down here, somewhere thru their long blue, lonely years of being separated from other gays, there'll be a whiff of information, a rumor in the air, the name of that street...that special street.... Lucy & Mickey hung out in the bars, in these funky streets, because they were free women —outlaws, and paid the price for that in the insults of society, the harassment from police; & the poverty.

Lucy had lived with rain leaking thru the roof into her room more times than she could remember.

They kept house in the day and got ready for night where they reigned as King & Lady of the gay bars.

Lucy was so awful that she didn't have regular johns and had to find some new sucker each time. Mickey put an end to this. Slowly the tricks would come back into their lives; they'd be in a semi-hustling bar with other gays, and a john would come by and look at Lucy like she was on display under the yellow and red bar lights; Mickey, man-dressed, aggressive, just threw her arm around Lucy, and the john would move off. 'I got to get a job,' the teenager thought. Snarled something nasty in Lucy's ear, and ordered another drink and forgot it.

Memory & inspiration. Creativity flooded back to her; images so powerful they couldn't be ignored.

Mickey'd been thru this before—girls & their games & tricks. Their coquetry and how they were in bed with her, whispering promises they couldn't deliver. Lucy was different.... Money wasn't a driving ambition that pushed her into whoredom like the others. The redhead could exist in poverty on the fringe of sanity in the midst of skid-row and watch the tricks parade by; go home alone and poor; so now she was with Mickey there was good odds for fidelity. For loyalty between them, and no third party to corrupt it.

The butch wanted that mouth and that cunt for herself!

CHAPTER TWELVE

At Grand Central train station that night, I bid the ushers good-bye. Going to visit my mother in a dream. Gangs of well-dressed people in polyester carrying suitcases; and hobos and insane people who live as rats do, amid the tile walls and benches made of wood. Walk down the platform, trains chug to a stop blowing steam, iron wheels clank. Last thing I remember, my girl says: "Well, dunk my weenie! Are we having pee soup next Thursday, Miss Piss Whip? That's an old burlesque joke, Mickey!" Lisa announces in a loud clear voice. "WHEN THE WEATHER'S HOT AND SULTRY IT'S NO TIME TO COMMIT ADUL-TERY, BUT WHEN THE FROST IS ON THE PUMPKIN, THAT'S THE TIME FOR DINKY DUNKIN!" I know them all! I should know them! I've heard the goddamn things enough backstage, waiting to go on and do my act!"

This was my life. I watched two seasons go by. First snows from the polar ice. Stars twinkle. Pluto's frozen fire. Heights revolve above us mere mortals, the frozen signs, and snow-banks; now melt, and my heart runs, and my body is sticky from Lisa's love. Blood on the sheets. She is menstruating & it's in my mouth, and smeared over my cunt where I've loved her. And Lisa is professional. She has equipment that less-advanced gay girls don't—a plastic dick. It's ringed with her blood, and she loves to put it in me, too.

"You don't understand me!"

"I feel bad, but I got to go! You don't love me, Lisa! You treat me too mean!"

"Everybody leaves me, Mickey! You're the first girl to be honest enough to tell me you were."

"Because I hoped maybe you'd change and love me, and stop hitting me, and being so damn mean. I'm like a prize fighter, I have to watch you every minute, 'cause you're gonna lose your temper and swing at me! And *you're* the lady! *I'm* the one suppose to be knocking you around!"

She left New York City with its raining days and nights and drizzly snowfall.

And Valorie. Another one of the review of ladies she had in NYC. In a lineup of spoiled strippers & hookers. Workin' as a part-time whore aside from the dancing, making $20,000 a year & catering to herself—indulging her every whim like a ten-year-old kid.

Anything she wanted, she bought. Instant gratification, like the money wasn't going to end. Like giving candy to a baby. GIMME! GIMME! And sported Mickey to food and hotel rooms and nice jackets and shirts from elegant men's stores. & they rode around town in cabs. But unlike Lisa, who stopped whoring, Valorie wouldn't.

"I got to go to work, Mickey!"

"Aw, hell, no! Stay!"

"I got to make some money! What are we gonna do? I can't live off what you earn in that restaurant! $60 a week! It's chicken feed! I can make that much in a couple of dates! I'm going! I'll be back by eleven!"

"Don't go!"

"If I'm not back in an hour, call the police station!"

"I'll call the police station, the hospital, and the *morgue*."

"Don't say that! You'll give me bad luck!"

I used to tell Valorie that. She'd be gone too long. When she sauntered in, tired, hair falling out of place, & counting her rumpled sweaty green cash, I'd tell her, "I was on the phone just now! I called the police station & the hospital!"

"Please don't tell me about the morgue, Mickey! Not that!"

So Valorie rushes out the door, but doesn't get far, because tonight Mickey wanted to take her. A grease-splattered apron and filthy cooks' pants lay balled up waiting to be washed. Her uniform. Mickey had scraped up the $8 for the hotel, and had $12 dollars left over from her job. Valorie knew the butch would follow her thru the streets & she'd never be able to work, so she gives in and plays the trick game with her butch that night. Took Mickey's $12, counts it out in her pale hands; solemn white face; red dress so short it stops just below her crotch with her sweet little ass stuck out; and breasts poking up.

"Well, that ought to be good for 12 minutes." Threw a nickel aside. "That's five seconds." The nickel rolled off the bed across the floor.

"That's my cum."

"Five seconds? You cum longer than that! You cum hard! You go, UHHHHHH OOOO UUHHHHHOOHHHAAA OH *GOD* UH UH UH UH UH OHHHHHAAAAA! That's more than five seconds! I'll have to charge you more!"

Valorie peeled off her red dress, and Mickey pulled off her pants, naked ass and legs, and saved her worn black leather jacket for last.

"You have a sweet body and a nice ass."

Under a yellow light bulb in a $8-a-night hotel room, lovers grunt on a mattress. Valorie was the first woman to show Mickey how to fuck her using her fist.

Her cunt opened up, taking three fingers easy, warm, wet and slippery; it's just the ring of muscles when she first went in that tightened; then pushed four fingers in; the big part of her hand across the knuckle span was hard; using her spit as lubricant. "Come out, Mickey." Valorie breathes. Her body is sweating from sexual tension; she lays back on the pillow, eyes closed. "Ball up your hand in a fist." She gives instructions. "Hold your thumb inside your fingers—yeah." And Mickey pushes in her hole again, goes slow, pushes hard, and her vagina opens, accepting the fist. "Push it all the way in, baby." Fist goes thru the wet, smooth chamber. Mickey feels contractions, and it's in, halfway up her arm.

Yellow light from a hotel room across the airspace. Neon from the street below.

Pounds inside her, pushes her fist up: "UHHHHH. OHHHH. UHHHH." Valorie groans in unison to each thrust. "OHHHHH. UHHHHHH. That's right, Mickey, oh, baby, keep doing it awhile."

When Mickey pulled out, Valorie's cunt didn't want to let go, sucking, held her fist up there, so Mickey had to pull hard, and slowly; then felt it slide down & out.

'That last week it's cold, rains alternately blows cold wind. I haunted streets outside the burlesque houses... The penny arcades—just like here on South State Street. The Royal Theatre; talked for hours with the gay night manager, caught the 7:30 and midnight strip shows, ran across the street, listened to music on the jukebox in a semi-beatnik joint—O'Douels, out of whose window I saw the Rialto marquee go off and on and off and on in red block letters.'

Mickey sat in a booth, sipped a 25¢ Coca-Cola, eyes furrowed within the power of a changing mood. 'If I leave town, I leave my woman, I leave my job. I have nothing but $125 I've saved. Lisa's not my woman; she hurts me too much.' Mickey's arm has black-&-blue bruises from block- ing the slaps Lisa bats out—BAM! Anytime she gets the slightest bit mad. She's tried to injure her butch inside her cunt, pinching her up inside there, which later leaves little pieces of dead attached skin which must be removed by a doctor reaching into her cunt with latex gloves & instru- ments. And Mickey won't let her in no more, and the relationship has gone to hell.

"Why don't you stop stripping if it makes you so mad!"

"I love my act! I love to dance! I'm a good dancer! I'm one of the best!"

"You *are* the best!"

"I'm not going to stop, Mickey!"

"Yeah, but it's driving you crazy! We can't never settle down nowhere. You got to travel the circuit and go from town to town, and I can't even get a job that fast; and when I do, then I got to quit my job! We spend all our money on this expensive hotel! You make big money, but you spend big money eating out, 'cause there's no kitchen in any of these hotel rooms, and on cabs and stuff—we ain't saving no money!"

"I have to live the way I'm accustomed to living!"

"And all these fancy dresses you throw your money away on, we could save something, and maybe stop in some town and get an apartment and I can keep a job and we can settle down! All you do is dress up for other people! Not for me! You walk around in a slip all day for me!"

"Oh, just shut up and leave me alone! I need my rest!"

"I hope God has mercy on you, Lisa!"

She tosses and turns in the bed—Mickey thinks she's just getting comfortable—then hears a small voice: "I don't believe in God, anyway… I don't need anybody!" Lisa says bitterly.

"You must need somebody!" Mickey wants desperately for Lisa to say yes; she needs her.

"Of course I don't need *anybody*! Not anyone! Do you hear! And you're gonna leave me, too! You said you're going to Chicago! And then California!—and there's no strip clubs in California—just this new go-go dancing, and it don't pay as much!"

So Lisa and Mickey lived on the stripper's work schedule—5 shows per day starting at noon, ending at midnight, with 3 hours' break in between—that was 10 cab rides per day, unless they hung out in the lobby of the theater; & couldn't spend time backstage because the owner forbid it.

Her costumes scattered over the room.

The owner of the theater—one of several theaters—was a bastard. He hated Lisa because she was the only dancer who wouldn't sleep with him, which he did routinely with every performer he could.

Mickey had experienced the hot orgasmic rush.

Romancing Lisa in between the strip acts at the Rialto.

It's a grand old theater, a showpiece of the high-class entertainment industry before it fell to semi-nude sex dancers; huge vaulted ceilings designed in baroque, carved cornices with medieval masks, red velvet curtains extending for the 30-foot drop from the arc of the stage—deep crimson red, bound by gold-braid ropes & tassels. It's palatial—covered now by dust and scratches. Stagehands climb like monkeys thru the overhead tangle of lights & beams adjusting spotlights and sound speakers.

'After I got to know her, we met up in the lobby of the theater—when she's dressed and has packed up her costume in a tote bag; I saw her flirtatious switch, round hips, her come-on, which excites me. She's bi. She goes both ways. And I'm so excited because this means I can have her—there's no stone wall up between us—that I can never get past. Lisa is part colored. She don't look it. Her hair is coarse; she uses a special treatment to make it straight. A cast to her skin—tan, just barely. These things are the only clues that she is not white, and if she confesses what she is. When Lisa treats me like a human being, it is fire! And my presence beside her discourages the tricks & johns who fade out of her life. We move in the hotel together. Her tight dress and nylon stockings over her pretty soft wonderful little rear end. On the inside of her mind, Lisa calculates how much money she's gonna lose with me around, and I provide protection, as a man; and we take cabs back and forth together; I sit in the audience, watch her act, eat out in the hotel restaurant together; and we are inseparable.

'Maybe I'll be a new person. Gay, but new.

'I hear life is better in California. I'm not sure where to go, Frisco, or L.A. I'm going thru Chicago first, or Miami too, on my way.'

First thing seen about these cities of night is the fog, which unites us in chemical evolution; a gaseous state, and we are a transition. Nothing permanent... Spirit. Like the vapors that must have risen when the world began. When polypods crawled out of the ocean, and Eve walked naked and dumb in a hostile 200 million B.C.

'Well, I've heard about this place of yours, California, it's at the end of the American continent. And it's suppose to be the beginning of lives at the end of the world. Maybe I will find happiness there, if I leave this place.'

So Mickey, soul in turmoil had these thoughts in the bar across the street from the blinking Rialto Theatre; red on, black off; red/on, black/off. Hands cupped her chin. A soft drink wet spilled a watery rim on the marred wood surface of the table of a booth.

Night fog was in the street, & snow drizzles. Marquee lit up for the last show.

'In the town, there's a street... Name of the street, funky funky Broadway. In the street, there's a nightclub... Name of the nightclub...fonky fonky Broadway...in the nightclub...there's a woman, name of the woman, Broadway woman.'

Remembered the town, the hooker that she loved. The transition from East Coast to West. The Rialto Theatre, the Regency Hotel. 'You got to fight in this world, I'm not equipped to fight originally, as a baby; but I learned to! I have! I was raised that way by my mother, by jail, by the street. But I still don't have the killer instinct! My heart is too big! If I leave here and go west, will I be leaving the best woman I've ever had? Kids will say in the gay club, "Mickey? That butch with the black hair and the men's suits, you know her, she went off on a wild-goose chase she never came back from and we ain't seen her since!"'

Light blinked off then on. Inside the cavernous theater, Lisa had the stage illuminated by spotlight. Rows of empty seats throughout which a scattered male audience—mostly middle-aged, drab, worn, with ugly gray faces—viewed near-naked female bodies performing their dance acts; & jacked themselves off secretly with furtive gestures.

Mickey sips her drink, solemn... 'And, when I get out to California, at the end of the world, and life still don't act right... Somebody tell me! Will I have to change it?—Life itself! The world's whole life? Change it if I can?'

Mickey, butch, experimenting in life. One of the gay children of the world, wanted to make this rough experiment that she was, work. The first draft of which there were few examples before her—recorded in history. A gay woman. A gay society. And not to have to depend on the old society that did them no justice. To have her own power & not depend so much on fate.

A withered crone ran the ticket booth of the Rialto Theatre tonight. Operated the turnstile with a switch under her foot. Wore a white uniform. Old crone with as many wrinkles in her face as a pane of cracked glass... A million slivers of mirror. White plastic dress, red lipstick, eyebrows tweezed into arches with peaks. She, too, was an ex-stripper.

Mickey walks down this seedy street; RIALTO! Hangs in space, featuring STORMY GALE!—WARNING! I. NITA MANN,

DUSTY D-CUP, AND MISS LISA LAMOUR. Dusty D was a transsexual; injected with silicone to create huge size 50 fake tits. Mickey was privy to these bits of information, and the audience of deathlike ugly gray men jacked off to them in stupid bliss.

Their last time, Mickey sat in the hotel restaurant, waited for Lisa to come down, buys them a quick breakfast. They'll eat, call a cab, and zoom over to the theater. It's their last time together, but Mickey doesn't say so. Lisa appears in the door in her blue coat, turquoise dress, hair all teased up, makeup on…. The Star with class. Mickey sees her, has fear and trembling. Don't want to leave Lisa, but her arms are black and blue & inside her cunt are dead brown pieces of flesh Lisa has pinched that will have to be attended to by a doctor in the free clinic in the new city.

CHAPTER THIRTEEN

So Mickey had moved in with Lucy & saved $11 for that week, and all the weeks in their lives to come. There was food in the house and money to spend in the gay bar.

SLAM SLAM! Of car doors on the strip all night over their room.

The table was set. Battered, with mismatched chairs & a ragged tablecloth. Lucy cooked biscuits, chicken, gravy, and some green-gray canned unidentifiable vegetable—all on the hot plate.

A pigeon that belonged with its army of friends flapping their wings under the eves. The two women had found each other.

Pigeons. She had watched them in prison, and in Times Square by a gang of Drag Queens who worked the tearoom in the subway.

Pigeons, brown, white speckled & gray flew upward from a ledge, into the eaves. Cornices of the tenements—once long ago fancy dwellings constructed in yesteryear with curlicues, artful designs—how they saw the fall from grace. The now-grimy torn-shade windows, the dirt unwashed from years.

Changed from expensive suites to single-occupancy rooms. Gay, they were like the pigeon that carries a straw in its mouth, building its nest. So in the straight world that didn't want to let them, these two women built their own nest openly, and made their own love.

In the back of her mind, Lucy remembered that last time moving. Herself. She'd been in a hurry. 2 sacks like semi-suitcases, one long coat tossed over her shoulders, another leopard-spot coat in her hand. Shoulder-strap purse bulging, crammed with dainty gold shoes falling out; the other bag barely filled at all. Hands full, red-nailed fingers clutching, carried it down the turnings of a worn out carpet on sagging stairs—to beat the rent.

So Lucy was at this hotel a long while now; hillbillies lived there, some families in a series of rooms together like it was their private castle. It was the same as all the other bare stick-&-board skid-row hotels. Ancient, leaky pipes. Lucy lived and accumulated a lot of things more than she'd brought in two sacks. Some she'd stole from other people, some tricked for, others the Welfare Department bought. Stuff given away by a church as charity. And still other stuff was presents from lovers.

"First time," Mickey said, "we hitchhiked out of New York. Second time I took the train. I remember the lights along the turnpike. New York's harder to survive—that's what the park bums say. So I came here. But I want to keep going out to California. It's the easiest to make it because it's so warm all year round. You can sleep on the beach. Nobody cares if you're gay or not. It's free. And there's jobs picking lettuce and strawberries in the Valley, and other kinds of jobs in the cities that anybody can get. *Anybody.*"

"Winter is cold here." Lucy saw the cracks between the windows and their frames, & knew the cold air that rushed in, her blankets stuffed around the windows & piled high on the bed, shivering, nursing a bottle of wine, and the breakers on Lake Michigan frozen solid in gray-blue ice.

Later that week, they heard about the raid. Police in blue-&-black uniforms with stars on their chests. Gone in the girl/boy club and hauled off half the kids to jail—"Case Dismissed!" by the judge next morning.

They were lucky they hadn't gone the three steps down into that club—The Silver Window—that night; poor because it was the end of the month, they'd amused themselves at home until Lucy's welfare check came, and made a brief appearance at the Fizz Club downstairs where somebody'd bought the redhead a drink she got a buzz of intoxication she so craved.

Police made Mickey tremble. Vice cops. It was hate. Police hatred of them as free beings. So, for another week waiting for that day the money came, they had something extra to worry about. Getting all dressed up, going out to a gay bar and it being raided; them taking Mickey to jail for male impersonation, and Lucy (as they did both female and male femmes) to jail in handcuffs on the phony charge of suspicion of prostitution.

Lucy wore her slip, satin, old—a strap kept falling down over her round shoulder; Mickey'd reach across the bed & pull it up. Lucy had her bottle of wine—Chianti, with the straw wrapping, and didn't notice the strap. Mickey wore boxer shorts & T-shirt—no bra, no binder.

They lay side by side, under yellow lights on, which muted the red blinking sign outside to pink, a pulse that throbbed thru the room, by now so accustomed; and told each other the story of their past while they lived each current day—as outlaw women.

Room hot, still, uncirculated air. Summer of 1959.

Lucy lay back, her tits under satin moved liquidly; bottle in one hand, mouth opens in a yawn.

Mickey thinks back... 'If I wasn't a woman-lover, would I have sucked off all the strippers; their cum in my lips in those hotels and back rooms? Behind the stage door, down the long cement corridor of the Rialto Theatre? Would I have rubbed their clits with my tongue hard & fast and brought them to orgasm after they'd come in from turning their tricks where they *couldn't* cum...and loved them no matter where they'd been? Or what they were?

'Ain't I a lover of women?'

She had serviced them all. All her women, with no disrespect for their professions. Had gave them head. Had mounted them, clit under her furry black cuntmound pressed to their cunt, slippery wet; no matter who had had it before her, or what they had done to it.

'And they pulled me on them, some, so hurried, like they were desperate for a woman's love, after.

'Like it was so important to them, to have somebody of their own—a woman, a butch that could make them strong. To show them that they were strong too, & not weak and just a piece of gash, a piece of meat getting fucked for a price.

'So I let them love me, and take me with their fingers inside my cunt so they could do to me what some john had done to them, and watch my face, and delight... She would just be delighted to see my face change its expression as she moved inside me, and heard me moan knowing she had the power to love me. The power to affect another human being.'

Lucy stirred on the bed; white flesh, satin gown yellowed by age. She was drunk, and pulls up the gown till her cunt shows, wispy brown hair; pink lips of her pussy; and her hips squirm on the bed. Then arches her hips up and pulls the slip up over them, to bunch together at her midsection, just covering her full breasts.

"Come on, baby. Love me." Lucy whispers.

Lucy held her ankles, feet up in the air, and wiggles her ass, her cuntlips are open wide; she smells strong & good. Held her knees back so Mickey, who was climbing between her legs, naked, could get her sex pressed up against hers & they could rub & hump and cum together.

First Mickey pulls the slip off over Lucy's head, then puts it back down half over her tits, to reveal them for erotic pleasure, as a whore had taught her to do—to get it off fast.

Mickey tucked the satin gown over Lucy's ripe tits, then slid down to the sea—tasting the entranceway of life, by which all humankind is born; began to suck; and reached her hands up over Lucy's belly to squeeze her tits thru the satiny material. Lucy relaxed her legs, soles of her feet down on the sheet, knees spread; and let the waves of pleasure roll over her.

Mickey licked, and put her fingers inside, and then, in a while, Lucy moaning, pulled the slender body of Mickey up on her; and Mickey's riding her, her hips pushed down and around, driving her wet thrusting cunt meeting Lucy's. "AHHHHH!" The redhead exhales, "OHHHHH, MICKEY! MISTER MICKEY!"

And Lucy humps underneath, thrusts her wet cunt along Mickey's cuntlips, moves hot, building the orgasmic fire.

The butch's going up and down on her, and around and round; upper torso lifted up by her arms, one hand on each side of Lucy; black hair mussed, a straining expression on her face; & looking at Lucy's ripe tits bounce about under the satin gown as she fucks; the motion of the bed on its springs, and her motion on Lucy juggling them around; and then Lucy draws back the gown with her red-nailed fingers, partially shows her tits; and seeing this, Mickey fucks harder; erotic arousal fires her lust...

Mickey grunts & groans and screws; a rush of desire floods over her body, withdraws back into her hot clit, then, in the next motion of their cunts, lust floods out again. Lucy pulls the satin gown off, her bare big tits with pink-brown nipples jog jellylike as Mickey screws her. Lucy squeezes her own tits & moans, one hand over each, kneading and holding them up for Mickey to look at; she sees, it makes her cunt drip with juice in feverish desire, and lowers her upper body down to place her lips against one breast and suck, and moan, then raises back up, sweat glistening over the rippling muscles of her strong back, to fuck hard & fast with rapid pumps and she's gonna cum hard & good.

Lucy humps her cunt up, slippery, rubbery wet under Mickey's clit; and continues to play with her breasts; streams of desire suffuse her body as she squeezes her own nipples, and her hot clit being pounded by Mickey's clit. "CUM, BABY! CUM, HONEY! CUM FOR ME! USE ME, MICKEY! LET ME HAVE YOUR CUM, MICKEY! GIVE IT TO ME, MICKEY! GIVE ME YOUR CUM!"

With each short thrust, the bed moved and Lucy's tits

shook; Mickey looked down, using the erotic sight of her tits to fuck lustily. Lucy squeezed her tits, moaned, turned her head from side to side, her nipples had gotten big and red. "FUCK ME, MICKEY!! TAKE ME, BABY! I'M GONNA CUM, OH, GODDAMN! I'M GONNA CUM! DON'T STOP! FUCK ME! FUCK ME! FUCK ME! FUCK ME, MICKEY! TAKE ME! TAKE IT! TAKE IT, BABY! TAKE IT!" Lucy's hips thrust involuntarily, giving up her pussy & Mickey's mouth opened, neck arched back, abandoned herself to the unchecked stream of desire that raced thru both their bodies flooding into orgasm.

They came. Hips twist, pump fast, like pistons, both hollering as their cum went on and on; sexspots pressed together in a climax, working in this intense feeling; spasms, stars bursting, lasting miraculously for minutes. Then Mickey dropped down upon Lucy, panted, and embraced her; weak and spent.

Mickey was glad she belonged to the race of females; that species within whom life began. Who feel emotions. Who cry. In whom nature creates life itself. Better than being male, forced to live an artificial life. Women were more real—if they let themselves be. But being a woman was very difficult in a male world.

Now was the beginning time of power & love in her life.

In the past, that had built up to this point, Mickey had been dominated by older more aggressive women. Her mother; the strippers who had much higher-paying jobs & world experience. The matron in jail.

This had put Mickey in a passive role, of sorts, which, as any butch, she bucked up against. Pulling at the reins.

Now, finally, she had a woman of her own who was passive. Tho older, Lucy did what Mickey said to do. And went to bed with her the way she craved. As a bottom lady.

Mickey was a dominant stud.

Being serviced by any kinky fetish or dirty words either one of them could remember from their past. And did it as often as Mickey wanted to do it.

And this gold mine of love & desire paid back all the debt of troubles fate had dealt her in the beginning.

With $45 from a freaktrick, they started their lives; loaded up with food; waited for Lucy's welfare check, and had a window in time—a space for Mickey to find a job.

Now every day Mickey would look halfheartedly thru the Sunday paper, circle a few jobs with a blue-ink pen, and hit the streets. The want ads were divided into gender categories, like society—& butches didn't fit.

In those days, the segregated ad section for women was the smallest. Men's was larger. They had the most interesting jobs, technical work, engineers; things a woman didn't know about.

So, from the pain, suffering and humiliation, came the strength. Forged steel inside.

Chiseled white features; face set hard, but a fire shone out of her dark eyes.

Now, Mickey had yet lessons to learn. Still a long row to hoe.

Got lazy. Whipped by failure to get a job, the butch relaxed. Decided maybe she'd get on welfare, too, like Lucy—but was torn by the idea of not having a future.

So every day after a feeble few hours attempt to find a job—reading the newspaper ads might account for half of this time—was boredom, waiting for night to come, and again she could be herself—a lesbian butch in drag & they could mix with their own kind.

1959; Chicago was not like New York, Manhattan— Greenwich Village, where gay kids came to assemble from all over & there was a culture of them out in the street, ready, visible, that a stray dyke or fag could get to; plus a multitude of gay bars, plus restaurants, a few thickly populated with visible gays; Chicago's hidden population submerged like the tip of an iceberg by day—scattered sightings of lesbians & homosexual men in certain streets a little more than other streets; to emerge by night; gay kids funneled from West Side, North Side, and South Side—of the blacks; alike, into a few jam-packed gay clubs that paid off the Vice Squad and managed to survive for a length of time.

And condensed into that time, they did party!

Waiting for night to come... Outside red blinking light

went off & on. Shadows fell across the room; pigeons cooed in their nests in the eaves.

Night fell.

Mickey had walked the beach this day. To forget, and to remember. "Sometimes I see gay kids there. But it's mostly men picking up each other in the bathroom on Division Street." Water blue. Lake big as an ocean that no eye could see the end of it. Smell of seawater & fish.

Waves beat into her heart, and opened eternity for a glimpse, so that's why she went there—Mickey had soul.

Lucy put on her fingernail polish. About the last item left over from the trick money some months past.

Plaster peeling walls. Noise of the old hag who muttered to herself in an adjacent room. Pretty painted wooden boxes Lucy had done under the influence of alcohol; filled with her things.

Mickey examined her own hands a moment. They were square, tough, with no nails overlapping her stub-end fingertips. Masculine. Capable of giving pleasure to a woman.

Shirt, pants, shoes, sox, tie & belt; ready.

At night, at The Silver Windows, the couple was a hit. Epitome of a gay butch/femme couple. Handsome & fine. Mickey, dark hair & eyes; in her suit & tie; stone drag. Slim lines, with no hips, down to men's shoes; and face set hard to fit her persona. And Lucy was beautiful. Her face, made up, the dangling earrings, and red hair teased up into a crown on her head. Under purple lights, dim; no one could see the poor quality of her clothes, the straps of her shoes cracked with age. Nor the rent threads in Mickey's trousers. Lucy was just a gorgeous woman and Mickey a handsome man. They made the perfect gay couple.

By 11, the bar was 3 deep with gay boys and dykes drinking beer & swaying to the music. They danced, but couldn't dance slow—female/female or male/male—that was a sure police bust. If any ABC or Vice cops were on the premises, they could close the place down & yank the liquor license.

It was things like undercover cops that tried the souls of gay people during this time.

"Where yuh meet her, Mick?" A bantam butch wanted to know. "Are there any more like her? I want one, too!"

Clatter of glasses; Bobby, the male bartender swished up and down behind the counter, drawing bottles from the multicolor lit shelf & poured liquor & made change. Music of The Supremes inflamed the souls of the party goers. "I got lucky one night on Rush Street," she lied. "I found her there in this beatnik club." Yes, she'd found Lucy, among all the broads, chippies and whores; a redhead woman to go home with & they stayed together. At first, for 11 months. This is the story of what happened those 11 months.

So, games people play: La Dolce Vita. Mickey had to invent this lie. Thru the alcohol blur few remembered Lucy's face anyway—from when she'd come in with male tricks, sat on their laps, drunk and with an Indian stone-face watched the gay party whirl on about her, which part of her was drawn to, but she didn't know why.

"I'd sure like a girl like you got, Mick."

"There's broads in here, Shorty." Mickey replied, throwing her a languid butch stare. A cigarette dangled in her lips, unlit. Had been forced to quit the habit in jail, and just wore cigarettes behind her ear, or dangling from her mouth like this one, to enhance her masculine effect. "Who's that blonde broad over there with the two guys?" Mickey frowns, hunching down, and squinting, trying to see thru the gyrating bodies of dancers.

At a round table by the dance floor they sat. Three well-dressed older people, smiles on their faces.

"ABC man. Or the Feds." Shorty snarled.

Soon word had buzzed thru the crowd, behind backs of hands, in whispers, that the party at the round table was Federal cops.

Dykes lined up in the bathroom with worried looks. "If you got 3 articles of women's clothes on, you're OK." Many of them, as Mickey, were in drag. One redhead dyke, Rusty, dipped at the knee, bending in front of the mirror, combing her hair back behind her ears man-style. "WELL, FUCK!" She glares. "Maybe I should comb her hair down over my ears and borrow my ladies' earrings!"

"Shit! I don't have my ID on me tonight."

"Well, yuh better get out of here then."

"But it's so nice tonight! Everybody's down here! It's a party!"

"Jo! What's yer birthdate on yer ID! Do yuh have it memorized?"

"Yeah. I'm Connie Collins. I'm 22. I was born August 5, 1946!"

Panic spread. Ripples thru the large gay crowd. Some kids left, to wait outside and come back later. Notes of music dropped in the smoky air as nervous dancers hung on the sidelines in terror, like puppets on strings. All because of 3 people who looked too straight and suspicious.

They stayed about one-and-a-half hours, then left.

Cold prickles of fear went with them. Gays came out of the shadows outside & the party resumed in full intensity!

"Them stupid fucks nearly ruined our Friday night!"

Mickey was handsome. Lights played on her in purple. Coughs, from the cigarette smoke.

"Who's that broad with Jan?"

"She's a straight woman. Jan's new lady."

"Straight? Why's she with a dyke?"

"She's got 3 kids to support. And Jan has a house and a car, and a good job. She'll tell anybody she's straight if she's had a few drinks."

Looked at the butch-femme couple down the bar. The woman was pretty; blonde, wore a halter top and tight pants over a curvaceous body; had on earrings and makeup. Jan was older. Dressed in slacks, an expensive jacket; man-rings on her fingers. Short hair smoothed back.

"I took her in the bedroom; I touched her all over her body. 'You'll get used to it,' I told her. And she has."

"That's what she told us, Mick! Uh-huh! Boy, what I'd do if I got a good looker like that in my bedroom!"

In a while, the meridian would be past—hands on the clock signal 1:00 A.M.; the Silver Windows had just a 2:00 liquor license. Soon paradise would empty out into the asphalt street.

Some gays had cars; others rode together with friends who were driving, or took taxis.

Some, like Mickey and Lucy, who were poor, had to walk, if they couldn't bum a ride. Very occasionally could they afford to take a cab.

So that was another harrowing experience lurking in the back of the butch's mind. Parcel in the part by part of their continuum of struggle. To get there with little or no money, to survive the police once inside, and to survive the dangerous streets getting home.

Tonight, in the dark, where neon slips its fingers under shadows that their feet make, they looked enough like a man and a woman that nobody in the few cars passing, or men walking by, bothered them.

They came out of the deserted area west, and headed back into the barracks of lower Clark—it felt safer because of being so populated. The wino clubs with 5:00 licenses were going strong & roaring drunk.

Lucy passed them up tonight, towing her drag butch along. "I can't go in there dressed like this, Lucy!" Mickey's tie was flying, and her shirt collar had popped out; a worried look knitted her eyebrows. "Under the lights they'll see what I am, and I'll get killed."

"I know."

The best part was when they finally turned into the entrance of their seedy hotel. Mickey threw off her jacket, put it over one shoulder, loosened her tie and hollered: "*FUCK!* I HAD FUN TONIGHT! YAAAA-HOOOO!" Like a hillbilly.

The two women climbed the stairs, arms wrapped around each other's waists. Mickey's white shirt stained in sweat from the hot summer night, and Lucy on her high-heel pumps wobbling from drink.

CHAPTER FOURTEEN

So Mickey laid Lucy every night, with the passion of a teen.

Pushed Lucy down on the bed; loved her by tongue, licking and mouth sucking her femme's salty wet womanhood;

then firmly put three fingers inside and fucked her hard for fifteen minutes nonstop. "So you'll know who's the boss." Mickey explains.

Now one time it's gotten late in the month; Mickey's over at the table where Lucy keeps the canned goods & hot plate & there's some meat in a tin & she's hungry, but Lucy hollers, "DON'T EAT THAT MEAT! IT'S FOR TONIGHT'S DINNER!"

Money got low; they had trouble eating. And Mickey still hadn't found a job.

So the half-breed Indian Lucy takes Mickey down to the Welfare office, & soon the butch is getting a check just like the girls in jail said they would do first thing upon release—a thing Mickey had vowed she'd never do because it symbolized giving up. In her mind's eye, welfare was for people who were so low in society or so messed up mentally, or had such a low IQ, that it was their only resort.

All day at home together in the room, or when Mickey took her walks out at the lake, she thought about the impending evening at the gay club; to meet and talk & have fun with other dykes and fags. And throughout the day & night fantasized the lovely redheads tits & hips, her curvaceous body up on all fours wagging her naked ass for Mickey to fuck her from behind like a dog. That most glorious moment of cunt. When the bed creaked under their weight & they let go their troubles and worked out their horniness & shed the loneliness of a lifetime.

Some long dragging days as when it rained & there was absolutely nothing to do, and their hormones raged in fiery passion; certain days of their monthly estrogen cycle, Lucy lay in bed all day with the butch and let herself be licked, sucked, finger-fucked, penetrated by cylindrical objects such as vegetables—cucumbers, carrots—or a hot dog; and ridden over & over, cunt to cunt; or thighs locked to thighs, clits joyously riding each other's thigh to climax; and give her butch oral sex; sleep a few hours, and then go at it again.

6 A.M.

Day begins.

Knocking of pipes in the decaying walls; shuffling feet in corridors.

Mickey stands at the window, curtain pushed aside. T-shirt & shorts. Black hair tousled. Wipes sleep from her eyes.

Huge amounts of rain poured out of the sky. A deluge. Bucketsful & bucketsful of water. Weather had shifted during the night; an overladen sky opens up, black clouds pour, lightning strikes jagged, cuts the sky; thunder rolls from the ends of the earth; then the sky turns blue & white, and it's over.

Events in the heavens, or crashing waves at the beach always awed Mickey. Wind pushed her hair back as she strode.

Made her feel alive, charged, as if from a bolt of lightning—sniffed from the wet ground the scent of grass and cement mixed with rainwater that floated to her nose.

This city life made her feel small & insignificant.

Not like the majestic summer storms of the East, nor the waves crashing onto the beach—which just placed her in proportion to the universal scale of things—a scale in which she had a definite place, purpose, and reason to be alive.

Near the lake, everything is blowing. Vision is clear, as rain has cleansed all the dust out of the air. Steady wind; shades rattle against their windows. It's like being on a boat.

Again, the past invades her thoughts.

Mickey had been real tired of life. Of eating scraps off the table.

Using the women after the men had cum in them. She wanted the best. Wanted a good woman—not to share, but to call hers. And tailed around the Stripper circuit; Kansas City, St. Louis; theaters in Ohio, New York & then they'd gone down to Miami, Florida, which didn't work.

Essentially was a kept butch. Showgirls laughed at the idea of living on her lousy $50 or $60 per week as a dishwasher or a cashier at the turnstile of the Strip Show; and they'd never been in one town long enough to hold a job.

So Mickey had worn paid-for fancy jackets and expensive slacks; tweeds, wool, silk shirts, gold & jeweled cufflinks; the finest that the hookers gave her as presents. And took their money out of their perfumed hands to put in her wallet so as to pay for meals and the cabs and the hotel bills, like it was her own money.

Would remember till the day she died the long scar across Valorie's belly from being attacked by a deranged john who felt impotent because of having to buy women & couldn't get sex any other way like Mickey could. Valorie had told Mickey the story after they first met. And how she had to paint it over with fleshtoned makeup nightly when she danced, applied just like the pasties they were forced to wear over their nipples—bright sparkling dots that peeled off because of the Vice Codes against showing the naked human female breast in an erotic fashion.

They were women laying side by side in the half-dark, had finished their lovemaking for the first time, & Valorie explained how she'd got away. Screaming so loud had unnerved the man, and there were people in the rooms beside them; she was fighting kicking & biting, and she'd run out into the hall trailing blood; naked; & the guy served time in a mental institution and she'd been fearful to turn tricks alone in a hotel room by herself since.

So Mickey may have cum after the johns, after the show was over, and the floodlights turned down; after the audience left their chairs in the vast theater; but she came the best; in the most intimacy, held and wanted by women for who she was; and so she came to the fullest extent.

'I'm so glad to have this time with you.' Kisses over the woman's body, together on a sofa in another hustling Lady's house. Mickey knew all the right, smooth lovewords to whisper. "I'm so glad to have this time with you." And Valorie had given her more time, then all her time.

So, the problem stopped being how to get women. The women taught her what to do. Each one showed the 16-year-old butch some new technique that personally brought her over the threshold of pleasure; and it started being that Mickey was mad now, about being a 4th-class citizen—in fact, a drag butch was a non-citizen—in the straight fascist winter of Amerikkka; pissed about picking over the pieces that everybody else left after they'd gone home. Sick of not having a home & having to travel after the money on the burlesque circuit. Her rights as a lesbian were real, straight from the guts, to the point of the heart real, with feeling.

Remembered Lisa, after the show went thru the door marked EXIT in red, into the dusty corridor with stage props against the wall... Embracing; and Lisa's sweating forehead furrowed with worry, makeup wet: "How was I? Did you watch me? What did I look like? Did the audience watch me? Did they pay any attention? Or were they just beating their meat?"

The butch had a growing resentment from eating after everybody else had been served. Working jobs nobody else wanted—and lucky to get that.

Maybe being confined within the reformatory walls during the formative years of her adolescence gave her the desire to walk and walk and walk and walk and walk.... Best place to do this was along the curve of Lake Michigan with its dream sequences of waves that rush in, in 3 dimension; the sandy beach, the green-black seaweed & above, towering blue sky.

Remembered hookers with their faces cut up by sadistic pimps—like emotion—it left only the scars.

Found out soon, in a progression of little girls making love on their cots doing jail time; 'There's no such thing as the right girl, there's just females—to love them, and hold them—no matter how short your time is. If you know this girl will be transferred out in a week, just hold her, tight, just for now, & love her as fierce & tender as you can.'

Valorie, who'd bought Mickey's plane ticket to Miami, with some other showgirl hustlers with gaudy clothes and luggage & perfume. 'Had my fist in her pussy, up to my forearm.' Felt the walls of her vagina contract, pulling her up and in. Fist pounding her in a good fuck. 'Lucy can't do it yet; she's afraid. But I'm stretching her, every night we practice.' This made Mickey feel more powerful, as she jumped over the rocks—giant white cubes of chiseled stone taller than a human being—in gym shoes picking her way down to the waterline.

'A lot of strippers said I should be a man. That I was what a man should be.' And they took turns letting Mickey love them, laughing, planting kisses on her face, leaving red lipstick marks, pulling her by her white shirtfront into their bosoms that reeked of perfume; pushing her black-haired head down between their sweaty thighs in eager excitement. A toy for them to play with, to find release after drinking the bitter dregs of life. A woman they could love, who looked like a man and loved like a Master.

'I could have a sex change and be a male, but the whole thing is about me taking them as a woman. It's all about a woman being with another woman—that's something a man can't have.'

They'd pat the fly front of her trousers to touch her clit—bold, or shy; faces musically alive under their worn makeup, high, mostly on pills or alcohol, but sometimes heroin shot mainline, from the nightlife. They used, to keep themselves running on the fast track.

'I knew them all, I loved them all. From fat to skinny. I wasn't a picky bitch like so many. I took them as they were.

'And some, their tits with milk still in them. I sucked the white liquid because their tits were painful, heavy & ripe, the baby gone, given up for adoption, or being raised by relatives, and the woman had to keep working to support it. I sucked the milk out of their tits so they wouldn't hurt. And the women touched my hair and held my head close to their warm bodies. I had my fill of their love, rode them till my clit was sore & I'd cum so many times we lost count. They'd have a contest, who could make Mickey cum the most; & my wallet was full of their money that I used to spend on them. It was fun for a while.

'And it makes no difference if she's on her menstrual period. Same love, same woman; needing my love then. We used a hot towel and kept wiping her cunt, and blood got all over us; blood on my fingers, on the sheets, clots of blood, thick, as their cunts opened in sexual heat; and I kept on, my fingers fucking her cunt, tongue licking her clit, blood over my face, until her hips raised up off the bed & she released her orgasm.

'I sucked them off! I fucked them all!'

Moon, invisible in the day sky, was full behind her shoulders; a million miles off. Wind swept thru her close-cropped hair, angular jaw set. Trousers and shoes and jacket; the tie folded in one pocket prepared for this evening's wear. Memories spill out of her soul, pushed by the oceanic waves.

Blue sky; puffy white clouds; it's still hot. Back behind her is the ribbon highway of the Outer Drive, the city of skyscraper building blocks. Geometric forms rise & fall in steps along the curve between lake and land, sky and earth. City of Chicago rises in the distance. Sodom & Gomorrah. Night fell; anticipation of gay life; blond beach boys & dykes in trousers & short hair with their ladies talking & laughing around the jukebox like a campfire site. Mickey's heart leapt with excitement, her guts turned over with acid in an adrenaline bolt of expectation of the play-party evening to come.

Women, removing their clothes in a slow striptease—lacy bra, satin panties. Their cunt aroma of love.

One-mile-long lines of waves come in after each other, roll over, over, under the bright sun.

Flies play on the seaweed. Green-black clumps. Seasmell.

Beach is so vast; opening up for as far as the eye can see in all directions. Space. Mickey's eyes witness waves of space breaking in a baptism; free from the inner city of building blocks blocking sight 25 feet in front of any direction of view.

Sun shining down on this place makes the whitecap-tossed waves silver.

First mirrorlike sand before the swish of tides, lays. Along the beach are piles of seaweed in 4-foot-tall bundles. Not a collection of vines the waves swept up together, but each pile is one giant 90-foot strand that came uprooted. These grow in the ocean; roots submerged on the continental shelf.

Mickey had walked them all: Atlantic; the Gulf, the Miami beach.

Stares into the glistening water, perched on gym-shoed feet upon a massive white rock.

Lives built like this: intercellular souls, bundles of lives twisting along a common core with only thin walls of hotel rooms dividing them. Membrane between individual consciousness and the mass tribal instinct of subconscious. Chemical, mineral, finite spirit, infinite Spirit.

Lucy & Mickey, their lives; and all the girls of yesteryear & all the girlies to cum; the gay kids dancing away the decade under the party lights red, blue, and green...

Superawareness sent a jolt to her brain. Slow waves opening, discovering memories, then close. The lake turns into a sea; water unfolds what had been veiled, in an image.

She had gone where spiral staircases with red carpets lead, past rooms shared with women of a thousand names; and she will go where sidewalks furl out in many cities of the plain; and follow laughter in the evening, as she goes where people who are gay are moved to be. Follow a woman's laughter, talking, dancing, touching, until she responds. 'Living only to spend a while with you.' And hopes that fortune deals her both loving intimacy, and public fame.

Mickey smacked her fist into her hand. "I DON'T KNOW! I DON'T CARE! I DON'T UNDERSTAND! I JUST WANT YOU! I DON'T WANT TO SHARE YOU WITH ANYBODY, VALORIE! STAY WITH ME!"

To get her out of this world of high-priced women.

"Why don't you just quit and come be with me!"

"You don't have any money, Mickey!"

"I can get some kind of job, and so can you!"

"I don't want to be poor! I was raised poor all my life, motherfucker! Don't tell me about being poor! Do you know what it's like to never have anything for yourself? NO! I won't quit the fast life!" Angry, stomps her foot.

"I got raped!"

"Valorie!"

"He held a fucking gun to my head!"

"You been there with him all this time!"

"We got up to this fucking hotel room, he pulls this gun out!"

"So you got no money."

"NO! All that work and nothing to show for it!

"THE POLICE! MICKEY, ARE YOU CRAZY? CALL THE POLICE? Because a trick beat a whore out of her money?"

"I'll stick a gun in the sonofa bitch's ribs! I'll murder him! It ain't right! That's the lowest thing! Cheating a prostitute out of her money! Goddamn!" The butch smacks the wall with her fist BAM! BAM! Mad. Mad at johns, pimps, and con men, with their big shiny cars, flashing big bankrolls of $1,000 cash they carry around.

"Hey there, it's me and you, little brother." The pimp calls her in close, next to the brick wall of buildings on the night-club strip's main concourse. "Me and you, we can take care of business. You have ladies and I have ladies."

A black pimp offers to teach Mickey the pimp game—and all she ever wanted was to be the husband of a wife in a happy, secure family.

Her shit is ragged.

"It's either steal or work the streets. I can't earn enough money to keep these high-priced ladies in line."

Valorie dials the phone frantically. "Ain't that the shits! He ain't even home!"

"Fine tricks you got, Gloria!"

She dials the number again, slow, carefully. No answer. "This is supposed to be his day!"

Valorie needed some money—$50. So one of the girls let her use her trick book, which was 2 seasons old in Miami, blue-lined names and phone numbers with instructions for each, and prices on soiled pieces of paper—a list of some 11 or 12. Descriptions, where they lived, how much they'd paid for specials, and certain precautions—"Don't call before 8 P.M., has a son who might answer the phone," etc.

So finally gets the john at home, and they have to take a cab and drive Valorie's body over there and make some money.

Valorie & Gloria and Scheherazade a weasel-faced whore with acne coated by tons of makeup. They all have unprotected sex for extra money, and Mickey picks up their infections, too.

Lay back nights in her expensive men's pajamas with open-fly front for her plastic dildo, in the hotel bed. Valorie—her bottom woman is asleep next to her; Gloria has the cot that opens up, and the whore gets the sofa. Wrung-out stockings hang from the shower curtain in their private adjacent bath.

And Mickey decides to let this money thing go. To find a woman who is clean in her cunt, and who will go with women only—not both—and with Mickey especially.

Fulfilling this long journey of her childhood fantasies about caring women. To examine the river of emotions that flow thru women, and experience their love—which she'd never got from her mother. To be surrounded physically by cunt, the same sex as her. To be in the realm of other females exclusively. Even dyke butches—knowing they had emotions under their shirts and pussy under their trousers, that got wet, and wide and juicy like hers; a clit that if she rubs or sucks it gives her an orgasm.

Knows, that she'd rather be poor, a thousand times over, in clothes that are threadbare, then what she has to go thru in this high-price, fast-talk, big-game life of the hookers.

Some girl whose cunt belonged to Mickey.

No threat of infections, or jealousy, or danger.

So Mickey's fancy suit, taxicab, nice restaurant & hotel world fell apart in Miami.

Girls blew off in the wind.

The weasel-faced whore Scheherezade left first—that left Gloria & Valorie, who knew each other and took turns making love with their butch. But they were sullen and couldn't get along. Sharing Mickey's butch tenderness, sexual power and firm command in bed had been the only thing that held them together this long. Mickey lay back on fresh-scented linen sheets in bed beside her bottom lady & the words of Lou the matron in the reformatory, came back, the wisdom she had told her: "The biggest problem, Mickey, is to keep the girls in line. Dick and dope. That's what they want. And you're the dick, Mickey. They admire a stud. And give her more credit than they do another woman. As a stud, they look at you as more dependable and in their corner. Not flighty, not apt to run off with no warning; not in competition with *them*. Not prone to causing so much trouble. A good stud woman keeps the bitches in line. A good stud keeps the women straightened out."

So here she was, walking along this waterfront town— another city near water (like California—her ultimate goal— point on a map at the ends of the earth). Beyond red-brick fire-escape buildings. With water stretching into invisibility, and sewage seaweed-choked smell of open sea.

From Atlantic to Pacific.

'Strippers, showgirls, B-girls, whores…. Came to me crying because of how rough the men were; I took their shaking bodies in my arms and made them quiver with my love instead.

'Men & lesbians won't leave them alone. With their wants… Chase them, buy them, trap them; because of their beauty, so they can prove themselves by having them; so glamorous women freeze up inside.

'Didn't demand anything for myself, but asked them what they need, and whatever that was, did it.

'Take nothing from them but what they gave. I'd rather starve. I'm not a pimp. So I was their pampered pet in fine suits, and a diamond on my pinkie finger.

'And…I blew all my women… I couldn't play the role…. I wasn't right for the part…

'Couldn't stand by watching them earn money they'd never keep; buying fine dinners and drinks, stepping in & out of new clothes, to make up for the poverty in their hearts—letting their whore money run thru their fingers like silver water & golden rain.

'So ain't I a lover of women? I proved it the hardest way! I didn't rob them when I could have. Did not make fancy promises, but did what I did for them in bed. What little I had, I shared…. Took nothing from them; there was no way I'd pimp—buying a fancy car and house in my name alone…. They always wanted a lesbian to ride them, to suck their pussy, and I was there.

'Thru mines of open space of dangerous neighborhoods, I had to cross on foot by night, going from one side of town to the other to be where they were. Thru adverse circumstances —gangs of men drive by in cars stare at me, and if they didn't think I was a man, I'd be in trouble. To get to women and give them my love.

'And it wasn't like traveling from one point to another point in geography on a map; I traveled uncharted territories because we didn't know where we were, or what we were. Society tried to hide that truth from us. All books on the subject were considered dirty, or were against us. Dirty in the doctors' text. Dirty in the preachers' sermon. We were sick. And we were rendered mute and couldn't answer—so we bowed our heads, and kept on being gay. Furtive, angry; but gay. Loving women, yearning for companionship, trying, until we finally found a way to express the urgency of our sexual needs with a woman.

'Ain't I a lesbian? Up in the motel room after, in a rental house, in a poor sector of town. Men coming and going; dwarfs, weird old men, sick tricks with fetishes; all day and night—in that house out in Jersey City, the date-book calendar of trick appointments; the girls came up after and laid down with me. Ain't I a lover of women? I proved it!

'And pumping my hips between their thighs, and driving my cunt inside the rim of their mouths, I got my fill, too. Deep thrust of my hips working my clit against theirs so we both got our rocks off together, deep and good. And thru the coarse laughter from downstairs, we were satisfied in each other's embrace.

'I fucked the strippers! I fucked them all! Their sweet juices ran thru my mouth, the stink of their sex on my fingers, their cum on my face; my cum on their thighs. Their sex wetting mine.

'Can't say I ain't a lady lover!—Or why would I do this? Be an outcast to the world? An outlaw! Can't say that I don't love them from my soul & from my heart!

'Can't say that I don't love women!

'In the end, it was even more than the sex—it was to the point of the heart—my love.

'I sucked them off!—In every position, way, and shape. With somebody else's cum in them that they'd washed out by taking the ho's bath, squatting on the floor of the trick hotel with a basin of water, whirling 2 fingers up their vagina, swirling the load out & came to me, & told me so, so they were clean enough. Clean enough for me. And I took them just like they were.

'And I was privileged to hear the bell-like tinkle of their earrings & bracelets and fine things. I inhaled their beauty, their fragrance.

'Some girls were imprisoned in The Fast Life—they had nowhere else to go. Had seen the world outside, cold & harsh, and come back. Society spit them up & out of itself in scorn. And the police burnt down this whorehouse, that trick pad; this strip, that stroll, the red-light-district nightclubs here; we moved from hotel to flat, in cabs full of suitcases crammed with dresses & lingerie & corsets & costumes, always on the run.

'Society spit us up out of its throat, coughing gagging, just like I spit it up—this Great Beast, this motherfucking world. But the small bodies of my women, so worn, their dresses soiled; removing their panties, caressing, giving my body to them, taking them; I did not spit up their juices, nor did they spit out mine. I wanted all of them & swallowed the wetness of their cuntheat.

'I delivered them, in a nightly fuck with my mouth, my fingers, my toys, my wet sex crammed in their slippery wet cuntlips; rolling in each other's arms; to fulfill the orgasm that had been stilled in them after night after night of tricks, or tease, shaking their ass, cum locked inside them, murdered in them, for all night, or a lifetime. I brought out the sex in them; my hands cupping their breasts, stroking their nipples till each got hard; looking into their eyes, face to face, soul to soul; taking my time, pleasuring them, nurturing them, massaging them; my lips kissing their eyes; then, at the right time, taking them in lust, in hard strength, serving them as I served my own hot rampant desire; our bellies slapping together; my plastic strap-on cock thrusting into their cunt, till they bust their own nut, wiggling & hollering along with my climax, and their eyes opened brimming with relief that yes, they could cum, they could get off. The relief they felt in their cunt—and in their spirit—knowing they weren't too frozen up.

'They boosted and they hustled & worked as little as possible. And some were dancers, and most, would-be dancers. They were go-go girls, and massage-parlor workers, and nude-encounter models, & escorts. I paid them—in the fine cash of emotion. And as they leaned their wig heads against the lapel of my mannish jacket—in the knowledge that they could rely on my personal strength—I watched the streets for them; told them who looked like Vice Cops, and Undercover Detail, and why a certain john had vibes of a killer psychopath, watching like a stranger in the all-night diner where we never spoke but in secret, pretending we didn't know each other; so as not to scare off the tricks; there I watched out for them.

'And they knew I would have taken them away from the street, but the glamour, the glitter and the high-ambition dreams were too strong. So I took them as they were.

'I didn't treat them in the way johns do when they buy it, like they own you; so it was free and easy to me. Because I knew them, and the feelings they hid. Wasn't I a woman, loving a woman?

'Some cum & go. I'd never see them again. Going up to my room, pulling off her tiny dress, opening her arms, spreading her thighs for 15 minutes of love; and then leave forever.

'Some 14 years old, skinny & afraid & lost, I touched them like a sister, & saw them go back to juvenile jail instead of homes that couldn't keep them. Some 15 years old with fake IDs saying they were 19. Some 25, hardened thru and thru. Some used up & dead at 45. Hags. I loved them, too, was moved as I saw the yearning need so deep inside these older women who no one wanted; as they crushed my face down into their furry sex; their makeup-caked expression cracking with tears, heads thrown back in orgasm.

'And I'd cum till I had my fill—there was no other end but my satisfaction. 2, 3 times with one girl, 1 time with another,

1 time with two girls. Some not at all. Yet I was still happy to receive their flavor, their touch.

'I used a rubber cock in them. In their pussy. I came in their back door, too. Used fingers; got between their legs and rode them, & some wanted to fuck me as well, kiss my thighs with a halting touch of wonder and penetrate me with their fingers; and after they'd fucked another woman were proud of it, and made merry laughter back in the parlor bragging to the other girls how they'd made me cum.

'And I'd let them enter my vagina, slowly because of their long, polished fingernails, & they loved me and watched the expression on my face as they did it.

'Tho they were straight, or had been at one point—now blurred in time and life-style; I frenched them and was frenched by them in settings with lingerie, and rehearsed conversations in a sexual drama, like tricks paid $250 to do—it was free to me.

'And I demanded nothing from them.

'All cum! Then, me. Us.

'Cum one time on top. One time orally. One time their fingers in me. Or the strap-on cock in my cunt—rubber; while I worked the plastic cock inside her butthole. Get back on top, and cum one more time screwing her ass.

'They bragged to see how long they could make me go.

'They were cast out by the world—outlaws, and so was I. Left by the wayside, by the world with its rules, its morals, its dying church. So they cum with me and break the rules. And we made our own world.

'Got as freakish as they could want. To reach for her meat under satin underpants. To bring it home, to bring her to my lips. All the stilled cum inside, all their dead emotions locked up, but not irretrievable forever....

'Worked on them on a mattress, in a bed, on the bare gray floor of the dressing room of the Rialto Theatre, that couldn't creak with the motions of our lust because it was set directly on cold concrete behind the stage.

'We lusted, & bedsprings creaked under our weight, by our energy; with 3 or 4 other girls looking on, then joking, offering an extra hand to caress, another tit to be sucked; some jumping in, too, their thighs for my waiting mouth.

'In bed in the back-room upstairs apartment of the whore-house in its current location.

'And I didn't judge whether they were drugged or doped.

'Like pages of diaries, like lines of a part in a script...so it went.

'Some had children taken from them by the State from which they'd flown, for being unfit mothers, which further destroyed their self-esteem so they could abandon hope & sink even deeper to the bottom of hopeless addictive destruction. They came from outlying areas to be here in the grimy inner city ho strolls, the capitals of sin & money & crime. Most had had abortions. Some had no sex left; it was cut out of them by surgeons.

They had disease after disease, & infection upon infection.

'Some played rape—and I used foreplay to make it better—hotter; then had to chase them, catch them, fake beating on them & then give them violent sex.

'Some I mounted from behind, on all fours. We played dogs; my rubber cock in her ass, while reaching around to thrust my fingers in her vagina, & jerk her clit simultaneously, in a bursting climax.

'In harness studding her with my cock, my thighs slapping against her ass, as the thick tool went in out of her cunt now; humping like dogs, & the best part was it was another woman doing this to her; an aggressive lesbian butch; and one who would do whatever she needed. That turned them on. Without shame. And they turned me over, wanting to take me again, and again; their fingers sliding in and out of my wet hole.

'Heard gossip some were pregnant. Especially ignorant young girls. Carrying a baby; I mouthed at their sex-smelling sea, between their legs; looked up over the growing roundness of their bellies—and I was looking at a woman and an infant, still a blob, a jelly, inside their womb & hoped by my love, just like a prayer that when the baby came out, it would not suck & draw upon vacuums of a shadow world of stick people who march about like machines, but would be a child of joy. Bastard, but loved. Made human by love, and not inhuman by coldness. And be sheltered somehow in this garish world of whores, bars, trade, drink, drugs & death.

'We had fun using the instruments of pleasure on each other. Several girls who owned dildos had obtained them thru mail-order catalogs. Dirty bookstores & porn shops were illegal in the 1950s. Slid it in and out of her and they did me.

I was strong for them, and I could lay down for them.

'Round and round the hustling circuit; Kansas City, St. Louis, Chi-town, L.A., Frisco, Seattle, Vancouver.

I masked any concern in my eyes so they could keep their pride when I saw the law, the world, fate, smash them in. Did not use words, but showed my caring in body language; they were all too cold & deadened for anything else but that.

'But as I bent over them, licking them, loving them, mounting them & fucking them fast with my clit in their pussy, trying to give them what few others would give them, I got inside their souls a moment, & they whispered, "I love you."

'As I labored over the party girls, groaning & sweating; their dresses thrown off, over a chair; naked and high, spreading their thighs for me, I cum hard, and they were guaranteed to cum. Fascinated by me; by my manner; by my butch clothes; laughed at my jackets & trousers. Lipsticked and short skirts, we played. Time when powder and makeup wears off & wigs and cocktail shoes have got to go. We transacted sex under the stars of night.

'All night the hollow shells of them gaming, playing the tricks, responding off them with clever parries & retorts. Now they told the truth.

I came to them cupping warm tits in my hands, releasing the bra that might not have come off nor been removed all night, just the lower portion of their dress—to give up cunt; turning 7 tricks per night in ghastly slow motion on speeded-up gear, made by my hands human and warm again and gave them their flesh back from ice blues; and the showgirls told me, "I would have brought that $100 john back here tonight, but I knew you'd be here, baby, laying in bed waiting for me, and I wanted you more."

'And I didn't ask for a marriage, just each moment counted between us—free. I took them as a butch, manlike, on top between their spread legs wrapped around my torso; I loved them as a woman side by side, my fingers sliding in and out of their soft hot holes. I used rubber cock, jammed in them as hard as they wanted & as long as they needed. They craved my mouth, lips; my tongue sucking, licking till involuntarily their bodies gave up cum. Let themselves go; and they were proud of it! Strutting around in their wilted show-girl finery, boasting to their girlfriends what a big load they've dumped with me. They wanted my love because it was just for them—not for me, selfishly. I went just a little while longer.

'I never had to leave money on the dresser.

'After hours, as dawn came to tired women & streaked the sky.

'Yes, I caught the diseases that they carried. Was treated for VD, yet in the bowels of the night was unveiled pain of a greater kind, to which physical disease is just an anthill. That dark Mount Everest of pain.

'I was one of them, not simply taking and going, but their sister, their mother, their mentor, their daughter, their stud, their lover, their lesbian butch, their confessor, their teacher, their plaything. I ministered to them as no clergy in black robes within ornate church structure can ever do. In the most intimate way—wet, & hot between their legs, and mine. By deed in the most basic way—sex. Loved, embraced—beyond cum; filling them in their innermost sex and soul need.

'Touched thru the greasepaint of their staged effects, the mascara, and silk, thru their panties, bras and stockings; I touched my fingertips red with menstrual blood to their souls.

'Some just beginning—almost naïve. Others, by then, most of the world had already passed them by.

'So scared, or so bold. The restaurant jobs, the offices, the schools barred their doors to them, they were just good enough to work the streets, but they weren't below me taking them to heart in my arms.

'So this was the floorwork—illegal by Vice Codes of the States of America. This finishes up the floorshow of an aggressive lesbian butch—an outlaw, an outcast, so long denied.

'If I wasn't a lady lover, would I have done all these things and more? God! If I wasn't a lady lover!

'Took all the risks, the disease; fighting to protect myself from dangerous freaks—men who came down to the red-light zone to gawk; and tried to get off at our expense. The fearsome gangs, the criminals from whom we got no protection —for we were criminals ourselves in society's eyes.

'Would have I gone thru all that if I didn't put loving a woman above anything else in this world?

'And my reward?—They spread their thighs and yielded to my lovemaking. And as they drove away thru the fog of early morn, out of the weary party night yellow red and green, they put their fingers to their mouths, blew a kiss to me and whispered, "Baby, I love you."'

CHAPTER FIFTEEN

Towering buildings, skyscraper spires silver & chrome. Chicago's Loop.

Felt safer in her territory of ramshackle buildings & over in what was becoming the Old Town district; by the lots of reconstruction.

"WHEN ARE WE GONNA LEAVE?" Mickey had asked, yelling across the small room from the bed to Lucy, who was seated at the table doing her nails.

"I think we should start getting ready to go at 8:00 P.M." Mickey added.

"I'm gonna be taking all day to get ready." Lucy replied.

Lucy was a true femme and enjoyed primping in the broken mirror over the dresser. Examined her hair for any traces of dark-brown roots & would immediately dye it red. Kept the nails of her fingers & toes polished, and applied eyeliner, mascara & used a hundred other feminine wiles.

Lesbians in 1959 had no places to congregate. Nor to be.

That was a bit unusual—to have next to nothing in the

whole huge metropolis of Chicago with millions of inhabitants; it was the 2nd-biggest city in Amerikka; to have no gayness—except after dark.

So they'd hang around their room all day until shadows fell, and go out—this was uppermost in the mind of all gay kids all day at work, or at school; to go to the club to see & be seen. To party.

Sometimes there'd be kids loitering around the entrance at still-day—sunshine & clouds blowing across the sky.

So Lucy & Mickey showed up in Show.

They made attempts to connect with their own people.

In gay life, bars changed from season to season as they were raided by police. First it had been The Beach Ball Club. Then The Turquoise Ribbons. Now The Silver Window.

Gays came in from all over—from suburban areas; sterile, with no gays visible. Same concrete, same look-alike people, with traditional values; male or female robots. Most dangerous in their attitudes of hate.

Hot summer. Gasoline fumes rose off the pavement. In Chicago, Mickey noticed the difference: 'It's not tons of gay kids milling around like in Greenwich Village during the day.... Just a few standing out in front of the club.'

They'd be there, waving, smoking passing good times. Then the police would come along (Along Comes Mary), and they'd fold up the scene like gypsies their tents and be gone. Then another place would be happening, and another summer. Then that would be gone. Someplace designated by word of mouth thru the grapevine, where gays could meet; it was hard to keep up with it, the police moved them off so fast—but the gays never stopped. And in another month there would be a new place.

Straight moral people & their cops couldn't see that nothing they did was going to change that.

When butch Mickey dropped her fare into the metal box on the bus, the driver said, "Why don't you get a man & try to change your luck? It's hard for you gay kids—you haven't got nothing going for yourselves."

Mickey & Lucy sat midway in the bus as it bounced along

to North Avenue. "As masculine as I dress, and we still get comments like that."

Her red-hot yen for women. The memory of Scheherazade, of Gloria, of Lisa—the hot meat of a fast, bad girl; wet cunt underneath her cunt, her legs up in the air, waving silver party shoes, was enough to drive Mickey out in search under circumstances both fair and foul. Not all the assaults of this world, not their lack of money nor the fact that nobody would hire her, nor the fact that she barely passed as a semimale, or rape, nor threats screamed by gangs of punks driving by—nothing would reshape this yen. And their desire to be among their own people now that they were together. They could break the butch, turn her into a drooling idiot—mouth frozen in a grim line of hate & become asexual; a retard, a zero. As had happened to the old crones inside the Padre Hotel. But to change her own mind of her own volition, never.

'So goddamn him.'

Goddamn the pompous sneer of the self-righteous world & its churches. Mickey spit whenever she passed a cathedral. They were almost there, and the only thing that made it better was their profane laughter.

Black-haired Mickey turned to Lucy, demure, straight in appearance. Without this hard butch sitting next to her, nobody would suspect her sexual orientation. "If I get beat up tonight, take me to Cook County Hospital. If I die, call the undertaker. I don't have any family, so just call up a prayer." Turned her head up to heaven. "That will have to do."

"Don't worry, Mickey." Lucy pats the butch's square white hand. "I'll protect you, baby." And isn't kidding. The half-breed has a butcher knife in her purse & has been known to pull it out & start stabbing when enraged.

"I've been called Faggot in my life as much as Dyke! Do you know what an ugly thing that is!"

As the bus sailed along, finally they brought up the subject. "People keep bugging me...they ask where I met you..." Mickey stammered, red-faced, her young eyes downcast. "I don't want to tell them. I'm embarrassed." She confessed.

"That we met around a bunch of dumb fucks." Her eyes flashed as she spat out the truth.

"Well, tell 'em we met in New York—in the Village. That's more romantic."

"Yeah. 'Cause nobody's been there to see what it's really like."

Now they were walking again, Mickey bounding at Lucy's side; she on high heels, demure, red hair piled high on her head—a royal queen—a female queen; going in procession down the asphalt turf.

A rough man staggered up to them; the butch's guard went up: 'Am I gonna have to fight this fool?' "Spare a dime for a cup of coffee?"

They stopped to buy a hamburger. Mickey opens the restaurant door. A counter, some booths with red-and-white-checked tablecloths. Few customers. "You go up there first." Mickey says. "I'll scare her off." The waitress has seen them already, but thinks they are a straight couple—male & female.

They order. The waitress smiles. Mickey nods curtly with her head, afraid to say "Thank you," because the sound of her high-pitched voice will give her away. Because she just didn't want to live thru it one more time—that change of expression on their faces, the shock, or disappointment; & this growing rapidly into anger—once they realize she isn't a man. The woman in the white uniform waddles away; she'd been so polite that Mickey knew she'd thought she was male.

Leans over the table. "Well, she thinks I'm a man." Whispers dryly. "She was all over me with kindness."

Ate hamburgers. Juicy red meat with mustard; big slices of pickle, lettuce & tomato; juice combining with catsup. Delicious. & drank malted milks to wash it down.

Every time the waitress goes by, Mickey sits there stiff, tries not to move & be too fluid of motion; tries not to say anything because then she'll hear how high Mickey's voice is. But then it happens, as it has to happen. The butch needs the key to the lavatory. On closer inspection, lumbering back & forth down the aisle, the waitress has noticed something strange about this person. Mickey asks for the key—either key will do she thinks to herself; hand extended out, palm up. The waitress's eyes narrow, gazing at this stranger. "It's not here! Neither one!" she adds hastily. 'The bitch don't even want me in her goddamn toilet.' Mickey thinks, turns around & goes back to the table.

They pay & leave no tip.

Walk. Just a few more blocks separate them from their own race of people.

Then, right there in the middle of the block, there it is! 50 feet separate them from paradise!

Younger kids will be out here first—hanging out because they have no ID or money & won't be allowed inside. All their socializing will be done at curbside.

One baby butch, crew-cut hair, under 5', a 12-year-old, hollers & jokes.

Then there's Shorty, a 15-year-old lucky enough to have a fake ID which states she is 18.

Shorty plays with the pipsqueak kids—baby dykes 12, 13 years old with no place to go at all, & with the older dykes with jobs and ID and cars who will arrive later at night & line up along the silver-lit bar inside with women on their arms, or hoping for women.

Shorty who took her girls into the bushes of the public park, or a gas station toilet, or a doorway to have sex.

"She lives with her grandmother." Judy, an attractive femme leaning on the side of a car discusses Shorty. "She can go wherever she wants. Comes back 3 days later, her grandmother looks at her and asks, 'Who are you? What are you doing in my house? Get out!' 'It's me, Grandma! I have the key! See! I let myself in! I'm your grandkid! Remember?' Her grandma's demented. It's weird, huh? Shorty's such a pipsqueak. She's lucky! She has a free place to stay and nobody hassles her. I have to go thru hell to get out of my house. Mark here comes by and gets me. They think he's straight." Judy indicates a pretty gay boy who's mincing in the circle of fags.

"The nerve! Who is that man dragging that woman thru here!"

"That's not a man, it's Mickey! It's a She!"

"Well I haven't checked it out personally. I don't usually go for *butches!* HA HA!"

As Lucy sweeps into the bosom of the crowd on Mickey's arm, several butches examine her—their gaze running from head to toe, including the 3rd finger of her left hand, as butches are trained to do—the wedding-ring finger. To get some indication of her eligibility status.

There's a black stud in the crowd; she's a perfect drag—nobody can tell he is really a she. Short processed hair, man's clothes, tits tied down, and a sock giving the impression of a cock stuffed in the crotch of her pants, bulging to one side.

Gays milled around in a rare street scene for Chicago. Mickey had noticed upon arriving, the heavier oppression of this Midwestern mentality. "New York City is bigger & gayer."

Gay life. Car radio on. Kids lounge against the buildings, parked cars, & in doorways. Music notes issue up into heaven from a convertible cruising past which will go round and round the block. Gay boys & girls. Nightlife nostalgia. They were ostentatiously here for a dyke to find a woman, a boy to meet a guy, & couple for a while, and dance together under the artificial stars of a tavern's ceiling. So, The Life was greater than they were; it became an entity all its own. To be in The Life itself, thrown together in an unforgettable galaxy, a community of brightly colored birds of a feather.

Lucy, for the first time hung out with the gay kids and was bona fide—by being with a true dyke. A few eyes recalled, etched in dim memory, that this redhead had been here before—with men. Drag them down here on her dates because she had a hunger to be gay herself. And those who remembered were suspicious.

"Is that a man and a woman?"

"It looks like a dyke and a woman."

"It looks like that hooker who drags her boyfriends down here! Remember her? And the butch she picked up that time? The three of 'em went off together! They were drunk!"

"Is it the same one?"

Gay boys prance in shorts, sun-tan-lotioned legs. Smacking gum. "Whoops! You mean that man's a girl! EEEEKKKK!" He slaps himself. "I'm cruising girls now!"

"Look at that pretty redhead—how'd ya like to have her, huh?" One butch confides to another.

Mickey stood, patiently as the crowd whirls around, legs spread, undershirt showing at her collar—tie still not on, man's trousers creased & neat, hair slicked back behind her ears.

A darkly handsome man goes by, bold male eyes cruise him. A fairy in skintight pants switches his round ass, races after him, screams, "BEAT YOUR MEAT! $10! BEAT YOUR MEAT, SIR! SIR?"

"GO TO HELL, PUNK!" The straight man whirls around, fists doubled. Then, seeing the size of the crowd, keeps walking.

"Jack-off bastard!" the fag hisses. "He'd rather do it himself." Turns to the rest of the kids who are laughing in sidesplitting mirth. "He goes home, goes in the closet & puts on his mother's wedding dress, & does it to himself. And he'll be thinking about *me!*"

"Well, I see Miss Blab-It-All is in rare form tonight."

Out in front of the building of the bar, the pussyriders were having a conference.

Cool winds of night descended. Mickey had her jacket on, buttoned, legs spread in a stance, men's lace up shoes planted firmly on concrete. Lucy had drifted off to lounge with Eva, a femme she knew, who wore leopard-skin form-fit pants and a halter top and hair as big as Lucy's.

A butch gesticulates with both hands: "The way my baby's built, it's just right. Her pussy. Lots of pussylips down here. When I get on her and ride her I'm right up in it and it feels real good & smooth & I reach down and stroke her tits while we do it, and she moves for me, boom, boom, boom, like that, and I can feel her pussy real good, and it's like magic when we cum. She cums when I do."

Mickey nods her head in agreement.

Shorty slid into the group. The tiny he-she was skinny, clothes too big. Hitched up her belt. "I pull her tits." She says. "I pull her tits."

The black dyke with a sock filling out the crotch of her pants watched with a superior air of amusement.

Meanwhile, in the femmes' circle, Eva speaks of a friend's experience. "So Barbara makes love to her, and then the butch rolls over and starts to go to sleep, and Barbara asks, 'Aren't you going to make love to me?' '*Oh*. Do you want me to?'" the butch answers her. And this other one's suppose to be the butch, and Barbara thinks she's a hot femme, and a hot glamorous movie star and everything, and the butch don't even want to do anything, and Barbara was insulted. *Royally*."

A drag queen switched by, with the high energy of a female/male; dressed to thrill, in semi-drag.

Shorty nudges Mickey in the ribs; "She lays down fer yuh huh?"

"Every night." Mickey says sarcastically.

"Got me two ladies that'll lay down for me anytime and anywhere." The black stud boasts.

'Colored people always lie.' Mickey thinks, pissed.

When the stud ambles away, Mickey asks about it.

"He's not lying—she, I mean. He's got more women than that. He has got 3 women. I seen 'em. A white one, too. A blonde."

"Yeah?"

"There's plenty of action on the South Side. Their bars are always full."

"We should go down there tonight when the Windows closes. They have a bar that stays open till 5 A.M."

"Let's go to Calumet City!"

"What's that?" Mickey, the stranger to town, wants to know.

"That's where anything goes. It's just across the border of Chicago. It's a red-light district."

The gay guys dish: "I hate to go, but I have to get back to my wife. Oh, well, she's a good lay. My wife has the hots for my body."

"Well, dear, go on, then! No man will have you! I remember in '58 when you were out here paying for it—and begging to do that!"

"Watch your mouth, Alice!"

"That wife of yours looks like a section of bad track. A track that's bad all the way, honey! I bet the only way you can make it is to use a little alcohol!"

"DETOUR! DETOUR!" blabs a fairy.

"HEY, BIG BOY!" Mickey yells, using her deepest male voice, at a fag she knows. He turns, excited, thinking his prayers are answered—a real man calling for him—then sees who it is.

"OH, MARY!" He flips his wrist. Contorts his face melodramatically, shrugs his shoulders, and swishes on past, exclaiming "The man that got away!"

After laughter their faces felt hard from being held in position. In the bar life, Mickey & Lucy were Lord & Lady. Back in their own environment amid this gay wild crowd, wrapped in music they couldn't slow-dance to; buying drinks for herself & the redhead from their welfare money, and feeling healing waves—internal vibes pass thru them from being with their own people again.

It was a gay girl/gay boy summer. Shorts. Tans. Gym shoes.

Mickey sees the look of envy the butches have for her, for her girl Lucy. And femmes, the same for Mickey. They are handsome & attractive.

Now, at 18, Mickey knows the score. She's been around the world both in the sheets & in the streets. And has long since determined that she doesn't have to worry about other butches with Lucy.

It's men that worry her.

And she doesn't want to share that part of her worries with her buddies.

"Gee! You two look so *perfect!* Where did you meet? Down here?" a blond guy asks.

Mickey gulps—it's hard to think—but answers quickly; "We met in New York. We knew each other there first."

Smoke from cigarettes, chitchat, revolves under the stars of a Van Gogh print.

So that's how the lie of Mickey & Lucy meeting started & circulated around the ever-changing gay bars for months, when in reality Lucy had seldom been on the gay Village scene, but had hung out in Washington Square Park with the park bums, and, in the protection of their company frequented the Lower East Side cheap-shot brewery & winery halls on the fringes of the Bowery, deeply enmeshed in the liquid fingers of alcohol—drink. And was down and out and knew no gay kids at all.

"Is she any good in bed?"

"She wants it bad—from me. & me alone," Mickey says coolly, examining her short fingernails. Then hitches up her pants, thumbs in the belt, and adds, flatly, like she don't care one way or the other: "I see the begging look in her eyes, and I give it to her." And combs fingers thru her dark hair.

Above them, pigeons were courting. One stuck its head under its mates chin, then between its plump feathery legs, nestling & cooing. And so gay kids courted, too. That's what it was all about.

Arm in arm, some bent over one another on a car hood, deep-kissing—until the police ran them off.

"LOOK!" A pigeon trod on the back of its companion, trying to get on top & fuck. Sleek-bodied round birds.

'Everybody's doing it.' Mickey thinks & pats her flat belly. And she was among the lucky ones.

"AAGGGGGGGGHHHHH!" screams a fag. A handsome gay boy in a black cut-off-sleeved shirt, blue-jean shorts; his skin bronzed by the sun, bare shoulders, thongs on his feet; and black hair coiffed at the beauty parlor to frame his hand-some face. "AGGGGGHHHHH! EVERYBODY'S DOING IT BUT ME!" Like that was the worst deathly thing in the world, which to a teenager, it was.

Mickey spoke to the circle of butches: "My ma works at a hospital; she's a nurse's aide. It's a shit job. She use to tell me it's the worst thing to be gay. Always some fag they bring in unconscious has a dildo stuck up his ass & got lost up there, that has to be surgically removed, or they find them bleedin' in an alley with coat hangers up their ass. That's why she hates gay people. And women shake up a bottle of Coke & make it foam so it's bubbling over ready to explode and stick the Coke bottle up their cunt and let it foam inside them as a douche to prevent pregnancy, and it kills them. She hates gay people more, tho. She's old-world. She's old-fashioned."

"Gerry and her gay brother are in Lincoln Park sitting on the grass." Somebody recounts a tale. "Gerry looks like a young boy—a *very* young boy—when she's in drag. These two gay guys come over and say hello to her brother, and then they say to Gerry, 'OH *hello!* How are *You*.'"

"Well, hell, me & Lucy was just in this restaurant, and the woman thinks I'm a man and snaps to attention the second we walk in and does everything for us, and is so attentive and treats me like a King, and treats Lucy so nice & polite, and keeps coming over and smiles, 'Do you want anything else?' And keeps looking at me, and not even looking at Lucy, and don't give Lucy all this respect because she's a female just like herself and has the same thing between her legs; it's so phony! So then finally she sees I'm not a guy, and the bitch won't even give me the key to the toilet!"

"I like the respect I get as a man," a big bulldyke says gruffly.

"Mickey dresses so nice, I bet they think she's a nice respectable man."

Baby butches. Butches & Bulldykes.

A straight woman walks by hurriedly; a lace veil over her head—the fashion of the day. "AGGHHHHHH! She looks like the Bride of the Living Dead!"

"TAKE IT OFF!"

"KEEP IT ON!"

When they got inside, a lot of gay kids would just sit, beer in hand, eyes fixed on the door—as out here in the street, cruising both ends of the block—and any straight woman walking thru was a disappointment. Alas, that Dream Person seldom floated or strutted in.

"A watched pot never boils," a fag hisses.

Twosomes kiss on the hood of a car, from whose radio emits musical notes.

"YOU BETTER COME UP FOR AIR, BABY!"

Girls & boys in a big gang. One that never was allowed to be in the playgrounds & sandlots—now, assembled itself in power!

In the maelstrom of life.

Two dykes discuss Shorty behind her back. "I hear she escaped from a mental institution."

"Yeah, they locked her up because she's gay. She was out on the streets homeless for 8 months—she goes back to her parents' house one night. One lousy night & they call the police and they take her away to the mental institution. She's a high-school dropout. Her grandmother is crazy, too. Shorty plays with dolls. Give her a child's doll, and she'll run her fingers over it—I don't want to tell you what she does."

"At age 15, plays with dolls. Does strange stuff with dolls. Sex stuff. Yeah. I was at her grandmother's house. All of a sudden it gets real quiet. I look in there, there she sits, she's got this doll, its legs in the air, lifts its arms, then she's crying, tears run down her cheeks. And she's brought this doll along in the suitcase & she wants to go home, back to her parents, back to her childhood, or she wants to kill herself because she's a dyke; she's going mental on me. 'I want to go back to my parents' house because I had everything there!'"

"'Well, you have me!' I tell her. And she starts crying again, opens that dolls legs up and sticks her finger in between 'em. I hate to tell you what she was doing."

Just out of earshot of the femmes, Shorty stares sullenly into space. Face flat, freckles. Sawed-off brown hair & emotional brown eyes. Rugged dyke in shirt pants, and boots, under 5'; a juvenile, still growing.

Had been a sunny day; blue sky, yellow sunbeams scattering along the shiny hoods of parked cars striking windows of the apartments. White puff clouds nod & duck.

Breeze carried their cheerful voices towards nightfall.

Shorty remembered the first time she'd had a nice girl—a virgin. She'd had bad ones a lot, but nice girls were harder to find.

Poppin' her cherry. Fingers pushed into the girl's cunt slowly, Shorty's long middle and index fingers. They had held each other; fierce. The girl trembled, her body grew hot, her hands squeezing Shorty tight; gasping for breath; then she cried out loud. Then blood, as her fingers emerged. It was the sweetest moment of her short life. That she'd taken this girl's virginity—that the girl had wanted to be with her, Shorty, a baby-butch dyke, for her first time. And now all that was lost. And the runt dyke was bitter. That she'd not lost her to anybody else, but to the vast, ugly, straight world. Her little tousle-haired girl was not a dyke anymore. Not hetero either. Not anything. Asexual. Afraid. Hiding in secrecy in her parents' home. Afraid to be a lesbian. But Shorty wasn't afraid.

A fag held a big gardenia by the stem in his teeth. Pranced around, bare legs, gym shoes, striped shorts & T-shirt —utterly clean, & peroxide blond hair.

The Gay Life. 15 to 23—the oldest. The 12- and 13-year-olds didn't count. They couldn't get in the bar.

A transsexual, whose big hands & feet were a giveaway, and whose electrolysis was a bad cheap job, walked among them, not really accepted. Living on the fringes of gay society, because she was not accepted into the straight/gay world. Living on a fringe within a fringe, somewhere near the edge.

People still arrived. Silver Windows wasn't open yet.

At once there were boys everywhere; smooth-faced boys in men's clothes—who were actually gay girls, styled as butches.

Mickey pushed up her sunglasses, SNAP, with a masculine gesture, her eyes, black, stared thru the blue tint.

Rusty, a redhead, bright red hair that turned copper in the sun.

Shorty; Jan; Sandy; Ace; Gerry, who is ki ki, to name a few.

Rusty; flaming red hair so bright, in contrast to her pink skin; had her sleeves rolled up, showing the tattoo of a rose.

"Got a job yet, Mick?" Rusty slaps her on the back.

And Mickey, dark, square-bodied swaggers; is saying something and inwardly thinks, 'Hell no! And be like that coward Ace, who wears lady clothes in a downtown office on Michi-

gan Avenue…then slinks home to change and become a butch
& smoke cigars and prop her feet up like a king in boots &
T-shirts and trousers with suspenders. I ain't gonna put on no
skirt & put aside my butchness just to get a job—unless I was
sure I could get the goddamn job.'

Shorty looks up at Mickey & Rusty. "We look sharp, huh,
Mick?" the runt boasts, including herself in this statement.
"We look like a couple of pimps tryin' to catch some whores."

Mickey winces & has a sinking feeling in her gut; but stern
features betray no sign. And she says nothing.

Back by the parked cars, with Eva and the others, Lucy's
itching for a drink.

The bar doors swing open. Gays kiss. Shriek. Blond boys in
shorts & pink shirts & tight tailored pants, willowy, run in to
be in their world.

For a few hours, gays come from all points of the city to be
here.

Mickey & Lucy were a couple of great fame that summer
of '59. Envious gay boys came up to them: "Oh, you two are
so *divine!* I wish Larry & I could be like you!"

"A real lady and a real butch. So good-looking."

"I use to have a woman like her," Rusty theorizes. "I get
her home, she won't do nothin'. It's all glamour—they want
to be out in the clubs to be seen. Get 'em home, they don't
care no more. Wipe the paint off their faces & go to sleep."

"In the future," somebody is philosophizing; "everybody'll
be a hermaphrodite. It's perfect. It's both."

Bobby the owner flicks on the bar lights. Inside stars flash
& the jukebox plays.

Eva wore a halter top, showing bare shoulders; accentuat-
ing the cleavage of her round breasts whose tops showed over
the low neckline. Sexy jewelry & perfume scent. Big black hair
piled high.

Eva's romance was a jane. A Jew around 50 years old
—ancient. Eva was 22. This jane was like the average john.
Old, had money thru her own business, & had courted the
young exotic dancer. Bought her a car, helped pay rent on
Eva's apartment in a residence hotel.

Some of the gay girls here were hookers. Eva had been a showgirl & a sometime prostitute. Then she'd met Esther. And the woman gave her everything she wanted. Eva's mascaraed eyes flashed. "She's good to me. Anything I ask for, she gets it. And I'm good to her. I respect her. Every evening belongs to her and no one else. Yes, I see a butch down here at the club, we play around, but I'd never, never bring her home to the hotel, not while Esther's paying rent on it. She can trust me for that."

Lucy and Eva talked about making money. Batted their made-up eyes, blew smoke rings; earnest.

"I wish more women would pay. Then we wouldn't have to go to men."

"I'm so glad I found Esther."

"I believe it... I had an old jane climbing the walls down at Shrimpie's."

"Ugh. I hate that place. It's a dive."

"She was climbing the walls and crawling over the floors for me. I couldn't believe it. I saw her a few times, just $10. I felt sorry for her."

Eva nods her head, understanding.

"Well, she gets the wrong idea. Thinks I'm her woman or something. Women are too possessive. They think they own you, & they don't really have any money."

"I know. You got to get someone like Esther who owns her own business. She's very intelligent."

"This old jane, the way we met, me and another girl are sitting at the bar at Shrimpie's; she comes up, asks, 'Is one of you gals single? Don't have a butch or a husband somewhere? If you're available I'm interested. I'm single myself. Can I buy you a drink?' And she gets us all drinks. Then she puts her foot up on the bar rung and says, 'Yuh know, they have prosties working in and out of here, but I never saw one I liked. Now if, say, one of you beautiful ladies was a working girl, I'd give every last cent I have just to be alone with you for a little while.'

"And the girl sitting next to me, she's so fast, she says, 'Well, how much do you have?'

" 'Ten dollars.'

"Then I says, 'No, I'll go with her!' And we're arguing over the old dyke and her ten dollars. I really like women that's the only reason. I would have done it for free."

Eva tells Lucy all about Esther. How she's rich and she has dildos. All kinds. Uses them on herself. Uses them on Eva, makes Eva use them on her.

"So now you got Esther."

"Yeah." Blows a smoke ring. "She's a gold mine. But I need a butch for down here at the club for good times, to be with and dance, 'cause Esther won't come in here. She says the place is hot. A woman in her position can't afford to get taken in by the police. So she drops me off and picks me up at the end of the night." Eva said with a twinge of bitterness. "Besides, she's always too busy making money."

"So you got a dildo?"

"Yeah. She makes me use it on her. That's the part I hate."

"Mickey says she'll let me make love to her anytime I want."

"You do it?"

"Yeah. A couple of times. Not butch, like she does to me…but…"

"I know." Eva says.

"Mickey and me want to get a dildo. We've been talking about it, looking in the back of one of those sex magazines from Europe, in the back, in the classified section."

"Esther can get you one. Give me the money and I'll tell her."

Party lights flashed. Mickey was still at the bar, one foot up on the rail, handsome face, olive complexion under the dim lights, hollering & swapping stories with the butches.

"Don't let her get to like it too much; she might switch on you." Eva says. "Esther isn't a real butch. She's a strong woman, but not a butch, like my guy down here, you know, Sandy."

To Lucy, who was new to gay life—but not saying so—this was an interesting bit of information.

"Yeah." Eva tipped up her drink with dainty fingers. "If

you make love to her too much, she'll get to like it, and she'll want to be the woman. Now just think, she's laid down for you a few times—well, can you do it to her every night?"

Lucy smiled, a big grin from ear to ear, quiet, eyes brimming liquidly, "No. I don't want that."

"She might go with men after." Eva says, appraising the redhead coolly. "And this dildo, it's the next thing to being with a guy. She might run off on you."

"Holy smokes! I never thought about it that way!"

"Well...maybe not. But, it's happened." Eva blows a smoke ring. "I know a butch, she had nothing but men's suits and ties in her closet & she went ki ki—found a butch more butch than her and left her woman and ran off with the butch."

"So that's why they do it."

"Not always," said the experienced Eva. "Some are just like that. Butch one minute, femme the next."

Eva examines her nails. Long and red. Lucy's mouth is in a line. Her deep eyes ponder & the jukebox plays dance music.

"I learned this, when you have a real butch—like Sandy here, or your Mickey, if you put it in her, make sure she's on top, that's all. She'll still feel masculine, and you'll have less problems." Waved her manicured hand. "It doesn't matter when I do it to Esther. We take turns. I'm exclusively femme, but she don't play either role."

"I've already made love to Mickey twice."

"Well... Just make her feel masculine. That's important."

Lucy confided under the din of music, and roar of gay voices: "Mickey makes love to me...sometimes...she says she don't even feel like doing it, but she don't want me to get horny. She don't want me to get the desire to go back with men again."

"Would you go back?" Eva questions, appraising her.

"No." Lucy lies, unsure. "Men never satisfy me anyway."

"Well, if you're really gay, you'll never go back, once you've been with a woman—if she's any good as a lover."

"Mickey's a great lover. Mickey's a total butch. The next thing to a man. I'm never afraid when Mickey's with me. I know she'll do something to protect me if there's trouble. She puts herself out in front of me. Mickey is courageous."

"She carry a knife?"

"We both do."

"Esther carries a gun. That black stud—the one over there? She carries a gun. She was raped when she was only 12. That's why she makes herself look so much like a man. Now, Terry, over there—she says no woman has ever touched her and no woman ever will. She goes in the bathroom and does it to herself—I swear!"

Lucy and Eva looked at each other and laughed.

Girl talk.

Eva lip-synced a Top Ten hit tune thru her teeth. It crinkled her face paint.

Girl-girl couples danced on the floor in a bath of purple light.

Slow record comes on, & naturally the girls fall into each other's arms.

"CLEAN IT UP, LADIES! LET'S SEE SOME DAYLIGHT BETWEEN YOU!" hollers the bearded fag Bobby. "YOU DON'T WANT TO SEE US GET CLOSED DOWN BY THE POLICE DO YOU! *THEN* WHERE WILL YOU GO!"

"SHOWTIME!" A drunk voice hollers.

"LAST CALL!" bellows another. And some woozy gay girl thinks it's time to go home—extremely disappointed because she hasn't found a butch to ride her in the bed sheets yet, amid the sea of purple and gold lights, and handsome masculine women in jackets and short hair & strong hands. Alcohol roars in her ears; the heart is a lonely hunter.

"SHOWTIME!"

Excitement. Blue spotlights play. Jukebox clicks on the next record; music of the stars floods the room. Bartender wipes a towel between the glasses.

During the late '50s, and early '60s another genre of gay girls/boys was to be seen in the taverns only once in a blue moon. Those to whom street life's hustling, fighting, drugs & crime were foreign. They were the well-to-do kids. Who went to college. Who had proper upbringing. These bars, and worse one with B-girls and strippers & their low class of patrons, was an alien territory seldom visited; but since it was the only public gay life in existence, every now and then they'd venture down, together in a big group for protection—slumming—to be with their own people.

Tonight the cloistered girl/boy clique arrived, in the company of an older professor—a faggot prima donna, head of the Repertory Arts Theater. Vain & glorious he chatted to his young companions, admiring the handsome gay boys of the club—all the while, as a criminal, his eye on the door—fearful of a police raid.

Some upper-class types ventured down to the ever-changing location of the gay bars, delving for their sexual identities here among kids their own age, but more degraded by the muck and mire; whose streets they could not escape, whose hustle was to survive.

Dykes, obvious and male, were outlaws, & many found outlaw women themselves as mates. Some in the sex industry, who earned big easy money to rival the income of men; who were use to being harassed by police & scorned by society, and so were thus free of the restraints of moralism, politeness, concern of what others thought of them; & so were able to take their pleasure where they chose. And the nice girls looked at them for a moment, in a sort of envy.

So they sat right next to the door, ready to escape; girls and boys intermixed, appearing to be straight; almost—the females in tailored jackets, moderate hair styles, or austere, barren of lipstick. As close to drag as they could get without actually doing it. Artful women.

Mickey was Doing It. She was living The Life. Nothing was hidden. And the others hid. In their art schools, universities, their citadel of academia.

A femme came in, tight blouse, short skirt, long bare legs, fluffy hair & earrings. "Don't look at her!" Lucy snapped.

Lucy grabbed Mickey, kissed her big, and left a purposeful lipstick mark. "So they'll know you're taken," she says. Later Lucy looks admiringly at another butch. "Look at that gold chain she's got on her wrist. We'll have to get one for you to wear." Gay music plays. The Supremes.

Butch Mickey admires the girl who's right near by. Lucy grabs her again. "What would you do for her?" Lucy hisses. She wanted to know. Mouth solemn, not smiling. "Would you support her if she got sick & not leave her?"

"Yes."

"Would you visit her in jail?"

"Yes."

"Would you let her have a baby for you?"

Mickey looks at Lucy so long that the room changes colors: red, then gold, then blue.

"I just want to know, that's all."

"Why? Do you want to have a baby for me?"

"Maybe, someday."

"You're drunk Lucy!" Mickey hisses. "I hate when you get drunk in public and start acting out of control."

"I *am* in control, honey!" Lucy stares back with big dreamy eyes.

"You're not in *my* control!"

"Mickey." Lucy tugs on the butch's sleeve. "Eva told me there's some butches in here, their old ladies had babies for them. Are we gonna have a baby, Mickey? I can get pregnant—we can have a family."

"LUCY! Let's talk about this when we get home! Not out in public. You always wait till we're out in public to say this kind of stuff—when you're drunk—& embarrass me!"

So they had many things to work out between them. And many, many days.

It's lucky if you find a good woman in this world.

And Lucy & Mickey were lucky.

CHAPTER SIXTEEN

Jan was ahead of them in the line to the toilet.

Overheard Sandy arguing with Eva, her part-time girl, about borrowing some money, and why should she care—it was Esther's money, after all.

"That butch Sandy—why don't she get a job?"

"Claims they won't hire her—unless she can pass as a man."

"She's been in the Navy, she should be able to find something. How old is she?"

"25. She's just using Eva for the money."

"I hate to see a butch do that. It's slimy. Taking money from her lady when she could get a job."

Mickey stood in line to the toilet listening & felt uneasy.

Sandy was tall, very butch with freckled face, gap tooth in front, sandy color hair. Men's slacks, jacket & tie. Looked like a big open faced boy.

Sandy floated free once she was forced to leave the Navy—with an dishonorable discharge, due to suspicion of Homosexuality.

She'd go check in a fancy hotel passing as a man, sit up there, order meals on room service, and then walk out of the hotel lobby after a week and not pay for it.

Had turned to petty larceny, cashing bad checks. Got a welfare grant as a standby, & lived off her women.

And had occasionally been known to pick up johns at straight bars, get them drunk, & roll them for their wallets, and even to turn a trick with men—something she hated to do; but had begun it in the Navy with commissioned officers for extra cash. To support wining & dining her lesbian lovers.

Somebody who knew she was gay and a hustler had approached Sandy about doing a freak show for $100 and she said yes.

Jan stands in line for the toilet, sophisticated in jacket and boots; rings on her fingers; scowls at Sandy over the distance, as she berates Eva, begging for at least money to buy drinks. "You can get anything in this world if you get a job and earn honest money." Jan declares, angry. Standing a few bodies away from Jan in the narrow hall to the toilet, Mickey felt guilt crawl inside the pit of her stomach as she overheard. "I don't understand these girls who don't want to work. Any lesbian. To see her lose her initiative, and get fucked over by the world. Or try to fuck up their women…hustling drinks and worse. It took me a hell of a long time to find what kind of job I could fit into and a place that would hire me, but I found it."

The line snaked up the hall. Mickey cleared her throat, nervous & spoke up. "Where do you work?"

Jan shot her a glance. So pissed she kept on talking. "All these kids hustling, it just hurts me to see it. I hate to see gay people act like this! You need to have something you can show a lady! Ladies like security!" Jan looks at Mickey; "They're hiring right now where I work. They'll take you dressed butch. Just leave off the suit & tie—the rest is OK—slacks, jacket, short hair, it's OK. Look at me." Jan lifts up her arms; man's jacket, shirt, bolo string tie. Big, expensive leather boots. "I just came from work." And then she writes down the company name and address on a piece of paper.

And Mickey's so stupid she didn't go.

Shorty knew everything. "Jan's got a straight woman. A real nice babe—that one there." Points back into the crowd to a woman seated at the bar.

"She belongs to me." Jan said with self assurance.

Jan had a job driving a forklift truck at a warehouse. One year driving, four before that lifting & packing cartons on a conveyor belt. Was Union. Jan had managed to acquire a modest house and a car. And now, this woman, who worked in the factory office.

Thru the gold lights and filters of smoke, the butches gazed at the woman whose back was to them; low-cut blouse, femme slacks, bleach blonde; she tossed her hair. Jan would light her cigarettes and run her hand down the woman's back like a possession. Jan had everything Mickey wanted to have. Right now, all the two miniature man/dykes had in common was butch prowess & a pretty lady in bed to prove their masculinity. 'I need a job.' Mickey thinks, and puzzles about this as the line moves towards the flushing toilets. 'I'm getting too used to not working...' And this problem never went away, but kept eating in the back of her mind.

Green walls on either side of them. Shorty is crammed under her arm. Jan, the older role model, stands ahead. Time encapsulated them momentarily.

Mickey fantasized Jan taking her woman. The blonde beauty spreading her legs—'her cunt is blonde, I bet'—she enters her with fingers. 'Maybe she uses her whole fist; I have with a woman. I bet hardly none of these butches do that. Maybe Jan has one of them rubber deals. Maybe she does it pussy to pussy like I do...'

"Jeez, Jan." Mickey asks finally. "How did ya get her to make love with you...being she's straight?"

"Well, we had already talked about it. She knew I would take care of her kids—she has three—and she couldn't make it alone. So she just decided she'd come over to our side."

"YEAH! ANOTHER ONE FOR OUR SIDE! NEW TURNOUT! *NEW TURNOUT!*" hollers Shorty.

"I got a house, so she feels secure there—for her & the kids; so, when the time came, I got her in the mood with soft music on my hi-fi, and fixed her a couple of drinks to her relax, and took her in the bedroom & she's high, and I take her clothes off & she just let herself go. It's been a year, & she's gotten used to me, & she's happy."

"SHE WUZ HIGH, SHE WUZ NAKED & SHE WUZ ON HER KNEES!" Shorty bellows. Jan & Mickey laugh. "I had a girl like that, too! Honest!" Shorty's open face, freckled; eyes big. "I fucked her in the ass, in the mouth, in her cunt, everywhere! She woke up the next morning and didn't remember what happened! It was at my grandma's house. I figure it's because she don't want the guilt—of being a lezzie, a slut, cumming with me all over the place." Shorty weaves back and forth on her feet like she's about to collapse or throw up; and Jan & Mickey tip their heads back, bellowing with laughter.

Shorty held her beer bottle; put her thumb over the top, shook it, then held it down below her waist so the bottle pointed out of her crotch like a dick, took her thumb off & liquid foamed out. "I'M CUMMING! I'M CUMMING! WATCH OUT!" Dykes in the line fell all over each other laughing & shrieking.

"I NEED A WHORE! I NEED A WHORE! The broads in here are too tame! I NEED A WHORE! LOOK AT ME

CUM! I NEED A WHORE TO TAKE ALL THIS CUM!"

Mickey winced. Her dark eyes focused down on the ground. And Shorty was tugging her arm with beer-wet fingers. "Do yuh know any whores, Mick? Mick can do anything!" Shorty brags to the crowd of dykes in the corridor whose eyes are all on her now. "Mick has had whores! She's lived in 3 cities and fucked 3 ladies at the same time!" And Mickey retreated like a turtle into its shell.

Now some stragglers in The Silver Windows definitely remembered seeing Lucy, the pretty redhead towing a man in a 3-piece suit & tie behind her. Bleary-eyed from drink... They just couldn't quite remember was it really the same woman.

"I'd do anything to have a dick!" Shorty moaned. Grabbed her crotch & twisted her body about gyrating in the crowded hall.

"I don't need one." Mickey stood, legs apart, blunt fingers tapped the front of her fly. "What I've got is damn all right. When I've finished with a broad, I've cum all over the place—just like any man. On top, my clit on her cunt, in her mouth—I cum good. I just go on and on and on cumming for 60 seconds."

"Did yuh time it?"

"My ladies timed it."

"How'd she time it when she's on her back? Wristwatch?"

"The other ladies timed it."

"How many ladies?" Jan wanted to know.

"I had three at one point." Mickey did not reveal that she'd been sharing those ladies with the entire world who had the ability to pay. "What I got is better." Mickey said finally. "If I grew a dick and didn't have my cunt no more, a lot of women wouldn't want me. That's what my 3 ladies use to say."

"Dicks can't do nuthin'." Shorty says, wild. Short hair mussed. A wild baby street dyke who had seen many battles both in the interior of her mind and on the battleground of the world. "How many fingers yuh get in them?"

Mickey stared coolly, then replied: "I get my whole fist in her."

Shorty gasped in awe. The hallway of dykes fell silent.

Even suave Jan who was 15 years older, in her 30s, turned to look at this experienced young butch.

"I ain't never done that before!" Shorty's eyes were big.

"My woman back on the East Coast, Valorie, taught me."

Purple lights, smoke filled, filtered down on the crowd who disappeared inside the toilet stalls one by one, then went on their way, weaving back thru party goers on the dance floor.

Mickey raised her arm up, made a fist. "This, one time a night." Then points to her mouth. "This one time a night." Patted her fly front, tapping her clit. "This two times a night. BANG BANG BABY!" Accompanied this by thrusting her hips out in short jerks.

"You lucky sonofabitch," says a dyke.

"My woman right now, she's Lucy—that redhead at the bar? She takes my cum two times a night, every night."

"I do it myself." Shorty wails.

"She'll ride anything," Rusty says, about the runt. "I seen her. Armchairs. Pillows. Doorknobs. You think I'm kidding?"

"I wouldn't be a man for the world. They loose their sex drive after 50. They die out sooner." Jan ran her fingers thru her hair; rings sparkling; and examined the crowded smoky room outside the hall behind them. Purple and gold lights filtered down upon laughing, talking & dancing gays. Looks at her woman happily.

"Is she good to you?" Rusty asked.

"Yes."

"So how's she in bed?" Shorty pipes up.

"She's good."

"Straight women are the best women in bed 'cause they're real women!" Shorty rubs her hands together in glee.

Rusty fixes her with a gaze. "Why do you say that, shrimp boat?"

"'Cause!…. I don't know!… 'cause they're still ladies."

"I don't care if it's a lady who's been a dyke 40 years, or a new turnout. If I see her rolling around on her back with her hot furry cunt spread for me, and smell her sweet aroma, I'll know she's a real woman, for sure!" Mickey growled.

"AND ME FUCKIN' HER! ME FUCKIN' HER!" The pipsqueak piped. "Oh, shit, let me fuck her, please!" Holding the crotch of her pants, spit drooling from her mouth.

Jan strode in the toilet, then came out zipping her pants & buckling her belt, & the next dyke, a femme, went in & took her turn to piss.

"She's got 3 kids, huh, Jan?"

"Yes."

"Then she sure is straight. And a pretty blonde. Does she suck you off?"

Jan looked at the younger butch condescendingly. "She does everything I tell her to do."

"And she *likes* it?"

Jan looked up into the ceiling, shrugged her shoulders. "It's OK to her. It's getting better to her."

"She spreads her thighs open with her legs wiggling up in the air and lets you get on her and fuck her?"

"Everything." Jan says flatly, passing thru the layers of smoke, out thru the hall.

"I'm eating my heart out!" Shorty cries. "Jeez! Yuh got a straight woman on her knees! A job! A house! A car! 3 kids, even!"

Jan smiled, said nothing; butches and femmes parted like the Red Sea to let her go by, back across the dance floor. There her woman wiggled on the bar stool, in tight toreador pants, buxom in a low-cut blouse, turning to meet her. Butches stood, marveling at the pretty woman from the hallway. And the woman shot back a glance, wondering what they'd all been up to and what had taken her baby so long to get back. Then Jan sits back down, throws her arm around her waist, and like a queen on the throne, the woman tosses her blonde hair & resumes sipping her drink.

"Show me pussy like that, oh, what I'll do!" Yearning was etched all over Shorty's face; she grabbed her crotch again, holding her cunt under the fabric of her trousers with a tiny square-fingernailed hand.

"Wowie-zowie, she can wiggle her toes up in the air for me any day." Rusty comments, appreciatively.

"I'd like to see her on her back holding her legs open for me by the ankles—& a look of pain on her face & know she's going thru it for me."

The line jerked forward. Rusty was in the stall now, and new women pushed from the end of the line to get into the corridor.

Shorty's face was blank. "You get your whole fist in Lucy? Don't it hurt?"

"Women like it. You have to take a while to do it. It can take weeks, or months."

Then Mickey's turn in the stall.

"Do you really believe she gets her whole fist up inside her girlfriend?" somebody asks.

"Mick can do everything," the pipsqueak piped.

When she came out of the hallway and strode across the room, Mickey saw Jan smiling, picking up her drink; her arm in its black satin jacket reaching over her woman's bare white shoulders, stroking her, moving her hand down her back to her rump & gave it a pat. The woman bent toward Jan, whispered something, & they laughed together.

As the teenager walked by, she felt a questioning, like she needed to be out at the beach with waves & open sky, to ponder. Here in the smoke-filled bar, her brain tried to reach a conclusion. 'Jan has a woman, just like I do. And she works. She has her own money. She takes her pleasure. She buys stuff—anything she wants. A house. TV sets.' Mickey admired Jan, yet part of her is torn. 'Jan is 35. She's old. I'm still young. I can't waste my life working in some boring dead-end job—it'll kill me! I'm too young! I have to live life first! Then, when I'm old and worn out—in my twenties, that would be a good time to get a job....'

Down the bar, past gay guys and girls talking, yelling, drinking & dancing, there's Lucy; red-hair falling in a stray wisp or two out from her done-up hair. She was mad. "Eva just told me that Sandy told her that you said about me in the washroom you were telling them about me! About that we do in bed! I'm so embarrassed!"

"BABY! BABY! SHHH! BE QUIET!" Mickey puts her

hands on Lucy, strokes her gently. "I like to brag about my woman because you're beautiful!" Pats her shoulders.

"I don't know why you can't talk about us with out saying things about our sex life! I can't take it! Every time you butches get together, you talk about sex!"

The two lovers face each other. Lucy shows her teeth, with an angry swat pats her wispy hair back in place. Mickey strokes her, pleading with her to quiet down. Neither notice that just down the bar beyond a haze of purple lights, Bobby, the bearded fag bartender who is the owner of the club has reached in his cash register, pulled out a wad of green cash, left the bar, gone up to the entrance; and there's a plain-clothes police officer, Bobby hands him a thick wad of money —a payoff, to keep the police from raiding the bar.

And the show goes on.

All too soon it's 2 A.M. So, after 2, when The Silver Windows closes, abiding to its 2 o'clock liquor license, a group of gay girl/boys might venture to the Twilight Club—a syndicate bar with a lot of heavy-duty prostitution, drag shows and Mafia men, and big brassy whores; or, go to the nearby restaurant, and with volume of sheer numbers, turn the place gay. Laughing, playing The Supremes on the jukebox, crying on each other's shoulders about their love lives; sobering up on coffee, eating platters of eggs & toast, & continuing the party until dawn.

So Mickey & Lucy slept during the days so they could go out all night.

And forgot about the job.

Passion of the long brief evening had subsided; the drunk worn away, the moon in the sky disappeared.

Dawn comes up in a gray sliver. Nearby street lamps shone, but for a brief moment longer, before day would engulf them.

They sat together in red-plastic cushioned booths, in girl/girl, boy/boy couples; those ones who were lucky and had found each other.

"Come on, old lady, let's go." Mickey said in a deep voice. Guided her woman by the elbow. Lucy's panties were hot.

Mickey's cunt was creaming in her boxer shorts; they needed to get their pussies rubbing together soon.

"GOOD-BYE YOU BIG BAD BEAUTIFUL BASTARD BUTCH!" cried a lonely fag, admiring Mickey's masculinity.

Out on the streets, making their way home. This hour was the safest of all. No other people around—all the fag/dyke haters; the bullies, were long gone; & few police.

A lot of times, at bar closing, Mickey saw dykes get in cars—they had money and jobs—and leave her & Lucy to stand out there alone.

She'd be 19 in ten months.

Couldn't join the Armed Services with her reform-school record.

Sometimes when the streets looked mean and frightening, it would have been nice if someone had just been friendly and offered them a lift back to their hotel. But few did.

'It's true, nobody loves people like just a few special people. Like Saints do. Hardly nobody else in the entire world of billions upon billions of human beings. Very few.'

Thought about the fights in the club, between women, and the fact that they had really no friends at all.

After her fears of society—hassles in the street with straight males, the snub, and turned up nose of women; to go thru all that to get to be in her own world, a gay-only context; 'then we see what we do to each other.

'A lesbian could die. She could shrivel up and die; there's no encouragement from others.'

They had begun to walk the deserted streets; soon they were near home.

Crescent moon over the orange-colored city; buildings teeming with money & pain.

Mickey had taken off her tie & jacket, preferring to walk in a shirt and trousers, than go to jail for male impersonation. So, they're strolling home, poor, with no cab fare & the bus has stopped running.

A car drives by in the deserted street; "DYKE!" Screams a voice out the window. "QUEERS!" It's a gang of men inside. The car zooms off, & Lucy grabs the handle of the butcher knife inside her purse. And when the car comes back around the block a 2nd time, they knew they were in trouble. Two youngish men yelling out the windows in front and back, making the Fuck Finger sign, and screaming at them, in drunk voices. Mickey's hand had dipped into her pocket, and her knife was open. The car screeches tires in the distance, slows, makes a U-turn and zooms back. "FUCKING BITCH DYKES! WHAT ARE YOU DOING WITH THIS PRETTY BITCH, YOU FUCKING DYKE? FUCKING QUEERS!" Screams pour acid out of the window at them; dull panic hits the women's guts as the car doors swing open and three of the five men stagger out, drunk, wild, enraged. Then Lucy & Mickey are running, afraid, not knowing where to find safety; simultaneously, Mickey's hand jerks out of her pocket with the knife, sharp 5" blade glinting in space; the men are charging after them. BLAM! Mickey feels a blow of a white-knuckled fist slug the side of her head, & she's slashing down with the knife—BLAM! Another blow from another man, as the knife jars in pulpy contact, breaking from her grip and a male scream rends the air. "AAAAAAHHHHUUUGGGGGGH-HHH!" He's wounded. And blood is flowing over her jaws in a web; she gains control of the knife, in both hands, slashing the cruel blade zigzag in front of her, keeping them back; Lucy's screaming "HELP! HELP! POLICE! HELP!" And has her butcher knife raised up 10 inches long, glinting fire in the air; as the third man staggers back glaring at her in pure hate. Mickey's down on the pavement, blood over her eyes, the injured man holding his wrist, bleeding profusely from a severed vein retreats back to the car, howling & cursing. The men back off. Afraid of the knife, afraid of getting cut.

"GET OUT OF HERE, MAN! LET'S GO!" The driver yells inside the compartment of the car, and it jerks forward as they pile into it, hurling insults.

The next thing they know, red taillights. The gang of thugs disappears. And here come the police.

Lucy puts away her butcher knife—which is illegal. Dyed red hair stands out of place on her head. Veins pop out on her neck; eyes wide. Mickey's rising to her feet, bleeding.

The gang is gone, and the policemen in blue uniforms & silver stars are asking Mickey & Lucy, "What are you doing out at this time of night?" Like they have no right to be out there.

Lucy lies: "We had to go to my sick sister's house, and we have to get home to get ready to go to work tomorrow. & police take a report, confiscate Mickey's knife, & leave."

Silver dawn riddles the sky.

"Cold-blooded bastards!" Mickey is so frustrated; mad about the police. Sick of bullies. But there is no fear in her. A state of shock like a state of grace floods her mind.

Hotel room is cold. Red light of the tavern is out. Yellow light shines out thru their torn curtain, Mickey in trousers, bloody T-shirt, barefoot, lies in bed. Lucy boils hot water on the electric plate and tends to her wounds.

Sleep.

Few hours later, Mickey is on top of her woman. Lucy looks old in the new day flooding in thru grimy windows. "Why are you doing it so hard?"

"Because I'm mad!" Mickey glares down at her.

"Well, don't take it out on me, Mickey!" Lucy tries to push the butch off. "I don't want to!"

But Mickey pushes her down and struggles, knees between Lucy's legs, and pushes her finger up inside her cunt. "I HATE YOU!" Lucy yells, struggling.

"Why don't you want me? You wanted to before what happened with the lousy bastards, damn it!"

And she pushes her fingers in her hairy pussyhole, twisting her leg over Lucy's to pin her down; hips humping, rubbing her clit on Lucy's thigh. "STOP, MICKEY! YOU'RE HURTING ME!" And Mickey keeps on, now pushing three fingers in and out of her wet cunt. "Does this make you feel more goddamn butch, you bastard?"

"I don't want you getting the hots and sneakin' out with some man behind my back!"

"We don't have to do it every night!" Lucy clenches her thighs together and struggles under Mickey's weight. "Not with everything else you do to me! You're worse than a man!

You're as bad as those men out in the street goddamn it!" Her red hair wild, snarled, face contorted.

Mickey forces Lucy's legs apart with hers and keeps pushing her fingers in & out in a hard, steady beat. Accompanied by the pumping action of her own hips, driving her clit back & forth in a wet spot on the femme's skin. Feels Lucy stop struggling and relax under her.

Finally Mickey's thru. Has cum on Lucy's thigh, figuring she'd never get it any other way tonight, takes her fingers out; they are wet with cunt discharge; scented with Lucy's womanliness.

"Mickey…" comes a small voice, after some time has passed. "Why do you keep pounding in me every day? I don't need it every day!"

The teenager's eyes lower. Replies gruffly: "I don't want you to get horny and have desires, and start going with men again."

"MICKEY! That's not what's important to me! If I went back with men, it wouldn't be for sex, anyhow. You do it good enough; you've proved that already!"

These words enraged Mickey. "What do you mean if you went back it wouldn't be for sex? You're saying you *would* go back? You *might* go back? WHY? Because they're bigger and stronger & don't get beat up on the fucking street!" Mickey hollers, sits up on her knees; the veins pop out in her neck. "You mean you will go back with men because they're richer and stronger and can do more for you!"

P O W! Mickey slaps Lucy backhand across the face.

Hurt eyes stare back at her, silent.

Next day Lucy walks around the confines of their room. Her cunt hurt inside & they didn't speak much.

CHAPTER SEVENTEEN

Because Lucy lived in one room with no kitchen, walked down the hall to the toilet dressed only in her slip with a coat thrown over it; a room sandwiched between a howling wino on one side, and a babbling crone on the other; a tiny room like the cabin of a ship—that she'd flop down in & sail out of nightly in her alcoholic voyage, her dope-drunken boat. The setting was perfect for her life-style, & Mickey wanted more.

Broken-down hallways; toilet was a cesspool & bathtub unworkable. Took rinse-off baths from a basin of heated water. 1 room with 3 rather large windows, a tiny hot plate and a stack of canned goods; also Lucy's makeup, on a table. Wooden cartons painted different colors stacked up on one wall held their clothes & possessions. Room just 4 feet wider & 8 feet longer than the double bed.

So they existed on welfare.

Frequented the Purple Heart Thrift Store; there got Mickey boxer shorts & T-shirts, and Lucy a black sweater with a silver design across the tits.

Mickey was always clean. Bathed a sponge bath. Slapped on men's after-shave & used deodorant under her arms. Wrapped the binder around to flatten her chest, under her T-shirt, if they were going out.

Lucy was not so clean. Soon Mickey came to accept it. 'It's an American Indian trait. They can be dirty. She's a million times better then my mother who's fanatically clean & germ conscious and spends great energy scrubbing everything until it dies, & hates me & wants to kill me.'

Lucy explained: "My mother was a non-functional Indian. She was too out of it to do anything. I went to the white people's school along with everybody else in my neighborhood, after we left the reservation. And that's how I saw things were different than what was happening at home. My mother would stay drunk with a bottle of sweet red wine. She would throw our garbage out of the window rather than haul it down 3 flights of stairs, which was not just a lot of climbing, but dangerous also because of criminals who lived in the building. We lived in a welfare project & all the other tenants hated her and thus me also. I was different from my older sister & brother; I had a white father. They're full-blood. Both of them are a mess. They're in New York; we stopped communicating when I left. They don't have phones and can't pull themselves together enough to write a letter."

"What's that smell? Cleaning powder? Not that you'd ever smell that around here! WHOOPS! Don't get mad at me, Lucy!"

The butch was always yelling at Lucy to clean their room, because she was the woman and that was her duty; & silently, stone-faced, Lucy wondered, 'She's the man—when is she going to get a job?'

Mickey continues push-ups, punches, leg raises begun in reform school. Trying to be like a man—hard muscled. To walk tough. And didn't realize she had something different—as a butch dyke; this special essence was what women wanted from her. Not a replica of the strongest man in the world.

So, halfheartedly, she applied for a few more jobs.

And put the scrap of paper away that Jan had given her; thinking, 'I don't want a full-time 8-hour job like that. I want to work part-time like I did in New York. I'm too young to be trapped in a job 8 hours a day or more with overtime. I'll go crazy. I'll wind up calling in sick every day like I did when I worked in an office.... I should take the job.... Goddamn! No! Maybe I won't need to! Maybe they'll blow this world up with the Atomic Bomb!... Everybody's out here lookin' for a lucky break. Don't you see it in their eyes? Some place, some woman, where they can just get their lives started together.... I've got a woman...' And a worried look crossed her face. White knuckles strain in her hands when they are clasped together.

'I've got to live now! Or I will have missed it all! We gotta go out every night! When I use to party until 4 A.M. back in New York, I fell asleep at the file cabinets at work. I can't do both! I gotta live now! Soon my skin will be wrinkled up and decaying. I won't be able to make love anymore...and the women I made love to will be dead and gone. The mysteries of life might be solved when I hit old age—that will be the only good part.' Mickey gazed out of the window at the skid-row torrent of people stumbling by on a single-minded quest for drink; or the just poor, in their poor clothes. 'If I was locked in a factory all day looking at a conveyor belt, my soul would die! I've got to be able to go to the beach and think! I must embrace life with all the love I have—until I'm worn out from trying!—then I'll get a job!'

They sat in their lone island; a room on the 3rd floor over a tavern in a ramshackle hotel, reduced by poverty.

Later in the week, stirrings of guilt came to trouble her. Mickey stood alone by the dirty window, gazing out into space. 'For one day I lost all faith in myself. This dull, small room closes in around our wild spirits. I am selfish. I got to force myself to get a job in this new city. My dreamland is gone—I'm here, it's become real. My future—and Lucy's—is all caught up in a net, depending on me to get some money.

'The only thing remains for me to do is to change myself, and keep practicing my karate punches and do 50 sit-ups and 50 push-ups. I have the backbone of a jellyfish without guts to hold its quivering mass. I am afraid to get a job and mingle in the straight workday world. They make it so difficult. Anger drives me. Pure anger. I walk thru the streets avoiding the staring eyes, the inquisitive eyes. If anyone touches me, I jump. If anybody pushes me too far, I'll strike out with a karate kick. I hate the lecherous men, and the nosy busybody women. And they have tourists in Chicago just like the asshole ugly wide-eyed staring tourists they had down in Greenwich Village.'

June 30:

I won't go home until night. Or until I feel accomplishment from just walking.

July 2:

Applied for all sorts of jobs. Clerk. Cashier. Nothing works out.

July 3:

Applied for a factory job, but have lost Jan's slip of paper. There's a sign that says Not Hiring so I don't go in. Have wasted a carfare across town. Try out for a job in a movie house which I used to do. Nothing. It's a hard town to find a job. Welfare isn't enough money to last because there's two of us spending it. And we spend too much in the gay club, that's why at the end of the month there's nothing to eat.

I want to get enough of life! And not be like my mother, a

dried-up stick who works overtime. Not be like old bitching people I see; the same unfinished specimens of young kids who grow old and stiff and get wrinkles around their mouth, and regret their life. Who never get enough. Don't fuck. Or do nothing good, or do anything that matters.

I cruise the streets, see a few faces I don't want & who don't want me. There's nothing but death at the end, so I got to live! The beach, love with my Lucy, and fun at the gay club at night! It's perfect. Except not enough money.

July 8:

Hit every shop on upper Clark. Look for work for 7 blocks on both sides of the street. "Hello, sir, I'm looking for a job. Where's the boss? Oh, you have a full crew, all the help you can use. Not hiring. Oh."

There must be a million souls searching for an exodus—right now—a way to get off this planet. Each day is an empty tombstone gazing up at me.

Austere mobile beams of soaring skyscrapers. Mickey mostly walked & walked. Saw Drag Queens in high fashion like painted dolls with silicone implant tits. And steel girders going up, creating some new hotel or commercial building.

Turned the pages of the newspaper for news of gays, and there was nothing.

Job Opportunities ad section was 15 pages long in the *Chicago Tribune*—completely worthless. Having but 3 lines of something she could do: Delivery Man, Man to hand out leaflets.

'Jan wanted to give me a job...but I never went.... Stupid fuck... She even wrote it down on a piece of paper.... That got tossed out a long time ago.... She wants to get other gays in there so she won't be the only one.' Mickey had these thoughts as hot air whooshed out of a subway grate. These missed opportunities, like the blown shots of a junkie's arm; missing the vein, and liquid dribbling down their arm and away into the sofa, the rug; and all the other precious stuff of life beyond her reach.

The gaudy carousel of money & lack of it rolled over them like a torture device.

Lucy fixed Mickey a beautiful dinner of rice, beef, greens, carrots & corn. Had a bottle of red wine—Lucy drank most of this. It was welfare day & they'd be rich for a week.

When this General Assistance grant came in, they ate like a Lord & Lady. Lucy would clean the table with a wet rag, and pile all their cans up, and fresh meat and vegetables too. The redhead could really settle down and cook up a great meal.

Maybe Mickey got lazy, or broke down & gave up trying. Days passed and they were broke again.

It happened like clockwork.

Lucy adds a pearl to her Add-a-Pearls—fake ones that cost $1 in the dime store. No one, especially not Eva, a Star Femme in the club, is fooled by these pearls, and Lucy don't care if they ain't. The Add-a-Pearls are for fun, that's all. This Native American daughter has bowed out of the competition, the rat race, a long while back.

Mickey takes walks on the beach. Lucy watches a lot of TV—*I Love Lucy* is her favorite program, and is where she gave herself the name Lucy, which is not her real name, but her heroine's name.

Lucy muses thru a lingerie catalog she found. Yellow lights high above them in the tall-ceiling old-style hotel; red, from the bar advertisement in the street streaks the 10 by 12 feet box walls; soon it'll be time to go out—or to go to bed.

Nights they have these long conversations: "I thought you'd like this, Mickey." Lucy places a carefully manicured red fingernail under a glossy portrait in the catalog. "It's got garter belts & kinky underwear. Women in slips and panties. You like that, don't you, baby?" Lucy grins in a gap-toothed smile.

Mickey lounges on the bed, bare feet, shorts & T-shirt; breasts hang full. Circle of sweat under her armpits.

"So we flew down to Miami to work the wealthy New York trade—the rich people vacation there in winter because of its tropical climate & to escape the snow, sleet and sub-zero cold of New York in winter."

"So you love 'em and leave 'em."

"I had good reasons," said the butch.

Redhead Lucy had finally been allowed inside Mickey. The butch at last trusted, and let her on a regular basis. Lucy felt little Mickey's sex melt for her, loose, hot and wet, on her back giving it up, thrust her hips up to her, moaning, as the femme's fingers worked inside her & Lucy's lipsticked mouth pressed to her clit simultaneously; Mickey's arms & legs churning; her head turning from side to side had cum hard in a vaginal orgasm.

"I use to let my girls do me all the time. It don't make me any less butch to get on my back for my girl & let her take me. I'm still her man. It's just that in New York, Lisa, the mean one, she reached up inside my cunt & injured me. It hurt like hell. I had my legs spread prepared to enjoy it; and she pinched me & twisted me around & I couldn't get her out—you know how hard it is to pull somebody's fingers out of your cunt when she's already inside, she's hurting you? And I had to go to the doctor and have it cauterized. Minor surgery. Free at County Hospital. And went back there 3 times before it was healed." Mickey shot a look at Lucy. Dark eyes blink, features solemn. "That's why I don't just let nobody in me no more."

So they sat in the room, Lucy fiddling with her TV set; or adding some new handmade decoration to the multicolor topsy-turvy palace, or doing her nails; & mad when the roots of her hair started showing their natural color & there wasn't sufficient cash for henna rinse to dye it red again; listening to the same jukebox songs pound up thru the floor from the tavern below; working in a groove. Daydreaming. Mickey being mad when Lucy went out to the lower Clark Street dives, so Lucy having to reassure her that all men including her drinking buddies were big stupid dumb jerks & she really loved Mickey & that's all she wanted to be with.

But this last time her hair had shown its brown roots—lamely had suggested going to visit a trick; one she knew—for cash. "You're too stupid to be a whore! You take the world into your heart—and the world don't give a fuck! Like Eva—her and Esther don't give a fuck about us! You'll start turning tricks & get old before your time, and broke down like the rest of those hags here on skid row!" Mickey snarls.

"Well, you should let me make love to you, Mickey, for a change! Then I wouldn't want to. You want to be so much like a man, I might as well be with a man. I hoped when I went with a woman, I'd get some thing different!"

"I don't want ya' selling your cunt in the street! Promise that you won't!" Mickey glares at her. Lucy is silent, stone-face Indian. And that's when Mickey lay down for her; to make sure Lucy didn't leave. And their relationship progressed forward in another dimension.

It's important to remember at this wild & drunken period of her life, Lucy considered herself to be unemployed—as an office worker, which she'd done for several businesses down-town in The Loop. Had worked in the financial sector for a brokerage house, and in a place inside the Merchandise Mart for two years. Before tiring of low wages & not having enough money or any time for herself; and then just dropping out.

Suit & tie; binder. A stunning gentleman. When the butch undressed, she was just Mickey. Fuzzy black pubic hair, ditto under her arms. White body muscular, square; full tits, sturdy hands & feet. Wavy black hair. Handsome.

Threw her boxer shorts & T-shirt to the end of the bed; legs spread; hot summer wafted in the windows; sounds of the street right outside; with winos & derelicts; plus a few beat-niks and student artists who lived poor.

Head on her soft breasts; full; to feel them, warm under the sheets.

Nibbled delicately, with lips and gap-front teeth over Lucy's hot flesh; square white physique loving her. Had hot sex on their periods, blood-smeared sheets & thighs and faces. They were hot and young. Lucy was high on the infatuation of love for Mickey—as an actress in a romance. One better than on TV.

Gets Lucy on all fours, spreads the cheeks of her soft ass and goes slowly into her tight butthole with a small cucumber. One hand goes around Lucy's waist & massages her clit & the redhead rears up like a bitch in heat, pumping her ass and hollering.

And Mickey wouldn't stop. Once she got a hold of that sweet thing, she didn't let go of it; and Lucy cum hard.

Then, for the finale, they did it the butch's favorite way.

2 tousled heads on the bed; red & black. Heartbeat—the bar sign outside; red pulse run into the room, turning pink in the far recesses at the end. Watching her woman who lay back on pillows; who lay under her; whose eyes did not turn away, nor mask emotion, but looked back up to her, receiving her gaze as she received her cum; as their bodies moved together & thrust, reaching for each other in sex and animus—and drank of the fine erotic force inside each other in their secret loving in their hideaway room; not like so many hardened lovers, weary, turning their head on the pillow to face away & cumming separately as they came together.

CHAPTER EIGHTEEN

Mickey kept her women because she played the man's role unabashedly.

Lusted for them—desired them sexually & took them as a top, bringing her lust to satisfaction cunt to cunt; took them vaginally with fingers and dildos. Filled their body cavities. Mickey was wise & knew many ladies wanted to be penetrated & royally fucked. Showgirls, strippers & nice girls, too. Used every part of their body so they were satisfied.

And didn't mind letting them go in the door first.

The two were in bed wrapped in each others arms. "Get on top of me." Lucy commands. The obedient butch was so excited she didn't know what to do first. Mounts her, legs intertwined with Lucy's, rides her, her clit against Lucy's thigh, up and down, wet; & feels coursing desire run thru her with each thrust. Lucy plays & toys with her butch; pulls her hair, & jiggles her leg so that it bumps Mickey's groin & is doing a dozen little things to turn her on. Laughter, & Mickey feels Lucy's big, full tits bouncing underneath, and carefully pushes two fingers in, then three, while continuing to ride; digging in with her bony toes. Then, hops off, jumps down in the sheets, puts her head between Lucy's thighs, tongue probes between brown cunthair—the two-tone difference from the dyed red beehive hairdo of her head—to her pussylips & begins to lick her woman's hot wet meat. "DO ONE THING, MICKEY!" Lucy yanks her black hair. Laughs. "Do one thing and stick with it!" And lies back, thinking Mickey's gonna suck her off.

Pussy. Just the word made steam come out of her nostrils.

Lucy lay back while Mickey pleasured her.

The femme is menstruating, but this makes no difference. Blood leaks down out of her cunt, streaks along her thighs; is absorbed into the sheets, dark red in color, and covers Mickey's face as she licks, her nose and lips inside folds of pussy; flicks her tongue into that sweet wet hot hole. Pungent aroma of pussy in her nostrils. Blood clots & cuntjuice all over. Licks down her thighs in feathery touches. "I WANT ALL OF YOU, LUCY!" she hollers. "I *LOVE* YOU!" Wipes the load of blood and discharge from Lucy's cunt off her face, & dives back for more. Licks hard, fast. Sucks, drawing her pearl-shape clit into her mouth, while flicking the tip of her tongue back and forth over it. Stops. Gazes up earnestly from between Lucy's blood-covered thighs; "Remember, tell me when you want me to come up and fuck you with the carrot!" But Lucy can't help it; already feels herself cum, pouring out in molten lava.

"OOOOHHHHHHHHHHHH UUHHHHH UHHH-HHHH OOHHHHHH!"

"I'm ready for you—my whole body is ready for you! I'm gonna make you cum some more!" Mickey climbs up on Lucy, wiggles her hips between her outspread thighs, & does what she discovered in 1955, in one of the gypsy-caravan string of apartments in Jersey City—that she can rub her cunt on the woman's cunt, their pearly clits and wet cunt lips mashing together & both cum at the same time. Lucy's legs are wide open, she holds them out by the ankles, and Mickey's heavy body is on top, crushing her down, so Lucy can't get away, which makes it better. Lucy scrunches her ass around underneath, getting her cunt in position. Sweet & hot, nasty little wet cunt, can't wait to have it. Toes dig in, hips thrust; butch Mickey's thighs are iron hard with tension. Still can taste the woman's cuntjuice; moving her hips up and down, a pumping piston driving her clit in the woman's cunt, pushing Lucy's butt into the mattress. Butch so horny, femme trembling in desire. Mickey proving her butchness with women.

A tongue licks up her neck, probes into her ear. Deep scent of her own cuntjuice on Lucy's breath. Rough ride; Mickey's furry sweet wet cunt—red-hot—pumps against Lucy's, studding her toward a 2nd climax, goes around and around, clit in the groove of pussy, as she lays on her, propped up on her hands in the position of dominance.

Every butch needs a whore on some level, to tease and excite them.

Motion of her hips rock the bed, now stop in mid-thrust; pause: "Talk to me like you talk to a man."

"I don't talk to men." The redhead gasps her reply with heavy breath, eyes closed.

"Talk dirty to me, Lucy!"

"What do you want to hear?" Lucy's eyes flutter open, bright, to look at her.

"Say 'Put your cock in me, baby, Fuck me!' That's what my girls tell me!"

"OHHHHH!" Lucy moans. Enjoying the rhythmic grinding motion of Mickey's cunt against her already-swollen clit. "Ohhhh. Fuck me with your cunt, Mickey! Fuck me, baby!"

"No, say cock!"

"No. You won't like that! You have a cunt, not a cock! Ohhhh! Do It To Me Mickey! Don't stop!"

Mickey was glad at bedtimes like now, glad Lucy had seen her share of The Fast Life; & utilized her ability to talk dirty. "COME ON! YOU DID IT FOR YOUR TRICKS, DO IT FOR ME!"

"FUCK ME WITH YOUR CUNT!" Lucy moans. "Take me!"

"SAY IT!"

"TAKE IT, BABY! SEE MY NICE TITS! DO YOU WANT TO SQUEEZE MY BIG TITS WHILE YOU FUCK ME, BABY? OHHHHHHH!" Mickey twists a nipple in her hand; ass continues to pump up and down, hot desire rushes thru her body in waves, toward orgasm.

"COME ON, MICKEY! GIVE ME YOUR LOAD! FUCK MY SWEET PUSSY! FUCK IT, MICKEY! TAKE IT!"

"Am I in the right place?" Mickey pants.

"That's It! OH, BABY! OHH, MICKEY THAT'S IT! DON'T STOP! DRIVE IT, HONEY, DRIVE IT! GIVE ME YOUR LOAD! BABY, ARE YOU READY TO GIVE IT TO ME? I WANT YOUR CUM, HONEY! GIVE IT TO LUCY! CUM ALL OVER ME, BABY! CUM ALL OVER ME! UUHH UUHH! OH, *SHIT,* MICKEY I'M GONNA CUM! ARE YOU GONNA? OH! I'M GLAD IT'S YOU ON TOP OF ME, BABY. I'M SO GLAD IT'S YOU!

"RUB MY PUSSY, BABY! FUCK ME! MAKE ME CUM! I'M HOT AND JUICY FOR YOU, BABY! FUCK MY CUNT, BABY. UUUHHH! THAT'S IT, SQUEEZE MY TITS. MY TITS ARE SO BIG, THEY NEED TO BE SUCKED—SUCK THEM HARD! OHH! MY NIPPLES NEED TO BE SUCKED! OOHHH! YOUR CLIT IS SO HARD, YOU'RE FUCKING ME! UHHH! MY PUSSY IS SO HOT! GIVE ME EVERYTHING YOU GOT, BABY!

"BUTCHY BUTCH, I KNOW YOU CAN CUM LOOK-ING AT MY BIG TITS BOUNCING AROUND! IT'LL HELP YOU CUM! LOOK AT MY BIG JUICY TITS!

"FUCK MY PUSSY, BUTCH! FUCK ME FASTER! HARDER! OOHHH! I KNOW YOU WANT IT! I'M A HORNY SLUT. I TAKE CARE OF MY CUNT, BABY! I'M GIVING IT ALL UP TO YOU! I'M SPREAD WIDE OPEN FOR YOU, BABY. FUCK YOUR HOT PUSSY ON ME! OHHH! THAT'S THE WAY! UHH THAT'S IT! THAT'S *IT!*

"I'M A SLUT! I'M JUST A WHORE, YOUR WHORE, BUTCHY! FUCK ME! DO ANYTHING YOU WANT TO ME! RIDE ME, BUTCH, RIDE ME HARD!"

Open legs, between them, a butch rubs her clit with a screwing motion in Lucy's cunt, fast & furious, jiggling the bed, as dirty words squeeze her libido toward climax. Femme so hot, going to orgasm again; arms reach around Mickey's butt, pull her closer to make hard contact; matching each thrust Mickey made by humping her cunt underneath; their wet pussies slid together, working together. Bodies were wet with sweat. "CUNT! CUNT! CUNT!" Mickey gasps, thrusts her clit up and down & around; wet, slippery, rubbery; banging her brains out, straight fucking. Had no money in her trousers flung over the chair, owned little but her bare flesh, her cunt, her hands, her tongue—and her love was pressing over the final sexual threshold.

Humping dyke gave everything she got.

Mickey completed with an intense orgasm; together with Lucy, in a fierce embrace, rolling in each other's sweat.

Rolls off, basks in the pleasant glow of relief. Heartbeat slows back to normal.

Immediately after, Mickey is mad: "You tell them fucking bastards all that stuff!"

"No, I don't!" The redhead's brown eyes flash open in surprise. "I just said it for you to enjoy yourself! I don't tell them anything! Unless I have to because they're taking too long! I give them as little as possible!"

"You cum with tricks?"

"I can't. The only way is if they do something to me afterwards, and they're not paying for that."

"You'd like me better if I had a dick!"

"I wouldn't *want* you if you had a dick, Mickey! If you go out and get a sex change like you keep saying you're gonna do, then I'll go out and find myself a woman! It'll be over between us!"

The room was still. Bed had stopped rocking minutes past. Cartons of food on the table; their clothes hung by the wall.

Mickey looked at Lucy, listened to what she said. To this young teen, things seemed a dead end, and like they'd never change. On this mortal coil & its grief.

Remembered being fucked on her back by Lou the matron. Fickle Lisa & the 3 whores in Miami. So much of life was out of her control; she had so little power.

"If you want a cock, Mickey, get one from Esther—Eva's woman that she goes with. Esther sells them in one of her shops—under the counter. Esther knows professional women: Doctors & Lawyers & Professors & stuff. They come in and buy them. It's $40. It has a belt to hold it on you."

"I had one in Florida, but that bitch ran off and took it with her. In reform school we saved hot dogs from dinner and used them—then ate them."

Later, Mickey continued to try to fist-fuck. 4 fingers was easy by now, but that ridge across the knuckles jammed at the pubic-hair-encircled entrance to her hole. Wouldn't go in— that's when it started hurting. "You're still too tight." And gave up to try later in the week.

Fucked Lucy with four fingers; thumb pressed on her clit & sucking her tits, till she felt cunt muscles squeeze on her hand.

And got oral service from the redhead on her knees.

Fucked her hard—so sometimes Lucy felt her insides were dropping out.

Lucy stared up at the ceiling.

Red lights blinked off & on in the hotel room—shades of evening had fallen.

To Lucy, sex drive was something she sold, or had strings attached—like getting somebody to do a favor for her in exchange. It was difficult to enjoy just for herself. Not the way she enjoyed drink. Sex meant the pain of giving herself emotionally; just to see that person walk out the door because they couldn't stand her personal life.

Was stuck inside, & couldn't always let go—& totally abandon herself; her sweat & body motions culminating in orgasm; often in heat she had sold her body, or given herself to lovers who didn't satisfy her, just satisfied themselves, then got up and left. She had twisted the carnal & financial until they were intertwined. Instead of being a simple animal need, to Lucy, sex was a very complicated problem.

So from the first months of eager joy with teenage Mickey, shadows began to intrude; and Lucy found herself start to withdraw from sex pleasure—to hold off, to freeze up; just like she had with everybody else.

Lucy wasn't a real whore—yet. Times of her estrogen cycle, when extra horny, she was more bold & free; and motivated by need of cash, she'd go out, sit up at Shrimpie's, try to sleep with the old jane, fuck & sell herself at the same time. Go find James, lay up with him—& even a trick, get the money & still demand the trick suck her off as well! And a few told her they didn't suck a dirty whore's cunt, they saved that for someone special.

CHAPTER NINETEEN

It was supposed to be a trick. A freakshow like any dozen variety of Sexual Scenes performed for pay down on the hustlers strip. Transacted between persons who have $ and persons who don't.

Some common variety scenes were:

Double Bubble—a transsexual biological male still having male genitalia, plus female breasts & emerging body type of a female from hormone shots fucking a woman who's down on her luck & needs cash, for the voyeuristic pleasure of an audience of (usually) dirty-minded male businessmen.

Golden Showers—a derelict man picked up off one of the homosexual cruise points on skid row—one like Duke—maintains an erection, blue jeans unzipped, being pissed on, and his mouth being pissed into by a gay man.

Freak Show—a woman servicing a butch dyke orally, & lesbian fucking for the masturbatory needs of men. The underlying reality which cut thru these fantasies was a pre-op Drag Queen needing to save enough money for her sex change. The partners in the Double Bubble are so called because of her female breasts already formed by years of female hormone injections in the long time gap it will take until she can raise the money for the surgery to complete the change, bouncing into the female's tits underneath, as she/he fucks her with a still-real dick. A trick is a sex act done for money. An alcoholic man needing $20 to survive on the streets. A woman without a job, bad luck, broke, who foolishly let her finances fall too far, while partially living off her girlfriend, got the idea to do this for money to keep from being thrown out of her apartment into the street—money to protect herself from that fate—what she got was far worse than being in the streets. It was the same act as had been performed countless numbers of times between outlaw street dykes & businessmen in 3-piece suits, or Mafia johns with their kinky warped minds. But this scene went wrong—having had from its beginning a hidden agenda she didn't know about. It turned out to be not a freakshow at all, but rape.

The woman who had approached Sandy had lied.

The minute she got up there, the woman with her runs back downstairs. A man at the door lets her out & turns the key.

And she knew something was wrong, bad.

She tried to run back downstairs to the door but two men rushed after her, grabbed her. She got twisted around, fell, & that's when she broke her leg.

Had already had a few drinks in The Twilight Club with the woman who was supposed to have been her erotic sex partner, who nobody seemed to know; so her cunt was loosened up more & responded to the forced entry of their dicks & gave them smooth satisfaction; a feeling of dominance, power and sadism. A bunch of men. Didn't remember how many.

A kick in the face, breaking delicate facial bones as she crawled on the stairs; felt the side of her cheek cave in, and their dragging her back up & throwing her down on a bed so they won't bruise their knees on the hard floor.

Felt her crushed face & her broken leg, a fire-hot hell of pain; rough hands pulling her shirt up, ripping her jacket off to get to her tits, yanking off her trousers. One had his dick out, shoved it in her mouth and she bit down. He screams and fists pummel her face; she screams, begins to pass in and out of consciousness; and there's more blood.

"FUCKIN' BITCH DYKE!" A heavy weight presses on top, forcing her legs open, a horrible pain in her leg twisted out of shape grows numb; and his dick screwing into her, hot bolts of pain in her cunt as it forces in; then he's hammering in her like a piston—then he's thru. And felt her pussy open up after him, to accommodate the next one—everything she didn't want to happen was happening, & she had no control over her own body; her own cunt was getting wet & responding, tho she hated it.

Tasted her own salty blood, a mouthful. Head spinning from cranial blows which had battered her skull. The lower side of her body numb from the tremendous pain of her fractured leg. Her nice clothes stripped & torn off so they could see her body, hairy hands pawing her—bare, naked, bloody. And they continued the sexual part of the ordeal—her body built toward an orgasm on its own; while in terror, mentally, a stone rolled over her; as if she was in a grave lying on bed sheets; wanting to climb out of her own body and die.

Ramming their dicks into her hard, and it hurt. 'I was a fool to come up here to do this! Stupid!' Frantic thoughts milling in a gray zone of shock. The next man couldn't get it up and stuck his limp dick in her throat & she couldn't bite him, and fight back & risk being killed. And the intolerable pain went on & on.

Felt the male sex organ pressing in her mouth get hard; rough hands squeezed her tits; then he shot cum, hot into her.

And the one that went last didn't want to touch her; he had been standing there jerking himself off to shoot semen at her as she lay; & then they left.

Sound of joking, laughter, heavy footfalls running down the stairs of the rented suite of rooms & a door slams down on the ground floor.

Taste of her own blood was sweet and sticky; semen, tears. She crawled out of there, back out of the bedroom, down the worn wooden stairs. The only way she endured, and escaped the pain, and effaced what was happening, was that it wasn't her, but another person, another body laying there on the bed getting raped repeatedly, not her; and she knew she must get away from it—get out of there, & get away from that person—if it meant she'd have to kill herself.

And, another person, a stronger woman in her, a woman as powerful as an eternal rock struggled to survive.

They had left her in a hotel suite rented under an assumed name.

When she dragged herself outdoors in a trail of blood, someone found her, called the police, & they went to the hospital. A report was taken. Her leg was set; a huge black-&-purple bruise spread down her cheek, and where they'd slugged her a chip of broken tooth had to be surgically removed from her cheek. Internal injuries caused her to bleed from the mouth.

Every inch of her had been fucked like a woman. Fucked like a woman she never thought she was. She had always been butch, strutted around, flexing her muscles. And if she'd had the gun then, she would have blown her brains out.

As she had crawled down the stairs, had thought; 'I can't be a man anymore.'

Spent days at the charity hospital and was released. Was afraid to go out nights. Leg propped up in a cast. Sandy's broken face, freckled, framed by Sandy colored hair stared back gaunt and gray in the mirror. A non-person with a shattered identity. 'They didn't kill me. I should do that myself.' Wanting to die; in rage, unable to live with herself—in the realization of what had been done to her.

And wanting to live.

Lay up behind locked doors, wrestling in a cold rage, until her thoughts focused on getting a gun. She really wanted to get a gun. So, time ticked on, with no money at all. Food donated by charity; & injured severely. But disability money began to arrive from the State, and she knew, somehow, she would get a handgun & go looking for them, one by one.

CHAPTER TWENTY

Night. To be with others of their own kind.

Silver Windows, the gay bar, was far away, and more expensive to buy one beer.

So the two went to a dive on lower Clark Street. Mickey in shirtsleeves, jacket over her back, looking hard, but not in total drag; to get Lucy the firewater which she so craved.

INTERNATIONAL LABOR WINO'S UNION. Was written in shaky black letters on concrete in the side of a building.

Skid row town, so many facets swirled into one. Gay men passed into it picking up the lowest trade on the human spectrum—derelict wino men. It was brutal—far from expensive apartments with flowers growing in window boxes and cats languidly stretched in the sun & prowled under the moon.

Blocks upon blocks that had fallen away into disrepair; squalling kids in tenements that were still one step up the rungs of the ladder. The lowest were hotels like Lucy & Mickey's, populated by single adults; insane, alcoholic, at the last gasp of life; with no kids, no possessions, nothing but their tottering ghostly skeletons.

Broken windows that let in the freezing winter blast. Transients & dope fiends scuttled in slattern-mouth doorways.

And the only love is love of a junkie for a bag of dope.

Lucy had this love jones. This romantic illusion about Lucy & Desi—she had watched on black-&-white TV; now, just like a prayer become real, it was Lucy & Mickey. Had craved the love drug—Heroin—administered by the firm control of the Dope Mistress Phyllis; and carried, like her own heart, in a brown paper bag, liquid red wine sloshing in a bottle.

She wanted love. After romance, the agape love of a group. Wanted to love & embrace the whole world. To burn her candle at both ends, to possess the greater flame.

So Lucy went down there full of dreams.

Bomber-29 Club was full of folks. West Virginia hillbillies who slap each other on the back, comparing anecdotes about their young'uns. The only last blue-jeaned group near the edge of civilization. With their French, German, English & Irish pedigrees. Aryan whites, reigning Kings & Queens of slumland.

There was no ashtrays in the Bomber-29; the hillbillies would use them to throw at each other, as weapons, in a drunken rage; so they dropped their cigarette ashes & butts on the floor.

Sharpies eyed the mark. A few hustlers plied their trade —but most were too far gone for that, and had been thru these things so long ago, that now they just sat, ruined by time and drink; faces of wrinkled discolored skin, pouring alcohol down in gulp after gulp.

The Golden Shower bums spent their crisp $10s and $20s here, and the toe freak—who had a real doctor's degree exchanged pharmaceutical scrips for the pleasure of sucking the nasty toes of the most hideous skid-row bums. Flicked his tongue cleaning jam from between their gnarled yellow toe nails. He was black, and he sucked only white male toes; worshiping male feet; groveling & subservient to their feet until he was done. No sex. Just a silent controlled climax staining his pants front. Duke had been with him & Freddy, too. A line of men, victims of skid row peeled off their filthy shoes & sox. To allow him to salivate over their feet. Each received a prescription for amphetamines or codeine—30 tablets. They had to buy it themselves.

Hags were scattered among the drinking men; their gray hair long, disheveled. Wrinkled skin. Beer mugs held in withered hands. Some had once been wives. Some were whores. Basically, they had been dumb. After the first lies they'd told were mastered to perfection, and their art of swiping change off the bar, or wallets from a sucker—for all their game of those past golden years, here they were down at the bottom of the nightmare sea with problems & nothing to call their own. They had lived a fast, dumb life.

Boom-Boom was in her late 30s. The prettiest woman— next to Lucy. A showgirl who worked over on North Avenue. Bush of blonde hair—dyed—black roots showed. Was jealous of Lucy because of having once lived with & been a lover of Duke. Fed him, ironed his shirts; kept him financially secure, saw to it he could get drunk without having to hustle except to screw her. Was jealous because Lucy had a private pipeline to Duke—as a friend only—and one who had known him years before Boom-Boom had.

The two women had made a truce; so tonight they drank side by side & would sail out together on safari thru the rummy bars.

The Stripper had a pretty face—beginning to fade fast due

to alcohol. Drunken hags watched Lucy and her party leave thru bleary eyes, muttering to themselves and fingering strands of long gray dishwater hair.

After redhead Lucy, sparkling eyes, bare heels slip-slopping on top of a pair of high-heeled golden pumps. & Boom-Boom, feminine, glittery, came butch Mickey in shirt & trousers, and the alcoholic male troops: Freddy, Duke, moron Lee, and Lester.

One had to be athletic to go on safari—to walk from block to block hitting all the most popular bars on skid row. Circling between sets of cowboy music, or leaving when a particular club's liquor license ended—2 A.M.—to hit the taverns that stayed open later. Most of the drinkers, their livers were shot & had heart problems advanced by the ravages of alcohol. If they got up & just walked out the mouth of the club into the street too fast, they might fall down and die. Only strength they had was to totter from the grim isolation of their hotel rooms upstairs to be down here drinking at the common trough, lined up at the bar side by side among the others, facing oblivion.

"She looks good tonight, don't she?" muttered a crone in a raspy voice. "Boom Boom, her & Lucy and that lezzie dame. They're all users, you know. Of course. Drugs. That's where they're on their way to now—this liquor is just child's play to them. Child's play."

Now Lucy had this weird metabolism—not like her relatives; those full-blood Native Americans draped in worn blankets; thick greasy black hair hung shoulder length; on the bench along the wall; stone-faced, staying drunk continuously on 1 drink per hour. Lucy in the same amount of time could sit there and have 4 or 5 shots of liquor and still be sober.

Lucy wasn't accepted by the Indians, not the women; she was not really one of them. Or maybe because she didn't accept them & their ways fully.

Later that evening, Lucy is hollering, wild, drunk, arms linked with the painted pretty Boom Boom. Lucy was very disappointed in life. To call it a rat race was mild. Life was torture. Didn't make sense, & was sad. Enjoyed her butch

Mickey better than anyone who'd ever crossed her path. Loved her. But Lucy had turmoils down deep in her soul, beyond where any human being could reach.

The Barron Club. Boom Boom arranges her leopard-spot coat on a bar stool with the flair of a stripper; tosses her bleach-blonde hair, ignores Duke, who's dancing around in moccasins telling a tall tale, and latches on to Mickey on one side & gaunt wild-blue-eyed Freddy on the other & orders a drink by standing in her high heels on the rungs of the bar stool and towering over the bar waving her hand and screaming in a gay mood at the big ugly mashed-in-face bartender.

Now Lucy goes over against the wall & sits by a squaw so drunk she can't speak. From a daze of alcohol of the decades —not any specific drink she's had today. Squaw pats Lucy's leg in toreador pants with wrinkled red-brown fingertips, feels the material, gums her toothless mouth & mutters & claps her hands delightedly, like a child. Lucy puts her arm around the squaw, who's short and plump and tiny; hugs her. Straightens the shawl over the woman's shoulders. And big Indian braves stagger up and down. Lucy & the squaw are communicating on an unseen frequency. Now the brown hand plays in Lucy's red hair. The squaw utters a laugh—eyes gleam in childish mirth; her wrinkled face lights up as she examines Lucy's red hair. Duke is watching up at the bar. Puts his hand over his mouth and yells a fake war whoop.

"Chief." Lucy speaks to a brave beside them. "Howdy, Chief. Yuh seen the Buffalo Chief?"

"Ugh." The Indian grimaces & leans back against the peeling plaster wall; his eyes covered over by a film of passing meaninglessness—like once his tribe had witnessed the ancient hunt of the buffalo and scratched it on the walls of prehistoric caves—watching the progression of time, until his run is out. A feelingless, bloated hand passes over his reddish baby smooth skin. "They all got killed." He mutters.

"I know, Chief."

"No more buffalo, Lucy. Daughter."

Mickey had been amazed the first time she saw them together. Wondered why the hell Lucy associated with these wino rummy-bum Indians. "Who are these people? What are they to you?" the butch had questioned.

"I'm part Sioux. Indian. They belong to me." Indicating the line staggering & nodding at the wall. "I'm part white. Duke & Freddy and everybody else—the whole world—I'm part of them. These are my sisters & brothers!"

So now, golden lights bathe the drinkers at the bar; Boom-Boom's arm is around Lucy; Lucy is squeezed in next to Freddy, Mickey, swaggering, butch behind Lucy, drinking only a little, to remain ever-vigilant; Duke with his teeth knocked out, moron Lee & Lester to one side arguing over a cue ball on the pool table.

Mickey's mannish self doesn't fit in here, belongs in a gay bar. A few patrons turn their heads, cast a bleary look at this crew, then go back to their drinks.

Lucy shifts her ass on the bar stool, turns to Boom-Boom, lifts some blonde strands of hair away from the showgirl's ear and whispers into it hoarsely, "I hurt from fuckin' Mickey. She's gettin' so rough with me. She thinks it makes her more masculine."

"They all think that." Boom Boom replies in a raspy voice & coughs, gulping a shot of hard alcohol.

"Think she'd know better."

Boom-Boom was a stripper & had been around butch broads but was basically straight. Her affair with Duke had not worked out. He spent all her money & didn't fuck well—but sucked her off excellently.

"I might as well have been with a trick as fucking Mickey. Then we'd have some money & could eat out and buy some clothes & have fun."

"We *are* having fun!" The white woman turns and fixes Lucy with a stare.

"We're so broke & so poor. I thought she'd have a job by now, like James does."

The knocked their glasses on the bar, yelled, and itched for more alcohol.

Freddy, her old buddy from New York was a cook—he was buying rounds for them all. Freddy was tired of standing 12 hours amidst the spatter of frying grease. He was in his late 20s, getting leg problems. Open, friendly face minus the front teeth punched out in a fight. Like many bums who drank with the public, he made no discrimination of Lucy because she was Indian, or part-gay, or a thief, or anything petty about anybody.

He had a room in Uptown near Lee, and they were always Under The Influence.

"Have to go back to the Slave Market Monday morning." Freddy wails. "My job ended." Had been paid $180 for his last two weeks working a cook's job out of the agency—he went wherever they sent him. "The guy's a faggot, I thought he was gonna keep me on; him and me, we went drinkin' together up in Uptown just a few nights ago!" Freddy howls.

Reds, amphetamines revolved in their veins & plenty of drink.

"COME ON YOU, GUYS!" the redhead roars, voice croaking in alcoholism; "HEY, BOYS! LET'S GO TO THE BARRON CLUB! I WANT TO HEAR THE BAND!"

"We *are* in the friggin' Barron Club, Lucy!" says the ever-diplomatic Duke.

"Then let's go *ALL* the way up on Clark Street!" Lucy's eyes gleamed. Held her liquor glass: "I want to go sit somewhere where they have those nice upholstered red booths!"

Freddy & Duke & Lester were playing 3 on a match.

Lucy's talking loud: "Let's go up to the Dixie Club!" Which is all hillbilly. And Mickey knows if Lucy or Boom Boom set foot out of wino territory, they are so far drunk & loud & outrageous, the police might pick them all up. And Freddy & Duke are roaring in each other's faces spewing spit as they recount some tale. "I PANHANDLED ALL THE WAY UP FROM THE LOOP TO WILSON AVENUE! ANYTIME YOU WANT TO GO, JUST TELL ME!"

"I WANNA GO! I WANNA GO!" screams Lucy. The ugly bartender in an undershirt just scoops up their green dollars and sets down more drinks; this is how people drink in this house—on skid row.

Boom-Boom leans her head into Lucy's; "What's Freddy going to do with all that money?"

"I think we're gonna shoot heroin—at Phyllis's house. She's a wonderful person. Phyllis is so cool. Phyllis—"

"Aw, fuck Phyllis." Boom-Boom snarls. "You been talkin' about the broad all night. Ain't Mickey jealous?"

"Phyllis is a spiritual person. You don't get jealous of spirits."

Duke's face had been cut by a beer bottle in a jousting tournament of yore down here on the skids. It had healed into white welts in his leathery skin. Telling the tale of that famous fight was almost as rewarding as getting up and dancing on the bar. "This motherfucker I use to get high with, he's got a lot of tattoos, real dark. Portuguese."

"Short hair?"

"Yeah, short hair. He'd got out of some kind of chicken-shit drug program, yuh know—Gypsy!"

Then, up thru the smoke & hot air, in her appetite for drugs, drink & love—the love of life; while laughing too loud & screaming over the din of howling alcoholics, Lucy's wild eyes recognize a familiar face.

"JAMES!"

Wobbles on her bar stool, stoned; waves her hand, ignoring Mickey in the gray pea soup of her brain, yells thru the smoky haze of barroom air at a blurry face.

The tall man moves down the bar, glowers back at her; then beckons: "COME 'ERE, LUCY! COME DOWN HERE!" Nodding his head, not wanting to go into her crowd of cronies; and Duke knows the score & is trying to whisper what's happening to Mickey, who nods her head in disgust.

Lucy disengages herself from Boom-Boom and staggers down the bar. Her feelings are strong. She's glad to see him. A great emotion of relief sweeps over her—like it did when Mickey first moved her things into her hotel room—as if to mean, now all her problems will be solved. Grizzly with 2-day-beard stubble, weak-eyed, the barrel-chested giant stares down at Lucy. Lucy the redhead woman leans against his giant form; words tumble out of her mouth. "I'm so glad to see you, James. Mickey is driving me crazy. She won't work; she hurts me at night. She's jealous of my friends! She don't like me to come down here!"

James ignores this plea; is whining, hurt. "What's wrong with my tongue, Lucy? I got a tongue too, just like that lezzie!"

"You don't mind, James! You & me split up a long time before I met her. You don't mind!"

"I might have thought we were gonna get back together someday."

"Can I go with her without you being upset?"

"No, you can't go with her, Lucy! I *am* upset!"

"She's just a companion, James! Just a friend! Honestly! I thought you'd understand! I thought you were more advanced and had understanding!"

"No, because I'm jealous."

"You are?"

"My jealousy goes both ways."

"What are you trying to say?"

"You know what I'm saying!"

"NO! I don't! Is there something so wrong with you?"

"There's nothing wrong with me, Lucy! I'm jealous of you! I want you and I'd like to be with Mickey myself!

"WHAT?"

"She's a woman, ain't she? It makes me mad thinking of the two of you together! And I can't have either one of you!"

And all the while, interior, in her mind, the drunk redhead thinks: 'Mickey can keep her hand up in me longer than he can keep his dick hard. She's strong inside. James is falling apart. Everybody on the street says so.' Meanwhile, exterior, Lucy's wide mouth smiles, eyes wide & dreamy; is going on and on about how Mickey is driving her crazy; and sneaks a look down at James's crotch & pictures his dick under the stained khaki trousers, having seen it dozens & dozens & dozens of times. She feels safe around James. He's big and frightening. Other men steer clear of him & respect her when they're together. Lucy is a star, hanging on to his arm. Also, as she looks, idly down the bar at her drinking troops—Mickey's head turned proud, pretending to ignore her & speaking with Boom-

Boom—she sees the butch's head next to that blonde wench and already she misses her little dyke. And is going crazy that she can't make up her mind, & has in fact chosen Mickey, but it's a damn hard decision to live with—to admit she's a lesbian.

James sinks into alcoholic paranoia; defensive; imagining his space is being intruded upon by sinister men, and having no control over women. If he just glares at a man, the man will turn away hastily, trembling in fear, or reach for his gun; one of the two. And here's Lucy, edging back into his life just when he thinks she's gone. And for how long?

Yellow bar lights, roar of drink in the ears, rivaling din of voices bantering back and forth.

So, here is Lucy, redhead, back in the fold of the Clark Street Troops—by sunshine, or in winter blizzard; making her way thru ice congealed slush thru which liquor fires burn.

Lucy & Mickey were lovers, & the redhead's loneliness was ended except for those lonely ghosts nagging from her past. And Lucy had someone to back her up out in the streets—a butch to claim, one who was tough, used a knife & showed her off, glittery, as ornaments on a Christmas tree, to all the hags and wanderers & psyche wardens who imprisoned themselves on skid row on a bar stool, in the sour smelling beer/wine joints. A stud to protect her from evildoers, rape artists, and Mafia goons. Who all knew there was two females to deal with, not just one, so they left them alone.

Mickey draws designs in beer foam on the bar with fingers. Very short nails; plain hands & strong. Boom Boom's stench of perfume is an intoxicant, and her female vibes are enough to embrace the butch until finally Lucy staggers back. Backless pumps slipping on her bare feet, red wisps of hair stick wildly out of her hairdo. 'We're all drunk on Cook Freddy's money. We were walking on top of the world, me & my lady...that's all. It's a mess down here on Clark Street. All the arms and legs sticking up, of people trying to climb up the side of the bar, out of their quicksand. They can't see what drink is doing to them. And Lucy can become the same as them. We were walking on top of the world, me & Lucy... But now I ain't sure anymore.'

An old hag looks at them goo-goo eyed. At James; then back at Lucy and Mickey. Back and forth. "She's with that lezzie. I remember when she came here to lower Clark Street in 1955. The Chicago Police Force put her in the wagon and towed her off to jail." The ghastly hag recounted, drinking her Budweiser beer. "All she does is use her hand on 'em, gets $10—that's a lot. Enough to stay drunk. And she clips money off the bar. I seen her so friggin' drunk, knocks over her bar stool & crawl across the floor, along the bar rail as a guide to get out of the place. Men think about following her—you know—to take it from her for free; but she's so friendly she always has some men, or a lezzie with her to protect her. She wears leopard-skin pants—the type you have to dry-clean; that's expensive. If you wash them, they shrink up; so she never cleans them, and she stinks like any of the troops down here, but she still gets 'em. Got that lezzie there—with the black hair—that looks like a man? That's no man, dearie, that's a lezzie. They eat pussy. They're the champions of pussy eating. Look at her crying all over that lezzie. Lucy can turn on the tears, and they forgive her. I seen her with a shower cap on her head, come down here lookin' for James—that big guy who never drinks alone?—In a shower cap. 'COME HERE!' she bellows at him. 'I WANT TO TALK TO YOU!' You know they don't have showers in none of these hotels. It's for her hair, that's why. She dyes it red. You think her hair's red? Look at it close sometimes—it's got roots. The only thing red about her is she's an Indian. Half-Indian, I hear. James is going crazy, I hear tell. He'll kill a man before the year's out. He killed someone else. If you're a man & you start off the evening drinking with James, you better end the evening drinking with him—or he'll kill you. Look at that Lucy; look how she's crying all over that lezzie. The lezzie believes it, whatever Lucy is telling her—it's all a lie. A lie. She tells good lies, and she cries tears, so they believe her."

Din of gin, roars. In the demented sub-city, derelicts are urinating all over skid row in her dreams. Women, their pants pulled down, squatting in doorways exuding a stream of yellow piss. It was like the Golden Showers of May. Lucy cried on Mickey for a long time. The cowboy band played another twanger. A psychiatrist would declare that Lucy possessed ambiguity.

'Love, true love is hard to find & harder to keep.' Mickey knows.

"I love you, Mickey, I love you, baby, I really do. It's just I'm so confused. I am. I don't know which way to go. I don't know what to do."

And Mickey knew how it would have to be to get Lucy home—by cab. She'd stolen some of Freddy's money off the bar; they never gave money, only paid things if everybody was going along together. Lucy was roaring drunk; would maneuver her up the stairs & shove her thru the door & she'd be worthless as a companion.

Just like NYC, & later what Miami had disintegrated into. Hooker who don't want to do nuthin.' Stand out in the cold, turn as few dates as they can, use the money to get high, become mental—bodyless; just mental; come home pretending they no longer have a body & they don't want to feel & they don't want to fuck.

Mickey laughed gruffly out of her closed mouth. It was as if the weight of the world was upon her shoulders.

CHAPTER TWENTY-ONE

Strippers, living on the edge in a sex world, were kinky and the first to have different toys: dildos, porn photos, SM equipment in their possession whether or not they used them.

Lisa had a plastic vibrator—the type to be inserted in the cunt or ass, which they seldom used.

Valorie had a strap-on dildo of hard rubber that didn't bend. Only 6", but thick in diameter—simulated—with veins & a dickhead which she & Mickey and later Mickey & Gloria used during play.

Sex workers were jaded. Ordinary sex was a bore after a while—they had so much of it. They were freaks. So it was important to have a variety of Kinky Things to Do. Women juiced in their cunts at the sight of butch Mickey like a large boy running after them, cock in harness stuck thru the hole in a pair of men's boxer shorts stroking her hand up & down her dick's fleshy shaft in simulated masturbation, yelling: "I'VE GOT TO FUCK YOU, BABY!" And readily allowed themselves to be caught, and yield to penetration & screwing by their teen butch and be fucked well.

It had begun with Valorie, come into Mickey's life—an older hooker of 24, who had been given the equipment by a former trick for sex-play—in the line of business—a jane whom she had stolen it from.

It was a sort of sexual high hilarity:

"When I split up from her I lost my cock. It was a mess in Miami. We had a broad named Scheherazade. She got it, plus my watch, my gold chain & cufflinks, and a bunch of our stuff when she ran off. I kept saying I'd get another one…. It wasn't as good as this one—this one bends better; it's softer but still hard. I'd fuck her with my tool & she'd yell: 'Harder, baby, harder, faster, fuck me faaaster!' So I expect you to do the same thing, Lucy! I always keep my fingernails of my right hand cut real short, as you can see—even if I forget to do the others. A good lesbian—even a femme—should have a couple of working fingers available, Lucy. Even femmes like Eva who have dildos. Have you noticed her two fingers on her right hand are always short nails—even tho she paints them red? There was a place in Times Square in New York that sold stuff—sex-play stuff, men's bodybuilding magazines, & nudist photos from Europe and the police were always closing it down. Since 12 I've always used carrots, sausages, hot dogs, candles—you name it. It's for when you want to go wider than fingers. It's kinky. I have to love my women in every way. That's why we have to keep working to get my fist in you, Lucy. Valorie loved it. She would only let me fist her in our bed at home, nowhere else because she said it was so intimate."

So the memory of this sex-play was strong—Valorie & Gloria under the satin sheets they made their beds with (carrying them from hotel to hotel)—lusting; Mickey thrust her hips forward, pumping cock in & out of Valorie's cunt from behind, past her smooth round globes of buttocks, as their other woman, Gloria, upside down, sucked Valorie's clit from underneath, in an orgasmic orgy.

They would have to spend half of Mickey's welfare money to buy it, & they'd be hungry at the end of the month—but they'd have plenty of dick.

Next time at the gay club when they saw Eva, her black lacquered hair starkly contrasted to a white face & painted red lips; dressed in a ladies sky-blue pantsuit & high heels daintily holding a drink and holding court among the single butches who hung on her every word. The couple talked to her and Eva went to Esther—and they got it at the end of that evening.

"Is your pussy hot, Lucy? Mine is just thinking about doing it!"

For three months they had been lovers. In and out of the gay clubs & restaurants. And sailing in safari down a skid-row tour of taverns.

Lucy's touch was so healing to Mickey, after her women of the past. Those bodies the butch had possessed in bed; but had had to share them with their business clientele. She loved Lucy so, because as she took her night after night in a bath of love. She knew nobody else had been in her or on her or used her in any way.

So, by mid-August, Mickey was back in harness once more.

Strapped it on, and was surprised how the more modern harness held it snug to her furry pubic mound, and its base banged against her clit during action, arousing her to more frantic motion. It was 10" from base to tip and capable of giving a lot of pleasure to a woman. Esther & Eva used this model and others in their loveplay, and the older woman had named hers Rose. "Let's get Rose out and play. That's what she tells me." Eva confided. The dick had a bulbous head with a tiny hole at the tip, veins, was dark fleshy pink in color, duplicate of a sex organ—one that would never quit.

"A big piece of meat like this and such a little girl like you—you sure you can take it?" Mickey leered.

"I can take it."

After they'd been together months they were no longer as

wild & horny; instead of diving under the sheets & eagerly stroking each other to wet cumming, they'd play awhile. Build up almost to a climax, then pull away, then build again & finally when they let it go, slapping their wet bellies together, taut, hips driving red-hot, pounding down to the finish line with superb control; the orgasm was more intense, and multiplied frequently into a series of orgasms.

Hands & mouths, loved all the erogenous zones on each other's bodies. Their breasts, hips, groin, tailbone might be covered with kisses before they entered the white heat of sexual meltdown.

Very often, Lucy would allow the butch to feel her tits awhile & jack her off with one finger for a full twenty minutes.

When her body was red-hot with desire, Mickey began her lugubrious task; harnessed herself up like a plow horse so the tool stretched out from between her thighs; lubricated it with gel from a tube, held it with her hand and stroked the tip in Lucy's pussylips up & down until her cunt was sopping wet, then inserted the dickhead at the entrance of her hole & began to press into her lover's wet opening.

"I'm gonna give you your treat now, Lucy." Mickey says. "And show you who's the boss."

"Yes, Lord Mickey," the redhead gasped softly. A smile played on her mouth; bright eyes fluttered closed; curvaceous body wiggled on the bed, spread her thighs wide, scrunched her butt down to touch the heels of her feet, knees outspread; as Mickey thrust her dick down into her, sending a shudder of ecstasy thru her body. Lucy clung to the butch's shoulders; soon she was tossing and turning, moaning with every thrust—a professional technique remembered from a succession of lovers not too long ago, and how they'd trained her to do what they liked.

Mickey smiled and pulled out. The big cock stuck out, glistening wet from mucus & lube, reaching out of her crotch of black pubic hair, to its tip that shivered as the panting breath of the butch inhaled & exhaled. The redhead lay back on the sheets, legs spread, wanting to be fucked so bad; Mickey knelt between the woman's spread legs, held her dick in her hand again, slipping its tip up and down between Lucy's pearl clit and the opening of her vagina; the hard rod glided in the sopping wetness; then pushing her hips down so hard that she smacked her belly down on Lucy's belly, drove it into the hilt.

One hand on either side of Lucy, palms on the mattress, bracing herself, pumping her hips in & out like the piston of a train, faster; she liked having Lucy's orgasm in her control. To stop, & wait, & tease—then do it faster, harder & to keep on doing it until Lucy came. And Lucy needing, moaning for love.

Tonight was no exception. The butch pushed her hips forward, drove the cock into her pussy, pulled it nearly all the way out, then jammed in all the way; then took her with short fast jabs. Lucy pumped her hips upward. Could feel how bad the woman wanted to cum. How desperately she worked to conquer, humping underneath, to achieve ecstasy thru the sexual act and have a vaginal orgasm.

"I'M GIVING YOU MY COCK, WOMAN! I'M SLIP-PING IT IN YOU! GIVING YOU EVERY INCH I'VE GOT! FUCK! FUCK! I'M GIVING YOU MY HARD COCK! I'M FUCKING YOU! YOU ARE BEING FUCKED! FUCK YOU, WHORE! TAKE IT! YOU'RE MY WHORE! YOU'RE BEGGING FOR MY HARD COCK INSIDE YOU! I'M GONNA CUM IN YOU, BABY! YOU WANT MY CUM! YOU KNOW YOU WANT IT! YOU'RE BEGGING FOR MY COCK, YOU WHORE! FUCK! FUCK! OH YOUR TITS ARE SO BIG, BABY! YOU GOT SUCH JUICY TITTIES! OH, LET ME SUCK YOUR TITS, BABY! OHHHH! SPREAD YOUR LEGS WIDE FOR ME, BABY! LET ME GIVE IT TO YOU! YOUR PUSSY'S HUNGRY FOR MY COCK! I'M FUCKING YOUR HOT PUSSY! OH, YOUR CUNT'S SO GOOD! YOUR CUNT'S SO GOOD, BABY! IT'S HOT & JUICY FOR MY COCK! I'M GONNA CUM INSIDE YOU, WOMAN! I'M GONNA SHOOT MY LOAD! I'M CUMMING INSIDE YOU! UHHHHHHH UUUHHHH!"

Bed rocked with deep thrusts, as a willing femme humped

like a workhorse under her butch. Bed frame went BANG! BANG! BANG! against the wall.

Hips jerked to meet each other. Mickey fucked her fast, beating hard, drove Lucy down into the mattress; the muscles of her thighs were rigid with tension as she rammed the hard dick straight into her cunt. The cock's base banged against her own clit which was hard & swollen with passion, driving her to go faster. Both females' thighs were wet with each other's pussyjuice. Sweat mingled on their skin. Lucy humped and shook & pumped under her butch, held her legs open wide, as Mickey pushed the tool in & out of her hole fast, beating into her hot & hard, so there was not even a chance to raise her hips up in a counterthrust; for Mickey was driving her back into the bed.

Like a train thundering, a plane soaring beautifully, orgasm began to roll thru Lucy; her back arched, her hips pumped involuntarily legs trembling body quivering as she was being taken—for she had been taken up to the threshold of a powerful orgasm—but couldn't quite cross over.

Sweat beads rolled off Mickey's back. The leather harness was soaking wet. She was exhausted. Pulled the dick out & lifted her legs out of the straps & held the cock in her hand. "I'M GONNA SHOVE IT INTO YOU AGAIN!" Lucy's legs jerked open, surrendering; her hot wet pussy took the cock—the fleshy pink tool plunging deep—now, by operating it manually, Mickey could thrust it in at a slightly different angle, so it's shaft stimulated Lucy's hard, swollen pearly clit.

"*AAAAAHHHHHHHHHOOOOOOHHHOO!*"

Lucy came. It was a symphony arising out of a fire pit of passion—like a free-winged bird escaping the prison of self.

The flesh-colored cock lay on the bed. They were finished with its use. Hard, as it always would be. Until they were again ready to play.

"Wow, you let out a war whoop, baby!" Mickey held a trembling Lucy tight in her butch arms, kissing her shoulders & neck & face.

"I'm so glad it's you in me, Mickey. I'm so glad it's you."

Mickey slid down the length of Lucy's pale body, buried

her face in warm cuntfur, pushed her head between Lucy's thighs and kissed her clit, while the femme twisted her fingers thru Mickey's black hair.

Mickey was a stud. A workhorse in bed who satisfied women completely:

In ways she'd learned thru experience.

In ways stumbled on by self-experimentation—so she knew how cock felt inside her own cunt.

In ways taught by hookers & nice women alike.

In ways endowed biologically.

By means purchased from porn manufacturers & hardware stores.

In ways.

All ways.

In every which a ways!

"Mickey, get my shoes—and my bra." Naked, the redhead pulled on the high-heels, fastened the bra, then pulled her tits out over it so they poked out, white & full with hard pink nipples. "Come on, Mickey." Lucy lay back, spreading her thighs; with rednailed fingers reached to her furry cunt & pulled her cuntlips open wide.

Mickey lay down, covering this warm female with her entire body; savoring this moment of surrender; knowing this time was for her, this woman letting her use her cunt, her body, her embrace for pure satisfaction.

Naked, but for high-heeled pumps & bra, acting like a kinky whore, redhead Lucy smiled dreamily. Mickey put her wet meat against Lucy's wet meat; they rubbed their pearl-shaped clits together up & down, & around hard, rhythmic; she felt Lucy's caress her back. "My stud. My stud. My stud Mickey." Fast, faster. Lucy held her fiercely; cum exploded between her legs.

CHAPTER TWENTY-TWO

When Lucy went out drinking alone, she wore tennis shoes—not high-heel pumps. Wrapped her red hair in a scarf if it was a mess & didn't have the heart to fix it nice. Men didn't bother her as much this way. And tennis shoes better for drinking; she could keep her balance.

Lucy was out.

Mickey was out.

Lucy & James sat up at the bar of the B-29 Club. James would choose a male drinking partner later, for the evening—buying him drinks from his earnings as a furniture mover. The only stipulation was, the man had to stay at James's side all night, till James staggered out the entrance, or until the man passed out. So an alkie could get drunk free—if he could pay James's price. Tonight he sat with Lucy, wiping a large hand deformed by fights & heavy-furniture moving accidents over the beard stubble on his chin.

"I'm not *trying* to upset you! I'm not *trying* to force you into a corner! I just want to *see* you & have a few drinks!"

"You're always buggin' me, Lucy, & you don't mean nothin'. You're with that lezzie, you should leave me alone." Ran his big hands thru his unruly hair, leaving it wild, then rubbed them over his face. A double shot glass full of whiskey in front of him. Music ricocheted off the bare, stained walls of the cavernous bar. Quite a few alkies were in attendance; like fixtures at the bar, drinking; tho it was still early in the day.

"I get tired of sitting up in that hotel room; Mickey expects me to stay home and be her wife, I'm nobody's wife, I need to be out around people I love. Spiritually love. Mickey don't understand how I can love people spiritually."

James tipped the rim of the glass of amber liquid over his lips & swallowed. Set it down clear & empty. He rubs his scarred hands over his grizzly face again. "So you drop your panties for that broad, don't you?" Lucy said nothing, sat at the giant man's side sips her bear, sways to the music, trying to ignore James's jealous vibes. "She comes home from work all day, hard work, like I used to do, and you're playin' wife to her. And you drop your panties, don't you?"

"Mickey don't work, I told you! That's the problem! She won't get a job! James! Let's talk about something else! Let's leave and go to The Barron Club—maybe the band's on!"

"Lucy, you wouldn't drop your drawers for me, but just once in a goddamn blue moon. Now you let that lezzie fuck you!" *CRASH!* James pounded his fist down on the wet-streaked bar. "That makes me a chump, don't it? And it a makes you a goddamn lesbian yourself! *You're a fucking lesbian, Lucy!*" The giant swiveled around and stared down at her. Hurt was in his eyes. "I been spending my time and money on a lesbian!"

"I'm not one! I swear I'm not! I'm *not*...not really...but I like women! You always knew that! I've always liked women! And I like her! But I don't like her any more than when I used to like you when we lived together!"

Lucy was gone.

Mickey looked for her in her favorite tavern, The Barron Club. Band twanged; guitar & bass thud notes out the entrance onto sleazy Clark Street.

"Yuh seen my girl, that redhead, Lucy?" Mickey asked a toothless hag who had drunk with them upon occasion.

Wind blew thru the doorway. "She's been picked up," the crone mutters sweetly; rocks methodically on her bar stool. Gray hair down to her shoulders; gray clothes; gnarled hands clutching a glass of beer.

"What!"

"Saw her get in the police wagon myself," muses the toothless hag, dreamily.

'I knew this would happen!' Mickey thinks. As she heads out the door, the bartender yells at her to come back & calls her aside. He leans over the bar and says, "Look, that dame is out of her mind. She ain't seen nobody get taken off by the police. She's livin' in 1940, not 1959. Just between you and me."

'There's always the Clark Theatre.' It's a dingy little hole down in the Loop. 'This is the last straw.' Mickey tells herself. 'I can watch a double feature of foreign films or classics like *The Rose Tattoo* and *Streetcar Named Desire*. Stay all night there, and let her worry about where I am! I can sleep all night up in the women's gallery for 25¢.'

After her daily walks the butch would feel good returning to the warmth of home. Felt masterful having a woman there, waiting; while she climbed over the rocks along the sky-swept Lake Michigan. Now she thought, 'This is fuckin' disgusting.'

"Thank you, ma'am." The salesgirl had said cheerfully.

Now Mickey'd been "sirred" and "ma'amed" all day. Was confused. Not within herself, but outside of herself—about how others saw her.

At the Purple Heart Thrift Store it was embarrassing buying male boxer shorts off a shelf marked "miscellaneous," but it was much worse at a department store, where she had to go into the men's department—looking like a little man— amid the stares of wives, mothers, sisters, or daughters shopping for their men; and nervously imagining what the salesclerk was thinking, and it wasn't fun.

'When I blew my whores in Miami and came to Chi-town, I had 5 changes of underwear, 10 pairs of sox, 5 shirts, 2 pairs of trousers, and 3 pairs of dress slacks plus 2 suit jackets to match. 2 pairs of dress shoes, and 2 pairs of gym shoes & a short coat.

'I'm supposed to be out lookin' for a job. Maybe that's why Lucy's not at home, because she knows I'm just down at the lake goofing off.'

They had spent sleepless days & nights, running. Barhopping. Sat up with gay kids in the restaurant till dawn.

A huge Catholic cathedral of spires and arches. Gray cement fortress walls with 25'-high floral colored stain glass windows. 30 steps upward to a grand entrance way.

Mickey spat on the sidewalk.

Upon passing a church, Catholics of the 1950s would make the sign of the cross over their head & chest; but when Mickey went by, she'd spit on the ground.

'Wonder if I could go in here and use their bathroom.' Mickey pondered glumly. 'That's all it's good for.' But the heavy wooden door was locked.

If she was in a restaurant having coffee & a doughnut or some breakfast, then asked for the key to the restroom, some waitresses would look at her suspiciously.

For Mickey being in drag—the way she lived her life, or

even semi-drag—going to the toilet in public was an ordeal, unless it was around her own gay people.

Balanced her weight on one foot, as wind blew thru her hair, and cupped her head.

Walked under the underpass, back to the beach.

Not knowing where Lucy was, she just kept walking up the road of life. She had had her face bloodied for the sake of women's love—from the fists of dykes, her own lesbian people—from brutality of the straights, & more—much more to her; by the blood of love; kneeling at the gate of the sea of passage, the labia of her lover, whose menstrual blood smeared her face.

Passed the closeted homos who lurked furtively by the Division Street Beach bathroom; built of cement & blown with sand; which was a gay men's tearoom.

Falsie-filled drags with their shirts tied up under their fledgling bosoms, tight slacks & sneakers, and no socks—so as to appear more feminine.

Mickey sees people from the club and they turn away & avoid looking at her. 'Makes you crazy—going by people that you know are gay, and they ain't being gay no more—'cause they're in public. They'll be in the bar by night; hair slicked back behind their ears with Vaseline, slacks & a shirt like mine; and have 3 women they're chasing after—and by day that same hair is teased up & lacquered on their heads, dangling feminine earrings. And they still have that same hard look under their lipstick and makeup & they march by me without speaking.

''Cause I'm a fuckin' homosexual, that's why! A fuckin' queer! And they're not queer, just chickenshit! YOU DYKES! YOU FREAKIN' DYKES IN YOUR GODDAMN MASQUERADE DRESSES! YOU'RE JUST COWARDS!'

Walk, walk, walk.

Walk, walk, walk, walk, walk.

No stars. The city is covered in brown smog. No exit. We are caught within ourselves.

Lucy is out drunk. Mickey has gone to an empty home & exits back out & night swallows her alive.

We are the people of the night.

Not like iron stairs welded into a cage outside the burlesque theater, where you open an iron door and go out on the fire escape to puff a cigarette or to be exhilarated by the night air—there is no way out of this life.

Fog. Foghorns. A fat ex-streetwalker, scornful and proud, with ruined looks, waddles past, coat pulled around her & shot a glance at the butch.

Five years ago, back at age 13, Mickey had begun wandering these streets, walking, walking...to the people that she meets....

Honky-tonk music. Skid row. Pawnshops with the three-bronze-ball advertisement of chipped antique paint. Breadlines by day. Families have scurried home clutching sacks of give-away food, & evening falls. The woman lumbers by, neither of them speak; but the air takes on a slow burning flame of sexual motion.

'Five years have gone. Have developed a nervous twitch in my left eye that comes on when I'm tired.'

The tic flared up as the butch squinted in thought: 'Can't get my welfare check cashed without knowing if Lucy has hers too & if she's down in a tavern drinking it up & sporting the drunk soldiers there.' Mickey cried in silent fury. 'Goddamn this cock-sucking lousy-assed city! Goddamn sonsofbitches! Can't try to save my check and know Lucy's spending hers like water!' The two miserable, tiny checks weren't enough to keep them in food until the end of the month. As it was, they'd be starving; they couldn't afford to waste any money.

A woman walked out of a doorway, unseeing. Mickey did not detour to avoid her, but plunged headlong. "EXCUSE ME, SIR!" came the woman's bewildered voice.

'I need to go shake down every last skid-row haunt & find Lucy before her currency runs out—she'll get happy and spend it all! I should kill those motherfuckers she drinks with!' Thought about families with mothers & fathers and homes—which is what she wanted her & Lucy to be like—a dream so long denied. 'So wanting your own sex, it becomes futile...complex beyond belief...we're the black & they're the white. We're the wrong & they're the right.' So Mickey grits her teeth & is glad she's stomped over the woman who looks like a mother with a family, not like her own non-mother with a twisted family, not like Lucy, who can't make a home very well—without the use of wine—Richard's Wild Irish Rose.

Concrete everywhere. Layered into buildings. Sparse trees. Few wild birds.

Pigeons nestle in concrete niches, perfectly at home without grass or trees or anything of nature; They are domesticated. Swoop down with beady orange eagle-eye sight after a scrap of garbage left by their human companions to subsist on what is thrown away.

The '50s is an era of teen suicides in hotrods.

Driving by in an old-model car, some teen boys—straights—see Mickey & holler out the window:

"LEZZIE! FUCKIN DYKE!"

'I'm more man than you are!' Mickey thinks.

"YOU'RE THE LOWEST SCUM ON EARTH! WE HATE QUEERS LIKE YOU! YOU'RE A CREEP!" Mickey has a steak knife under her jacket; now clutches its handle in her hand; keeps walking, avoiding a confrontation if she can. Bolstering her ego, her mind engages in a private stream of her own hate; 'I'm more man than you'll ever be! And I got a bitch at home who grovels on her knees & sucks me off to prove it.' Then remembers the bitch has flown the coop. And she doesn't even have that.

The police force has developed into a battalion of sharks with ultra-modern equipment cruising by all the gay bars and quasi-gay/beatnik places. You get to a club & are in for a sad surprise; a sheet of paper taped to the window reads:

LIQUOR LICENSE REVOKED PURSUANT TO STATUTES

X, Y & Z OF THE ALCOHOLIC BEVERAGE COMMISSION
—Some fun.

The Underground—a beatnik joint where a few gays hang out—is closed because they couldn't pay the juice. This happens periodically. A lot of counterculture businesses can barely pay their rent; can't pay off the cops so there is a raid. They're busted on some phony charge, which is usually dropped by the judge next day. Unless they catch a minor —under 21 for boys, under 18 for girls—on the premises. A few patrons are taken away & locked in jail for suspicion of selling drugs, or suspicion of felony lesbianism. The place can't survive and becomes a dismal gray boarded-up door fronting on an alley off the avenue, a dingy hotel above it; gates folded across in accordion bars, where passersby immediately start tossing refuse & newspapers & it becomes a garbage dump.

JOIN THE POLICE FORCE! A sign proclaims. TOP SALARY, TOP PROMOTION, SERVICE! And some street person has scrawled an addendum: "TOP PAYOFFS FROM PIMPS & LOTS OF GRAVY!"

Gray walls of a prison. Thru its bars, wan faces and garish-color skin arms & hands of the incarcerated are visible— waving mournfully to the outside. She walks back to skid row. The day is become night. Starting from clean white & blue sky, then fog, now darkness.

Past colonnades of government buildings designed from a previous era, gray pillars of the Post Office; a library. And bushes glistening of summer turning toward autumn. Modern workhouses twisted out of steel & processed rock. The office buildings. Here within lie corpses, tight lips; in whom the cloud of life has gone out. They are nothing evanescent; just a stiff, rotting corpse; muscles jangling at attention working 9 to 5, ready for the Coroner's Office.

The butch looks in a bar. A few heads turn to gaze at her, then go back to their drinks. Reduced by poverty to the cheapest alcohol that rots their guts out faster. Bar floor filthy, broken chairs. Mickey goes back to the women's toilet. There's no lock. Quickly drops her trousers & squats over the filthy white bowl, piss yellow urine. The inside of the stall is covered by a Golden Shower. Piss. A few coins to get wine. That's what remains for people here—what's left of the human rat race: The Game, the big talk, the hot wind, the good intentions, or bad moves; the castles in air. Amid die-hard memories—this is the end of the line.

No Lucy.

Alkies cross her path. Mickey blinks, forgetting names.

"Say, Lester, have you seen Lucy?" A brief conversation, no sight of her. Wild gestures—maybe she's at the Dixie Club uptown, if she's got money.

A ducktailed lesbian with pursed mouth walks along like she controls the world. Mickey recognizes her from the weekend party—wants to speak & doesn't. The dyke passes by and the chance is gone.

Sweat rolls off the butch's face, as feet pummel pavements. 'I guess I forgot what I was aiming at! To get a job! And support us! And have this home! Me & Lucy!' A sort of yellow sunshine fills the butch when she thinks of getting something she wants. 'I need a chance—a job. To make honest money and have a big paycheck, like other Americans.'

Chicago's temperature sweltered at 102°.

Night fell. The butch joined the circle of park bums. The lone female wolf at the encampment. Waited awhile, shifting from one gym-shoed foot to the other, hands jammed in her pockets; boyish hair tousled. They were talking bum talk—breathing alcoholic dragon fire—of what they could have done with their lives & didn't. What they shouldn't have done & did. These ghastly companions, victims of society's Cold Shoulder.

The Tenderloin of Paris, the skid row of Rome—these were the fellow travelers. Mickey was full of wanderlust...so had tarried a whole summer in this Midwestern city on her way out to California—either LA or Frisco, hadn't decided yet, having heard innumerable stories and pros & cons of both from the park bums. And on her way met a redhead woman who flatbacked for her every night, met her physical desires & who was untamed in spirit wanting to sail out into the tavern-lit sea in wanderlust of her own. A woman whose love she'd yearned for in a nameless description, which had driven Mickey on her quest from the beginning; now, had found the woman, and this love was making pain.

Hit The Palm Gardens. No Lucy. Terrific loneliness of bars. Rhythms. Smoke. Lesbian winos hissing curses from their interior darkness. Jukebox flashing red, gold. Makes you want to light up marijuana to get loaded. Or to shoot up, a pain-killing substance, as a guaranteed escape from the cold women, faces aloof, so impossible to get to know.

This semi-gay bar managed by a Mafia front man. Tough old butches with ringed hands turned to look at Mickey as she disturbed their minds for a moment. Up at the bar, pausing, looking around.

Music with threat & danger in it. Lesbian sex music with rhythm to match body motion in bed during lesbian intercourse. SHAKE IT, BABY! SHAKE IT! You have nothing to lose.

Woman with a shorter woman; crew-cut hair, shirt collar turned up in back, tough; the other in satiny shirt, longer hair, sprayed in place; earrings; bathed in gold light & jungle beat. "NO KISSING!" the Mafia man screams. "WHADDA YUH WANNA DO! GET THE PLACE SHUT DOWN! *THEN* WHERE WILL YOU BROADS GO!"

Music adds excitement to the evening. Notes drip out, drip-drop onto the libido. Gay kids move in place as if the dance floor is one writhing body lit by a spark & we want gay life to go on forever.

"NO DANCING! STOP DANCING! WE DON'T HAVE A DANCE LICENSE! YOU WANT THE POLICE TO SHUT US DOWN?

"NO TOUCHING, YOU DYKES! I'M GONNA HAVE TO THROW ALL OF YOUSE OUT IF YOU KEEP ON! WHADDA'S SHE HIGH ON? PILLS? SHE AIN'T BOUGHT A DRINK SINCE SHE BEEN HERE!"

Type of tomboy 13-year-old Mickey had been. She remembered walking past taverns she knew were funny-that-way, near the fringe area of the slums. The neighborhoods would get really dirty, littered with debris, houses in disrepair, paint peeling; then "HOLY SHIT!"—here's a band of faces peering out of the entrance of a murky tavern; butches & their girls, obvious lesbians; arms around their mates protectively.

Embryonic butch. Prenatal lesbian. Destiny—Gay.

Had popped the cherries of one little girl after another in juvenile hall during her incarceration. When they were thrown together by fate. Now, almost an adult, here she was under the Elevated train tracks at The Palm Gardens. Inside herself, deep in thought; while standing in the doorway looking out.

So Mickey was going to California, & the idea was to take her wife Lucy along. So it had been also, to take Lisa to Miami. And Valorie from Miami to Chicago—none of it had worked out that way. 'I was King. I saw a woman, she saw me over the smoky dance floor, and we just came together. Our bodies first, pressed in a slow dance at some after-hours dive, then naked loving in bed; then our minds. We talked, shared our dreams, made the plans for the future which included each other; hearts oozing together in a bond. Then all of a sudden, there's problems, and I'm gone and come here to this not-very-free town. It's not that women here are snobs, it's just I don't know them... And I'm back in my element, the gay life, up to the hilt in barroom buddies & bar times, and cunt.'

Scheherazade had just come in off the street from turning a trick. Skinny, scrawny has ache which she hides with a lot of makeup & stuffs her bra. Mickey watches her across the dark room from bed. Slow, limbs come out of her coat; one arm, then the other; her hair is smooth. She has washed. And her fingers slowly open the little coin purse she carries in her bra; a $20 bill is there.

"So what did you do for him?"

"As little as possible."

"Give me ten dollars."

"NO!"

"Come on, Scheherazade! You got twenty! You're suppose to split it with me!"

"Now you're making noises like a pimp!" Scheherazade exclaims. Her pale face tenses uncomfortably. Blue eyes strain to see Mickey in the dark. Then reaches back in the little purse and pulls out 5 singles, hands it to her with no other explanation. Then pulls off her dress, and comes and sits by Mickey on the edge of the bed in her slip. This is her first butch. Is fascinated.

Mickey's dark eyes smolder. Strong white hand caresses the young woman's arm. "You said you want to be with us, 'Zade."

"Yes I do, Mickey."

"OK, well, time will tell. I'm gonna give you a month & see.

Now gimme $5 more. We got bills to pay! We're a family!"

Scheherazade beside her to the left, Valorie on the right, Gloria in the front seat of the cab; they head out to the ocean. Valorie looks out the window in an ultra-transfixed way as if she wasn't seeing the things that passed by, but the things that flash across her interior eye.

Mickey read a newspaper.

Fog; lights blur thru it. Sea crashes. Waves spread. Smell of fish. Seaweed. Mickey wears a black leather jacket & expensive tweed slacks. They walk into the restaurant. Valorie has on a fur coat, low cut satin dress, heels. Her hair in ringlets. Takes the butch's arm. A Lord and her Ladies. 'We had dinner that came to $15 apiece—$60 total. Then took a cab to the show, then back to the hotel. Took a hot bath.'

Mickey has a deep mind that likes to be absorbed by things like movies & books. Other people. Valorie likes math and she has a good head for figures. She remembers numbers; they stay with her. Has a photographic memory & has memorized her & Gloria's trick list:

John Smith; black $10–$15 PL 8–4692
John Wong: China $10–$15 FA 4–3731
John Doe: white $20 WA 3–2627

This gift for memory is there for her use; but all she enjoyed doing is to go to motion pictures, watch TV & get high, smoke; and hates the time when she has to go to work at night with her body.

The Eight Ball, after being buffeted about, finally settles by a corner & we are all behind it. Our money is funny 'cause we spend too much & Mickey don't drive her whores like a stud is supposed to do to keep them in line, because secretly she don't want to share them with any men for money, or women either. Also, Valorie chippies with the hypodermic needle, shoots heroin in her veins every week or so & is useless for a day. She is unhappy but continues to exist; and Mickey is her human highpoint— plus having fun at the movies. Valorie wishes life was a big gumball machine she could put pennies in & always get a prize.

4 A.M.

Bedroom dark, butch Mickey sits in bed under the sheets, red ember of a cigarette, waits for her women to return home.

This was in New York, when times were still good.

Hear their voices tinkling up the hall, burst in the door happy to be home, carrying cold air & perfume & cigarette smoke on their leather coats.

Run over to the bed, climb all over Mickey, rings on their fingers get caught in her hair as they run their hands thru it, pull on her, two kissing trying to get to her mouth first, another gets serious, tongue-licks down her flat white belly & dives into the black fur of her cunt.

"LET'S GIVE MICKEY A SHOW!"

"*YEAH!* I LET'S GIVE HER A STRIPTEASE!"

"SWEET DADDY, WE'RE GONNA GIVE YOU A SHOW YOU'LL NEVER FORGET!"

Now, Lisa had been Mickey's private dancer. Would do the same act she did at the theater—with overhead light in the ceiling of their hotel room as the sole spotlight; flash pink pussy & tits & roll on the carpet doing floorwork which was illegal in the theater; and then hop nude in bed and fuck with her now-steaming-horny butch.

Lisa's show for Mickey was private pleasure. Compounded was the show three girls could give.

Stately Gloria removed her gloves to put a sexy record on the machine—a fast beat like pumping bodies.

"KINKY!" Valorie says, approvingly.

"WE'RE GONNA GIVE A FREAKY FLOOR SHOW FOR OUR DADDY MICKEY!"

The music pumped; the three girls began their dance. They'd been tired from standing outside all night in the shadows under buildings; waiting; walking; working, but Valorie had ingested some drugs in pill form, and Scheherazade had spent more time dropping dimes in the telephone trying to find a secure regular than hustle new customers; and the fast music gave them new life.

Night was young once more.

Music punctuated every other beat with a GONG, and Valoria did a hip thrust, right to left at each GONG sound.

Guitars strummed a metal sound & heavy drums. Valorie wore boots up to her knee, and left them on till last. Began to strip; pulled her panties down & off; showed her naked ass, slow; rotates her ass; her tits shake. Twirls the panties around in air & throws them down. Hip to right, hip to left in time to the music. Works up a sweat scenting the room. Back turned to Mickey, stretches a scarf over her round ass; bends over, spreads her cunt with fingers. Music pumps. Comes over to the bed holding her tits juicy & big, thrusts her pussy up in Mickey's face, then sinks down to the floor, wiggling at her feet, exposing her wet pink cunt.

Scheherazade jerks the zipper to her zip-front dress—it falls down to a glittery pool at her ankles, kicks it away.

Yanks down her bra, so her tits, large & smooth bounce out like melons jiggling as she wiggles to the beat; licks her fingertips and slaps spit on each tit so they glisten, nipples pink, hard under the yellow light. Mickey gets hot as she sits beside watching & wearing a lecherous grin. Scheherazade rolls her cunt in Mickey's face, rubs her pubic fur into the butch's nostrils—making her sneeze. And bounces her tits up/down in her hands in rapid-fire motion. Mickey wants to bang her women bad. Sex heat spirals up from her clit & cunt throughout her youthful body.

Gloria is kinky. Wears a garter belt under her short dress & no panties—pussy naked.

Starts with a full-length coat—of hooker leopard spots, and ladylike gloves. Drapes the coat over her shoulders, lets it slide to the floor, pulls a glove off, twirls it around & pulls it back, stretching like a rubber band, then shoots it at Mickey. Removes her short skirt, grinding her hips & working ass; and is stripped down to her garter belt & lacy bra. Inches the bra down off her tits, inhales, hissing, "Sssssssss," closes her eyes and rubs her nipples, fingers spread between each. Her other hand rubs her pussy, while she gyrates to the music in ecstasy.

Clothes off, strewn over the floor, the three are on the bed deciding who gets to do what with their spoiled butch.

Those nights the four females freaked out in every way they could think of.

Valorie, Mickey's main lady, rode her butch's cunt—butch style. Mickey lay back, spread her legs; sweet hot furry black-haired pussy upturned, cuntlips opened up to Valorie's thrusting clit; the hungry mouths of their cunts grinding together. Gloria lay with her dripping-wet pussy over Mickey's mouth, working her pearl-shaped clit in a frantic rhythm; Scheherazade lay at an angle, pushing her cunt upward into Gloria's mouth, who savored that delectable pungent rubbery flesh, sucking and lapping with her tongue, keeping her tongue & lips hard, & moving for 'Zade's pleasure; while at her other end working her clit in her Daddy Mickey's mouth toward an orgasm. And Scheherazade lays next to them moaning & panting as Gloria sucks and licks her cunt well.

When the three sex workers had had their fun at last, after a tired night of work, Valorie had brought Mickey to a climax by rutting her clit into the butch's hot, wet pussy. Then stately Gloria had gone down between Mickey's spread thighs—feasting at the banquet table of sex—to suck her off with expert frenching. Finally, Scheherazade, Master of Cock, was allowed to penetrate Mickey with her magic plastic wand, while Valorie rubbed her clit industriously, bringing her to a mighty climactic vaginal orgasm causing the butch to shoot a wad of female discharge 3 feet into the air, out into the center of the room as her whole body shakes & turns & toss & she cries out: "OH, GOD! OHHHH! UHHHH! OHHHHH! UHHHHH! I'M CUMMING! AW, JESUS!" And frantic to lap up her cum, the women lapped the sugary liquid off the sheets, laughing & tumbling over each other in a tangle of naked arms & legs.

As Mickey looks out the door of The Palm Gardens, the last bar on her destination in the search for Lucy, listening to El trains ricochet overhead with the lonesome sound of traveling; these were some of her thoughts & memories.

One of the few times the couple was apart, & Lucy was God only knows where; it was so god-awful lonely. 'Lucy, it's death with you not here.' Abruptly realized the redhead was the only human being she had in the world.

CHAPTER TWENTY-THREE

Summer, with gayboys in shorts & bleached blond hair.

Emotional music that makes us think we'll make it right; oh, yeah; came on the jukebox, & we picture the erotic sex acts we'll do on the sheets; then hold me till the morning light.

Sweltering heat; unusually high temperatures, even for August.

102°.

Body of a Mafia crime boss was found dead in his driveway. It was a professional job.

During the subsequent turmoil, payoffs in the syndicate bars grew momentarily shaky; police & Vice cops were getting greedy—put the squeeze on the little bars to make up for it. Kept coming into The Silver Windows with their hands out for more.

The Mafia had put one of their phony pinball machines in the club; they weren't suppose to have gambling and pay winners, but they did. Just go see the bartender if you did win. And still gay kids couldn't slow-dance.

"I know a dyke who got varicose veins from standing up playin' pinball all night."

Kids are inside; they laugh, pop their fingers to the music, shriek, talk; then somebody runs in from outside and yells: "THE POLICE ARE RIGHT AROUND THE CORNER!" It sends a chill down their spines. Here's the police van creeping up close to the entrance, but back from view, right around the end of the building.

Blue & white; shield & star of the Chicago Police Force painted on the side of the van. It sits.

"It's a raid!"

"DON'T ANYBODY LEAVE!" Bobby yells frantically waving his hands in the air. "THEY'LL PICK YOU UP THE MOMENT YOU GO OUT THAT DOOR! JUST GO ON! GO ON LIKE NOTHING'S HAPPENING! KEEP TALKING! PLAY SOME MUSIC!"

So, here it was in 1959, police waiting in their cop traps; kids inside the bar sweating like fish pressurized down below the waterline, delving into the subconscious & discovering FEAR there. Knowing that that wagon—and there would be another one soon for the opposite sex—had room for about 20 people in it. Gray metal walls, metal benches, a door which padlocked closed; to take them to jail—for passing in drag; for allegedly assembling to commit prostitution—tho nobody in the place was over 25 but Bobby, and no one had any money.

An army of young blond boys in superclean beachwear prances; the hormone-shot Drags rock & role; all within the bondage of the times—like a fleeting ghost in the bar glass, they saw a second van passing.

But the police still didn't come in, waiting while negotiations were made between a plainclothes cop & the owner, Bobby. So the kids danced on gaily, pretending nothing was happening.

Cops, two in blue uniforms sat up in the front section of a van behind the locked compartment that waited for its human occupants. One male pig said to the other, "Good-lookin' women in there. Why do they go with something like that —dykes—don't they have no self-respect?"

"They want cock from a woman, that's why."

"They want the exact same thing a man does, but they want it from a woman—that's all."

Femmes & butches, guys and drags kept coming in the front door, expecting to find a lively party going on within—if they approached the building from the left side and couldn't see the police wagons waiting around the turn of the corner.

Once inside, they were trapped. They couldn't go back out, and had to wait thru the ordeal in cold, frozen sweat.

The interior of the police van was cold, metallic. A police CB radio crackled in frequency low over airwaves. "They need a man to make a real woman out of 'em. Don't they ever get enough of this dyke shit and want a real man?"

"I don't know what they do to each other, but there's more of them every year."

"How'd yuh like to bust one of those cherries?"

"Hate to tell yuh, but most of 'em ain't no cherries. I dropped a big load with one of 'em back when we raided The Turquoise Ribbons—that other club? We drove the women over to that deserted section near West, where we park?—and told them, 'One of you sluts is going to let me fuck her, or all of you lesbian queers are going to jail.' So one of 'em gave it up."

"Yeah!"

"And the lesbian slut took it in the mouth."

The phony charge could be anything: male/female impersonation; being in a house of ill-repute; suspicion of narcotics; the list went on & on.

Bearded Bobby doubling as bartender, ran to his cash register in a hurry. Negotiations were a success. Pulled out a handful of cash—that evening's till—ran out front, gave it to them, and the police vans circled slowly & pulled away.

Another shakedown & profits were going down the drain. Was barely worth keeping the club open.

One patron, a drag, when she heard it was a raid, left so fast she left her gunboat-size high-heel pumps and a rhine-stone-studded jacket behind.

Another couple got out, vowing never to return, afraid if their names appeared in the newspaper the next day in reports of a crime bust, they'd lose their jobs.

So, when Mickey & Lucy danced in the club, they were warriors.

Lucy sighed relief, slumped in her bar stool. Held a drink, legs crossed, a wan smile on her face, patted her beehive hairdo where red wisps of hair fell loose on the side.

Mickey stood, feet in men's shoes, one up on a rung of Lucy's stool. Had a bottle of beer in her hand—Lucy drank from a glass—splitting one drink, which was all they could afford.

Deep within the bowels of the bar, gayboys and girls in shorts & tans, boys in colorful shifts—near-drag, got their hearts back again; the music went up loud & people loosened up.

Suddenly the mood changed. Right after the fear & threat; people started to get violent.

Two fights broke out.

Dykes fighting over their women; a dirty fight; eyeball gouging, bites; & some dyke broke a bottle on a chair, held the bottle neck with the menacing jagged end sticking out & ran after another, with the idea of cutting her flesh to ribbons.

A femme twitched her hips flirtatiously, a butch went after her—abandoning her own date; and a jealous lover slugs her in the face. ONE TWO! The femme pulled the rival by her hair—it was a wig weave—a clump of it came out in her hand. "KEEP YER FUCKING HANDS OFF MY OLD LADY!"

"It's dykes always fighting. I'm going to open a bar just for gayboys next time!" Bobby yelled, impatient—flipped his bar towel down the wet counter. "The dykes are too much trouble!"

"Aw, Bobby, they've got enough boys' bars already!"

"It's the girls that fight! Not the guys!—GET OUT OF HERE AND TAKE YOUR TRADE WITH YOU!" Bobby screams, eyes big. "They'll get us busted for sure! You never know when there's plain clothes cops in here!"

Music blared so loud, Mickey couldn't concentrate on her own thoughts anymore.

Perspiring; body clothed in light purple shirt, trousers & men's lace-up shoes, Mickey jumped into the sea of gay life.

Mickey had this idea after dealing with Lisa & Valorie: 'They're used to having somebody in their cunts 2 or 3 times a day, so I got to keep sexing them long & good, or they'll run off and look for it somewheres else. Fuck her hard with fingers every day—it'll keep her on her back, satisfied, & passive and she won't have any extra energy to go screwing around.'

This mental plan had worked with Lucy to a degree—at the time the redhead wanted only Mickey on top of her, naked in bed; but her yen to drink & sail forth in the night sea of tavern lights did remain. And when this yen hit Mickey traveled at her side, as a sober bodyguard.

Lucy & Mickey were very good-looking, despite the fact they had little $. Theirs was a gift of Nature. They sat together; butch ran her hand down femme's bare back & patted her round ass, in a stolen gesture. Lucy sat with the painted fingernails of one hand resting on Mickey's thigh, hidden by the bar counter—they couldn't slow-dance—so this was the next-most-intimate expression of their erotic love in public.

Ocean of gay kids; bottles & glasses clink; high-pitched laughter; smoke from cigarettes swirls around them. The nasty low-down sexy rhythm of a Hit Tune reverberates, gives power to the moment. Mickey's heart pushed under her shirt—causing her white fingers to reach down the smooth, glistening wood of the bar counter, over the space which separated her & her woman—into intimacy. Touched Lucy. To bridge the moment, going from just companions seated side by side on identical red vinyl bar stools—to the urgency of passionate lovers.

That summer of 1959. Especially that summer—before their lives fell into disrepair. They looked so good up there. They shared a bottle of beer, the admiration of their crowd; & at home Mickey giving it to Lucy hot & hard, and the femme was accepting it. Opening her arms & spreading her thighs in wanting, every night.

They looked so good that a woman bought them both drinks. She was a supervisor at a plant and made $25,000 a year and had to put on a skirt to get it. Mickey held up her glass in acknowledgment in the smoky bar.

So Lucy & Mickey had been together 8 months; a lot; more then many stray kids who congregated in the string of gaybars on the Near North Side—being famous, infamous.

And their love was waiting for a freer time & place.

Front door opened, blast of black night air; out thru it ran smoke from the interior; the entrance issues in a group of women; one, long blonde hair wild & free—femme, wearing a butch black leather jacket; blue jeans & a bored expression on her face. Another, black leather pants & vest, with silver buckles & studs. "You can't tell who's the butch & who's the femme."

"Those people are dopers. They came out from California, They're traveling thru, on to New York—hitchhiking. Then they'll hitchhike back. They're spending the summer on the road seeing the big cities."

"I don't like the way they slide around. It's the drugs. I don't like the way they come up & talk to Lucy the minute I leave to go to the bathroom. Their femmes aren't that femme! That one likes femmes herself!"

"She's a switch-hitter."

"A switch-hitter on the regular side or the funny side?"

"She likes 'em both. The funny side more; she likes broads more. Femmes! When they leave here, they go to the straight clubs & sit at the bar and try to pull bisexual women. It gives them a thrill.

"They sell drugs—that's how they're paying their way in this town. They're hot, actually. Sexy. They have sex appeal. That's why everybody in here is talking about them. I use to hate butches that messed around being femmes, being that I strictly get on top. They wear a shirt & pants on Monday, & short shorts & a halter top on Tuesday. But I got to admit they got sex appeal. I guess that's how life is in California. Everybody's free and does everything & lays around in the sun all day & you can sleep on the beach at night all year around because it's warm."

Door opened, a middle-age woman, large, well dressed filled the entranceway a moment; stars hung over her shoulders, and a crescent moon set in the night. "EVA'S HERE." Mickey says. The large woman escorted her companion into the bar, saw her down the 3 steps, said something, waved good-bye, then turned and left.

Eva came in at 12. She was slender, her hair bigger than her body; bubble tits pushing up under a low-cut top. Secretly in fantasies played out on their minds eye, butches pictured her skinny legs thrown over their shoulders & them fucking her. Eva moved like a fashion model, jangling jewelry & was pissed that she was late; but Esther had just left Temple finally to come by and drive her to the club & give her drink money, and half the night had passed by while she waited up in her hotel room in a fancy section near the lake.

"She goes to Temple. She's Jewish; they go to Temple instead of church." Crossly pulled out her compact & dabs powder on her nose. In better times, when Esther left, Eva's stud would have run up, pulled out a chair and grabbed her, sticking a pink tongue straight down Eva's throat. To make the best of the few party hours they'd have before the jane returned to gather Eva up and transport her home. That was better times.

"I saw Sandy." The women around her waited, silent, to hear the news.

"She's bad. Real bad. Sandy's a mess. They hurt her bad. She's lucky she's alive. I just started shaking when I saw her. The bastards got her up there and raped her & broke her leg and smashed in the side of her face."

"Is she gonna go to the police?"

Eva turned, blank face, powdered, in disgust, then blew a gust of smoke. "Are you kidding?"

"I'd like to know who did it."

"We have an idea. Some of them definitely were Syndicate. They lured her up there, using some woman. Somebody nobody knows. Sandy was suppose to get $100."

Mickey froze inside; her dark eyebrows scrunched into a frown. Thinks: 'Was it the same guys that watched me & Lucy back at the beginning of summer?'

Eva blew smoke, sips her drink. "When she got up there, it was a whole gang of men—it wasn't what the woman told her it was suppose to be."

"It was a goddamn rape fuck show!" somebody says, mad.

An odd prickle of horror shot down Lucy's back; hand with a drink stopped in midair, her jaw hung open a moment.

"...which is what they pay you to freak off with each other." Eva was explaining to the more naïve listeners; "And they jack off watching you, or have sex with the woman. It's the woman they're suppose to have sex with; most butches won't do that."

Lucy remembered the butch's smooth cunt in her mouth; the butch sliding her love into her lips, her thrust weak, afraid, becoming strong, hungry, needing Lucy's lips and mouth because she had not had a woman for so long. Lucy. Redhead. Remembered what she had been then; moving along lower Clark Street carrying her mental baggage & hang-ups, dreaming secretly of a woman as she tipped up a glass of beer in some honky-tonk dive, postponing her love still another night; feeling uncomfortable & alone in the gay bars she seldom ventured into—and then, Mickey, hard & handsome stands over her, loosening the belt on her trousers & suddenly she, Lucy, is at the wellspring of life—her lips and tongue servicing a butch's swollen womanhood, and all she'd desired all those lonely nights, tossing & turning on her sheets alone, had come true. '6 or 7 men? And no women? It don't sound like the same guys. We were so stupid! But, I wouldn't have gone up there if it hadn't been for Lenore—she set it up.'

"Then the woman takes off running down the stairs, & a man lets her out of the front door, then slams it shut and bolts it; and there's all these men—& she's thinking she's gonna get paid to do it—and not this, not what's happening…"

"Another woman lured Sandy up there?"

"Christ!"

"Probably some hooker, and she got her price."

Tinkle of glasses, merry voices from nearby tables. Mickey was sullen. The gay guys pranced around, not a worry in the world, it seemed. Here was this heavy, ugly business, its weight sitting on their table. What could they do about it? And the band played on.

"It sounds like a Syndicate john to us—a weirdo, and some more freaks willing to pay big money for it. It's sick. The Syndicate john probably fixed it up. And Sandy met the woman in The Twilight Club which is all the more reason to believe it was Mafia. So the rest of the men are probably fucked-up violent johns from the Twilight; they paid good money, & the Mafia set it up for them." Eva blew a gust of smoke venomously.

"Sandy crawled out of there. Next thing she remembers, she's faceup on a gurney in the hospital, an IV tube stuck in her arm. The doctors called the police. The fucking police came and took photos of her & she saw the police report; it said 'Female Transvestite' on it. That's what the fuckin' cops wrote." Eva was mad. "That's all they see is—'Female Transvestite'—not the fact that she's bloody & broken; they figure it must be *her* fault it happened. You think they're gonna do anything? NO! They won't do nothing! She's the last on their list! The whole thing started as an act of prostitution, & she's in drag. So anyway, we took her to my hotel, & she lay in bed drugged & slept for 10 days & I tried to get her to get the whole thing out of her mind."

Eva took care of Sandy while she was helpless those first weeks, & Esther tho jealous of the manly drag butch who had romanced Eva at the club for so many months, was angry enough and outraged enough by the brutal assault on another female to overlook what had happened in the past & lent her financial support.

Sandy had packed up and moved the minute her disability checks began. Was weak where she use to be strong. Wasn't a man anymore, & this anger had suffused into a gray depression down swinging into black moods of destructive intensity.

"I use to go with her. I know what she's like. Sandy's not the same person."

In the weeks gone by, Sandy had taken charge of herself & her affairs in a vicious manner.

"Now she's up there in a cast turning tricks."

The drag butch felt so low as a dyke; eyed sharp kitchen knives, could have slit her wrists. But some kind of weird inner drive kept fueling her forward.

"Sandy's got a pair of those plastic vinyl boots, a couple of dresses. She gets high on pills & sits up at this bar on Diversey Parkway & hooks one trick, then sits there & gets drunk the rest of the night."

The grim circle of dykes listened, shook their heads.

"I didn't tell Esther," Eva continued, blew smoke. "I told Sandy, '*yes,* this is the reason I'm here in your bedroom. Do it for me! Prove it to me!'

"She has this gun, says she's gonna kill herself. She's not fit to live because of what they did to her body. She can't live with herself. Every time she thinks about it, she wants to run and get the gun, or a knife and tear herself apart. That's what she told me. Confidential. I talked her out of it. She's crying. She's holding me & just so angry she's shaking & falling apart. 'You're a man, you still are!' I told her. 'You can't help what happened. It happens to a lot of women! It happens to drag butches! It happens to men. It happens to men in jail, in hospitals and at war. You're not weak because it happened!' She switches off and on on me. Then Sandy grabs me and says she'll give me $50 to go to bed with her because she's going crazy. She can't get a woman—she hasn't tried. She only meets men, and she won't come back to the club because everybody in here knows what happened. I went up to her place and told her, 'Put your $50 back in your pocket.' And that's when I saw how bad she was.—She shows me the gun and boxes & boxes of ammunition: 'If I'd had this, none of this would have happened & I wouldn't be here now. I'd still be down at The Silver Windows with you kids. Now look at me! My legs in a cast, my face is messed up forever, & I'm going to bed with some man every night & saving as much money as I can. Don't ask me what I'm getting ready to do because I don't know. If I can just keep my finger off the trigger and not kill myself first, I'm gonna go kill those bastards.' "

"I tried. I wanted to see Sandy enjoy herself. I wanted it to be like it was between us before; sneaking off from the club to her place, and she loving me before Esther came back. I kept trying, she wouldn't. 'I'm not a butch anymore. You don't understand, Eva! I lay on my back and let men fuck me!'

" 'Are you straight, Sandy?'

" 'No. Hell no.'

" 'Do you still like women?'

" 'Yes.'

" 'Then you're still gay, and you're still a butch.'

" 'No, I'm not.'

"I lay down for her, but she wouldn't. I told her, 'Sandy, please! For me! Give it to me! Esther can't do nothing for me, not like you can!' Sandy just shakes her head. She's frozen up inside, and it's bad."

Later, when Mickey had a few seconds alone in a stall in the toilet, she made the sign of the cross over herself. "Thank you, God, it wasn't me and Lucy! Thank you!"

A dizzy gay boy; a semi-drag, kept tagging along after the gay girls, asking about Sandy, taking it all in secondhand, by eavesdropping, in a kinky fantasy play. He'd beg in his soft voice, "*Please* tell me about her rapes."

"What are you? A boy or a girl?" Mickey growls.

"I'm a boy, but I'm really a woman like you are. I have a pussy; I'm a girl." The pixie-sized boy gestured effeminately; his face was white with makeup his eyebrows plucked out and drawn back in with dark pencil, less like a lady, than a clown or a performer. "It's so romantic... I wish it had happened to me.... It's so terrible, all the difficulties girls have to go thru.... You are so beautiful! I think I love you! Because of all your rapes!"

None of them were free.

So the night went on.

Fade toward 2 A.M. Dim-lit bar, black, gold, red bar lights. About 2 weeks had passed. The handsome young stocky dyke in men's trousers & shoes—and a suitcoat with padded shoulders, black hair slicked back over her ears, beside a beautiful older femme, slender, white skin, huge coiffed beauty-parlor hair, red lipstick & nails. Open-toed spike-heel pumps on her delicate feet. Mickey & Eva are discussing Sandy. "She's just shooting up these pills all the time.... Boils 'em down in a spoon and mainlines 'em.... If you could have seen her a month ago, in the hospital. She was bleeding when I got there, was in shock. Didn't even know her own name! She couldn't talk or move her jaw after what they'd done. And her brain was too punched up to think. Then I drive out to her apartment last week, ask her how she is, she won't even admit she was attacked. She says nothing happened to her. I call her on the phone. 'Sandy, did you go to the hospital so they can check your leg?'—it's still in the cast. She says, 'What for? I feel fine!' A month ago she's cryin', bleeding; now she won't admit it. Maybe she's ashamed. But I wouldn't be! And she shouldn't be! It's not her fault! She didn't even know her own name; now, this week, it's like nothing happened.

"'At least go to the hospital! You got to have tests! See if you caught VD.'

"She says, 'I've never had VD in my life.'"

"I says, 'Well, you may have now! Sandy, go to the hospital, get some penicillin shots!'"

"Then she calls me on the phone 3 A.M., two nights ago. 'I can't sleep! I'm going crazy! That guy tried to choke me! I keep seeing it in my dreams!' The guy was raping her & choking her, trying to kill her at the same time. 'He's got his hands around my neck. A big guy. I was half-dead.'"

"And she's crying. I told her, 'Sandy, he'll go to jail; they'll get him. If the police don't, somebody else will get him. He's crazy. He's sick. They all are, they can't live with themselves—you CAN live with yourself!' So I went back up there last night and tried to get her to be strong again. I asked her, 'Sandy have you been with a woman since this happened?'

"'NO,' she tells me.

"'Then I want to sleep with you…*Butch*.' I told her. "Don't turn me down! I'm a Lady, and Ladies don't like to be ignored." I did it for her because she needs to be strong again.

"I let her make love to me three times. She told me she felt better. Felt at peace. I told her, 'See, being a lesbian is not so bad.' I got her to be a lesbian again, Mickey!"

"How'd she do it to yuh? Like a man or a woman?"

"I pulled her on top of me! Her face was numb, her body so cold, it was eerie—like a corpse. It's the drugs. She's mumbling. Her leg's in the cast caught up in the sheets. I pulled her on top of me. I'm pulling off my clothes. I told her, 'Take me like you use to take me!' I told her, 'Esther pays me $100 a week for this!'"

"You did it out of mercy!"

"You want me?"

"'You want a woman? Then you're still a butch! Now prove it to yourself! COME ON!'"

"She cum?"

"Yes, and she made me cum."

Everybody was proud of Eva.

CHAPTER TWENTY-FOUR

"Let's go to the South Side. They're always partying down there."

The South Side was the black district.

3 A.M., Silver Windows had to close because it had only a 3 o'clock liquor license—tonight was Saturday—and two tables full of gay kids planned to hit another bar that would stay open until 5.

"Let's go to the South Side. The Coloreds, they have some clubs down there that are always *full* of people!"

"Something's always happening down there, even on Monday nights!"

So a band of gay boys & girls piles into two cars, and heads down the Outer Drive past the Loop thru the Near South Side, farther into the black area to a bar on 63rd Street not far from Stoney Island Avenue.

They came out to the ghetto that night past high faded broadsides of unpainted-wood 4-story apartment buildings; two cars returning down the Outer Drive prearranged to meet, careening along side by side. Now they stood in the street in a big group, in high energy among the African-American passersby—the same as up north—the streets belong to the night people. A loquacious fag squeals in falsetto, his voice pierces the night. Jungle drums. Strong beat of African music. Mickey looks around warily.

Smoke fills the air like a building was on fire. It is sheets of smoke from an all-night barbecue. The sweet scent of meat hung in the air.

Within the hot black night, the black stud Stella was in her element. Junior butch Shorty hollered, "I'M A PIMP!" Hooting & mimicking the nightclub denizens transacting their trade along 63rd underneath the spiderlike shadow of the Elevated train track which ran there; staunch, the baby butch provided her share of muscle; she hoofed along. They walked to the club in a tight band side by side, Lucy in the middle; making them seem even more invincible on this strange territory. Their voices hung in air trailing them as did the sound of the clicks of their boot-heels sharp staccato, then dissolved. As lax cats the blacks in colorful clothes pushed sinuous thighs in conjunction with their rhythmic, trash music, talking soul jive & pausing to watch the queer newcomers as they paraded past. Then they were there. A female transvestite in gold jacket and trousers sauntered into the doorway to the club ahead of them talking to a faggot, and the way they talked to each other—in vernacular & in a smooth musical way was as if to remind each other they were black as well as gay.

Mickey let herself into the door & into a din of music & noise. A round bar ran thru the center of the club, tables alongside; the whole place packed with mostly gay black males. A stage was set up behind the bar in the middle with a Drag Queen DJ who played hit records, sang, & alternately was a band with a live singer & shows. Mickey stood within the cluster of white faces and watched them. They could really dance. Really put their bodies & souls into what they were doing.

Drag butches like Stella, their crotches packed with socks, like males; and glamorous dark women in satin dresses—a smattering few thru the crowd. And some of them were men. Sweet soul sounds surrounded by the boogie night. "Do you want any diet pills?" A half-knowing look on her face, Stella went about her work. "Do any of you people want to buy some reds?" Apologetically. "I get them from my doctor, they're good..." She lied. Diet pills—commonly known as speed.

A sea full of black outlaws—gays & nightlifers; and here they were, white rebels with a cause. This was the sector rumored about in the conversation of whites. The black ghetto. It was like a plague of locusts buzzing in a hive in the inner city. Slums here were worse than up north. A place of newspaper headlines; where rats ate up an unwatched child's face; and teenage girls leaving a church dance are killed by gangs' cross fire.

A sissy dipped and prance; black muscular body stripped to the waist, light on his feet; with a gay blond boy who was his momentary companion.

Woodlawn. A manic corner on 63rd Street. Windy City. Psyche of the black universe; a current of conversation buzzed thru the crowd with the same lisps, and identical falsetto as white gay men, but with a black accent. Gin, whiskey, a bottle of beer. Sodas. Their table filled with glasses. People go by, sinuous, with a leopard's relaxed air down here in this jungle under the El.

"It's under the El tracks, just like Shrimpie's!" Shorty observes. Quieted, awed, the baby butch was reserved tonight, and hovered close to the safety of their almost-all-white table.

Mighty, mighty Woodlawn night. Womb of civilization. Black love. The gays sang as they danced, chants inherited from tribal destinies ingrained into their genes in an undercurrent. Songs that sounded like hymns, synchronized to a lifting, inspired beat. Lucy, her red hair shimmering under a bath of purple lights, sparkling as if diamonds were set in it, sat up close to handsome Mickey in shirt & tie watching the sight with open eyes. Shorty danced beside the table, on guard.

For all the powerful deep love & soulful music, this was also a maniac corner. Cutthroat blacks. A prison population. A poverty land of little promise, and death before The Birth. The end zone.

Got near dawn—fog winding under ankles in bars was smoke. Soon they'd be back in the streets, walking under the sheltering structure of crisscross iron beams, their little band huddled together for protection; whites in no-man's-land; the winding streets that evoke a psyche of a society all to itself. Magnificent, the sun would burst at the end of the train track at Stoney Island, up over the beach there, rise to the fire-escape building scope and the din and clatter of the regular day begin—black gay folk dispersed to their homes all over the South Side; gray morning & niggers hollering in ignorance, fussing on the curb; whores dragging their ruffled plumage. Billboards blinked thru the fog from over the lake in a foreign symbol of Capitalism—Cash—a stranger to this hard-luck economy—picturing an expensive car that only a few government workers or successful criminals could afford; down here within the poverty & inhuman conditions. Lucy, dreamy, patted her red hair into place, walking between two butches vigilantly on guard; she pictured the Apache, the python, the heeled buffalo—a herd running in isolated time-stood-still. Extinct. Aurora, of the eagle. "The white man promised the Indian land. Territory. And peace." Lucy mumbles. They're nearing the cars. "Just like he did to these people. The Coloreds. And they went to his reservation, and were confined there—in death. A slow dying of the race. The Apaches didn't make no bargains. They fought with bows & arrows & the white man's guns." These were her alcohol-frenzied thoughts. Lucy, of a subgroup; composite to the frantic mirror of white civilization that cast its death hand, & its shadow over this dark society in a negative.

Walked up to the cars & piled in; headed back up the Outer Drive. It was dawn. The writing on the walls of vain fame—BLACK LOVE!—reminded them they were in alien territory. Then it gradually would grow white. Mickey had seen how the poor people lived under the El tracks southeast, like they did beneath the El tracks north. Blight of houses, the poor, the same everywhere, but that these were called "niggers." They had come up from the ghetto in a little while. Mickey wondered, 'Is it worth living in a poor flat raising children just for them to become permanent poor? People with short lives, drug addicts, prison inmates, prostitutes? We live in a room as poor or worse, but I am going to find a way out of there, & I'll take Lucy with me when I go. I'll make our lives worth it somehow.' Lucy was at her side in the back of the car as the lake whizzed by them. "Lucy! This is where women like The Supremes got their start! All that music & dancing? All those poor people out in the street—you know how they sing & walk & dance & talk jive all at the same time? That's where their soul comes from! I think they have more of it down there than we do up here!"

CHAPTER TWENTY-FIVE

So Mickey Leonardi ran home to the warm center of Lucy's thighs; to be at home with her; at peace.

Warm eyes; arms encircled each other. Mickey would penetrate Lucy with three fingers, fuck her hard & fast as a pumping piston until she moaned and twisted her body & trembled & shouted, then pulled Mickey's hair and yelled "DON'T STOP!" as the thrills kept shooting thru her vagina; and she burst loose with a vaginal orgasm. Then the redhead would slide down Mickey's thighs and lick her tongue into the butch's pussyfolds so fire spread all over the teenager's body; & when she was ready, Mickey got on top, bearing down with her swollen womanhood on Lucy's receptive cunt; who received her cum, & would then roll off; lay side by side, totally relaxed in her soul.

Go on long walks by the beach & think. Problems assailed them—but her aggressive sex drive had not given out. Returned to Lucy with renewed lust in her loins, and kept the redhead sexually satisfied so she wouldn't look at no one else during her days & nights of safari thru the bars of hell in winoland & gay bars of The Life.

"Be careful if you fuck Mickey with the dildo. If she likes it & it brings out the woman in her, she'll get weak, and lay back & you'll have to do everything." Had been Eva's words.

The butch let Lucy fuck her with their cock, lay back, was a woman, and showed no signs of losing her butchness. "Mickey is as much butch as she ever was, but she won't get a job. She's happy with welfare, I guess." Lucy was talkative; it showed her worry. Something she never liked to admit she did—be in the rat race. Take life seriously, or worry.

At home she watched *I Love Lucy* on TV.

Not five weeks had passed since the attack; Sandy had got her life back together the best way she knew how—she was whoring.

Lucy was full of news that afternoon; she had talked to Eva. "Sandy is turning tricks uptown out of some straight bar on Diversey. Has a deal with the bartender there. She sits up in the bar all day & turns 'em out of there. And she's still a lesbian, and she's still angry about getting raped, & she's just making money. A lot of money, 'cause her leg's broke, so she can get a Disability Check from the government as well as hustle; and she don't know why the hell she wants all this money, but Eva says she bought another gun. A 5-shot .38 caliber revolver. And she's thinking about putting her stuff in storage & leaving the apartment—she hates it because she turns the tricks there, it's right near the bar; and stopping tricking, & then she don't know what she'll do."

"She still sleeps with Eva?"

"Yes. Eva's laying down for her so she can get her... manhood back...as you call it, *Mickey*. Anyway, now she's fucking Eva, and finally it's the right way—Eva use to give Sandy money Esther gave her, remember? Now they're like you & me; they just make love, they don't hustle each other."

'Ha. So she sits up there, turns one trick and drinks the rest of the night, alone in a straight bar. What a hell of a price to pay for the easy life!' The butch thought privately, but didn't say anything because, as usual Mickey felt guilty for not trying to find a job.

Lucy talked on blithely, imitating a trick: "They come in: 'My wife doesn't understand me! I've got this problem!'"

"How does she get 'em? Is her hair still short?"

"She's got two dresses; she wears earrings and makeup —it's a good disguise, but she still looks butch—Eva says. And she gets prescription drugs from the pharmacy & she's like a zombie. Eva goes to bed with her whenever Esther isn't around, and half the time she can't fuck, she's too high. Eva tells Sandy: 'You been in the Navy, you know how to work a regular job; you're not like these young kids down at The Silver Windows who don't know nothing.' But she won't work. She sells pussy to men, then takes off her dress, wipes off her makeup & puts on men's trousers and a shirt & tie and Eva comes over & they take a cab & sit up somewhere and Sandy gets very high on pills & liquor. That's how she does it. Trick. Gets high first. The drugs lower her inhibitions. Then she can let herself get fucked. So by the time she & Eva go to bed, she is too stoned to fuck Eva most of the time; and when she can't hates herself when she gets up the next morning, so she takes more pills & wants to kill herself whenever she looks in the mirror—and Eva says she has two guns now, a .38 and a

.45, and boxes of ammunition, and she's gonna make herself psycho if she keeps on, and that she's dangerous."

In her mind's eye, Mickey saw the scene: a straight bar on the Northwest Side of the city—yellow lit, mellow music of a crooner on the jukebox, a mannish female, short hair, in a dress, drinking a glass of scotch, holding it her same way, with tough short-nailed hands.

"Lucy, if I went up to that bar and offered Sandy $15, she'd go to bed with me?"

"DON'T YOU DARE!" Lucy slapped Mickey's arm. "I'm jealous! Mickey, you wouldn't really take our last money and do something like that! I don't deny you! You don't need anybody else! Besides, it would kill her! Sandy don't want nobody to see her like that! It's suppose to be a secret!"

Now the last week before welfare, when the food was gone, they'd have to get in the breadline & wait in a line of stinking, drunk, sick or feeble people to eat a meal which had to last them all day. The last five days before their checks came were hell.

And of course these times, Mickey'd get a strange reaction from her femme. "Let me lick you."

"No."

"Let me use my hand, then."

"No."

"OK, just lay there and spread your legs & move for me then!" And Mickey climbs on her and goes ahead.

"Damn! You didn't cum so fast, did you!" Lucy says peevishly, then is silent. Mad.

The things we do for money. Mistakes the two women made & how sorry they were after. Sorrow is a great humbler of people. It brings them to their knees. So there was sorrow in the respect that Mickey never should have let Lucy do what she thought she had to do—but gave in because it was supposed to save their home, but it helped destroy them instead.

It was the end of the month. Too many missed meals.

"There's a couple of janes down at Shrimpie's—what about that?"

"I DON'T CARE IF IT'S A WOMAN, I DON'T WANT
YOU FUCKING NOBODY BUT ME!"

"Well, one only used to buy me drinks if I let her put her
hands on me & sit next to me all night. It don't matter if I'm
with a butch or not! Let's go down there, Mickey! She'll get
me drinks! I'll let you drink out of my glass, and we can listen
to some music and have fun!"

So, here's Mickey standing in the doorway of Shrimpie's—
known as The Palm Gardens—watching the El go past, shake,
rattle & roll; creaky cars around the rail, turn at Halsted
Street. Behind her, inside, at the horseshoe-shaped bar, Lucy
laughs; red hair piled up on her head, earrings flash a prism of
lights; her best fashion clothes, her hand under the bar
stroking the trousered thigh of a wrinkled, toothless old dyke
whose sporting her to drink after drink & Lucy is filled with
love, & estrogen & is having a merry time on the jane's
money; and it's a shame, but it's shades of NYC & Miami,
even if is a woman; and there's another old geezer jane who
Lucy use to sleep with & swipe extra cash out of the woman's
wallet after sex when she fell asleep, who wants to see her
again, seeing Lucy's fair game tonight, tapping her on the
shoulder urgently, & beckoning & whispering, when the
other old crone-dyke's back is turned—she misses her & her
loving arms. 'I should tell her, "Go ahead, turn ten tricks a
night"—there's men in here, too—there's no short supply of
them, ever. If we get the money, fuck everything else. That's
all that matters!' Mickey was so mad.

So that period of their lives, Lucy & Mickey went down
North Avenue into the sun over in the rough area near
Halsted Street, populated by poor whites, blacks & Puerto
Ricans; there where the El lets off & the gentleman's tearoom
there is known & frequented by male fags; and the two
women sold their blood, swiped change off the bar, got
welfare—Lucy was determined to keep her brown roots red,
and also, liked to chippie with drugs purchased at the drug-
lady's house once in a blue moon and nod off in a junkie
dream.

CHAPTER TWENTY-SIX

They'd been dancing, talking; gay gals & guys swimming in a sea of music at The Silver Windows, when suddenly the lights went on!

Eight men, big, older, simultaneously opened up their jackets to reveal their silver badges; CHICAGO METROPOLITAN POLICE DEPARTMENT.

It was a raid.

Some of the police were pretty. Fags in face & form, but living a lie because they didn't allow homosexuals on the force.

It happened around 11:45 P.M.

The lights went up, which made everybody stop. Deathly silence. Two minutes pass; a buzz of conversation resumes. "Somebody says we can't get out of here!"

"It's a raid!"

Then a voice barks: "REMAIN WHERE YOU ARE. NOBODY IS ALLOWED TO LEAVE. STAY WHERE YOU'RE SITTING." At the bar next to Mickey is a big barrel-chested man—a weight lifter; his face is powdered; eyebrows tweezed in narrow arches—a fag. Pulls open his dark blue sweater & there's the badge: he's on the police force. Plainclothes. A Vice Cop. A freakish smile plays on his lips. Adrenaline from the scene is exciting him in a weird enjoyment. And the butch hadn't even noticed him there before.

Two police wagons wait out front to haul gay kids off to jail. Two squad cars; cops in blue uniforms & guns swarm in the door.

When the blue & white uniform police came in they meant business. Bullets on gunbelts, nightsticks. Keys swinging at their sides. Official star emblazoned on their chest.

A cop blocks the entrance; three steps up, he towers over the room—all eyes look to the exit & back; realize there's no escape.

The club was crowded with young gays. Some underage, like Shorty, who carried a false ID. Most 18 thru 24. The owner, Bobby was only 28.

The cops went thru the crowd selecting all the femmes. Females & effeminate males. Made them stand in two separate circles facing out & handcuffed each person in the circle to their neighbor. The charge was going to be suspicion of prostitution & frequenting a house of suspected illicit activity.

Police think nothing is so low as a lesbian or homosexual man. That they are criminals & should be treated like whores, tho no soliciting could have been happening—it was simply a crowd of kids having fun. In the eyes of society, lesbians were lawbreakers and scum & sluts just because they fucked each other.

They let one person go free.

Esther said she'd been driving by & had just stopped in to use the bathroom. Esther was so much older than the rest; a middle-aged Jewish businesswoman, that the police believed her, and the cop at the entrance unlocked the door, stepped aside & let her out; her alone—leaving Eva standing in the circle handcuffed to Lucy and ten other femmes.

The police unlocked the handcuff on one side of each woman, led them out in pairs; then one by one they had to climb into the back of the wagon; door slammed shut & they were driven away to jail.

Same with the effeminate men in a separate wagon. It was a nightmare.

Three hours of processing everybody left in the bar. Police set up a table with report sheets; all the patrons were made to come thru single file, and show identification. The cop wrote down descriptions, information, address, phone number. "Because what you're doing is illegal & we need to know everything about you in case we have to come looking for you again."

Line slowly processed past the cop at the table to the door—and freedom.

Mickey was released at 3 A.M.

Wind rustled her hair & she walked away from the club, fast. She could still see Lucy's eyes looking back in the black night under the star-filled sky.

Somewhere in interstellar connections—the grapevine of

the underground—a lot of gay kids had been warned a raid was going to happen, and many of them had not showed up, or were tipped off at the last minute by friends and got out early. But bearded Bobby didn't warn the patrons inside his club because he had to let the Vice feel they'd caught somebody, or there'd be hell to pay the next time the club opened.

Eva got released in an hour, Esther was waiting at the Police Station, bail money in hand. The rest of the kids had to stay locked up all weekend until the judge saw them Monday morning and all charges were dropped.

The charges were shoddy & insufficient. Not enough for a judge to take them to trial. But getting a conviction was not the purpose of the raid.

This was harassment. A police tactic to keep gays from ever having a public life.

"So now where are we gonna go?" Mickey snarled. Red pulse beat across the room from the tavern sign outside. Seemed lately the butch was perpetually angry. Knowing there was nothing for women. Gay men were the lucky ones; they had a few bars for them alone, dotted among the millions for straights.

So, soon, a lot of them were down at Shrimpie's, for the interim; for want of a better place.

A few black pimps, a few white bisexual hookers and some old janes hung out here regularly. Jungle life. Under the El tracks, with some knifings & brawls.

This gathering point was not a focus of gay power. A cut way below what the other club had been. Many of the kids wouldn't go there & they dropped out of the nightlife, so the gay crowd was dispersed.

Mickey had a habit of standing out front by the doorway to watch the night & think. See a car of gay kids pull up; they'd take a look at the front of the place—the neighborhood it was in, littered, shabby; the kind of rough straight men walking past, or maybe a hooker; and they'd pull off and wouldn't even go in.

The Twilight Club, the notorious syndicate bar where big money exchanged hands picked up some of these searching cars full of gays; and the Show & Tell, a nice bar up on

Diversey Parkway; almost all women, but with no dancing at all; & much too far away & difficult for the poor Lucy and Mickey to get to.

So here they sit, right next to the gutter on the lunatic fringe of the world as it spun thru the galaxies on the rim of the Milky Way. A crescent moon. Stars dot the sky. El train rumbles, shaking the buildings below.

Dykes with their tiny muscles & no reserve cash built up in the bank to protect them; here in the city street life, in role, in the '50s. Unless she would hide in a skirt behind her closet door, meeting some girl on the campus of a university, she'd be alone. And Mickey wasn't so privileged. And with few places to meet, without a woman, just dying on the vine; juices dry up inside; growing bitter-mean.

Been a murder committed outside The Twilight Club.

Lucy & Mickey sit at Shrimpie's, alum: when they hear the news.

"SANDY SHOT THREE MEN! SHE'S BEING HELD FOR FIRST-DEGREE MURDER IN COOK COUNTY JAIL! NO BAIL!"

"Sandy took a cab down to the Twilight high on pills, talked to some men there; they didn't do nothing, just tricks looking for sex. She was fuckin' mad—she hates men. She was very angry and not high enough to put up with their bullshit, so she gets a couple of 'em outside, pulls out two guns from under her coat, and starts blazing away; BAM BAM BAM BAM BAM! Shot three men. One of 'em's dead!"

Two men went to the hospital by ambulance; one critical. The third went out of life; strapped to a stretcher, a stiffening corpse, white face now ash gray. Lifeless. A puppet in a business suit—zipped up in a body bag—that went directly to the morgue.

A blaze of bullets reigned in a 15-second synopsis of time; the johns bled profusely. Blood stained the cement sidewalk in front of the Twilight.

Anger was gone. Her face flat, emotionless, hair wild. Sandy was led to the squad car in handcuffs.

As the Coroner's Office prepared the corpse, the third man, who had a minor wound, gave his frightened testimony. He was blue with shock & fear. The second victim was in critical condition; his blood had drained away, soaking dark crimson red into the pavement; he was wheeled on a gurney into the back of an ambulance which, siren screaming, rushed him to a hospital.

Face set hard, pale, Sandy sat in the squad car; her leg in a cast poking out from under men's trousers. Sandy, brown hair slicked back behind her ears. Handcuffed, a strange smile on her face.

A grille separates Sandy from the front section of the police car; an officer, cap with badge tilted back on his head, writes up the report on a clipboard & they pull off. The dyke turns to the barred window & takes her last look at the streets for a long time.

"So drunk, says she don't remember any of it."

"Blood splattered everywhere. There's still bloodstains out in front, I went by and saw it myself!"

"They should put a plaque with 3 stars on it & Sandy's name in front!"

"Everybody's talking about it! Kids are going by the club to look at the stains on the cement. They don't go in, just stand outside & look at where it happened!"

"She was high on pills! She was out of her mind! She don't remember doing nothing!"

"Sandy's had firearms training—she's been in the Navy, remember?"

A dyke told a dyke told a fag told another dyke—soon the whole gay Near North Side was telling the story of the assault & murder. How Sandy had been arrested and taken to jail—it was a major topic besides when the next gay bar would open—and the story changed every time you heard it, and depending on who you heard it from.

"She's gonna claim self-defense!"

"Naw! She was attacked herself 2 months ago—she's gonna plead insanity!"

"SHE'S MAKIN' 'EM STIFF AT THE TWILIGHT

CLUB! BANG! BANG! BANG! *RIGORMORTIS!*" Shorty yells.

All dykes at the club were vindicated by what the sandy haired butch had done. She became a role model behind prison bars. Strong, to go as far as murder, to punish her unknown assailants, to vindicate herself against a lousy straight fucked-up world. Had been so far down on her luck, then; a strong, bad butch, she had pulled herself up and got back her masculinity.

"BLAM! BLAM!" Shorty swaggered around drawing imaginary guns from the hip.

"SHE'S MAKIN' 'EM STIFF AT THE TWILIGHT CLUB!" Shorty shoots her imaginary revolvers from hip holsters. "BLAM BLAM! BLAM BLAM! BLAM BLAM! She pumped 9 bullets into 'em!" And went round & round the horseshoe-shaped bar amid golden lights & amber liquor bottles retelling the story of Sandy's fame & shooting 'em up.

"Sandy is becoming a legend. It seems like she was right here in the bar, just yesterday. She blew those bastards away. And the Prosecutor is going for life in prison."

A dyke had slipped & fallen, but had regained her manhood.

Shorty's voice hollers above the din of the crowd; "SHE'S PUMPIN' IN THE TWILIGHT!—PUMPS 9 BULLETS INTO 'EM! BLAM BLAM!"

Sandy had risen up against her oppressors, committed a murder.

And set her soul free!

Chapter Twenty-Seven

As if doing push-ups, Mickey lowered her body down between her lover's legs; forced her swollen womanhood down on Lucy's cunt, got hard contact and rode. Lucy pulled Mickey's firm, warm ass into her & thrust her clit up underneath. Their pussies were the hottest part of their bodies & they were pressed together, juicy, wet. Mickey cupped one of Lucy's breasts briefly as she worked, panting, sweating; their bodies matching movements with each other, fell into their familiar easy rhythm, Mickey's butt going around and around between Lucy's legs, fast, faster, thrusting her clit into wet pussy & the two joined together in a powerful orgasm.

After they were done, Mickey loved the way Lucy might slide down, put her face right next to the fuzzy hairy mound, sniff her sex, and just lay there, nose & mouth in the triangle of her thighs and mound & breathe her aroma—as if she couldn't get enough of woman-scent.

"Mickey, honey, let me love you."

After penetration by the matron in jail, Mickey had had doubt about herself as a butch—but discovered tho she lay on her back, she did not lose her aggressive butch strength, not at all. It was an extra dimension to her sexuality to take private pleasure in this hotel room Lucy had decorated into a tie-dye palace. To drop the swagger along with her trousers, and lie back, nude, head on a pillow, thighs parted, in anticipation. Sexcitement. In uncertainty of what Lucy was going to do to her next. To give up control & surrender. This yielding made it even more enjoyable. To feel her nipples sucked until they grew hard; and feel a plump wet tongue licking between her thighs as hot currents of pleasure ebbed over her from head to toe.

Her submissive femme did it good. They'd lie side by side, Lucy would hesitate, lick the head of their dick, erotically, wet it with spit, then slide it along inside the lips of Mickey's pussy; stroke up & down; as the butch stares up at the ceiling, hands folded behind her head, tingling in white-hot lust of expectation. Then the butch felt her fumble around with the cocks' rubber dickhead at her hole. Lucy pushed it in with a revolving motion; shoved it in & out a few inches, in & out, then screwed it in deep down inside. She'd then bring the cock almost all the way out, & plunge it all the way in to the hilt. Mickey moaned in ecstasy with each thrust.

Lucy's fingernails were long, except for the 2 middle fingers of her right hand which were absolutely short. This had started upon instruction, just after she met Mickey. All the rest of her nails were long & painted red; totally feminine, but these two were for Mickey's cunt. It was a clue for anybody who might see, when Lucy had both hands on the bar; and they might ask in mock innocence; "Why are those two fingernails always short?"

Often times out on safari thru skid-row haunts, Lucy would get very aroused and need to feel Mickey's pussy so bad.

Bleary eyed at the bar, a shot of vodka gaping in front of her, surrounded by toothless hags and alkies and immersed in a blue mood—that old loneliness of the past—when she had wanted a woman so long, so long—and here was a butch at her side! The redhead would teeter at the bar on her backless gold pumps, pull Mickey's sleeve: "Come on, baby! Please!"

So the two would stagger back to the toilet, go inside, throw themselves up against the door, since it didn't lock, and the butch let Lucy do anything to her.

Alcohol on her breath, breathing hard, Lucy's hand petted Mickey's nipples; pressed on the cloth of her white shirt & the binder underneath, till they stood out hard, like little knobs on her full, flattened breasts. A blast of alcoholic breath belches out of her red-painted mouth; "I wanna be a butch! Lemme feel you! Lemme! I'll try your job for a change and see what it's like!"

"You can put your fingers in me, baby! The short ones," the butch replies calmly. Unbuckles her belt buckle & lets her trousers slide down to her knees. Lucy weaves on her high heels, leans down stroking the butch's wet pubic hair & penetrates her carefully.

Mickey leans against the door. Her dark eyes squint closed, head arches back, mouth opens in a gasp; handsome, reflecting passion. Feeling Lucy's fingers in her pussy in the skid-row club.

Urine on the floor in yellow pools, stuck pieces of toilet paper; the lovers amid the stink of piss.

Lucy's fingers slid in the butch's wet hole. The redhead lusted, wanting the pungent smell of her mate; dropped down on her knees, gold pumps skid on the floor, & buried her face in furry black cunthair where she worked off her lipstick for 20 minutes sucking & licking the butch's cunt & clit, then climbs back up Mickey's body. The butch holds her tight & Lucy goes in again with fingers, fast, probing her wet smooth channel, fast, faster, at the same time banging the heel of her hand on Mickey's clit as her fingers go in & out moving inside. Then using her thumb on the pearl-shaped clit as Mickey had taught her to do in the love of a woman; in an intense fuck, full of love & drunken kisses while pressed against the toilet door in defense from hell outside of drunken hags & boozers clamoring to gain entry so they could piss; fucking her cunt, stroking her clit till Mickey's pale thighs trembled & jerked upward in orgasm.

On the run to the next bottle of alcohol.

Mickey & Lucy used cock as much as Mickey ever had with her whores in Miami. They used it in ways they couldn't if it was actually a man's dick. Not even strapped on. There was an angle of entry that stimulated Lucy's clit and gave her a guaranteed vaginal orgasm every single time. And the speed of thrust maintained by Mickey's hand in precision piston action brought her over the cosmic threshold repeatedly. They could twirl it around, run the shaft all the way between her legs up her butthole & back; keep it hard for hours—forever. And thus the cock took on a life of its own. And an identity which diverged from being a male facsimile mimicking hetero-sexual sex, into a vagina-defined object used for ecstasy.

"Now I see why Esther calls hers 'Rose.'"

It was theirs. A new adventure in lesbian sex; a new frontier in self-discovery & in each other.

Mickey had never been kissed all over her body so much before.

Lucy went round the world 2 times. Feathery licks of her tongue all over the butch's body; & kisses, too, so the next morning her mouth was sore.

A slow & steady glow of sexuality permeated their days.

Basked in sensual touch. As days grew late toward evening, the hours became underlined with a consistent horniness whose promise would be fulfilled late at night—in Lucy's arms. Love's stinky jungle flowers, their cunts busting loose in fiery mutual orgasm.

At first butch Mickey took her woman over and over all day long, so Lucy finally put a limit on this & allowed Mickey to have one daily fuck—which might result in five orgasms between them.

At the end of the month, when food ran out and Lucy was despondent from not having cash to go have fun in the bars & sail the night sea of drug houses, Lucy didn't want to have sex at all. And Mickey would force her & cum roughly. Not very fulfilling; & feel guilty. And desperately lick and stroke Lucy, wanting her to cum also, & the redhead would push her off, mad, and then wouldn't speak to her.

When times were flush—cans of food piled on their table, room rent paid—then Lucy knelt on the floor, giving oral sex to Mickey who held on to the iron rail of the bed, hips pumping in vigorous motion, moving her clit-cock into the mouth of her woman; and felt gusts of hot breath from her nostrils on her thighs, in a wonderful dominant experience.

And continued working on the fist-fuck, loosening her cunt nightly.

Other things began to change in their relationship.

Just as before, when she'd tried to go to the bars alone, Lucy was getting sick of the gay life. Sick of police harassment & petty bickering of gay kids. Yet fully, undeniably, loving Mickey.

So, after one bad evening at The Palm Gardens, Lucy spits it out; red hair falling on the sides of her bedraggled beehive, green veins sticking out in her neck from anger, eyes big: "MICKEY, I JUST DON'T WANT TO GO TO THAT BAR ANYMORE! I HATE GAY PEOPLE! I HATE THEM! I HATE THE WAY THE FEMMES LOOK AT ME & TALK ABOUT ME BEHIND MY BACK! AND EVERYBODY'S HAVING PROBLEMS ALL THE TIME! AND THERE'S NO PLACE TO GO BUT THAT ONE LOUSY BAR! IF I'D KNOWN BEING GAY WAS THIS ROUGH, I'D NEVER HAVE LET YOU GET ME INTO IT!"

Mickey wanted to slug her. "SO YOU WOULD HAVE STAYED STRAIGHT?"

"*No!* I'm not straight!" Lucy cried, quieting somewhat—

realizing her mistake. "I just wouldn't live a gay life! We could just love each other at home and go to straight bars and pretend we're normal like everybody else. Except you're such a butch, it ruins everything!"

"THEN GET A GODDAMN FEMME LIKE EVA TO SCREW YOU, BITCH!"

"*NO!* I WANT YOU TO SCREW ME! I WANT YOU TO LAY ME, MICKEY!—IT'S JUST THAT I CAN'T TAKE IT NO MORE! THIS LIFE! THE WAY PEOPLE STARE AT US! THE WAY THEY TREAT US LIKE DIRT! *I CAN'T STAND IT!*"

All the churches, media & institutions of society were aimed at destroying their love. Using scorn, hate & violence to try to take their life's blood. To not allow them to live.

And the final straw that broke the camel's back. By the end of the month, when the two women were desperate, poking under multicolor tie dye curtains for a radio Mickey had found on the beach; picking thru the wooden boxes painted rainbow colors which held their things for soda bottles they could return to get the cash deposit, looking thru the room for stuff they could sell to buy food; & the last thing they saw was Lucy's body, & Lucy thinks about selling herself; & Mickey's soul cried out *NO!* Because she knew Lucy wasn't above doing it.

Men live in a rough & insensitive, brutal & active world. They have sex differently, as direct gratification—at any cost. Some are violent & like to kill people. Mickey had passed as a man enough—she knew how roughly they treated each other. She didn't want Lucy turning tricks! "Then I'll have to be right there with you & guard you!"

"Oh, wow!"

"I don't want no men putting their dicks in you. I'm the only one going in you—don't forget!" Angry, jabbed her finger against Lucy's pubic mound. "This is mine!"

So that's when Mickey lost her confidence & began using her nightly fuck to get between Lucy's legs and have sex with her until she was raw. Not just animal need, but an urging in her mind to do it, sex, then an hour later turn Lucy over again, rough—breaking the rule—get on top, fuck her cunt till after the 3rd orgasm she couldn't cum quick no more & Lucy had already cum & is waiting for her to finish. But Mickey is straining & instead of being a masterful Top Butch, has lapsed into a desperate fantasy that she is raping Lucy which she ordinarily doesn't have to do to get off, but must; lying on her, taking her legs by the ankles and jerking her legs wide; sweat rolling down her shoulders; teeth gritted like a grinning skeleton as she humps, and finally makes Lucy go down, suck her clit for a half-hour—proving futile—and at last straps on the cock and sticks it to her from behind—in her pussy while using an index and middle finger in her ass & fucks both holes for another half-hour, till Lucy's body is convulsing & she's crying: "PLEASE, MICKEY! NO MORE! You're so rough, you keep on doing it! I don't know why! What are you trying to prove? I've never had a man as rough as you are, or do it this much! You're worse than anybody! PLEASE STOP!" And held her, crying, mouth contorted in a little line crookedly attempting to dam back tears. *"PLEASE!"* Hugged her butch in a tight embrace. "I don't know you anymore, you're a different person! You scare me! I don't know what's happening! This sex thing is scary! And you're so aggressive! You're threatening! You're not gentle like you use to be!"

And Mickey would grumble, jealously; & grab her by the shoulders & push her down on the bed for more. Mouth grim, eyes focused on Lucy's body with a serious intent.

Lucy says, "Well, if you're so damn jealous of me turning a trick, it's stupid! They never get this much of my time as you. I *never* did it this much with a boyfriend. You're way ahead of everybody! So why do you have to keep proving it? I'm yours honey, and you're hurting me! I'm worn out! Please stop!" And Mickey's holding her like a shield from the world, like a protection from the cold-blooded pain there; but twisting Lucy & hurting her like the pain she felt inside—in the process. Squeezing her so tight. "PLEASE!" The line of the redhead's mouth quivered and broke. Tears rolled out of her big eyes.

So Mickey stops.

Falls asleep; and wakes. Hours have past. A terrible dream left its input, fresh in her conscious mind—that she was losing Lucy.

Room runs red; lights flashed thru the tie-dyed curtains and torn shade. Mickey hurts emotionally. Lay tossing and turning at her side of the bed. Lucy slept covered by a sheet. Back turned. Tears roll down her cheeks that the teenage butch doesn't see. Mickey is tense inside. Both females haven't had feelings this intense since their troubled childhoods.

It was the pain of an animal for its mate. A much higher, more sensitive primate who had a big red heart; this human being.

In pain for her mate she felt she was losing.

CHAPTER TWENTY-EIGHT

One day Mickey's out on a walk, waits at a stoplight; a red Cadillac convertible with the top down drives up, a man inside; car jerks to a stop—it's a Mafia man. He yells out: "HEY! YER' ONE OF THE KIDS FROM THE SILVER WINDOWS! THERE'S A NEW CLUB GONNA OPEN NEXT WEEK—AT 169 DIVISION STREET! TELL ALL THE KIDS! TELL EVERYBODY!" Then the Cadillac zooms off.

Their dancing feet had been stilled. The laughing, gossiping crowd had lost its power of assembly; their right to be together was gone—to talk, to love—snatched from them by the long blue arm of the Law; since The Silver Windows had been closed. A sign on a piece of paper tacked to the door, fluttering outside: CLOSED BY ORDER OF THE ALCOHOLIC BEVERAGE COMMISSION—LICENSE REVOKED. Now, again, their dancing feet were set free!

The 169 Club was a real toilet.

Slowly the word got out. Shorty, the miniature mannish dyke with a crew cut & lumber jacket, recruited gay kids whenever stumbling on some—in a semi-gay restaurant, or seated at one of the hard-core Mafia clubs.

"SAY! Yuh heard since the Windows closed 'n' everybody went away—well, the Syndicate opened a new one for us! They got a jukebox, women, the same as before. Everybody's comin' back!"

The new club was run by a front man for the Syndicate; his name appeared on the license, but they really owned it. Bobby, a gay male and former owner of a real gay club had been bumped out of the picture.

This new place was a sewer. Dim lit, black walls with white plaster showing thru, they were so worn. Seedy. Red lights, a door that drooped on its hinges. No sign in front, just the miraculous numbers 169 on the front. "ONE *SIXTY-NINE*? They must have PAID somebody to get that address!"

So all the same kids are partying once again. A pool table. A decrepit place; rainwater drips in thru the ceiling and has eaten away a large piece of the floor. There's a hole in the women's toilet cubicle with a chair placed in front so drunken dykes won't fall into it; and the neighborhood's worse. "It's a cesspool! But it's the only cesspool we got."

Everything is frantic; a whirl, a blur.

Seemed all the summer was going. Taste of autumn in the air; you could see it in the leaves. Feel it in intuition just around the bend.

Gay kids were whirling in the wind. And Sandy had gone to jail for manslaughter, a lesser charge than murder one. A hero, framed in gold. She rose out of the fire of hell, in triumph.

Mickey said; "She rose out of hell to victory!"

Shorty said; "She's got the biggest dick of 'em all, huh, Mick? BLAM! BLAM! SHOOTIN' 'EM DEAD!" The sawed-off runt thrust her hips in & out in a motion of fucking; & drew the imaginary six-shooters. "SHE'S SHOOTIN' IN THE TWILIGHT! SHOOT IT, BABY! SHOOT YER WAD WITH ME, HONEY! SHOOT IT WIT' ME ANYTIME, SANDY! I'M ALL YOURS! BLAM! BLAM!"

So Shrimpie's, with its El train clanking above, lost its gay crowd—all but the stragglers & prosties & part-time lezzies & their butch pimps.

"I want some money!" Lucy stated, angry. Hands on her hips.

The Palm Gardens was a part of Mickey's recurring nightmare; Lucy liked it. Now that the majority of gays had abandoned the place, leaving just enough queerness to make her feel comfortable there with her butch, she felt right at home.

Dreamed about it—nightmarish clatter of the iron wheels of trains heading toward forgetfulness in the underground tunnel. Mickey had ridden the elevated train from the North Side at Wilson Avenue to the end of the line at Stoney Island on the South Side; hours and hours, in order to have a place to sit & sleep; and found shelter there when she'd first arrived in Chicago. Maybe this is why she dreamed of it now.

Great huge cavernous bar with a round counter, an island in its middle of clear, amber & brown bottles, and two cash registers which could easily have accommodated four bartenders in better times. Big expanse of floor. Now the higher-class clientele of gay kids had gone, it left the skid-row types to flavor the setting. Lucy sat with a glass of wine, elbow to elbow with some whipped prostie come in from the streets, taking a break. Black male pimps kept a low profile on the sidelines, and so few people were scattered here and there that the bartender had to close a section down marked with a sign, & cluster the patrons together to shorten the distance between them so he could serve them.

The butch had come down the runway of the bar scene. Saw a difference between a real gay bar and what passes as a gay bar.

The Twilight with its Transvestite Drag Shows; patrons 4 deep at the bar, full-blown whores in big wigs & satin dresses & mink coats like Lenore; Johns in 3-piece suits; a few gay boys and dykes, many, many street drag transvestite prostitutes. And the age range of patrons went from 18 to 80 instead of 15 to 25.

There's a lot of drugs going around at Shrimpie's, and the redhead is too close to drugs for comfort.

'The guys have more places to go, and a lot more things to do,' Mickey thought.

So, inevitably, at the end of their rope, canned goods are gone; the two look at each other ugly:

"What's wrong with it, Mickey? Everybody you like does it! Sandy did it! Eva does it!"

"Eva does it with women! With women only! And just one woman! And look at Sandy—what a mess she got in!"

And the half-breed Indian is real mad; makes her occasional show of fiery temper. Veins pop out in her neck.

"*WE* DID IT, GODDAMN IT! YOU AND ME! WE TURNED A FUCKIN' TRICK TOGETHER. THAT'S HOW WE MET—REMEMBER!"

"WELL, MAYBE THAT'S WHAT'S BRINGING US BAD LUCK, THEN! WE SHOULD HAVE MET IN A GODDAMN CHURCH OR SOMEPLACE NICE LIKE STRAIGHT PEOPLE GET TO DO! LUCY, I'M TELLING YOU, IT'S NO GOOD!"

"I SUPPOSE NOT HAVING ANY MONEY IS BETTER! AND YOU WON'T GET A JOB!" At this remark, Mickey dropped her eyes and glared at the floor, jaw stuck out in a pout. "YOU THINK IT'S BETTER SITTING UP HERE WITH NO MONEY? WELL, I'M SICK OF IT! IT'S THE SAME AS WHAT YOU DO TO ME, EXCEPT I'LL GET PAID! *WE'LL* GET PAID! YOU TREAT ME WORSE THEN MY TRICKS USE TO DO! *MICKEY!* I DON'T DO IT ALL THE TIME LIKE YOUR OTHER GIRLS DID! I NEVER DID IT BUT ONCE IN A WHILE—BECAUSE I CAN'T STAND IT!"

So, the way Lucy & Mickey met was at a freak show; maybe this didn't bode so well for their future—maybe disaster was set up in the cards of fate. 'It's important how people meet—thru a friend, at a nice party, or a cookout at the beach over the holidays. So, we met in the gutter & return to the gutter. It don't portend well. It's symbolic. Like the union of star-crossed lovers in a romance novel. Like history. Like the stages of generations led up to the birth of Jesus in a special chain of events. Not simply some haphazard incident in the gutter down at the bottom of the world.'

CHAPTER TWENTY-NINE

Another day when Mickey was out on a walk, halfheartedly pretending to look for work, Lucy disappeared.

Mickey looked down thru all the lower Clark Street taverns for the redhead femme; all the drinking palaces with screeching hags & alkies; & finally found her in a bar she didn't usually frequent.

Lucy was with her cronies Duke, Freddy, Lee & Lester; she never liked to drink by herself & she could not find this compatriotism with dykes, who either wanted to fuck her & jealously guard her from anyone else, or would completely ignore her once they thought she was straight. Lee was good for drink after drink; an alkie who needed a crowd to party with him. The Chiefs & Counselors—the rum soldiers the same. Freddy was a zombie floating around having shot scag & had zero sleep in 3 days from working his mandatory 12-hour cook's shifts, & then going directly out to the bars to party afterward.

People on the scrap heap of life.

So they were paying the high price of living on the edge—substance abuse; but in a joyful din had fun.

Lee was a semi-moron currently employed in a glass factory where they melt down mountains of blue & white glass fragments & make new glass. He was a sweeper—swept broken glass; jagged pieces of bottles & tiny slivers back into the edge of the mountain—20 feet high, which was forever creeping out, spreading back over the factory yard. Wore a mask over his nose & mouth, but inhaled glass particles anytime he took it off. His skin itched from invisible fibers of glass circulating in the air above the shimmering glass mountains, & it got hot under the mask so Lee could hardly breathe; and often he took the mask off. Pay was not bad for the times—$4 per hour. But it was killing him. So he drank himself to death first, in a race of human consumption vs. fate. Thus Lee is sporting all his friends & cronies to drink at the common well. He wore a plaid shirt and orange trousers from a Purple Heart Thrift Store & looked like a fool.

"Dumbbell Lee will sit up here & get so drunk he'll shit in his pants." Duke says in a low voice, discreetly.

And Lester's brain is fried by amphetamines; zonked out; walking stiff-legged around the pool table except sometimes it's his right leg that limps, others, his left.

So here Mickey found Lucy. The winos step aside so she can slide up on a bar stool next to her woman. The disheveled redhead rocks back & forth, happy, timid and pulls the butch to her sweet bosom in a hug. Nourishment of being next to Lucy—the healing aura emanating out of her woman's body & soul—what Mickey had yearned for all her life. Emotion flooding out of her heart. Quick as lightning, there is a beer foaming in a mug set in front of Mickey, which she nurses slowly thru the long grueling night, wanting to stay sober so she could watch out for the two of them.

So Mickey would go anywhere Lucy went; to be near, & to protect; no matter how low the circumstances.

There she sat, wide legged in butch trousers, white shirt open at the collar showing a T-shirt. Handsome features; & black hair slicked back behind her ears, drinking courtesy of Moron Lee, who, when he got high enough, belching liquor breath, would automatically piss in his pants.

Winos battled a bald-headed cue ball on the pool table. Click, click, click; it struck, like the dice of fate.

"The Trotters is a nicer club. They got some Cherokees there." Lucy mutters half-aloud. Now! Lee is white & of English descent, and is just smart enough to be prejudiced.

"I don't want to be around no Injuns. No niggers either."

Everybody else who knows Lucy is part Indian, falls silent. The redhead drinks on, blithely, unembarrassed. She's heard it before.

Red lights play along the bar. Inside Lucy's innermost thoughts are visions.... Naked forms just inside her alcohol-blurred mind's eye, as jukebox music thumps its echo back from barroom wall to wall.... Sweat beaded on Lucy's brow; toys compulsively with the fake rings on her hands.... A butch mounting her instead of a man...white body.... Small boyish butch with a rubber dick strapped around her thighs fucking her passionately, like a stallion.... Slender fingers inside of her, lips sucking her tits. Lucy had had sex with females before. But only twice.

She'd bragged and exaggerated to Mickey when they met; but for all her interest in lesbians, she had been too shy & too afraid to get in deep.... Drink after drink Lucy tipped up and swallowed it all down, Indian style—pouring the liquid straight down her open throat without pausing to gulp; then the liquor hit her in a wave. Her head whirled in confusion like a record stuck in a groove or a sleeper caught in a recurrent dream. Red lights streaked the naked walls.

Mickey looked sideways & caught Lucy biting her wrist. Yanked her pale arm away from her mouth & shook her. "STOP IT NOW, LUCY!" She yells over the din. Fully drunk, the redhead has escalated from fidgeting with her rings, to biting pieces of the flesh of her lower arm. It's how Lucy had tried to commit suicide when she was a teen, biting her wrist, cutting herself with the tip of a knife. Little scars—she was afraid to push down deep; but was in so much pain, emotionally, felt trapped in life like a prisoner tossing & turning with no escape. When she worried & was in an alcoholic haze, she'd pick up this habit again. And Lucy was worried.

Duke eased himself onto a bar stool. His ass hurt from being fucked in it. $10 bought a lot of drinks. And he passed syphilis down the human chain in a gutter by the subway station which was a gay male cruising area; and Duke wasn't gay, wasn't worried at all.

"We're gonna meet that Phyllis chick down at Shrimpie's and cop some scag! At 12 midnight!" Freddy bellows thru his toothless mouth; his blue eyes water.

"YEAH!" Lee chimes in, & Lester stares at them from just a body width away, yet hovering far off in outer space.

"You're my King, Mickey." Lucy bows her head, snuggles up briefly, whispering love words. Pats her butch's leg in a reassuring gesture. Red wisps of hair fall out of her piled-high hairdo. Mickey had been thru the phase of sexually objectifying Lucy, also, from the beginning, simultaneously, had begun to love her, too. And was a soldier, weary of fighting off her suitors, liquor, poverty, & now—the ominous specter of dope. "Don't worry! Don't use much, just a little bit, Mickey! Just a very little bit! Don't deny me my little bit, Mickey! Don't deny your girlie-girl her little bit of fun! You're my King! Don't worry so much! Everything's gonna be OKEY-DOKEY!"

'I'm gonna have to seriously look for a job.' Mickey tells herself. Then the thought went out of her head.

"REMEMBER THAT TIME WE ALL WENT TO THE RACETRACK 'N' FREDDY PUT HIS WHOLE PAYCHECK ON THAT HORSE—A LONG SHOT—& IT LOST!"

"$250. He played it across the board. He would have been a Fifth Avenue Millionaire if it had finished in the money. It was fifty-to-one."

"Ain't that just like somebody from the Village to lose their whole paycheck on a lame mudslinging nag! We can't win! We're losers!" They laughed together. Lucy laughed, too. Under red & yellow bar lights, the soldiers recounted these memories that haunted them—their past delusions of winning and grand mansions & chauffeurs & an Easy Life, flew like bats out of a bottle of Richard's Wild Irish Rose.

Flunkies settled down the bar in blue work shirts, rolled-up sleeves; looked to the bandstand. A trio had come on & was playing Country & Western.

Mickey sat at the bar, her hand on Lucy's thigh.

A man comes over, 2 heads taller than Mickey, 100 pounds heavier; his hand reaches over space to touch Lucy's blouse pocket like he's trying to put something in it & he's feeling her breast & Lucy turns and grins, puts her hand on his, pulling it away & talks to him.

"GET YOUR HAND OFF HER! SHE'S WITH ME!" Mickey growls.

"I know," the man replies matter-a-factly. He turns, looks her in the face: "Mickey"—He knew her name—"I'd like to give you $15 for 20 minutes of her time."

P O W! Mickey's hand shot out, reacting, before she had

time to think. Clipped the man in his chest. He backs up, just stands there, hands up in the air, surrendering. "HEY! I'M SORRY! THOUGHT SHE WAS WORKING!"

"FUCK YOU, MOTHERFUCKER!" Mickey's pushing the man away, but it's like going up against a rock, an immovable object. "FUCK YOU! KEEP YOUR HANDS OFF HER!" And the man shoves Mickey's hand back in her face, and dangles his huge hand there, teasing her, so Mickey lunges off the bar stool, swings & clips him on the side of his face. P O W!

The man shoves the butch back hard, into the bar, a mean look on his face. "WHAT DID I DO, BITCH? WHAT'S WRONG WITH YOU! ARE YOU CRAZY?" And Mickey flings herself at him, trying to pull him down on the floor, & they wrestle in space a moment.

"GET OUT OF HERE! TAKE IT OUTSIDE!" screams the bartender. He leaps over the bar & is pushing the wrestling two towards the door. Bar stools tip over; bottles overturn, breaking; Mickey's bleeding & pushing the man, he's enraged & bewildered. Somehow Mickey is going to seize power—even if she winds up dead. And outside in the street swings again, & again, misses, & the man backs up, his face has turned beet red. "YOU FUCKING DYKE BITCH!" Everybody in the house has piled out of the entrance to watch. Feet are flying, running out; as others duck down out of sight & harm, not knowing what is happening. Mickey swings and battles; clips the man in the jaw a grazing blow as he dodges: "COME ON AND FIGHT, THEN, SONO-FABITCH! KILL ME, THEN! BUT YOU AIN'T TOUCHING MY LADY!"

His fist punches at her, & she blocks it, then ties his strong arms up in a clench. They've wrestled out into the street between two parked cars. Crowd cheers from an arc of yellow light around the entranceway & inside the deserted tavern with overturned chairs, somebody's scooped up Lee's money from off the bar & stolen it. The troops have run out after them, but the fight is all Mickey's.

"HELP! HELP, SOMEBODY! DUKE! DO SOME-

THING!" Lucy screams. "SOMEBODY STOP THEM! HE'S GONNA KILL HER!" Mickey holds her own, wrestling the big clown, & kicking his shins. Traffic speeds by; he tries to slug her, but she catches his arm & ties it up with her arms, & they grunt, locked, wrestling up against the metal tail of a car.

"GO, MICKEY! GO, MICKEY! KILL THE MOTHER-FUCKER!" Duke yells in glee, dancing on the balls of his feet. Lee is hollering; eyes bright, spittle drips from his stupid, excited face. Freddy looks very upset, panics. Lucy screams. The fight doesn't get anywhere; the man tries to shove Mickey away, finally peeling her off him, & limps along the side of a car. Mickey is bleeding and breathing hard, hand-some face contorted, chest heaving gasping for breath; & clothes torn. Lucy grabs her around the waist & they slowly make their way back inside.

"I tell you this: she's gonna do some time," a hag declares. "She's gonna do some jail time."

"She's already done some." Duke responds casually.

Lucy helps Mickey back up on a bar stool, wets her hand-kerchief in beer suds & pats her bloodied face.

The minor riot subsides; the soldiers of Clark Street shuffle back to their stations & resume drink. To them, this was just one in a series of ongoing fights. But to Mickey it was a major event—the flame of her spirit upheld. And Lucy was so drunk she soon forgot about it.

Yellow lights; cowboy band didn't miss a beat. Shirtfront torn open shows a bloodied T-shirt stretched over her flat-tened chest; puts the jacket on. Side of her face swells. Solitary, the butch stares into space, drinking in earnest now.

"I feel freer with James. Nobody hassles us." Lucy whis-pers drunkenly. The old hag nods her head in agreement.

Problem for Mickey & Lucy was, society was making a lot of Lucy's mind up for her. Tells her she is wrong to be a lesbian in inferences: facial expressions and curses snickered behind backs of hands at best, and violence; blocking her path, throwing a punch at her jaw, at worst. Had even the disapproval of the denizens of wino alley. A hag ancient as

Methuselah from the Vodka Dispensation queried Lucy—her lipstick smeared pale pink in crooked strokes above her lip line onto her skin; "Are yuh gonna shack back up with James? He'll be in here tonight, dearie. Is that girl doing you any good?"

Only place Lucy was respected with her mate was in gay clubs—for a few brief hours—for a few brief months—before the clubs collapsed and their kind went off onto their diverse ways. Gay life ceased altogether when the club shut down by day, till it reassembled the next night—if the club was still open and hadn't been raided and shut down by the police—this act of force also telling her she must be wrong by making her an outcast.

Lucy is delirious. The barroom revolves around her.

'In the streets we're super—me and James. He's big & strong. Men are afraid of him. I'm safe. Men don't respect a female—a butch. And more than that, it's the fact that he's a man, even if he was smaller than Mickey, he's still the opposite sex & straight people, the whole world thinks we're OK. I'm free. When I'm with another woman, people look at us strange. Despise us because we're queer. I have a great freedom when I'm with some man, running around from tavern to tavern hanging on to his arm and spending his money.... But the damn problem is—& it's the real problem, down deep—is in bed. When I'm with a man & he's doing it for his own pleasure, it's a turn-on as long as he keeps going, but it's never long enough; and after this James spends an hour trying to get me off, but whether or not I cum the first time with him, or later when he eats me out, I'm still wishing it was a woman. I'm wishing it was a woman even if she can't fuck, or doesn't know how to eat me out. Yes, I wish it was a woman. And now that I have Mickey, and she can fuck and eats me out in much less time and makes it so damn good & I'm hot for her, I'm happy in bed because she is a woman, and I'm in her heart and she's in my heart; any woman is, any butch, any female. When I'm with one, I'm happy. And that's my goddamn problem.' The redhead sighs deeply, heaving her shoulders. Slams her glass down on the counter in finality.

Tells the hags of Clark Street one thing. Tells James one thing. And now in her heart knows something entirely different.

Mickey felt vaguely like a hero. Remotely so. Drained. Pain is what she felt strongest.

They sat side by side, not talking. The butch touched her face gingerly; her bruised arms were darkening in purple splotches. She decided to drink to lose the physical pain & keep the problems tucked neatly away in forgetfulness; and to make worry get behind her. Swallowed it down—grateful for the bliss liquor gave.

After a while, the two women, incommunicative, were so thoroughly drunk they felt no pain & all their worst problems had disappeared. Couldn't feel the hurt now—or think back down into that volcanic red sensitive place inside—& observe what was in them. The blatant feeling of inferiority—of being women without power. Or see the scars, or hear the screams, by time emotionally gagged. So it was an aching poison pus in this secret pocket—anesthetized.

Sat among diseased alcoholics. The mentally ill. Non-writers; their novels unfinished. Non-singers of songs unsung. All locked up inside in their brains like a vault & so they dragged leaden steps all night long on safari thru the garish squalor of cheap hotels, barrooms, wino parks & vacant lots in nightmarish pursuit of the bottle & drugs.

While Mickey struggled to fight off the world of winos, here come the alien intruders from the planet Junk.

Phyllis came gliding into the tavern wearing a short skirt, & white plastic vinyl boots with toes curled up elflike. Mickey is startled, turns to see her as though she was a ghost.

Lucy's head snaps around immediately; all smiles & reaches out to touch Phyllis as she does with people she loves.

Phyllis endures this touch with gritted teeth; stands there like a shirt on a hanger; spooky, silent.

Drugs have taken over her body & possessed her. She hovers, in the way heroin junkies do; it's their chemistry—dope re-creates their vibes, restructures them with its own metabolism, like a chemist.

"Phyllis, this is Mickey! Mickey, this is Phyllis!"

"Come by the apartment sometime; you're invited." A cold smile spreads on her face. An underseas junkie.

Phyllis was important in Junk World, for down in the dregs of the gutter, she rented a drug house.

Lanky, white, scarred face, long dark hair; she spoke in a calm junkie tone: "Leah is on speed & alcohol, and she is convinced that outer space—or something *from* outer space—is going to fall down on her and kill her. Leah's been running around crazy all week, giving everybody in the house the jitters—real bad news. So I said, 'Look, it's gonna fall right here—in this spot.' I pointed at the sofa. 'You're safe everywhere else.' And the fear left her."

Mickey came out of an alcohol nod, rubbed her sore face & blurry eyes, just in time to catch the tail end of the conversation.

Phyllis hovered, feet in plastic boots almost unconnected to the cigarette butt–littered wino floor of rough boards.

"We just need some money. We can cop again." Phyllis says sweetly. "I have a foil package." She smiles. "You know what's in it Lucy. Would you like a cut? Huh? Just a little cut, with me—for free? Shall we go in the bathroom? Is it safe here?"

Lucy shook her head.

"I think you're right; it doesn't look safe. Hmmmm!" Phyllis is very intelligent and knows everything about drugs there is to know—like a pharmacist. Stands ghostlike; an ectoplasmic substance.

'She gives me the creeps.' Mickey thinks.

"I've got a record." Phyllis is saying. "I can't afford any problems. They'll put me away in the Federal Penitentiary in Lexington, Kentucky. Come on, baby." Phyllis snakes her junk-scab hand around Lucy's waist, hugs her for a second, then lets go. "I've got to warn you, Leah is acting strange. I know you like her because she's one-quarter Cherokee. Leah has the prettiest straight black hair. I know you want to talk to her, baby, you want her to be close to you—but don't say anything about outer space: it'll just work her up."

Phyllis runs this drug house which has windows boarded up, tie-dyed curtains & sofa covers, & bric-a-brac dope fiends drag in to give her. The rest of the houses on the block are abandoned and slated to be demolished by city reconstruction in the growing area of Old Town. It's spooky.

ZANG ZANG ZANG! Band picks up rhythm and it's traveling. Cowboy outfits with fringe & silver studs. Blue & gold lights flood the cesspool with a heavenly amber touch.

Mickey hisses in Lucy's ear, blowing aside red strands of hair, "I want you to stay away from her! She's nothing but a freakin' dope fiend!"

"You don't own me, Mickey!"

Mickey can't see what Lucy likes about Phyllis—knows there's a physical response between them. The junkie has no body—is skinny. Abscesses from blown shots splotch her legs, arms, neck, and even her face. She shoots drugs into her face when she's desperate to find a vein that still works.

Guitar picks up; metal TWANGS; bass thuds; all the instruments sound like one of those lonesome trains that rocks & rolls thru the Appalachian hills. Traveling music.

"Nobody owns me!" The redhead mutters.

Mickey sinks back into this yapping in her ears; resigning from the outer surroundings. Alkies stomp their feet in their world of hell. Colors flash. Din. And the butch's spirit rises above it to higher worlds.

Feels her heart pump blood every few seconds; her chest rise under the torn shirt in breaths that keep oxygen in her lungs; & then starts to cough. Lucy, blithe at one side, ignores it. Phyllis's hand strokes down Lucy's satin-covered back & comes to rest just above her ass, firm, presses the sweaty flesh of an erogenous zone; cold hand, firm; & Lucy feels this, is aroused, but tries to keep her composure cold, because the junkie Phyllis is non-emotional & hates the sight of passion & flits away on elfin boots the moment things look like they're out of her control.

Mickey coughs, spits up blood, red, into her hand—from the fight. As an idea spits up from memory. A dyke at the 169 Club has told her about a job opportunity. A theater is reopening under new owners; gays can apply. The old straight-aced owners have passed on and it's a new, colorful beatnik kind of art-film house. Mickey holds onto the thread of this thought, and tosses back a gulp of beer.

Phyllis removes her hand from Lucy's back, leaving the woman wanting more. This cold junkie is Lucy's mentor. Gives her a lot of credit. Phyllis is 35. The only completely independent female she knows besides Mickey. She is a lesbian bisexual who dwells on the drug side of life—not sex. A weird kind of freakish non-emotional psychosexual eros. Too high to have sex usually, Phyllis's sex drive is muted into mental kinkiness. In her cold-fish touch that ran along Lucy's back from shoulder to ass—on the other side where Mickey can't see—a harsh caress, so Lucy would have no doubt of her intentions.

TWANG! The band picks up a beat, ran at a rapid clip, the male singer's nasal sounds, mournful; decked out in cowboy fringe & silver metal, he twangs the guitar.

"A toe freak OD'd down the street from me in the alley. It was sad."

"A toe freak?"

"Yes."

Mickey's in the middle of split conversations; Duke & Freddy complaining in their paranoias about being World-Class Losers; & her woman Lucy and this coldhearted Phyllis.

Out on the lunatic fringe.

Behind them a backdrop of slaphappy hillbillies, & psychopathic city-made men whose fierce hands crush a whiskey glass—who bury their murderous tendencies in alcohol—as one buries some corpse they don't ever want to find again, deep in the earth.

Cunning eyed, too groggy to be dangerous. Unemployed hillbillies who collect more welfare cash than they could back over the Missouri River in Kentucky; interject a streak of blue—jeans & shirts. And broken-down work boots.

"I'M A LOSER! I'M A LOSER!" Duke testifies to Freddy. He found his place at last. On skid row they've lost everything. No bills, no worries, just drink. It's a relief.

"Not a dime in the house, nothing to eat..." Phyllis touches Lucy's hair in concern. Her mask face reshapes itself into an attempt of a pang of expression. "I lay on my back and get fucked by Mickey for hours, and I could be using my hand on Terry—that guy she tries to beat up just a while ago, and get $10—just my hand, and pay rent on the room, plus food & not have to worry."

Phyllis strokes her for one second—no more. "I think it was a very good idea, Lucy—to turn that trick to save your home & your things & have money for *fun*." And the redhead's wobbling on her bar stool.

Society could criticize her for her addictive personality; her booze—but actually Lucy was engaged in a far worse battle—to survive. And her yen—it's strange, this yen wasn't quite for drugs, not yet, but for *life*. To live to the hilt. To be with people without fear. The redhead was not trying to die, she was fighting to live.

Lucy wobbled off the bar stool and made her way, groping thru the crowd of people down the bar, to where a tall man had moved in & had beckoned her to come over.

Mickey's head is woozy; vaguely hears a couple having a loud argument right near by—one was a familiar voice; but she didn't respond. Was lost in a private mental retreat.

"LUCY, I AIN'T GONNA GET NEAR YOU WITH THAT LEZZIE BROAD YOU GOT! SHE MIGHT HAVE GAVE YOU A DISEASE!"

Lucy played with his sleeve.

"WHAT'S THE SCORE?"

Her mouth was clenched into a line, eyes too tired to twinkle. "Just for old time's sake, James! And I want $10—now. I need $5 to take a cab over to her house!"

"Is she a lezzie, too?"

"Yeah, sometimes."

"You drop your panties for her, too?"

"No, she hasn't asked me."

"Hell, no! I won't give you $10!"

"You worked a job, didn't you!"

"I only made $25!"

"I *told you*, I'll come see you later in the week! I can't *now!*"

"I won't see my $10, and I won't see you!"

"YOU'LL SEE ME!" Lucy bellows tugging on his shirt, drunk. "Then just give me \$5, James! COME ON!"

Grizzly face stared down at her. "Lucy, do you want to get laid, or you want to get paid?" But he hands her \$5.

"Both."

James just stares at the redhead.

"I'm horny!—for you! I'll come up to your place, I promise! You can show me a good time!"

"You're horny? Why? You got that lezzie broad to take care of it, don't you?"

"Yeah, she takes care of it, goddamn her." Lucy is drunk, talking without heed, out of her head.

James pounds his hairy white fist down on the counter, trembling. Spit flecks his grizzly cheek. Drunk as she is, Lucy knows she's said something wrong. "SHIT! YOU LET HER IN YOUR PANTIES EVERY NIGHT!"

"She makes me do it! I don't want to do it!"

"YOU LET THIS LESBIAN BITCH IN YOUR PANTIES EVERY NIGHT AND WOULDN'T LET ME IN 'EM HALF THE TIME WE WENT TOGETHER! LUCY, YOU AIN'T CHANGED, YOU'RE THE SAME LOUSY LIAR AS ALWAYS! EVERYTHING ELSE MIGHT CHANGE, BUT NOT YOU!" James glares down at the pretty redhead. Lipstick blurs pink over her mouth from drinking, blotted on the edges of too many glasses. And her blue-shadow mascara ran at the corners of her eyes from crying. Sweat stains had grown under the armpits of the giant towering besides her; here was a real worker who moved furniture for a living—and constantly was hustled by leeches so they could drink, party, & have fun. The stink of adrenaline-rage-induced sweat was far worse.

Lucy tips back her head, shouts up, harshly, thru her teeth: "YOU KNEW IT! JAMES, YOU KNEW IT! I TOLD YOU I'D BEEN WITH WOMEN! WHAT DID YOU THINK WHEN I KEPT TAKING YOU BY ALL THOSE GAY BARS!"

"WHAT DID I THINK! I THOUGHT YOU WANTED TO WATCH THE FREAKS! IF YOU WAS TRYING TO

*MEET A LEZZIE TO TAKE HOME WITH YOU, YOU
RUINED YOUR CHANCES BRINGING ME ALONG!
NONE OF THOSE SELFISH COLD BITCHES EVEN
LOOKED AT YOU!"*

"Now I realize that. I made a mistake!"

"WHAT DO YOU SEE IN THOSE SELFISH COLD
BITCHES! YOU'RE TEN TIMES THE WOMAN THEY
ARE!"

"I can't take it! I can't take anymore! I can't stand these
men! I can't stand these women!"

Phyllis stood in plastic boots, like an elf; observing from a
safe distance. The winos in their habitat yell & scream, drinking firewater. Not at all behaving as the denizens of her house
over in the reconstruction area—in a peaceful junkie nod.
James pounds his huge fist down on the bar, accusing Lucy of
giving him gonorrhea a year ago. And Phyllis hangs in space; a
haunt; all head and no body, no feet,—just smoke; plastic
boots connecting her to earth—not attached to mortal soil.

"WHAT'S THAT DYKE GOT THAT I DON'T HAVE? I
GOT A TONGUE, TOO, LUCY! YOU LET HER GET
PERSONAL WITH YOU! YOU NEVER ASK *HER* FOR
ANY MONEY!"

"You 'n' me, we're personal, too, James!"

A hellish look flickers on his face; hell-bent; all other
emotions had left him but destruction. BLAM! James cuffs
Lucy across her face. And immediately her body is down on
the floor. He stares at her. He's a big man with a lot of weight
behind him, & tho he didn't hit her ferociously, the blow has
knocked her half-unconscious.

"I bet he's jarred some teeth loose," mutters an Alkie. "I
bet. They're loose now, her teeth…. The next time, all he has
to do, he'll just give her a tap and those teeth will fall out.
That's the way to do it. Loosen 'em up with the first punch &
take 'em out later, with a tap. So nobody can say you took out
their teeth & haul you off to jail."

James turns and stalks away to a different side of the
bar—afraid of what he might do; feeling his space severely
intruded upon, & settles down safely between two male

cronies to begin his drinking night on the $20 left from what he's earned—& to forget.

Lucy was being picked up off the floor by Freddy & Duke. Had felt a watery crunch as close to her as something can get to a person—on her own skull. Heard a THUD. Saw stars out of her left eye & now her head was jarred askew. The left side of her face stung. Lucy merely gave up. As the two walked her back to her bar stool, Lucy bled; red drops of blood drip onto the barroom floor mingling with long-ago stains in its wooden boards. Inside, a ten-year-old half-Indian girl let go, ran free like the buffalo; free, like the Compassion of Christ, from all that imprisoned her in that time & space of 1959 at the summers end; and she, adult, age 23, was giving up fast.

"SOMEBODY SLUGGED YOU? WHO? *WHAT HAPPENED!*" Lucy fingers her swelling face feebly. "I CAN'T KEEP MY EYES OFF YOU A MINUTE!"

And Mickey is following them out of the club, bleary, stumbling; Phyllis hails a cab & tells the rest: "No, you can't come with us—it's girl business! We'll right back!" Outdoors is swimming with tavern advertisements; traffic whizzes by; climate cool. "YOU'RE GONNA SHOOT UP! I KNOW IT!" Duke howls. Lucy has the $5 crumpled in her hand. Liquor pounds inside between her ears, her balance is gone; mind spins dizzy, glad she started out this evening in gym shoes instead of high heels. Mickey, Phyllis, and Lucy pile into the cab.

So they drive over west ten blocks to the drug house, where Mickey can watch a cold-fish woman tie up her baby's arm and shoot it with heroin.

Phyllis sat, eerie; and serene as the cab bounced over the blocks. Secretly the fish-eyed Drug Countess was glad Mickey didn't use because there'd be more for them. And Mickey's slouched to the side, her shirt torn, bloody, body in pain; thinks: 'Why am I going thru this again?'

Lucy had obviously been there before—she gave instructions to the driver & settled into as much comfort as she could, next to Phyllis; they were like two femme girlfriends.

Mickey didn't fail to miss the touch of Phyllis's cold white junkie hand on Lucy's thigh.

It was Mickey's first time at Phyllis's. The minute the door swung open, she saw something—an atmosphere, more than anything specific—something which lingered in the back of her mind, like a puzzle she couldn't figure out.

Dusty drapes from floor to ceiling perpetually blocked out light. Completely dark, except for rays emanating from a lamp on a stand. Throw pillows. Rugs. Sofas covered with dust. Floor spattered with junkie blood from bad hits.

Bare. Nothing that can be sold. No radios, TV's stereo music players, clocks. Just 3rd- and 4th-hand rugs—stolen from abandoned buildings, blankets, bric-a-brac. 3 men in a junkie nod had had a needle workshop; picked over their scabs. One had a shoe on, the other off; scratches his toes for an hour. One stares into outer space tho he's indoors. "These are my friends." Phyllis smiles and glides like a ghost to the stairs. "They are full of reefer and have shot up something. Paregoric or something you can buy over the counter." The brown rug was trod to shreds. Mickey stumbles in the half-light; no windows, curtains hiding the walls. Light hurts dope fiends' eyes. They sat there scratching & twitching.

Upstairs in an anteroom beyond, with a bathroom, was a perfect place to shoot up.

Tiny room enclosed the women like a womb. Walls painted red, in streaks of unfinished areas—Phyllis painted it herself; with paint one of the junkies had found discarded in an alley. Junkies with time on their hands all day drag home a variety of things.

Phyllis glides to the bathroom, opens the door, breathless with expectation, wanting to get her own hit. There hangs a collection of ties, belts, rubber hoses on a tie rack.

Upstairs room, is like the rest, its plaster falls, gaping holes; but Phyllis has gone ahead blithely without plastering or preparation & painted anyway. Walls sky blue, with shelves, and door frames lemon green and the baseboards red.

"This is new, Phyllis." Lucy remarks, gazing about her. Still holding her sore face.

"Oh, yes. One of the boys found a gallon of red paint.... I even made a faux baseboard—see?" A gaping stretch of wall with baseboard missing; Phyllis had simply painted it in—red strip 8 inches off the floor line, that continued around the room.

As Lucy and Mickey peered down at the red baseboard, it came to the butch: 'This is where Lucy gets her ideas. These tie-dye curtains, these painted boxes. She's always fixing & painting our room...this is it...like our room but ten times bigger....'

The two women left Mickey gazing & thinking and Phyllis glided off, arms wrapped around the drunk Lucy like a prized possession; And thru her alcohol haze—in the other room, Mickey sees Lucy wrap her arms around skinny Phyllis; the two giving each other a long, deep kiss. Two femmes. 'Lucy wants to make love with her.' Mickey thinks morosely. And have the love she'd get with a drug hit.

Cold caresses with fishlike hands. Phyllis didn't give sex; it was psycho sex. Enhanced by drug yen instead of bodily horniness. Drug-Psycho-Sex. Then the scar-faced addict ties up the redhead's arm, pulling the ends of a rubbery hose till the vein bulged. Green/blue under white skin. Licks her lips. "You have such nice veins!" A vampire. Pricks the skin, pumps the contents of the hypodermic in, then pulls it out combined with Lucy's swirling blood into the glass cylinder then shoots it in with fixed determination. Pulls the needle out; a smile on her face. As the dose hits her system, Lucy goes reeling into the toilet, slams the door & she's disgorging everything in her guts—wine, beer, emptying.

Mickey doesn't care. In a weird way, wants to see Phyllis take her woman Lucy—in a dream state, lay her back, half-naked; pull her pants down and her shirt up over her tits and fuck her good. In a freakish way, hasn't been with two women since Miami. And Phyllis smiles with a superior air, knowing she already took Lucy—with the hit in the vein of her left arm.

Phyllis cut the dope down so bad, but Lucy rarely used, so it was strong to her. System unused to mainlining drugs. Sat on the floor, back against the wall. Mickey had crawled over to her side, face puffed out where she'd been punched in the fight, black hair tousled. Phyllis sat next to them; had to jab herself over and over with the needle to find a hit in a vein which wasn't collapsed or abscessed. Mickey combs black hair back thru her fingers; lightly presses the side of her face. Pain. Thinks, as she watches Phyllis in fascination, that she'd like to fuck the woman herself. Bleary-eyed, runs her gaze up the skinny legs, thighs, junk-shrunk tits, weasel face with long brown hair; a strong face & big eyes & hands. Wanted to lean over and say, "Think you could spread your legs for me, baby? Let me get to your cunt—I want to bang it bad." And Mickey's not horny at all. It's a mind trip.

Soon Phyllis's arm runs with blood from a dozen needle pricks; she can't get a hit. Sticks the needle in again, again. "Damn it!" Postponing her enjoyment. Lucy is too out of it to tie her up. Has the end of the rubber hose between her clenched legs now, to pull it taut; now, between her teeth. Mickey watches her struggle.

Phyllis gets her hit. Pumps the works up and down, blood into the syringe, shoots it back into her vein, back up into the glass cylinder mixing with the drug, then shot back in in prolonged ecstasy of a junkie rush. Tie falls loose in her lap. Phyllis, an underseas ghoul gazes with fish-eyed superiority. Used Lucy to get a cab ride home plus a few dollars for this hit. In return, Lucy is starry-eyed in infatuation with ghoulish Phyllis, attracted to her masterful cold, aloof, kinky drug-induced psycho-sex. And Mickey has been told the $5 was swiped off the bar—change belonging to moron Lee, or Freddy.

So it's an exchange & everybody's happy. And Phyllis has orchestrated it all.

Lucy loves Mickey.

Lucy is infatuated with Phyllis. Has the beginning yen—of a novice. Still it's just a mental yen. Is taking her drug apprenticeship under Phyllis & would like to be under Phyllis's cold white body, learning to move with her rhythm—but this will never come to pass. Phyllis appraises this undercover need—she is a pusher of people like pawns, not just a dealer of drugs. Lucy admires Phyllis, who opens up the medicine cabinet of opportunity in green and yellow pills. Lucy's lust for life is mutated into a yen for love-drug-sex riding on a fantasy of White Horse; none of which can be fulfilled.

They took a cab back to The Silver Spur, thus completing their safari that night.

Old Indians sit in their same place. Semi-gay strippers fallen with age. And an army of alkies & wino hags. The bar fills up with patrons from the closed 3 o'clock license dives. They all congregate for this last stand. "ANOTHER DRINK FOR MY FRIENDS!"

Liquor houses; barns for alkies of cut-rate 5¢ glasses of beer, Hasty Tasty's cool lights in a blur; Duke discusses his syphilis over a glass of drink. Dearborn Street chili parlor. 4:30 A.M., now fires of liquor burn low. Only a few ghouls left over in the graveyard of Clark Street—dead ashes. Frantic or methodical; gulping drinks. Cigarette glow. Vomiting at curbside. Red taillights of cars vanishing. Now 5 A.M.—it's over. Just the last ghouls left, picking over the bones of the skeleton of night before they stagger home; tip up dregs of a wine bottle; the rest collapsed on the sidewalk, in doorways. Paranoid troops. Clicked off; the blue & yellow lights of neon lamps. The moons gaze is gone. They drink in the night air as the black walls of The Silver Spur spit them out.

Body revolving with drugs; the redhead had passed out at the bar.

Just fell out. Hand uncurled, spilling a drink.

Lucy kept passing out & Mickey had to shake her & slap her awake. Lucy grumbles, hair is falling down wild to her shoulders; Mickey is angry, black eyes flash—acne makes her face rough; Mickey pulls the woman she loves & fucks out into the night & the bartender padlocks the door.

Shout & scream in the street; Mickey slaps Lucy: "WALK, BITCH!" Richard's Wild Irish Rose. Lucy on the nod. West Erie. Hollering & yells; red hair fallen over her shoulders long & loose come unpiled from the beehive that sat on her head—floating wild in the wind of motion; "I'M NOBODY'S BITCH! NOT YOURS! NOT JAMES! *PHYLLIS* IS MY

MAN! PHYLLIS IS THE ONLY PERSON I LOVE! SHE DON'T WANT NOTHING FROM ME! PHYLLIS WON'T PAW HER HANDS ALL OVER ME! PHYLLIS IS NOT A CRUDE PERSON LIKE YOU, MICKEY! *FUCK YOU!*"

Sun beyond the building tops. Instead of heat beating down from above, it's still vibrating up from the pavements beneath, & off walls. Their faces swathed in sweat. Miserable folks crawl out of the tenements in the heat, fighting depression.

Their voices echo thru the streets of day; reverberate down corridors, bounce between fronts of 5-storied buildings.

Neon lights & liquor-store signs are off. No passing cars.

Up the stairs, door shut behind them. A room to themselves.

And at last, again, they were alone together.

CHAPTER THIRTY

When she woke up, dizzy, with a hangover; it was 4 P.M. Had been down to the hall to use the toilet & didn't remember it. Forgotten most of last night but scag, the dope house & some kind of fight that she was very close to.

An aggressive lesbian butch was loving her—not Phyllis with cold caresses, aloof, with no body. But Mickey, throwing her legs back on each side, so as to jam her hairy pussy against Lucy's pussy; with fingers opening up their pink sexlips under pubic hair bringing to unison their hot, wet meat; and began to fuck her.

It was a blur. Face hurt on one side; red hair wild to her shoulders. Only knew that she obediently held her knees back, as she was supposed to, and humped her cunt underneath to meet Mickey's and felt her sex grow hot; blood swell in her clit, going around & up and down; in final moments as Mickey is cumming, wraps her legs around Mickey tight to pull her cunt down tight into her for hard contact. "UUUU-UHHHAAAAAAAAAAAAAA!" Mickey hollers, and it's over.

Lay in bed in sweltering August heat; two fingers playing in the wet, sticky meat of her cunt; next to Mickey. Sun heats their room to a feverish intensity.

It wasn't working. After seeing James on the sly; having clung to his male strength, his no-emotion evenness, Lucy still wanted a woman. Still missed Mickey. Was infatuated with Phyllis. More than ever wanted pussy like her own.

Lucy felt worse than she had since teenage. Felt herself having turned gay. Finally. All the way gay & was afraid. Afraid of being this different species. This outcast of the outcasts.

Soon TV flickered black & white serial dramas. Jackie Gleason & Audrey Meadows. Retreated into TV land; half fantasy land, but not as strong as last night's drug-induced dream nod of a junkie.

TV time. Mickey held Lucy in her arms, her hand in Lucy's cunt, massaging fingers stroked her vagina, juices wet the sheets and the fingers going in & out & Lucy is annoyed, tries to watch TV. "Baby, you didn't cum! I want you to cum!"

"Not now! *I Love Lucy* is on next!"

Outside the window, sky, clouds in the day; blue & white & breezy.

"Want me to cock you, baby?"

"Sorry, it's not my week for boys."

Mickey had the harness out and the dildo slung in it. And all Lucy wants to do is watch TV.

Lucy's lips fixed in a tight line; studiously. Lucy & Desi flickered across the screen. Straight sexuality is everywhere. Female-to-female sexuality is very deep; both spring from the same well. And Lucy had to make up her mind.

Few days passed; it's a terrible thing to be hungry. Butch sat in the chair in her boxer shorts & T-shirt. Last cans of vegetables had been flavored with an 83 cent package of neck bones. They'd sucked the neck bones dry. A little bit of pink-brown meat, then the white fat; sucked each last splinter of bone, and not a bit of meat, fat, or muscle was left. The sharp edges of bone cut her lip. Then took the pile of bones, swept them into the garbage. Mickey got in bed next to Lucy, who's watching TV with a bottle of 50-cent wine. Went over and over in her mind—food. "Did I eat every last scrap of meat off those bones? Was there any left? No. Is there a can of beans left in one of the wooden boxes somewhere?"

All gone. Rice gone. Bread gone. So, Mickey too left reality & fled into fantasy. A steak dinner. Yum Yum. Thick, juicy; mashed potatoes with butter; a crisp green salad with red tomatoes. Finally she went to the medicine stash in one of the crates and took two aspirins to get high and give herself a blast of well-being.

Good-food smells of cooking—but it wasn't coming from their room.

The very last and final days near when their money would arrive; in starvation—which is the mother of innovation— Mickey came back to that idea. That place she'd heard about, the movie theater, to get a job. Toyed with it, but was afraid. Fear of the loathing she might see on their faces when she applied for the position—because she's queer. Fear of change, also. And again, let the idea slip back down into the dark well of things postponed.

So Lucy's old life kept barging in on them. Like the trick who came up to see her in the bar, who Mickey fought. At least Lucy had found out where he was living before the butch pushed him away.

Mickey knew the Fast Life well. Days blurred into nights hustling to play above the poverty line; doing drugs. Getting money to sit in bars.

"Hold it in my hand, jack it up & down." (Till his white cum spurted out). "That's all." Lucy tells her, mournful. And then Mickey recalls the doorways and the game run down— like they did in New York. She had not thought of this idea before, but times were desperate.

"I did it in Times Square with Valorie."

"Did you get the money?"

"No. He ran away when he saw the knife. We needed a gun. Other butches used knives & it worked."

Lucy grimaced.

Now they'd first thought of it in New York when Valorie was bleeding & Mickey didn't want her to work.

So, they planned to lure a john into a doorway and rob him at knifepoint.

Used a deserted entranceway, unlit, about 5 blocks from their hotel.

Spent an hour waiting around until they found the right-looking trick; Lucy going up to him smiling & talking.

The redhead brings him in there. Mickey's waiting. "GIMME YOUR WALLET! GIMME THE MONEY!" But the man isn't afraid of two women—there's anger in his face—so Mickey slices down the front of his chest so the knife cuts thru the cloth of his suit coat, skin & flesh, and sticks. The man screams, holds himself, and the women flee, run off into the night, and get home safely.

Mickey's proud of herself. "I SLICED THAT FUCKING JOHN! I DREW HIS GODDAMN BLOOD!" They hole up in their room. Left the knife behind & got no money.

Next day the bravado turns to fear. Cold fear. They're afraid to go out on the streets and possibly be recognized by the john riding in a police squad car hunting for her. This and other terrifying scenarios bombard her imagination.

Red lights blink off & on. Again, she sees the john spurt blood and basks in an uneasy triumph. "HE STOOD THERE & HOLLERED! HE COULDN'T BELIEVE IT! HA! HA!"

"I hope I don't see him again!" Lucy declares. "If I do, I'll tell him you were a robber, that you jumped us! I didn't know you! I'll say you were a man! A stranger!"

Mickey knew what it was like to be a fugitive, & to be uprooted. Never staying more than a night with the same woman. Being out of doors & having to look over her shoulder & be ready to disappear around a corner & to always be afraid.

For she had done this at an early age, fleeing the police her mother had sent to pick her up off of the streets of Manhattan, New York. Fleeing down side streets when squad cars screeched to a stop beside her, sirens wailing, blue lights flashing. Climbing up fire escapes and running over rooftops to get out of girls' houses. Fear in her heart. Panic. Just remembering it made her breathing increase, eyes water; she felt like a rat in a trap with no way out.

They didn't have any money. Mickey's afraid to go out. Lucy's depressed.

2 more days of hunger before welfare.

Lucy & Mickey brave the streets to get in line for dinner, free, at a soup kitchen.

Panhandles a few coins eon route.

They come home. The little butch works on Lucy, massages her, tries to revive life into her.

Soon the room smells like cunt & sweat.

Sex. That's all they had.

Lucy's bleeding from her vagina—she's on the rag. Empty wooden boxes where they kept the food. Cunt. Sweat. Blood. And tears.

And time passed. Life was a hard motherfucker riding them down. Low-class dykes—some go straight. Others are dead. Others are brave, live gay life in the open. So at the 169 Club they would meet again. It was the weekend, after a long unendurable panic of daily days.

Braved the dangers of the streets of night to get there. Hustled a beer from a dyke as poor as them.

On the dance floor. Lucy and Mickey. Mickey and Lucy. Suit & dress. They touch hands, romantic. Run fingers thru each other's hair, twirl around. A magnificent couple. Mick in a big-shouldered suit, dark, to match her black hair; black lace-up men's shoes & a tie, deep red. Lucy in a red dress, high heels and a coat that had wrapped her up—emerging from it like a phoenix, to dance, dance, dance!

They did all the things that cement a relationship together. Had erotic sex, Lucy floor-showed at the club & Mickey was the stud. "Will you love me after five years?" Mickey asked Lucy. And a clear voice seemed to come out of her soul in answer: 'Is it worth losing your love with all your fighting & arguments?'

Mickey sought advice from older butches. Just telling her side of the story.

The handsome stud lounges in line to the bathroom. Rusty tells her: "Find yourself another woman—if that's what's going on. Bi ones; they never change. They're nothing but heartbreak. That, or get used to her."

"Take it like she gives it, Mick," counsels Gerry. "I've had playgirls. Take it when she gives it to you & find another woman the rest of the time."

A bar stool was empty at The 169 Club. Sandy was in the Women's Pen doing 16 to life. Manslaughter and use of firearms in commission of felony assault. The judge took into consideration that she had no previous record; her admission of guilt early in the case; and her recent victimization. Gone were the men's suits in exchange for a uniform: a blue prison dress.

"I remember Sandy once told me she'd turn tricks herself & not have her old lady do it."

"YOU'RE NOT GOING TO DO THAT, MICKEY! I WON'T LET YOU!"

"I won't lay down! I'll murder him first!"

Then they set up a date for an older butch lady to use her woman for an hour.

Esther had met her at Temple—a visitor to the city. A Jew about 55, a lesbian and Judge on the Circuit Court of Appeals of New York City. This Judge can't afford to risk her professional reputation, so she must be discreet where & how she meets women. Eva sets it up. The two girls giggle, excited; Lucy has polished her nails, toes, perfumed her body, dressed up, borrowed jewels from Eva's stockpile of glittering femme weaponry; having a great time giggling, primping in mirrors, fixing their hairdos at Eva's hotel apartment. "MICKEY!" The redhead shouts over her shoulder while seated before the vanity mirror. "I never want to do it with men again, not even that show with them watching! I just want to do it with women!" Eva & Lucy clutch each other happily. Mickey observes drolly, 'It's like she's going out on her first date.' They leave the apartment and go have several drinks at the club first, then go back up to Eva's hotel.

And Mickey stays back at the bar. Thinks about her woman, cunt swollen in love, flat backing for another butch.

$50. And they can ride high all month.

"YOU SHOULD HAVE HAD SOMETHING STRONG TO DRINK FIRST!" says Eva.

"I did! But it wasn't enough!"

"NO! NO! If Lucy got drunk & don't know what's happening, she might wake up dead!"

"Not with a woman I won't! Not with a Judge of the Supreme Court of Appeals of New York City!"

She had been so excited about turning a date with this lesbian Judge, but afterward Lucy has become a bird dragging its spoiled muddy plumage. Feels empty. Her makeup worn off. Tired. Stays wrapped up in her coat. They sit together, three dykes at the bar of The 169 Club, glittering in the gutter. Mickey broke the $50 hours ago & is buying a lot of drinks for women who bought them drinks when they were broke. "We'll go to the gay restaurant with all the kids when the club closes and buy the two expensivest blue-plate-special dinners & take a cab home!" Mickey had declared. "So tell me, honey, how was it?"

"I didn't like it!" The redhead buries her head on Mickey's suit-coated chest.

"Baby! She didn't hurt you did she?"

"Mickey! It was terrible!" Lucy's eyes got big, face like a sad clown, wearing a frown upside down. "The minute we met, she talked to Esther in Hebrew & looked at me up and down like I was a piece of meat, & I couldn't understand what they were saying! And she wouldn't look at me in my face, not the whole time! Just my body! Eva & Esther left, they went to dinner…. Oh…it was terrible! The Judge got up after and she just put on her clothes and left the room. She didn't talk to me, or hug me, or kiss me after. She treated me like a used paper bag or something you throw in the gutter!"

"Did she get off?"

"Yes! A couple of times! And I didn't get to cum at all! And she wouldn't look at me! Not in my face, just my body! She kept staring at my tits while she did it!"

"Well, maybe she's embarrassed!"

"She didn't kiss me or caress me! I could hardly get ready for her!"

"It's suppose to be a trick, Lucy! She's not supposed to fall in love with you!"

"Women are suppose to be different, Mickey!"

Mickey showed her teeth. At 18 she knew more about the hustling game than Lucy. "She gave you $50! That's all she's suppose to do!" The butch reached up & tenderly patted wisps of hair that fell down into her femme's face back into place. "Lucy, honey, yer not really a prostitute. You want to give yourself emotionally—that's for a lover. That's for us."

"I know, Mickey. I'm finding out."

Lucy's trick. All the mental garbage she's ever had to deal with; it had been the same with this woman. So Lucy took her answer out of the needle. Summer was turning to Autumn. $50 had been her reward for going thru with it, yes. But money is crude & doesn't satisfy the spirit. Sexually, Lucy had put out for this woman, and had been looking to get something back.

Mickey did her sit-ups, push-ups and karate punches as usual. Went out for her walk. When she returned, Lucy was gone.

Note on the table reads: I'M AT PHYLLIS'S HOUSE. TAKE A BUS OVER & MEET ME.

Lucy usually kept a routine. Nights she went out afloat on the eternal sea of taverns, all-night restaurants, after parties, and recently, maybe end up at Phyllis's shooting gallery with her butch in tow, tie off & shirt collar open, trying to stay awake.

But this time, Lucy had just said, "Shit." And took a cab directly to Phyllis's and started off there in the beginning.

The neighborhood was hot. Drug hot. Police going around kicking down doors of suspected dope fiends. Tearing up the whole contents of houses into tiny bitty scraps in a search for narcotics.

Lucy nodded next to Phyllis, whose cold arm had long since slid off her shoulders.

They are seated on the filthy rug in that antechamber at the top of the stairs.

They shared drugs, not intimacy. And if Lucy felt it was love, she was wrong.

The redhead nods in the junkie crib having shot up nearly the last of the trick money from the lesbian Judge of the Circuit Court of Appeals, who by now has flown out of town.

'1959. 4 years into Chicago. I came here in December 1955. I wanted a woman way back then. Mickey is my new woman. I'm on my back as usual. I love Mickey & my life is a great disappointment. Tell me why, somebody. Tell me why!' And her head falls to one side, oozing into a pleasant drug glow.

A junkie answers the door downstairs; his ankles swollen up & abscesses along his arms.

Teaspoons lie around, & belts & straps. Odor of marijuana lingers in the air; it suffuses the rugs & drapes and tie-dye decorated sofas.

Dope fiends develop an animus: a ghost, visible, that fills them & walks around in place of themselves. Tho their feet walk on the ground, they are zombies tuned to a different channel. On a different level. Mickey noticed these strange vibes when she stepped in.

Leah looks down from the top of the stairs; hollow dark eyes floating in her head; clung to the banister to see who'd come in. Drugs build an artificial center in her mind—which she hated to leave—& seeing it was Mickey, Leah glided back into the antechamber.

Phyllis acknowledged the butch with a cold, bored expression & pointed to the corner. Junkie Leah twitched and held Phyllis around the waist; yearning for dope. Dope!

Lucy would never forget how she'd come here & fell into a drug-induced quicksand. Drug fingers straining to pull her down out of conscious into a morass; to tear at the fabric of her sanity.

Odor of marijuana hung on the air upstairs too, a herb, acrid. All these drugs had washed their money away.

Lucy was in the corner, seated on her haunches, rocking back & forth. "LUCY! WHAT ARE YOU DOING!"

"I'm looking at that face."

"What face?"

"The one over there."

A bolt of terror shot thru Mickey as she encircled her Lady with strong arms, smoothed back her now-loose red hair, felt the cold, clammy sweat stick to her sweater. Tried to comfort her, and reassure her & make the faces of nightmare recede back into Lucy's haunted unconscious from where they'd come.

The redhead faded in and out like a bad TV channel or a faulty radio wave. "Take an ax, Mickey, cut my head off. Take one for each of my two faces—Sandy took two axes—Two. I can't go on like this. I quit."

"YOU'RE PARANOID FROM BEING UP 2 NIGHTS IN A ROW & DRINKING & SHOOTING DRUGS. It's normal—you're not crazy. You need to come down from these drugs and go to sleep for about 48 hours."

Mickey was strong. Masterful. Piled Lucy into a cab— grabbed a plate of food to go from the Hasty Tasty as Lucy waited outside, slumped in the backseat, took her home, made her eat & threw her into the bed.

So they'd spent $15 in the bar that night past; $10 in the restaurant & cab home. And $20 at Phyllis's plus dinner & cab. There was a few crumpled dollar bills & change in the bottom of Lucy's purse, & in Mickey's pants pocket. So the butch went out to the store, bought $5 worth of canned goods, and they were poor again.

Huddled in Lucy's arms—sprawled sleeping. Moon rose thru their window. Peeling plaster peeks from under tie-dyed curtains walls. Chunks of ceiling falling in. Bed that dipped in the middle—breaking down from the weight of a thousand transients.

Huddled in this older woman's arms, Mickey felt herself tremble again—just as she had in front of the spectators back at the apartment where she'd first had her clit in Lucy's hot loving lips. Just like the first nights here in this city when she'd been alone. The redhead was older, but weaker. So their survival seemed to rest on her butch shoulders. The 18-year-old felt very afraid. In a big strange world that ground on and on without stop. Didn't know how she was going to stay alive, or to keep a place on earth to plant her two feet. How was she going to protect Lucy as a female? Keep their small bodies from the streets? Food would run out again & the manager of the hotel yelling at them for rent & they'd have to sneak in & out the back door from the alley; huddled there in the loose embrace of a sleeping female spread open in a slip, tousled hair and painted toenails and fingernails; and felt the trembling in her sturdy body. A huge fear rolling over her.

The bravado that had carried Mickey here from Miami had flown.

CHAPTER THIRTY-ONE

Lucy came out of the nod—momentarily.

Now when she'd come back down to the real world —she'd find she was farther & farther behind.

Rent wasn't paid, clothes not washed.

Her hammer & pieces of cloth and wooden boxes and dyes she'd been working with sat idle.

Mickey kept exercising. Preparing herself against the ever-present threat of male (or dyke) violence. Grunts, doing sit-ups & leg raises.

Then they received their checks. With that little money, everything is better for a while. Got a list of places where there's free food. Mickey goes for her walk, comes back to their room, Lucy's there, and it sends a shock thru her; a cold chill that ran down to her toes. 'Welfare...this is what people with no hope get...'

Went shopping in an A & P supermarket; they had to take a bus to get there. The Odd Couple; Lucy, curvaceous, tore-ador pants over her ass, high heels, tits bouncing under a pink sweater; & hair wrapped up in a babushka. Butch in slacks, man's shirt, gym shoes; very hard dyke. The supermarket Sample Lady left the lid on her tureen full of samples as the two went by pushing their metal shopping cart. Mickey happens to turn around & look behind her, and there's the Sample Lady staring at them with a frown on her face. One of those perfectly dressed church-believing ladies who kills with acid looks instead of knives. Mickey goes off down an aisle. When she returns to the cart, Lucy's munching—her jaws are full of food. "What're yuh eating, hon?"

"Some stuff that lady has over at that table." Mickey is enraged. Lucy had gone back & gotten some samples. It was bacon crunch on toast, which the lady is now dispensing; chitchatting with a nicely dressed housewife. Mickey strides back—the Sample Lady's back is turned! The tureen is open! She starts to snatch the whole pot & stuff it in a bag—but doesn't: The butch is too proud. Turns her face into a scowl and struts on by. She did not want to eat off the master's table.

"THIS CART IS CRAZY!" Mickey howls, pounding her fist on the cart. Cart rolled crooked on mismatched wheels; & they'd got in the wrong check-out line by mistake; and Mickey's howling for a reason she knows not what.

And all the straight shoppers turn to stare at this tough butch; hair slicked back behind her ears.

A month passed. Again, the sound of things going haywire.

It wasn't just their poverty, it was Lucy's willingness to do it. Money was more important to her than to Mickey. To buy alcohol, or drugs. She was sick of being poor. Life lit up her eyes again when she thought of Phyllis & her junkie palace. And that took money.

Ideas she got from Phyllis at her multicolor crazy-built junkie crib were appearing in their room.

Lucy had a hammer picked up at the Purple Heart Thrift Store, & was nailing fabric into the wall. And expected her butch to help. So Mickey's standing on the table, & frustrated—she's never held a hammer in her hands before. Doesn't comprehend how to do the job. "HIT IT! HIT IT!" her redhead woman yells. And the nail bangs off onto the floor.

"I CAN'T DO ANYTHING RIGHT!" Hit many nails over and over; Lucy handing them up. They went in crooked. Or missed. She hadn't been trained to do this job. Was so frustrated she finally pulled her arm back and slugged the wall. It felt good.

Threw the hammer down on the floor & slugged the wall once more. Busting up her knuckles. And all the hate-energy came out, & she felt just empty.

Mickey gave up on some level. Didn't care anymore. 'It's worn me down.' Lucy is turning their room at the Bristol

Hotel into a palace, & Mickey suspects she's gotten the extra money from James. And she gives up a little bit. And secretly now, thinks about what the extra money could buy. 'Lucy's gonna sneak out anyway, she's a crazy half-breed Indian, & do anything she can to get that firewater.' —That is her strongest passion. Oblivion.

But this hustling is very rare & petty, & mostly they starve. 2 women trying to scrape together a life down at the bottom. One too young, not sure about jobs & responsibility. The other having given up & surrendering to fate & wherever it might lead. Mickey's face is scarred with acne, which makes it look hard. Eyes black, intent. Her emotions were big; and at that point she moved away from Lucy by a degree. And later moved farther away—a few degrees at a time. By October Mickey had begun a fantasy—building a fantasy woman. One who was bodily clean & strong of mind & didn't drink, & didn't fuck anybody but her. And simultaneously constructed a fantasy Mickey to accompany this woman—a Mickey who was mentally powerful, physically strong, and worked an excellent job; who owned a car, a wardrobe of fine butch-clothes & boots; & who experienced the love of the fantasy female plus had several other ladies on the side. And, finally, constructed a fantasy place, where they would be. Be safe & free & in power. And then there was just the remaining problem of how to get this.

Right now, she felt the constant disappointment.

Tenants loud BANG! thru the walls; winos fighting all night. It was frightening.

Then Mickey actually applied for a job, went in; thought she was going to get real work, only it wasn't legitimate—it was some kind of fraud done over the telephone.

Went to the theater & they had already hired a full crew. But the manager did say, "Come back in a few weeks, in September. Some of the employees are students & they're going back to school."

So, didn't think she had anything. Having been fed empty promises in the past. And if she'd had a gun, would have killed herself right there.

Lucy took a drink & a pill. 'I'm not going to feel this. In fact, I'm going to enjoy it. This money is for Mickey & me.'

And went & got $15 from her old trick Terry, the one Mickey had physically battled in the skid-row streets; and Mickey finds out about this and is sad, angry & disgusted.

And Mickey's fantasy woman isn't going to do this; isn't going to prostitute herself. Nor drink red wine & beer. Secretly wished for this fantasy time & place.

Mickey sits on the stairs of the crummy hotel outside their room. Tousled head buried in her hands. She will eat no food—going into her 2nd day. Faint with hunger, passed out, awoke, staggered back in the room, head reeling. Lucy's there, the food is still there, also the memory of what she'd done to get it is still there, & she won't touch Lucy. And stumbles across the worn-out floor & falls into bed and lapses into unconsciousness again & Lucy can't wake her and she's running a fever.

"HONEY! EAT! MICKEY! EAT FOR ME PLEASE!" The redhead held a spoonful of dinner up to the butch's mouth.

Mickey struck it away. "I'D RATHER STARVE!"

"If anybody's jealous it should be me! You and all those girls you had in Miami! You took their money didn't you! You ate their food!"

So, next day Lucy has a dull pain in her uterus. Non-stop. A throbbing hurt that makes her wince & double over. Pain pushed by each tide of blood pumped thru her body by her heart.

Lucy limps around and has to confess she hurts inside.

"YOU'RE NOT BUILT RIGHT TO DO ALL THIS FUCKING! SOME WOMEN CAN'T TAKE IT! YOU'RE SUPPOSE TO BE A LESBIAN! YOU CAN'T JUST GO OUT FUCKING LIKE SOME STRAIGHT WHORE!"

"You almost have your whole fist up me!"

"Well, then, why does it hurt?"

"I don't know!"

"Because you weren't relaxed!"

"Maybe I have an infection!"

"Didn't you wear a rubber?"

"Yes."

"Then you don't have an infection."

"Somebody went down on me. Maybe that's where I got it. Unless I got it from you."

"Phyllis."

"Yeah… Maybe."

"PHYLLIS! YOU LET THAT BITCH SUCK YOUR CUNT! YOU PROBABLY DO HAVE AN INFECTION! SHE'S A WALKING DISEASE!" Mickey's eyes flash, her black hair slick with summer sweat. *"YOU FUCKED THAT BITCH AND DIDN'T TELL ME! I HATE YOU!"*

They stop speaking. There is only one battered wood chair in their cramped quarters; no comfortable places to pass the time but the bed. They lay on the sheets back to back inches apart, feeling the rise fall of each other's breath but not touching. But Mickey gets up to go with Lucy down the dangerous hall to the bathroom. Lucy gently lowers herself down on the toilet seat, in pain. Lays in bed all night mildly drunk on a bottle of wine, & Mickey eats.

"Was he big?"

"No."

"Then why are you hurting? I'll tell you why! It's because you should be with me only! That's why!" Mickey's forehead furrows. And she rubs Lucy's thighs back.

Next day, the pain in her insides is gone. "God answered my prayers!" Mickey declares. "But you can't do this anymore! If you did it every day, you'd be creeping around in pain all doubled up!"

"I'd stay high and wouldn't feel it." Lucy replies with a devilish grin. "And spend his money with Phyllis."

"LIKE HELL YOU WILL!"

"I won't." Lucy says, tired.

The moon passed over the building tops toward morning, and Lucy confessed. "We did it in different positions—that's what hurt. I was trying to cum, Mickey."

"What?"

"Just to see if I could. He kept a hard-on. I wanted to try it.

I've never cum that way—vaginally with a man. Don't worry about it! It didn't work!" Secretly the redhead thinks: 'If I can't cum with a man, there's no point ever being with one—even if he does suck me off. Mickey can do that, plus she can make me cum with her cock, but she's got to hold it in her hand. I've got to get one of those French Ticklers Eva talks about. Maybe I can cum then when Mickey's got the cock strapped on her. I could put the French Tickler on James. But if a man can't make me cum, I'm not going to waste my time putting a French Tickler on him—if he can make me cum straight fucking, it would be better being with him because life is a lot better when you're straight.... But that's the least of my problems because I still want a woman....'

And Lucy's listening to her outer voice holding a conversation, trying to make some feeble explanation to Mickey— she needs to share this struggle that's tearing her mind & soul apart.

"And when I told Phyllis about it, she sucked me off. 'To heal me,' she says. 'To heal you of your mental & physical ordeal.'" Lucy finishes her half-lie. "It was love. Pure love on her part. An act of sharing. You don't have anything to be jealous about. She's not the type...a person....gets close to—not like you, Mickey. I'd love it if we could both live there together with her—see, you don't have to be jealous at all."

"Did he fuck better than me?"

"No."

"Did she suck you off better than me?"

"No."

"I'M SO FUCKIN' *ANGRY!*" Mickey passed a hand over her eyes to hide the tears, brimming. And turns away so Lucy won't see. Roughly wipes her fingers over her smooth adolescent cheeks; yells: "IT'S FOR ME! YOUR HOLE IS FOR ME! YOUR MOUTH IS FOR ME, BABY! YOU'RE MINE!—OR I'M GONE FROM HERE!" Mickey forced Lucy down on the bed, wrestled her there until she was still, holding her wrists. The butch wanted to cum, but felt dry inside, shrunken up. Felt all her sex power was gone.

Next thing she remembered, she was waking. Sat up. It was 4 A.M. Lucy slept.

A while back she'd felt close to giving up her life in frustration of having no money, no job. Now, tho she had a woman, couldn't care for her. Felt she had no power.

Felt like returning to the supermarket and stealing something to make up for. The Sample Lady's rudeness. And every other bad thing that had happened to them that week. To get a piece out of it—some goods out of that multimillion-dollar supermarket chain; to get a piece out of it like they had got a piece out of her soul.

Best thing to do was to go to bed with Lucy in their hotel-room palace & screw her hard; in her pussy, ass & mouth. Sex had been the antidote since before the butch could remember; to give her back her power, to put her on the throne again. To love her tenderly. Then fall into the arms of sleep's oblivion. But desire was gone.

She was totally emasculated.

CHAPTER THIRTY-TWO

In November, fierce winter winds set upon them from the north, and from over the lake, bringing icicles. Flu & fever. Mickey bundled up inside their freezing hotel room in 2 pairs of sox, pajamas, sweat pants & shirt, blankets & a cap over her thick black hair.

And Mickey had been promised the job.

However, it was shaky with Lucy. Lucy didn't want to let Mick screw her anymore. Just sat in front of the TV, not speaking, wan smile crooked on her face, in a dreamworld.

It was one of those gray days in Chicago that starts out dead: coated, in cement, no sight of sun. Totally leaden sky, gray clouds.

Tip your head up for a moment and wonder where infinity ends.

Lucy did their laundry in the sink piece by piece. Strung on a clothesline across the room, to dry. They had so few underclothes, she had to keep washing them out every few days.

All her boxer shorts had turned dingy gray from no bleach. And all Lucy's little pink silk things had been worn to shreds.

Drugs Lucy shot, & drink (it was the only reason she used) was a crutch to limp thru the days.

Their first two months in summer had had plenty of love. Plenty of oral sex. Penetration by fingers and a variety of fresh vegetables—carrots, squash, cucumbers—& hot dogs. Finally they got the sex toy—10" of pure female cock. And now Mickey had a job to go with it.

And it was all falling apart.

All the gay kids at the club still thought they made a great couple & wished to mimic their successful relationship. But as the two sat at a table littered with glasses & bar napkins, in the dim party lights; lovely Lucy in a dress & high-heel pumps with fancy straps, hair piled up on her head; and butch Mickey in a suit & tie, deep blue, dark hair contrasting to handsome features; nobody but them knew they barely slept together.

"Please, honey!" Mickey tried to turn Lucy over to make love; warm breasts & round hips sleek in a silk nightgown wrapped like a seraph; slid down her body, tried to lick her thighs; to go all the way. "Have a heart!" Sometimes she did. A lot of times she didn't.

The redhead spent money at Phyllis's house—when she could sneak over there. Escape emotional problems that seethed inside. The unreconciled conflict of her childhood in a broken home. Her unresolved identity as a woman from two different racial heritages—was she a Native American Indian? Did she belong to the whites? And, her problem living with the fact that she was a lesbian.

It was too much.

Soon money would funnel into the household from Mickey's job—& she had not notified the Welfare Department, so they received her check as usual.

Phyllis & Leah & Lucy were licking each other's clits.

Three nasty pussycats with junkie fantasy-illusions playacting that they were lovers.

And Mickey was in a frustrated rage because she wanted to be the one doing it—licking & riding all of them!

Lucy at 23, was still older & more experienced in some

ways than Mickey—tho she was quiet. And found ways to slip thru the butch's grasp like quicksilver & go about her destructive life-style in the drug house & in the taverns.

Chicago. Glaciers of ice. Part of an archaeological trough from the Gulf of Mexico, thru which air comes down cold; and Illinois is the pits. So heat & cold change more severely than in other Midwestern cities.

The sky is black with birds speeding by like pepper dots over the sky in a ribbon.... They keep coming, floating, flying down.

Another streamer of birds flew past, a mile long.

A band of birds fluttering: travelers shimmying on the sky.

Mickey wished she could just keep walking out over a pier into the blue-green water & die. Couldn't escape her love problems & what to do with the future. She was almost 19.

Angry! She wanted to leap out & kill the next man she saw!

'I can stand Lucy and her alkie friends. But the tricks—I'm not going thru this again! And Phyllis. That cold, heartless wench scares the shit out of me! And Lucy's in love with her—in some weird kind of way!'

This was different than before, when she was butch companion to hookers & showgirls on their territory. Different because Mickey was older now, and life wasn't just a game for players. It was something of substance. And because Lucy was her wife.

Walked by the frozen blue-gray lake; didn't know what to do. Feet stomped over snow, crunching & her breath blew fog clouds; didn't know where to turn. Nobody would have realized this by looking at her—just that her mouth trembled a bit; but she forced it into a line, so she seemed in control.

Twinkling waves that had folded over and over; now frozen in a solid block of dirty gray ice. 'Holy Virgin Mary, don't let me lose Lucy!'

And as if from heaven, clouds part to let thru a twinkling beam of light; a clear assurance flooded her for an instant: 'Sorrow is just for a little while.'

CHAPTER THIRTY-THREE

Suddenly, Mickey's on the inside looking out.

A job.

Earns enough per week to pay for their room & eat, & she can walk to & from the place, saving bus fare. Janitor. Cleans up the theater lobby, office & toilets; & sometimes cashiers & handles the candy counter & popcorn machine. There's food she can eat: Hot dogs, candy, sodas. It's warm inside. She's getting paid more than welfare; so in a newfound security, she looks out thru the yellow window at the snowbanks & ice & freezing passersby.

Began to see that dressed as a female butch rather than trying to pass as a male who had to put up a drastic imperson-ation, she had more freedom. Tho she had fewer choices where she could go, and what she could do as a man; as herself—a mannish dyke she was beginning to be more accepted—espe-cially in this semi-artist, quasi-gay area.

Stared out from the yellow window and thought: 'The rich people ain't gonna help us, that's for sure. The ones that have the most give the least. If they give you anything, they want something in return—be sure of that. If they sport you to dinner once, they expect you to go dutch with them. Halves. Equals. Even tho they have $1 million in investments and you are penniless, they think it should be the same rate of exchange, but it ain't.'

The new frost had fallen in their first winter together & no heat. Wind whistled in a broken windowpane stuffed with rags. All they could do was stay wrapped up in each other's arms under a pile of blankets & coats.

So here, huddled together under a mountain of covers, Lucy gave in & let Mickey stroke her soft tits, and enter her with fingers & kiss her long & deep.

"The money's more important. More important than anything... To keep our home."

So when Lucy had began turning tricks, Mickey accepted the money. But after the trick was turned, Lucy wanted to spend the money on heroin and drink. Spend it on her beginning habit. Not on their home. Not even on herself to buy clothes or jewelry.

A problem brought them back to poverty. Mickey had to have her welfare checks cut off because she was working. So now, tho she had a job, was earning only $20 more per week than when she was getting charity.

And she had to buy new gym shoes to work in. Men's shoes wouldn't do. And a few pair of men's nice slacks & male shirts from the Purple Heart. Miss Lester and Mr. Cooney from the Welfare Department had scared her so bad at her last evaluation that she hadn't gone back, nor filled out the forms—so the free ride was over.

While she's at work, evildoers visit their room; and they boil down some pills and shot up mainline into a green-blue vein in the curve of Lucy's arm.

Phyllis, as a thief, has come to ransack their hearts.

When Mickey gets home, sweat rings under her armpits from a hard shift of labor, the redhead had crawled into the inside of her body. Was just a head, listening to her blood vessels hum.

Mickey notices Lucy's eyes; makeup is rubbed off; blue-moon circles under them hid by powder. Eyes puffy and swollen. In her armpit a red circle & blood dried into a black clot. "LUCY! LUCY! IT'S ME! MICKEY! LUCY! IT'S ME! YOUR BUTCH! MICKEY!" Fear answers her.... Lucy's white hand, ghostly, squeezes hers—silent. Taking the breath out of her throat. Mickey trembles to see her like this—& is unable to do anything about it. 'It's trouble when she lets those broads into our room.' "LUCY! SAY SOMETHING! CAN YOU HEAR ME TALKING TO YOU?"

Lucy had become a weekend junkie. A joypopper at this point—not an addicted heroin addict who is forced to use every day.

Flirting with hell.

Mickey had Fear & Trembling about the world. A fierce society circumscribed her. In which she felt she was powerless to a fate as random as the click of billiard balls on a green felt pool table.

She wanted this relationship desperately.

Wanted someone who was warm & good, like Lucy used to be—tacking tacky pieces of fabric on orange crates; who cooked little dinners & held Mickey & stroked her wavy black hair & gave the tender love of her body at night. The redhead femme was rapidly withdrawing from the circle of their love.

Mickey was gruff; silent & strong—to mask the hurt within. Mornings did exercises, building muscles onto her stocky physique. Went on walks at the beach to think privately. Went to work. 'Maybe when we have money she'll feel more comfortable & want sex more.' Mickey had a plan: 'If I can get more work and move us up off lower Clark Street away from the denizens of the deep who weave their grasping fingers around her soul, and square up (in a gay way)…. There's nothing to hold us here…. Nothing.' B-lights flash off and on. 'And budge Lucy out of her old habits. She always wanted to be high even before we met. She was loaded the first time we were together.' So the butch put up a fight for her girl Lucy. Tried to get more work, was patient, stayed by her side thru safari nights & junk mornings. Did the best she could do. But it wasn't enough.

Lucy came out of the nod. Reality intruded its cold, stark edges. She lay on her side facing the wall. 'Drugs.' She turned in the bed like a rider on a merry-go-round. 'Drink.' Lay on her back. 'Mickey.' Lay on her stomach. 'James.' Turned to face the warm smooth skin of Mickey's back. 'If I turn another trick, will it be the one that makes Mickey leave me?' Whirled over again. Snapped back, tugging the blankets in frustration & carried half the bedclothes with her. Everywhere people were asking for money. Manager of the Bristol Hotel. Lady in the grocery store who'd advanced Lucy some cans of food on credit. Mafia bartender's big hairy hand reaching over the bar to grab the few dollars she had remaining in her wallet to purchase a drink. And over 20 blocks in the reconstruction area—Phyllis. 'That bitch Leah, she's suppose to be Indian like me, but she's in the rat race. Thrives on money. She can't wait to see me—to see how much I have to spend and how high we all can get. Mickey is in the rat race. How she wants success. She wants to get 2 more jobs and earn enough money to get a nice apartment. "You'll be working the rest of your life." I told her. "You won't have time to walk on the beach & dream like you do when you go off and ignore me every day. You're only earning $1.50 per hour. You'll be like I was— working 10 hours a day just to have an apartment you can't afford, and no money left over, and no time to enjoy it. That's the rat race." Mickey wants to climb up the rungs of the ladder of success; but I'm safer right down here in the Hotel Bristol. It's cheap, my time is my own, no damn lady boss bitching, ordering me what to do, and telling me how to dress; & I can stay up drinking until 5 in the morning & don't have to worry about falling asleep over the file cabinets at work the next day.'

So life is nasty & angry without enough money & they're existing on the bottom—periodically the bottom falls out & there's not too many blows a human spirit can stand.

Mickey put on her gym shoes to go to work—the best ones—& slacks & shirt and a worn 3rd-hand coat from the Purple Heart. She was going to work—to feed this monster whose voracious appetite could be fed only by money, that was nipping at their heels. It was near the end of the month. Paycheck 5 days off & welfare a week away.

Lucy told her flatly that she had arranged to be with this man she'd known from the past—a friend. So Mickey mops up the theater, her guts in turmoil of acid; furious. Tends the popcorn machine stuck behind the brightly lit rancid-butter corn-smelling counter, making small nickel-&-dime change for candy bars & sodas at $1.50 an hour, wishes she earned $8 like even some of the Clark Street troops—men—earn, so she could buy Lucy's time herself & keep her at home watching black-&-white TV & maybe take a cab to the gaybar to party with their own kind.

Lucy was pissed that Mickey was going to follow her to the trick's apartment and wait outside in the freezing street. "To make sure you don't get killed," the butch had informed her. Or was it to make her ashamed? Lucy wasn't sure.

Ran between the toilet down the hall thru the paint peeling stretch of decrepit walls and a tattered brown rug, back to their room to their sink behind a tie-dyed curtain & the table with her makeup & bracelets on it. "WE'LL GO TO THE CLUB AFTER, MICKEY! WE'LL HAVE MONEY FOR A CAB! FOR DRINKS! WE'LL HAVE FUN! Don't worry so much! If I wanted them more than you, I'd do it five times a day and we'd have lots of money! It's just the fact I know you don't want me to, is keeping me from it!" Goes down the bathroom for privacy; hastily inserts her diaphragm; a rubber sheath covered with gel to prevent pregnancy. Lucy has this well hidden; the butch thought she had thrown it out—not needing it once they'd vowed to be together as a couple.

With this money they can party & buy canned goods, and a sack of potatoes and some meat which will last until they get their checks. "It's OK! It won't take that long, honey! I already know him—it's safe! Baby, I know I haven't been treating you right, but I feel good already, I feel so happy because we're going to go out and party & have some drinks later! I'll wash my pussy good & let you fuck me. Do anything you want."

"Come to me, Lucy!" Mickey said and opened her butch arms. And Lucy came.

"Now! Let me go! I said I'd be there at 10!"

Swallowed two pills on the sly, a present from Phyllis, to make the task she had to do bearable—in fact, even enjoyable. Lucy got in a freakish mood when drugs hit her system. 'I'll get drunk after.' Lucy tells herself, to fortify herself to go thru with it; and they go floating out on the sea of night.

Mickey waits outside on the steps, shielded from the cold Hawk—Chicago's icy wind from over the lake. Stomps in the cold, blows gusts of icy air. Lucy's already been up there 20 minutes; & Mickey's thinking about it, gets enraged. 'Lucy's laying up there in bed with a stiff dick in her for 20 minutes & she don't mind doing it—claims the money is for us both.' Mickey waits, stomps her feet; shoes & trousers & worn 3rd-hand coat and black hair flecked with snow. Hates herself. Feels frustrated that she earns only $1.50 per hour & that they are always poor. Rage of jealousy and anger. And, in the back of her mind, also, is a hunger to join the faces of the night. To sit at a bar with cronies. Party lights, red blue & green. Knew they'd buy drinks & have fun with gay kids and afford to eat dinners at the restaurant; a straight establishment by day which they'd transform—the whole bar would descend upon the place en masse & turn it gay until dawn; then take a cab home after. And thinks: 'I don't have to be jealous. Lucy is coming home with me, not him. And if Lucy was a whore, she'd be doing it five times a night five nights a week, like she said; not once every other month.' Then, feverishly wishing it was her—Mickey—with their dildo strapped on giving it to her—cock, and handing Lucy $15. Snow flurried around the cement entranceway. Cold wind has sliced into the marrow of her bones with its butcher knife; her red blood runs cold. Time didn't seem to be going by. 'Is something wrong? She's been there 40 minutes! My God, maybe she's hurt!' And knowing Lucy, maybe the man has a bottle & they're having a party & have forgotten about her. She didn't know what to think.

Cold wind blew. Frost dries; animation suspended in icicles.

Huddles in the brick entranceway. Toes going numb. Wants to put her fist into something—Lucy's cunt. Or the wall. Wishes desperately she had a dick like the johns & could take Lucy to undreamed-of heights in bed & out to dinner in nice restaurants; instead of being short in stature & skinny and having a cunt that Lucy doesn't even bother with anymore and having no money. Mickey gets more and more frustrated. Enraged. And time marches by steadily; it's after 11 now & gay kids are beginning to party at 169 Division Street. 'What can I do to escape this trap? Maybe I should go back to school and get a degree and become a professional person like Esther & that Judge, who can get anything they want. Maybe I should get one of those Sex Change Operations everybody's talking about—like Christine Jorgensen in Denmark, & then it would be just my luck to be stuck with a dick that don't work like a lot of men.' The turned & stomped in the brick entranceway. Gusts of cold air brought flecks of snow to her shoulders & black wavy hair. Icicle breath. 'At least I've got a job! When she gets down, I'm gonna fuck her, too!' Just when Mickey was ready to break down the door with kicks, here comes Lucy, exhausted, red hair stuck to the back of her neck. "YOU BEEN UP THERE SO GODDAMN LONG! WHAT HAPPENED!"

"He couldn't get it up," she explains. "We tried everything! I played with his nipples like a woman. He put on my dress! Everything!"

Lucy had been struggling with the man, both of them trying desperately to get him to come. Trying every trick they knew, but nothing had worked.

"I thought he was raping you or killing you!"

"I wish he had raped me and gotten it over with! He couldn't get hard! We tried everything!"

"But he's just suppose to get 20 minutes, Lucy! If he can't cum in 20 minutes, that's his problem!"

"But he's a friend of mine!"

"You *did* get the money!"

"Yes." The redhead held out $15. A ten & five singles, damp, rolled into a cylinder; and handed it to Mickey.

"All that time! *Shit!*"

"He didn't get off!" Lucy replies, pissed.

"Well, it ain't your fault! As beautiful as you are! I could have come twice in all this time!"

Hawk was beginning to blow snow. Outside in the fierce Chicago cold. Summer fun was over & the time they trusted each other was gone. The wicked winter. Alkie's blood, red, on the crisp snowbanks. Derelicts swirled by, hags with gaptoothed snarls. "All this time, Lucy! Shit! Me freezing & worried! I got a better tool—fingers! I got something hard—at home, to put in you all night long!"

"IT'S NOT HIS DICK—IT'S THE MONEY!" Lucy screams in a silent hiss over the wind. "When will you get that thru your thick skull? You're so jealous! It's not the Indian way to be so possessive and materialistic! And I'm tired of not having any money!" Lucy's out in the middle of the avenue; foggy headlight's yellow beam frames her, passing; she flags down a cab.

And then they were riding, riding once more, like Miami,

Times Square, feet propped up, in style—on their way to party fun. And under her handsome profile were murky doubts. A loss of self-esteem. There was nothing in the news of homosexual people like herself—their history was a blank. Mickey wanted to scream & rage against it. That was the world in 1959. And, her personal inability to take care of her woman financially & barely able to protect, or hang onto Lucy. Turns to her over the space of the cab's backseat which separated them; "You're high. I can tell."

"I took some pills. Phyllis gave them to me. Hustling johns ain't half-bad—when I'm high."

"You need me in you," Mickey growls. "You don't need to get high to have me love you."

The pretty redhead smiles wanly from a makeup-painted face; reaches over and puts her hand on Mickey's leg. Then slides over the expanse of plastic seat & cuddles up next to the butch, under her arm in its big coat. "No, Mickey, not you. I never need to get high to have you."

Nearing The 169 Club, hysterical squeals of too-gay Drag Queens.

Black walls, red lights. Inside Mickey stands in line to the toilet. Confessing her latest problem with her lady to a fellow butch: "Lucy's nuts when she takes those drugs. I never know about her from day to day anymore. She's sweet and gentle on Saturday, & on Sunday she's plotting behind my back."

"Drugs change things."

Meanwhile, at the bar, down a ways, three dykes glare at Lucy. "I should go in there right now and tell Mick, while I can. I hate to tell her."

"Spare her the pain," says another.

"But somebody has got to tell her! Her broad's turned junkie, & she's selling herself to johns!"

"Yeah, and Mick even has a job now!"

"She's a good butch. She don't deserve such a rotten bitch sneakin' behind her back."

"Mickey's got no competition but this"—the dyke indicated jabbing an invisible hypodermic needle into her arm—"that heroin."

So Shorty takes a risk, goes into the toilet after Mick. They stand by the hole that rain has made in the floor. Shorty stares up at her, stupid, a minute, then spills it out: "Mick, I hate to be the one to break the news to yuh, buddy, but some of the guys and me, we heard yer broad is...well....hustling over at Shrimpie's for drugs."

"POW!"

A blow grazed the top of Shorty's head as she ducked. *WHAM!* Another punch. "SHUT THE FUCK UP, RUNT!"

Shorty's back is up against the wall; her hands cover her face. "NO, MICK! NO! I'M SORRY! I'M SORRY!" The rebuke stung in Mickey's mind, spread out in a blushing fan of shame into her nose and hit the nerves in her eyes last, making tears form; but held it back. Her face hardened.

As Shorty scuttled out the door into the gaping crowd, Mickey pushed her way out; felt the need to strike out with fists. Hit. Feel contact of dull thuds of her knuckles on flesh. To punish them. To punish the world that was against her from all directions as far as she could see thru the funnel of time.

Black walls spun around her; the world was suddenly revolving; three dykes are on top of her; BLAM! POW! CRUNCH! Feels the weight of bodies press her down into the side of the pooltable. Blood runs from her nose. The bartender screams: *"OUT, YOUSE GIRLS! OUT! OUT! NO FIGHTING! YER OUT!"* And Shorty backs off Mickey's slumped form. Her two friends pull back in mid-punch. "SHE HIT ME FIRST! MICKEY ATTACKED ME IN THE CRAPPER! LOOK WHAT SHE DID TO MY FACE! AND I WAS ONLY TRYIN' TO HELP HER! HONEST!"

At the bar, Mickey leaned on Lucy, who held her head to her chest; and she's bleeding. Bartender throws them a wet rag. Seems like it's always something blocking her way in life—even if it's just a runt blocking the washroom door. Has a cut lip, which swells. Her right hand swells up like a balloon with fat fingers—so you couldn't see veins or delineations of bones & knuckles. Alcohol soothes her. Lucy helps hold the glass; her hand over Mickey's hand. Blood drenches her shirt, stains Lucy's satin front leaking thru to her bra. Mickey leans there safe, in her woman's arms, in a snapshot of time. Bright red blood on a cold bar towel. Black walls spin, and the laughing din of gay kids proceeds.

When the 169 closed at 2, they'd take a cab to The Bomber Club & maybe see Duke and Freddy; afraid of running into Shorty & the two dykes in the restaurant.

Out in the street under a film of winter snow, Mickey brags: "I punched that runt in her fuckin' face!" CRACK! Slaps a fist into the palm of her hand for emphasis, forgetting her injury in a passionate moment of anger; then winces with pain. "If I hadn't pulled my punch, it would have broke her face!" Mickey glowers.

Mickey had $10 left of the $15. Thinks, privately: 'Damn me! I slugged my pal Shorty for calling my old lady a whore, & here's the trick money right here in my wallet.'

Duke was there; front teeth out from a bygone battle. "LUCY AND MICKEY! How the hell are you!" Limped over, swung his leg over a bar stool & sat down gingerly. "Motherfucking faggot, I should have killed him.... Gee, Lucy, you look nice. All dolled up. Not like we use to be down in the Village, huh." Duke didn't like to talk about his hustling, since he was straight; but when he'd been drinking, everything came out. He'd allowed a fag to use his rectum to ejaculate and thus spread syphilis thru still another link in the chain. Duke was being treated by the VD Doctor, but he needed money to drink. Had got $10.

"Well, mine couldn't even cum," says Lucy, brushing a wisp of red hair out of her face with a swipe of chipped red finger nails. She fell apart slowly as night wore on. The two big spenders discussed it alongside the bar. Duke wasn't any part fag and he hated turning tricks as did most of the skid-row men handsome enough to add to their income by going with fags. And Mickey sat like a Lord between them, drinking 7UP.

Later, around 3 A.M., Lucy's bent her elbows, hunched over the bar, serious, in conversation. A grease monkey in a blue uniform stands next to them; dirt under his fingernails and smudges over his skin. He makes a good living working on cars. Can support himself & have money left. Has bought them all a round of drinks. He asks, "Well…will you?"

Lucy leans to Mickey, eyes blurred; straps of her dress fall over her white shoulders, & stains from Mickey's blood have dried on her satin-covered tits. "Baby"—Lucy pulls on Mickey's arm—"tell him to go fuck off."

"She can't, she's on the rag." Mickey tells him. "She's sick."

So they keep spending their own money. Duke looked into space. He didn't have a skirt, nor would he wear woman's clothes; but it was remarkable to him how easy Boom-Boom & Lucy and women like them could earn a living—just by sitting on a bar stool minding their own business.

The grease monkey in blue uniform could be seen down the bar; moving on down the line & was talking to somebody else, elbow bent on the bar, holding a bottle.

But Lucy was the best-looking woman in the house.

They're spending. The money is going—down to $5. They were going to go home broke—the price of fun.

Mickey drank mostly soft drinks to remain sober & have clear judgment and be able to tow drunk Lucy home safely. Blows struck on her body and her crash into the pool table and subsequent fall to the floor have left her in a floating state; felt she might pass out. Bright lights flashed in her brain from nowhere. And spasms faded in & out, jerking her arms and legs every now and then. Lucy spoke drunkenly to a hag nearby.

"An Indian is the next thing to a nigger, practically. They're evil and you can't trust them!" the hag mutters.

"NO!" Lucy's saying. "NO! This is not true! I myself am an Indian."

The hag looks at her thru squinty, bleary eyes & laughs. "'Yeah, dearie, yer a redhead squaw." The hag's laughing, & her hillbilly drinking partners roar. "Redhead Injun." The hag mutters in mirth.

Lucy turns to Mickey: "She don't believe me, honey." Mickey holds her tight a minute. Then they just sit side by side. This isn't a gay bar, they aren't free here, or anywhere. 'I put too many demands on Lucy. I forget she is part Indian. She thinks things the Indian way—she got it from her mother; even tho she looks white. And talks white. I have too much expectation. Lucy is simple hearted. She just wants to live her life from day to day. There is no Right or Wrong. No sense of Duty. She don't want to get a job and feel like a red rat in a cage.'

There's a noise, like the big yawn of the ocean; it's a mass intake of breath; as collectively, in one animal, the bar patrons duck & run for cover. CRACK! SLAM! A wino brings a chair down over somebody's shoulders. Any people with sense, or who aren't seeing double from liquor, have climbed over tables of benches, if they can't scurry over to the other side of the tavern.

Dark red beads of blood have dried on her satin dress front. Lucy and Mickey run from fate hand in hand—they run from another fight.

Lucy's eyes are moist; thick black mascara has blurred; she was hurt—in her feelings. "Nobody can have a good time without fights."

Ringing in her ears; Mickey remembered nights, not long ago, before this town; her body covered with slaps—stinging her flesh. Could feel it—slaps on her arms, neck, face. Pain. And at that point she'd decided to stop the affair with Lisa; like she'd decided to cut the ties from her mother & that abuse, and not remain there anymore.

Violence. It ripped the cum right away from her.

Peace is another fantasy—longed for, in Mickey's world.

Yellow-lit tavern; folks were crying in there. Balling up their fists & screaming.

Mickey went outside into a blast of cold and hailed a cab. It pulls up in the snowy gray slush. They got in, collapse in each other's arms. "One of those dykes stuck her finger in my eye." The world was raining blows on them. Dykes' fists. Men harassing them in the street. Acid churned in her stomach. 'If Lucy was just here for me & would be my righteous Lady.'

The sweet being nestled in her arms as the cab raced

toward the Bristol Hotel. "That lady said we were drunk Indians." Lucy tips her head up quizzically. "She didn't believe me! That I'm an Indian! She called me a redhead squaw!"

By the time they got up the crooked stairs, past rooms of winos and insane muttering; down the corridor into their rainbow palace; here is this real butch need inside Mickey. Her clit throbs under her trousers. She wants to fuck. No longer emasculated like the nights before.

Went to her, loving her; half on top, kissing, fingers working in Lucy's cunt. "I'm glad that motherfucker didn't screw you. Glad!" Mickey snarls. "I want you to save it for me!"

Soon Mickey's bucking up like a stallion; hot, wet & wide. "I GOT TO FUCK! OH, *FUCK!* OH, CUNT! CUNT!" Pounding on her baby's cunt, clit red-hot.

"Cum, baby! Cum! I love you, Baby Mickey!"

Chapter Thirty-Four

Lucy is doing her eyes with eyebrow pencil at the table in front of a piece of a mirror.

"You're putting on makeup to go to the Welfare Office?"

"I'm sorry, Mickey, I just can't go in there without something on. I'll be sitting there the whole time worried about how I look... See! I just used a tiny bit of lipstick. So I don't look too awful, but I don't look too made up!"

"You got to look poor."

"I *am* poor!"

To a stranger in town, the 2nd or 3rd landmark they know is the location of the city jail. To visit if they are lucky. To do time if they ain't.

Not far is the DEPARTMENT OF SOCIAL SERVICES OF COOK COUNTY. To reach it they had to pass by the jail. A ten-story building of gray cement with slits for windows that run the length of several floors, and are not wide enough to let a human being out; & thru which prisoners can catch a glimpse of blue sky. As a fortress of antiquity: with slits out of which warriors could shoot their arrows. "These buildings are taller than the tallest castle was, way back in medieval times—this is the progress of civilization. A fucking jail.

"They got big fat hillbilly guards in jail who weigh 250 pounds and more. And some places they got niggers who hate everybody white in their charge. The hillbillies were so stupid, it's the only job they can get—so they take it out on the people entrusted to their charge who are smarter than them— Shit! For the first time in their lives, they have power over somebody, & they can't use it to do the right thing because they're so dumb. These social workers, a lot of them are no good. I hate to say it, but some of the black ones are OK because of being oppressed themselves, have more of a heart. But all of them are phoney because they don't know nothing about gay kids. That's why I'm glad I don't get welfare no more. They can kiss my ass."

Farther along is that solid 2-story gray brick cube under the rolling freeway. The Welfare Department built on government land, its title chiseled in stone blocks.

It's so cold, their hands stick to their gloves. The redhead was blue. This event was part of their Life Struggle. She had to get evaluated by the Welfare Department every so often, & it took up the whole day.

To Mickey, these caseworkers who processed the General Assistance claims were accomplices & collaborators of jail guards—or were of the same mentality. They were all fragments of an unjust System. "We're nothing to each other in their eyes! You're not my husband!" the redhead snaps peevishly. "They can't prove you're helping me!"

"Good, because I hate to confront some nosy bitch behind her desk poking around in my life asking questions—I'll go wild!"

Gray stone archway 2 human heights tall looms over them in an architectural sacrifice to style. Everything else about the building is utilitarian.

They enter the tyranny of the Cook County Social Services Agency. "LOOK AT THAT!" An obese woman with several children in tow howls. "That lady there—she fainted—and got to get up in the front of the line!" Indignant. She'd been waiting for hours.

"The niggers do that," Mickey whispers to Lucy. "But we got to stand here like everybody else."

The line snakes forward; Lucy gets her papers; has to fill them out and come back at 2 P.M. for a class.

When she returned from the class, the redhead reported: "The guy in front of me had a bible on his desk. And the lady says to turn the page in our booklet? And this guy's turning pages in his bible instead. He's crazy. And the lady from Social Services who's leading the class—she's crazier than anybody. She yells: 'NOW TURN YOUR PAGE TO PAGE 23!' And she gets somebody to read out loud. Then she hollers, 'DID I SAY PAGE 23? WELL, IT'S PAGE 26!' And another guy, I don't know if it was a guy or a girl—he looked like a she, who knows?—says, 'I have to see a doctor!' And the lady says, 'I AM NOT ON *THAT* PAGE! I'M ON THE ORANGE PAGE!' And she keeps mumbling, 'I'M GOING TO GO THRU THESE PAGES. IF YOU HAVE ANY QUESTIONS, ASK!' So everybody starts asking questions. 'What if you're in a Mental-Day Care Center?' 'What if you're just out of prison?' And the next guy—or girl—this one next to me asks, 'What if you're an alcoholic? What if you're a drug addict? Can you work?' And the lady yells, 'WELL, I DON'T KNOW! CAN YOU WORK OR CAN'T YOU! YOU HAVE TO ANSWER THAT YOURSELF!' And the drug addict, I don't know if it was a man or a woman—she looked like a Drag Queen—he, she sounded like a University Professor; she says, 'I researched various welfare programs and found I wasn't eligible for them. I think I'm eligible for this one, tho.' And the lady gave him a look to kill—it was unforgettable. So then, another lady comes in—another Social Worker—bends down & whispers to the other Social Worker so close she practically kisses her. Coloreds, those two. And the first one says, 'Oh, well, I'll see you later, *baby*...' They're worse dykes than I am."

"It don't mean nothin'. They all call each other 'baby,' the Coloreds."

"Well, *then*, she tries to hug her, but she couldn't reach over the desk. 'Come on out in the hall, *baby*,' she says. And the lady gets up and disappears out into the hall and she's gone for ten minutes! Then she runs in, straightening her skirt & pats her hair, all out of breath and sits down and picks up the book and gets the wrong page & is all hot and bothered. It wasn't just that they were Colored, they were *dykes!*"

They walked past the Coroner's Bureau on the way out of the Government Complex. 'Maybe I could go to school & get a job like a Social Worker.' Mickey's mind lit up like a light bulb & flickers feebly.

'…You start out; then you get shot down & stepped on. Everybody keeps stepping on you as they proceed on their own course. Even dykes and fags from The 169 Club.' And then they were running for the bus.

'We are utterly alone. Nobody knows who we are but the manager of the Bristol Hotel, some bartenders, & a couple of dykes who secretly want to fuck Lucy behind my back, & the skid-row bums. The police, the Mafia, the straight people, and the church; they are all against us. What we say or feel inside makes very little difference to them. I should go to school, maybe, and study, and get a job that's a career, and make more money & buy all the women I want. They will come flocking to me because I have a car & a house & a lot of nice clothes & jewelry and can take them out to eat, & wear a lot of expensive men's after-shave cologne, so when we have sex and my body sweats, it won't stink; & I'll have a private bathtub.'

Passed a huge church half a city block big; alabaster Doric columns of chiseled Greek architecture; & stained-glass windows. FIRST PRESBYTERIAN CHURCH chiseled in granite.

Mickey spat.

CHAPTER THIRTY-FIVE

'It's not so bad if I was coming back,' the butch thought. The trap was a mental jail, a point of no return, as the sick feeling hit her again. 'But when I leave Chicago, I won't never pass back thru here. This city is too rough on gays. So, if Lucy can't come with me…I'll never see her no more….' Shrugged her shoulders & the weight of Atlas must fall off.

'I got to make it to California; that's the answer. Where it's free to be yourself. And the people aren't full of so much hate.'

Constant grinding away as if she was strapped to a big wheel; turn, turn, turn…with no control—but her restless spirit to rebel.

A restless anger. Permeated thru the days. Anger. Mickey felt something had to happen. She couldn't be like Lucy all the days of her life; she'd move on up—or die. To climb. To achieve a better place on this mortal coil—or to get out of it altogether.

They all knew the anger of days; Lucy, Duke, the Clark Street troops; Gays who lived The Life, not just visited it down on the weekend, braving danger enough to stick their head in the door of the club and cruise it for a few minutes. Anger of days with its slaps, punches; its curses and condemnation. Till a human soul became a blank nothing. Emotion had drained—leaving the rind. The crescent moon. The empty bottle of wine.

So Mickey had become stuck in Chicago, but then remembers she had really been on her way out West. And realized that currently she was in a trap. In chains. Pressed down at the bottom of a nightmarish scene—sweat beads broke out over her forehead; for the pressure was great.

Now the whole club of gays knows it—Lucy is a whore. This makes Mickey a pimp. So the butch's image is shattered in the eyes of some, & raised up to be larger than life—a hero—to others. It's serious. Who will she lose Lucy to? Phyllis? James? Some trick/friend? Some dangerous john—a maniac—killing them both. Or will she find Lucy with a knife sticking out of her chest in a dark alley? Dope? The bottle?

There was Lucy, sucking from a wine bottle—the release valve of the society that had expelled her—at the foot of the city; the spewing mouth of skid row under red & blue lights & steel guitars twang; in a tawdry satin dress with straps falling down over her pale shoulders; fragile as a dove who was protected by Mickey; and James before her, and always by her band of Clark Street troops, and, ultimately by God. By the fickle hand of fate—how much longer did she have before her luck ran out?—before her front teeth got knocked out. The veins in her arm got blown, & a monkey on her back. Or was a corpse in the morgue?

Mickey cursed God, but her words fell back on her. The heavens said nothing. The answer lay in the fruition of time.

One day soon she would pass out of the state of Illinois, and leave the B-girls, the club dates & take a train to the ends of the earth.

Occasionally, a human voice comes to her that means something: like Jan; who had said encouragingly, "Look for a job. You can find one; you just have to keep trying." Some voice, amongst all the liars, who told the truth.

A short, baggy-pants dyke stands before her, again, in memory. A runt; her face hovers in space; its expression made hideous by fear. 'YUH SAID I INSULTED YUH IN THE TOILET! I DIDN'T INSULT YUH IN NO TOILET!'

'Or maybe when I leave her she'll turn cold & callous & get smart. Painted scarlet with ugly makeup. Whore is short for horrible.'

'A lot of sand under ice. This is a great beach. A vast lake. The bottom floor is far…green algae in summer… Gray-blue ice in winter.' Mickey was on her walk, along a round about path on her way to work; exploring the geology of her mind.

Carries, ideas with her, with a hot, jubilant glow. 'Jan says anybody can get a job somewhere—some kind of job. Especially in California. I got this one, didn't I? And it's working OK. Even as a dyke. They depend on me. And I had that job in New York, and could have got one in Miami, too. I don't have to stay here if I don't want to. And this is killing me.' The teen trudged, hands in pockets, back hunched against the cutting cold. 'I'll let Lucy decide. I'll wait & let her punch my train ticket like Lisa did with her slaps. And like my girls did in Miami. I can't get away from her otherwise—unless she makes me hate her. Because I love her. If she does something so bad as to betray me, that will punch my train ticket and get the wheels rolling out of here. Jan says to use my head and not my feelings, but I've got a heart. I'm weak that way.

'Lucy says it's gonna be rough out there in California alone. That I won't get a job—look how long it took me to find this one. She don't want to pull up roots & go. Wine has made her too content. Too afraid of the future.'

"YOU MOTHERFUCKER!" A slap in the face. Lisa yanks Mickey violently by the collar of her butch shirt. "YOU GO TO HELL!"

"You're not my old lady no more, Lisa! This does it!"

Lisa stalks to the hotel room door in her golden high-heel pumps, filmy negligee blowing in stride, yanks it open: "GET OUT, BITCH!"

Mickey tells her in a controlled voice: "I'm getting my things Lisa! My clothes & stuff!"

"DON'T *TOUCH* IT! YOU'RE NOT LEAVING HERE WITH NOTHING YOU DIDN'T BRING HERE IN THE BEGINNING! WHO BOUGHT YOU ALL THESE CLOTHES & THAT WATCH AND YOUR FUCKING PIMP RING? JUST LIKE A BIG GREASY PIMP! *I BOUGHT IT! ME!* AND IT'S STAYING WITH ME!"

First thing God created for the gay world was black walls & a red light. Then some bar stools with red vinyl covers. Then a lady. Then a butch.

'Name of the club? Funky funky Broadway. Name of the woman? Broadway woman. Name of the butch? Broadway man.'

So, all hell was rioting in the frozen gray sky; 'I got to get out of here.' And the cars are driving around the Outer Drive with their little swords of light ahead of them; a beam of headlight lengths longer than the car.

She'd be passing out of adolescence soon enough....

If Lucy wouldn't come along to California, if Mickey couldn't find a girl out there, her room would be cold at night. The strap-on dick would sit idle—no fumbling its rubber cockhead between moist thighs guided by her clenched pale fingers of one hand; pushing, stroking into her, raising her to pleasure, higher, higher.... Would have to do it all herself. Everything. The job, the sex, the schooling, the surviving; until she could make life better.

The walk to the theater was some ten blocks. Had no money for bus fare, so Mickey had plenty of time to think about Lucy: the skid-row bums and all the rest on her way. 'Her thing with men, she whores because she's used to being with them. And our marriage is not working. Some dykes, it's their job to be a lookout. A pimp who stands in the Hasty Tasty, looks sharp out the plate-glass window to watch their woman work, & if she's hustling the streets to protect her from some bigger pimp who offers to break one of the ladies' legs if she don't comply. But I'm not a fighter, I'm a lover. Lucy's got to come with me and cut lower Clark Street loose, and the troops with their alcohol loose, and Drug Princess Phyllis loose—leave it all, and come with me!'

'He had a gun pointed to my head, the muzzle cold steel against my skull, and I told him: "You're gonna have to shoot me then, motherfucker, if that's what it's gonna be, because you can't have my old ladies, none of 'em and I'll tell yuh why." And his eyes are going back & forth in his head; wild, high on Cocaine. A black pimp—his eyes were yellow. "Because they ain't mine to give nobody. They are Independent Ladies. They work when they choose & where they choose. They keep me in diamond rings & silk suits when they feel like it, and I might have to go to the pawnshop tomorrow & sell everything if they flake out on me & disappear tomorrow. I got no control over them. So you can have them—if you can find them."

'And then we had to get out of New York. Times Square was too hot. Too much Vice. Too many bad pimps. And it was winter, just like this—cold, sleet, wind driving rain into snow down, down, down.

'And I just I just didn't have the heart, not the heart to pimp another woman—for the violence it does to the heart. Even for the sake of a pocketbook full of money big as Wrigley Field. Money. Love. Survival. The axes like poles of the earth thru which is wrapped a terrific confusion. So, in

Miami there I was doing it again. And now, in Chicago, again, too. When will it end?'

CHAPTER THIRTY-SIX

So one day Lucy just walks over to James hotel room. Mickey's added 2 more hours on her job and she's not around as much, so the redhead's free to roam.

Climbed steps to James's hotel room; clung to the giant's arm—huge muscled biceps—felt secure. Lucy saw his cock bulge, poking up under his gray work pants. She couldn't help mentally comparing it to the ten perpetually swollen inches of their lesbian dick at home.

James had body hair—his chest was thick with curly hair, fur down his stomach to his pubic hair, rubbery sex.

And love was not like when she ran her hand over Mickey's hot furry pussy as they got ready. Lucy barely touched James at all.

First James sucked Lucy's luscious breasts; he fondled her a long time as they'd learned to do together in the past. Squeezed her nipples, his rough beard stubble nursing at her tits, as she got wet & his cock got hard & hot. When he entered her with his 6" dick, Lucy knew from the memory of many repetitions she would be in for a good time, but not for long. Always expectant, usually disappointed—with men. Knew it wouldn't go as long—Mickey could cum 3 or 4 times in succession & keep fucking for two hours—not go as far, or as deep as the dick she & her butch shared in their rainbow palace of love.

"OK, James," Lucy had said, giving permission, signifying she, too, was ready, and lay back. With him she had even less work than with Mickey. Didn't suck him off; didn't feel him up. Time she had to spend instead by going in the bathroom to insert her diaphragm; then lay there. Scrunched her cute little pussy up to James's cock. His face was blank over her; taut, serious, with the look of a mission to accomplish.

As he thrust his throbbing manhood into her, she felt the ecstasy. Arched her hips up to meet his. At first she had hoped

to cum with James—Lucy had never got off from a man fucking her; only with Mickey fucking her with the strap-on cock.

Passion flickered as he beat inside of her. Arousal grew; He
rammed it in her cunt into a high level of excitement. It was
over in about 15 minutes. He ejaculated into her, rolled off,
and rested a moment at her side. 'He has to make me cum like
a woman does.' It was getting more and more confusing.
'Mickey goes longer with the cock then James can. Ours is 4
inches longer & it makes me cum. And his can't. It never has
all the time we been a twosome.'

After some minutes had passed, James slid down her legs
and began to suck her pussy—he'd been thru the routine
dozens of times & was well trained. 'And even with a tame
man like James, I want Mickey. And with her I'm afraid of the
world…. Would it make him mad if I brought our cock over
& let him finish with that instead of eating me out? He's so
sensitive about his fucking cock.' Lucy felt the hot, hard
motion of his tongue bringing her to climax. Her face
contorted with the energy of her release; pale voluptuous hips
thrusting her hairy cunt into his mouth with a bittersweet
emotion. Those nights after nights with James & other men,
in which she'd really wanted another female to love. The
memory rushed back. Her lack of success in lesbian life—until
finding Mickey. Night after night spent in the shadows,
mating with physical satisfaction, and emotional hollowness.
Her body jerking to orgasm—just to feel the hunger still
remaining in her, for a woman's scent. A woman's cunt.
Wanting the action of a woman's thighs interlocked in her
own. The pain of not having a woman lover & so many years
of wanting to. It made her feel she'd flunked a test. As if she
was not enough woman to be a lesbian.

They had even gone to The Career Club. A nicer bar on
Division Street where young executives, & office workers &
business professionals—straights—went to meet & pick up each
other. Had forced James to shave & wear a cleaner pair of gray
work pants and a white shirt. Was vindicated for the last time
she'd ventured in there alone and the bouncer at the door
wouldn't let her in because she looked like a tramp. Red hair

losing its dye, showing brown roots, messy, hidden under a scarf; soiled toreador pants, dirty feet bare in a pair of open-toed high heels; drunk eyes glowing eagerly—in pursuit of safari nights. Lucy had fixed herself up also; like those two years she'd been a file clerk in an office, before falling from grace to tottering one last step above being a homeless streetperson. And they bought drinks & stayed. James uncomfortable, looking around at the mostly shorter, younger, clean cut men. Knowing he didn't belong & neither did she. And Nancy Sinatra sang to them thru the gold & blue jukebox: "THESE BOOTS ARE MADE FOR WALKING! AND THAT'S JUST WHAT THEY'LL DO! SOMEDAY THESE BOOTS ARE GONNA WALK ALL OVER YOU!"

Arm & arm they toured Division Street, which runs a fine line between the skids to the south and the more affluent area of the north. Which suited them, for tho they belonged to the former, at this time there was still a chance they could rise up to better things. Went in a restaurant for coffee & a Greek salad with lettuce, olives, tomato, mint, oil, & feta cheese. The redhead felt relief to be straight—or to pass as straight in the normal world. It was the way people treated her (low) when they found out she was a lezzie. The fear of being two women alone. In all respects it was better to be straight—if she could really carry the act off—to herself.

James & Lucy made the perfect straight couple.

James was big, strong; had a mean look and people feared him; yet their fears were dispelled by him having Lucy on his arm; a beautiful, gentle fluff. So they accepted them both with smiles.

She was safe. A man to lean on. Promoted immediately to a higher notch on the social rung by being a couple. And bona fide in the eyes of society's vicious & violent clucking hens. Lucy felt she could do no wrong.

A burden was lifted off her.

It didn't take long for their path to veer back down into the comfortable dregs of their crummy skid-row haunts. The couple made their choice after the grating demands of the more upwardly mobile & sophisticated world of upper Clark street began to push thru their facade; they abandoned the nice bars, and, on fire with many belts of alcohol, headed down.

Everybody on lower Clark street was drunkenly happy to see them back together. Reasons differed. The hags liked it because now Lucy—one of their own—would not be an embarrassment to them with her sexual preference; those gray-faced witches drinking gin, retaining to the last the moral righteous image of propriety even as their livers lost the battle against cirrhosis from a lifetime of alcohol abuse. The men realized that with Lucy around, the giant wouldn't be as violent. Only Duke & Freddy didn't like it—they thought they had lost Lucy as a companion and they would have to fade back into the background of boring Clark Street nights.

In all respects, they were as a Lord & Lady.

Under this facade, as the strap of her dress slips off her shoulder, & she, impatiently pushes a wisp of red hair out of her face, for it interferes with drinking—her inhibitions lowered—Lucy's libido began to run its course. Lucy knew she must be straight to keep her sanity. And knew, furthermore, if she didn't have lesbian intercourse regularly & constantly, she'd rather die. As rhythmic music moved its fingers thru her brain, stirring desire, envisioned how they'd moved together—holding the panting slippery-wet butch in her arms; being moved—erotically in a way men didn't do. The hot sexhole of her lover; what her baby had for her to penetrate. Her cunt, dripping its scent of pungent desire, which Mickey thrust into her mouth again and again, climaxing eagerly. Lucy missed that in a man. But that was all her heart soul & body.

And such a hassle to her brain.

Bar lights revolved. The giant is into his 5th drink—in this establishment; his 10th of the evening—& is buying for a man beside him to his right. This man would become his drinking companion far into the night after Lucy left. Now Lucy had a reason to go home drunk, as James paid for a cab, & she climbed into it. Their tryst was over, leaving her to count the hours until she could remove her diaphragm, wash out her cunt; & be embroiled in great disturbing feelings about being a lesbian. Had been with Mickey 8 months. The sad truth was, she was no longer a free spirit who floated over the Near North Side being with men, striving for women: and passing across the borderline back and forth; who could pick & choose from opportunities either sex offered—to sleep with one person one night & somebody else the next; but was slowly, inexorably being drawn to the truth of who she was. Drawn over some invisible line to be the same as Mickey in her hard suit & tie, and tough swagger—but femme. Pretty. Womanly. And a lover of other women.

Lucy had never been with a woman this long in her life.

Mickey got a job in the 2nd theater in a chain of several; as cashier, & suddenly was working full time. Tonight, sweaty, arms flew as she furiously shoveled popcorn out of the machine; sweat covered her white face. Made change, and passed hot dogs & candy over the counter to customers. In a while intermission would be over, the audience would head back thru the red vinyl–padded doors & the lobby would be empty—leaving her to her thoughts. As music sounded faintly; to press against the glass and see stars above in the night sky & wonder what Lucy was doing.

Lucy couldn't afford to get her hair done—when she worked in offices, it had been a luxury to visit the beauty parlor once a week—so she had to buy henna rinse & do it in the sink herself (it was a mess) to keep her hair red. They had more money. Mickey came in smelling of the night air, and a nice meal was cooking on the hot plate. A empty box of hair dye was on the table, and the femme was doing her nails with red nail polish.

Mickey wolfed down a delicious dinner. "I brought you some candy bars from work. You been home doing your hair all day?"

"Yes."

Privately Lucy thinks, as she snuggles back on the bed under a crazy-quilt blanket & electric heating pad (new), 'Mickey is as stupid as a man. I can fool them both. Maybe I'm really fooling myself.'

"I love you, Lucy."

"I love you too, Mickey."

The redhead shifted uneasily under the covers. Round feminine curves in languid motion. 'I really do love her. Here I sit in this room with a female who resembles a man. I'm really sitting here with a lesbian. A queer. Who loves me every night, intimately, thoroughly, and fully; knowing every inch of my body. She is my lover. And it's not like it was before. I'm not sorry. I'm not searching. I want to be with her—forever. I want us to stay together and to have peace.'

Lucy painted the table, the bureau and the shelves light green & a blue & red & yellow stripe down one end of everything, so they were similar colors. Matching furniture suites of the poor. When Mickey trudges in from the cold, her 3rd-hand coat covered with snow, Lucy's standing with a paintbrush in hand, and a bottle of wine.

"See? Matching furniture!"

"Yuh been at Phyllis's house, ain't yuh?"

They went out that night to a straight bar; then Lucy, high & drunk, lost her head. "I want you, Mickey, & nobody else!" Teeth gritted, eyes got big, pleading. "But I can't stand it anymore—living like this! Never sure of how much money we'll have! And what people think of us because we're gay!" Mickey's trying to shut her up; Lucy's ass slides on the bar stool. "I'm afraid, Mickey! I don't know why. I'm afraid you're gonna leave me, 'cause I act so bad to you!" And she's pawing the butch, thus getting hostile attention from the patrons of this straight bar.

Mickey yells, "STOP IT! You're gonna get us thrown out! Or me beaten up!"

Lucy breathes an alcoholic blast over Mickey's face and tugs her by the lapels of her suit coat. "Come here, honey, I got to tell you something." The butch leans over. Lucy strokes the black hair that's slicked back behind Mickey's ears & whispers: "I'm not straight!"

"Well, that's a relief."

"Now...I'll just get loaded and forget it all."

Later, when the bar was ready to shut down at its 2

o'clock liquor-license curfew, Lucy demands to go to Phyllis's.

"No. No drugs. No!"

"YES!"

"*NO!* People take advantage of you over there! You're sporting the whole house to fix, Lucy! That Phyllis is getting you hooked so she can get high herself! You spend all our money over there!"

Lucy and Mickey were having a terrible battle in the middle of the street!

"I let you fuck up all our money in the bar to keep you from going to Phyllis's!"

"You just hate her, don't you!"

"You're sleeping with her!"

"No, I'm not!"

"She probably can't do nothing, that's why! 'Cause she's a goddamn sexless drug addict! Everybody's been seeing her with you! She's stealing your money! She's turning you into a dope addict just so she can get high when you get high—and you're paying for it!"

"I'M GOING TO PHYLLIS'S HOUSE!"

BAM!

Mickey popped Lucy hard on the soft part of her arm. She screamed in pain. Mickey twisted her arm and held her hand up ready to deliver a slap. "YER GOING HOME WITH ME! *NOW!*"

Near morning, when the redhead was sober, Mickey rolled her over on her back for their nightly fuck.

"Cum with me, Lucy!"

"Yes, Mickey."

She lay over her. Lucy opened her legs wide and hunched her cunt up against Mickey's cunt, tight; & the butch is moving & moaning as they made love in the last desperate act; knowing she'd chosen Mickey & this meant a lifetime being a lesbian. And the choice wasn't hers, anyway, but only as it was to understand the depths of her own soul and what was in there. Her body jerked with pleasure to Mickey's thrust, moving rapid fire against her cunt & then Mickey raises the upper part of her body up, hands on each side of Lucy on the mattress holding her up, cunts fused together. Mickey cums; throws her head back, neck arched. Lucy wraps her legs around Mickey's ass, pulls her in tight as she's cumming, hollering in relief.

Lucy lay wiggling in bed. "I didn't cum when you did. Do me." Her sweet, hot pussy wiggling there, waiting for love.

The butch runs her hands, stroking, over Lucy's body; comes to her vagina, parts the pubic hair & inserts two fingers, then three, jams them in and out, fast; hard. Pulls out of her wet sexhole, runs her fingertips around over Lucy's swollen clit, then plunges back inside. Now, with her other hand works her clit; & pounds in and out of her cunt, hard, in rhythm. "OHH. OHH. OHH!" Lucy groans. And her hips begin their circular motion as her pussy opens up, then tightens. Faster, fingers massage her clit while the other hand jams in deep, hard & fast, pumping pistonlike over and over. "AHHH!" Lucy cries. The soles of her feet slap down on the mattress; hips thrust rhythmically to match the furious pumping of Mickey's hand penetrating her pussy; and the other rubs fire out of her clit. Lucy's stomach quivers in visible waves, trembles, and then her head goes backward, mouth opens in a yell; "AAAAAAAAAAHHHHHHHHHHHHH UHHHHHHHHHHHHH AAAAAHHHHHHHH!" & cum gushes out of her soul.

"Baby, I plowed you & didn't even get to use the dildo!"

James moved back another notch into the backdrop of Clark Street & was gone out of her life.

CHAPTER THIRTY-SEVEN

Winter snow in the air. A hole was growing in the toe of her shoe. Soon the pair would be worthless & she'd have to buy something else they couldn't afford.

"In California you don't even have to wear shoes!"

Mickey saw the changing seasons. Was still brooding in the cold shadows. But the other side of the American continent was sunny. And there a dyke could obtain the American Dream.

'I need to feel free. A breath of fresh air.'

The redhead felt similarly: 'I need to live life! Not be trapped in this little room watching TV.' So they went down to The 169 Club early, while it was still light; by bus, thru the gray slush streets & snow fog & starpoint flakes of snow fall from heaven.

It was so close—everything ran down to a finish line neck & neck like trotters at the horse races. Seemed like things were going to fly apart. Ice-cold wind blasts, snowbanks shoveled high; they walk, backs to the wind. Back at the hotel, the hillbillies have taped broken windows shut with cardboard; their place is an icebox painted in gay colors & Mickey has bought a small heater that raises the temperature of the room to bearable. 'I can't stand another winter like this one, not here in the city of Chicago.'

She remembered home & her crazy mother, Mrs. Mary Alice Leonardi. Who had not loved her & had favored her brothers & used other rude treatment in a mental torture to the little black-haired Italian girl. And as she grew, learned about desire.

And that's where it all started—between her legs.

Images present themselves to be examined:

Jailhouse matron with a phony diamond ring on her pinkie.

'If I can just keep my self-confidence and play the waiting game & seize opportunity the split second it comes. Be prepared. There's a way to do everything, & I know there must be a way to a better life.'

The same women were passing thru Chicago as a rest stop on their way back to California.

They'd been on the road for months, been delayed by a case back East—arrested for hitchhiking & possessing pornographic lesbian photographs. Which had been later dismissed from court. They were in a hurry to escape winters blast and get back home.

Four women: one with long blonde hair to her shoulders, wearing an imitation leather jacket & boots; another with curly hair wild like a mad scientist. The third, a femme with a knowing smile who'd lay down with anyone if their vibes were right. 2 others, plain & nondescript. They looked very wise, relaxed. Had a laid-back manner. "We're on our way back to California. This town ain't nothing, man, this town can't do nothin' for me." The wizard with wild hair summed up Chicago in scorn. "Something's happening in California that you can't explain."

Three of the women sat in The 169 Club; having stopped on their journey for some days of rest. "Dena is hitchhiking south. I'm headed due west with Sherry. We're going thru Frisco & then we'll all meet up again in L.A." Glamorous. Air of the road, of freedom, of world travelers.

"This is all you have here? In a city as big as this?" Sherry scoffed. "There's some bitchin' clubs in L.A. Nice clubs. *Women's* clubs."

They laughed together. Privately Mickey thinks: 'It's the gay males that's lucky. They have everything. They own clubs where no dykes are allowed. They have it because they're males. And because they're white, and not American Indians like Lucy. Or Colored, like Lisa. And they think life is a fucking game. Just to have fun & peroxide their hair blond—while we women are down here fighting for our lives.'

Days fluttered down like calendar pages torn loose. Snow packs. Icicles hang from windowsills; drip in frozen silver glass to the frozen ground.

After Mickey's barroom fight, she just saw Shorty one more time. The runt was cold; turned her back on Mickey and didn't speak. The idol had cracked to the 15-year-old's eyes. Then, the baggy-pants baby butch was gone.

"Shorty had to leave town. Her parents caught up with her & they're gonna put her back in the mental institution because of her being gay. She's gotta stay there until she turns 18. She escaped on a weekend pass before, but if they get her back they're gonna keep her on a locked ward drugged out of her mind. She's been staying at her grandmother's house all this time—ducking & dodging whenever her parents showed up. The old lady's crazy, too. First she says she's seen Shorty, then she hasn't. Then she says, 'Who the hell is Shorty?'

Shorty's a little bit crazy, yeah, but not that crazy. Not enough for them to lock her up in the loony bin. Yeah, she plays with dolls. And all that stuff. Their whole family is kinda crazy. First time I seen it, it was freakish. She gets this doll, takes off its clothes, lifts it up by the ankles, upside down & starts licking its crotch."

The lesbians from California had gone barefoot that summer when it was warm. Dressed in black & purple. Black slacks. Black sleeveless blouse. A black satin sash. Naked arms, freckled skin, long hair & bare feet.

Born of dirt-poor stock whose parents had been farmers from the Dust Bowl. Poor white trash. Sharecroppers whose weather-beaten faces were creased and red from always being in the sun tilling the soil; walking & not being able to afford to drive. Salvaging. Mending old clothes. Patching pants & dresses in a crazy patchwork of odd color scraps. Make do. Born of parents & grandparents who'd labored too hard, enjoyed nothing—& now their lesbian children had let go of the plow. Turned loose the hoe, & they traveled free.

They were flesh and blood. Womanflesh, warm.... When she was near these vagabonds, teenage Mickey was infatuated. She listened to their seasoned words of life.

And Mickey had sex with one of the women.

In the toilet of the tavern, the slender Dena, a femme, who wore a black pullover sweater, black pants and delicate black shoes; leaned against the wall, a half smile on her face. She spoke: "Mickey, I've been noticing you. You're a special kind of person." And Mickey's hard glance wavered, she swallowed hard, clenched and unclenched her hands nervously—and came to the lesbian from California. Put her strong hands on the woman's tits, rubbed them thru the fabric of her sweater till her nipples were hard. The strange half-smile plays on Dena's face; she looks down—her nipples are poked up round under the black garment. "See what you did to me!" Her vibes are very laid back. Wise. Slender, pale, in the bright light of the toilet; she briefly runs her fingertips under the lapels of the butch's suit jacket. Mickey's kissing her, stroking the inside of her thighs. "I'm all wet! My panties are soaked! It's all your fault!" Willowy, she presses the full length of her body against Mickey and moves rhythmically. "I want to give you a treat since you're such a special person, Mickey." Undulates her body full length against Mickey. Dena laughs, a high, tinkling voice: "Are you wet, baby? I am!" Runs her hands thru Mickey's wavy black hair. Light caresses like the breeze. Feminine hands with painted nails like the butch is used to. Dena tosses her curly black hair which falls in ringlets to her shoulders; takes Mickey's hand and puts it to her crotch—the fabric is hot & soaking. Mickey feels the soft wetness of Dena's pussy. "She's wet—for you Mickey. Are you gonna love her?" And Mickey wishes they had time, to do everything; and a place—because the girl is on the road, & has no place, & Mickey has only the room she shares with her redhead femme. And neither one of them has money to rent a hotel room. So she slides down to her knees; clenched grip of white knuckles pulling Dena's slacks down her legs as she goes & the wild femme wears no panties. Has curly black pubic hair; and a strong scent of a female on the road who hasn't had the niceties of hot showers and safe living spaces; but who is free, free and passionate. And Mickey's tongue licks her hot wet meat; her mouth sucks deep of the sticky-sweet love flower. As she leans against the peeling plaster wall, Dena pumps her hips, moving her clit in Mickey's mouth. Fast, faster; Dena's hips thrust frantically in orgasm.

Mickey rises up, cheeks & chin wet with the juice from Dena's cunt. Wipes her face on the back of her suit coat sleeve; her hair is mussed by the effort. Dena breathes hard, relieved. Her chest rises & falls; her lean flat stomach quivers. Now Mickey pushes her hard against the toilet wall; leans full against her, unzips her trousers. Dena's fingers go into Mickey's fly, seek thru the hole in her boxer shorts & begin to stroke between the butch's wet cuntlips. Wearing a serious expression, Mickey jerks her hips fast, heat builds in her swollen womanhood & pumps; surrendering to Dena's moving fingers, receiving her orgasm.

It was with this woman that Mickey committed adultery the first time.

Gave release to a stranger; and with her, cum herself.

Winos have urinated all over the lobby of the Bristol Hotel. Two dykes; one mannish, the other in high-heel pumps, slacks, a stylish but threadbare coat & a babushka covering her red hair; one weaving drunk; make their way upstairs.

They got to the 3rd landing; Lucy looks at the corridor to their room—some 25' & thinks (if it could be called such in her blurred state of mind) 'Can I walk down this hall & make it to the other end?'

She couldn't string together the words to a sentence.

Lucy cries like a baby; nestles in Mickey's arms, red hair falling into her face, & they walk embraced together. "Plain-clothes cops are worse." Lucy informs Mickey. "SHHHH!"

Hallucinating from drugs; from drink. "JINGLE BELLS! JINGLE BELLS! JINGLE ALL THE WAY! OH, WHAT FUN IT IS TO RIDE IN A ONE-HORSE OPEN SLEIGH!"

And Mickey burning with fire to move on; leave this cold town. Lucy's in a no-sleep delirium; her overworked mind sings to itself: "I'M DREAMING OF A WHITE CHRISTMAS!"

Undressed under silver starlight in the cold room; tumbled into bed; their red & black hair mix together. Mickey reached to Lucy with her special touch, showing she was ready to take her nightly fuck. "Come to me, Lucy!"

"Yes, Mickey."

Mickey's tired, so instead of standing, dominant above the kneeling submissive Lucy; lays on her back, knees spread; Lucy between them, licking her wet cunt with long, drunken strokes of her tongue from clit to pussyhole & back; head wobbling, face wet with her own saliva & the butch's pussyjuice; then buries her head deep between Mickey's thighs and sucks & licks, moving her mouth fast, in a forgetful, disjointed rhythm. It takes about ten minutes. Hears the loud moans emitting from her lover lying above her, and has to wrap her arms around Mickey's ass and clutch onto it for dear life—and keep licking, as the butch humps hard in cumming. Lucy looks up, wet, scented by cunt; "Did I do OK, honey?"

Put her head on the pillow and slept.

CHAPTER THIRTY-EIGHT

'Got to get the dead lead out of this town.'

In the past, when Mickey packed up & moved, just did it quiet; during the night; maybe owing back rent. Packed her tote bag, a suitcase, & stole out.

This world of Chicago & its showgirls & freaks and snow—once had been new. Now, it had gotten old.

Been out here a season, and the dialogue began to repeat itself. A trail of bleach-blond fags repopulated itself over night. The same designer selves, but with different names. And the new ones didn't have faces yet—Mickey didn't know them. Old characters being replaced by new actors—who said the exact same thing and were going thru identical trials & tribulations as the former, so that it was déjà vu to be amid the blue & red party lights, and outdoors driving sleet & hail of snow; & a sense that she'd been thru it before, had been there before time, out of time, and there was just time left—to move on, to get in the wind, to catch the tail of the Hawk, to get out of Dodge....

'My life held still for an instant; when I was 13, 14, & 15; pulling away from my lousy home, running to escape the police my mother set out to find me, like a character from a French novel fleeing thru the sewers of Paris. The gaps when my life wasn't in my control, but in & out of jail, waiting to be released out into life again & face the challenge. Then being in love...a new love. Lisa says, "Yes, Mickey, I love you, too—and I mean it! From the very lower portion of my anatomy!" Then we fuck. Our love is this rhythm in the figure 8; sexuality in motion. And I left her because she was bad to me. And I have pride. I must have my respect from a woman. Not what Lucy is doing—seeing other people on the sly, & tearing us apart with drink. I depend on me in this world. And nobody else. Not my mother, or my brothers or my lover, not the schools, not the people in authority—nobody. I depend on me. I've traveled far and wide; always with me is fear. Fear recurs. Of the streets where I must walk as a dyke/queer. Fear of pain. And the horror of being alone with no woman. Facing this world by myself is no fun. I will go out & find me another broad if Lucy can't be a wife as she is suppose to be. As poor as I am, accept what I got to offer her and be my wife, so I can cherish her nude body & know nobody else has been with her. There are so few women in the world that will take on a butch lesbian like me that are any good. Not pill poppers or bad girls who go in & out of jail for shit like stealing & passing bad checks. There's got to be somebody *looking* for a mate in California. Somebody who'll do the right thing for me. There's more opportunity to meet a nice girl out there. A nice girl. Maybe we can have a baby together. And have a home & a marriage, and be like straight couples. So that's why I must go from all these familiar things Lucy has spent time building here. The board painted green which makes a desk. The rainbow painted boxes that hold our clothes. The tie-dyed curtains over the sink. The people in the bar who know me. How am I going to be able to take making this change without losing control? I have to leave my job!—'cause I got to leave my *woman!*—'cause I got to leave this *town!* Tonight the pressure is killing me. This thinking about leaving—like I never have before. I want to howl! My head's spinning. Stars in my eyes. I'm afraid to leave. I'll die if I stay.'

The lines on the soles of both of her feet were different. Fingerprints unique only to her. And was identical to billions of other human beings with heads and feet and hands; but in her boots & trousers & shirt & cap was unique—as other women/men who love women down thru history cross-dressing, acting a role; aggressively seeking love. Lines creased into her face as time wore on. Genetic code creating Mickey—her unique hands and feet—with boots—the same as an army of aggressive butch lesbians over time....

Everybody's waiting for the happy ending to the story.... Somebody comes along, sweeps the hero/heroine off her feet. Or they go off on separate paths, never to meet again; or commit suicide.

'Why am I leaving this town? When I have a job? And have Lucy who gives me her body most of the times I reach out—who don't deny me my pleasure. It's because of the police harassment. It's too rough in the bars. In this town homosexuals don't help each other, they hurt each other. Fights every night. Threats. I can't stand it. And because my woman is a drunk, a drug user & a bisexual who can't commit herself to me alone. Those women from California say there's freedom there. Freedom to live a gay life and be natural. I'm not a baby butch no more. I'm almost an adult. I'll be 19 very soon. Then 20, which is just a year away from voting age of 21. But...if Lucy chooses to go with me, I'll accept her. I'll take her. I owe her that much respect. She has given me sex faithfully & given me 9 months of her time. Maybe she'll go square and behave out in California. We'll live together like man & wife; I'll go to school and learn some kind of profession that pays so much money I won't have to ever again share her cunt with a paying customer.

'And here's Lucy laying in bed with me; her dirty slutty pussy has fucked half the lesbians, women and men on the Near North Side of Chicago I bet! And I'm sick of it! I'm almost 19 years old! I can't go on like this anymore!

'Let her go! Stop trying. Why is she still here with me when she can have James, who earns $25 a day instead of $10? Or shack up with Terry, who can do more for her than I can?'

Lucy; dyed redhead, wrapped under sheets & a blue electric blanket (new) restless, not asleep; having reached the knowledge finally at age 24, that she's not straight. And is afraid to be a lesbian queer. And just happy Mickey's earning more money so she can stay high on wine & pills—and seeing that even her straight world ain't so straight. Like Phyllis turning out to be a lesbian; over in the artist sector where the city is tearing down buildings like cardboard boxes; the wrecker's crane & iron ball knocking open walls & exposing rooms in demolition & Phyllis's squad of dope fiends carting off any remaining furniture, cans of paint, drapes, boxes of whatever was people's lives that they were forced to abandon as they were relocated to other parts of the city, so that Phyllis's house grows into a palace made of their leftover scraps; Lucy's room, too, in a junior model—of a Junk Palace. And going over there, hair covered by a babushka, in gym shoes, plain slacks disguising her very female form so as not to be harassed by men; & coming home thru the blocks of totally deserted abandoned buildings clutching a butcher-knife handle for defense; drugged with heroin revolving in her veins, afraid of getting assaulted & gang raped, but her yen to be with Phyllis is great enough to drive her; and Mickey is stupidly at work at the movie theater looking out of a safe lobby, by a warm popcorn machine, into the snowy, chilly star-filled sky, dreaming. Risking life & limb to go over there, to climb the red-carpeted stairs, to be taken into those skinny junk arms in an embrace, with all her desire for a woman; to experience Phyllis's touch, her smell, the eroticism of her; and to moan at her cool, detached caress and the light, thrilling semi-bored licks of her tongue over her clit. Knowing she is a real lesbian to desire so deeply this totally feminine woman—who is not any kind of male replica, but as female as herself. And then, when she needs her pussy fucked good and hard, Mickey her butch is for that. And Mickey's got this rod as an accessory; a fact that makes Phyllis blink cold eyes in a mixture of hatred & weird fascination.

The redhead had hung around dykes 2 years, but they snubbed her; were too good for her, didn't desire her pussy bad enough because Lucy always had a man in the background & they felt threatened. Slept with a few butches who deserted her after a night of hot lust. So had retreated, gone back with men into straight society & didn't feel powerful anymore. Felt she'd given up. Had slowly begun to curl up & die; yet felt safe with a male on her arm. And then, meets Mickey & lesbian life begins! The gay mad whirl of party lights in the dance of life! Lays back, thighs spread, passive for this man/woman to fuck her, which Mickey does faithfully every evening. And Lucy's active hand, searching the hot, wet hole of her butch; finally being allowed to experience this female wonder—cunt—that the other hardened butches hadn't let her penetrate.

And Mickey's looking at her, thinks she's sleeping, thinks: 'It's all shades of Valorie and Lisa and Scheherazade. Older girls I can't control. Their desire for big money is too great. Their desire for drugs is too deep. Moving in and out of my gay life—where I'm stuck—'cause I'm obviously a queer. So I'm going to blow this one, too. Along with this fucked-up town. Am saving my money from work on the sly, am gonna buy a train ticket & get out of Dodge & find a nice girl in California who's not a whore, never been a whore, to whom whoring is not an alternative—who would rather starve, like myself—but who can fuck like a whore in bed.'

Chapter Thirty-Nine

The 169 Club is a toilet, black walls & red lights. Roof that leaks & holes in its floor. A shabby door facing on Division Street which must be slammed shut periodically when violent street thugs are standing outside fighting each other; while the staff & gay kids wait inside breathing hard, eyes wide, listening for the commotion to die down and pass off down the way.

The special circle of gays who sometimes came thru had been afraid to go there—this neighborhood was worse than the other location, of The Silver Windows. But tonight a pack of them came in, seated in a circle of boy/boy, girl/girls, for protection. One, a little female 5', curly blonde hair and shy demeanor, looks with secret glances, appreciatively at Mickey. The fluff wears a lady's jacket with jewelry, slacks, demure medium heels. She's an artist, & a student at the Art Institute of Chicago, as are the others in her group of clean cut gay girls & boys. Mickey is paying for a drink at the bar & notices her gaze. Thinks: 'How I'd like to have a girl like that, all mine, who's going to be something someday; & we can work & stay in a nice apartment.'

Phenomenon in 1959 was, that when a slow record came on, nobody would dance in the dance area in front of the pool table, but a couple might grab each other's hands and run into the bathroom to clutch each other and grind in a hot embrace to the music, out of the watchful eye of the bartender. Most would go sit down on a bar stool & wait for the song to end because it was illegal for same-sex couples to dance touching. Mickey waited impatiently thru a popular torrid love song, then chose a fast tune to stride over and ask the girl to dance. Shyly the girl said yes, & they went to the floor & began to move, & Mickey wanted to crush her to her suit-jacketed chest, feel the pressure of the girl's thighs wanting hers between them; and push her clit, hot, on one of those thighs, and work her thigh against the girl's sex in rhythmic motion together. And could take her right there, she was so hot. Lay her down on her back on the pool table and pound on her & they could take their share of orgasms together.

As they dance, Mickey's eyes travel the length of her body over the short distance between them.

Pretty. Curly blonde hair. A green velvet jacket with a red brooch on the lapel. Underneath saw the rise of her tits; nice size. Gray lady slacks—sleek slender thighs with a gap in between like her pelvis was built wide & easy to ride. In the butch's imagination, she could taste her cunt, feel her fingers go in slow; and wanted her juice, her kisses; the movement of her body; desired the girl's caress on the back of her neck at the hairline. And to know as they were doing it that she was with a nice girl at last.

'Here's a nice girl who's going to school to make a future. And probably lives in a nice apartment.' And it made Mickey wonder why she'd fell down so low—into the gutter—where she'd been crawling since.

"You come here often?"

"I've never been here before—I'm with them. We usually go out together to the boys' clubs." The girl was nervous.

"This place just opened. It ain't as nice as The Silver Windows was. Or The Turquoise Ribbons was before that. There's holes in the floor by the pool table and inside the ladies' bathroom, so be careful."

"We went by that place, and we saw the sign on the door

saying it had been shut down. We don't usually go out to places like this, but there's no women at the boys' bars.... This place...it's scary. Nobody wanted to come in."

"Scary?"

"The neighborhood... And...the police raid places like this. I can't afford to get caught... I live with my parents, and they're sending me to the Art Institute. My parents would kill me if they found out if they found out I was gay. They'd stop paying my tuition & put me out in the street. I know because it almost happened once when I was 20."

Mickey devoured the sweet blonde hungrily with her eyes as they hastily jittered out a rock-and-roll step in the pretense of dancing. Pictured her cunt, pink, blonde wisps of pubic hair. Party lights played down over the dancers; the girl turned & wiggled her ass suggestively, then turned back on the beat of a step & looked into Mickey's eyes to see her reaction. 'She's wild!—a little bit wild! She's shaking her hips for me! She's coming on to me! She's made it plain—she wants me!' Mickey suddenly felt tough and bold and in command; like she wasn't running around searching for things to make herself happy, but that joy was coming to her; pleasure & opportunity were knocking on her door! And she wanted to go to bed with the girl. Lay her down and give her a good long screw.

"Are you really gay? Totally? You're with all these guys!"

"NO! I'm not bisexual! I'm gay! Like you are!"

"Oh. I just seen all those guys—"

"NO! I do not sleep with guys! I'm a lesbian! These guys are gay! They're nelly fags!"

"Well, a lot of these women down here, do." Mickey said gruffly.

"*Yes.* Because a lot of them are prostitutes aren't they? That's why I'm afraid of places like this. A lot of these women have been in jail. And use pills...and are burlesque dancers.... It's scary—I wish gay women had somewhere nice to go."

"Yeah."

"We stay together like this, it's a front. People see us together & they can't tell it's actually girls with girls & boys with boys. We all go to the Art Institute. We've got everybody there fooled, too."

Mickey's impressed. 'She's smart. She's more gay than Lucy. She's not a street girl, but she's sexier than half the broads that hang around in here.'

"I'm going to get my degree, in Art Education. And then nobody is going to tell me what to do," the girl said emphatically.

They arranged to meet downtown in the Loop.

"But you can't wear this and meet me," she said, referring to the suit & tie.

"OK," says Mickey. "I don't go out like this during the day, anyway. I'll wear gym shoes & slacks & just a shirt, and a zip-front jacket."

She wouldn't give Mickey her parents phone number. "I never know who I can trust," she says softly.

After the gay gang whirled out the door into the snowy night, following party lights in a safer club, Mickey stood at the bar, one trousered leg up on a bar stool, ran a hand thru her wavy black hair. Silently took stock of her complete set of working lesbian parts: 'There's my fingers, tongue, my own cunt, clit, thighs, & I'll pack my cock in a tote bag. Wonder what she's gonna want to do? I'll fuck her first. Then go down on her. Will she want to touch my cunt? Will she try to get on top and ride my thigh?' Mickey even envisioned the slim girl strapping the harness around her own thighs to fuck, using the cock. It shot a thrill thru the center of her being. 'I'll probably do all the work, & that's fine. I'll fuck her hard! I'll take her good. Up to heights unknown!—Until she's begging for it again and again!'

"See yuh got a nice little girl there. What's her name?" The redhead mannish butch Rusty wants to know.

"Alyson. She's a student. One of those kids who always come in here—they always stay together & don't talk to nobody but themselves—& then leave."

"Yeah, I'm surprised she talked to you."

"Charm." Mickey replies.

"She's a nice girl. You make a good couple."

"Yeah, but she's different.... We went to the bar to buy a 7UP, and I gave her some cash—$10—and told her to keep the rest, for drinks for herself & to play the jukebox. Most girls would be happy, yuh know? But she looks at me like I'd spit in her hand."

"You can't do that with those high-class types. They think it cheapens them."

"Just when I finally get women figured out, they go and change on me!"

An evening later in the Bristol Hotel, Lucy confronts Mickey at the door, red hair wild on her head, green-blue arteries strain in her neck: "WHO'S THAT WOMAN YOU TALKED TO AT THE CLUB!"

"Nobody! One of those kids who comes in, and they always stay right next to the door in a little circle."

"WHAT DO YOU WANT TO TALK TO THEM FOR? THEY'RE A BUNCH OF SNOBS! THEY NEVER TALK TO THE REST OF US!"

Lucy was mad and jealous. "YOU DON'T WANT A GIRL LIKE THAT! SHE'S A TRASHY BITCH AND A BLUE-NOSED SNOB! THEY'RE NO GOOD IN BED, ANYWAY! THEY'RE COLD!"

They met on Michigan Avenue, in windy snow; on the steps of the Art Museum, as prearranged. Right under the twin lions that guard the palatial building.

Mickey wore slacks, shirt & T-shirt showing at the neck. 3rd-hand coat; ducktail hairdo. Just a few heads turned to stare; she was not in complete male drag. Alyson was nervous, embarrassed & glad to see her. Shivered. It was so cold, her expensive rings had begun to slide off her fingers. "Let's go, Mickey." Shy, she gazed at the butch a second, then looked down into the snow.

Alyson had rented a hotel room for them for 1 night. It cost $75, which to her was nothing. It was what Mickey's salary was for a week. "Father is one of the Captains of Industry," she explained.

The hotel is expensive. It has power. Is silent. Wall-to-wall carpets; mahogany wood trim burnished golden with a fine polish. Chandeliers refracting light in multicolor prisms and a bank of elevators along one wall. Mickey was in awe. There's is a pink/white room with TV, double bed, room service and a view of the lake and downtown buildings. Pigeons flap on ledges of the 30th floor.

The girl takes off her clothes. Pale body, small hips and breasts, not as well endowed as Lucy. Brown-blonde hairs wispy, soft over her wet cunt. Bolts of lust hit Mickey's groin; she can't wait to have sex. Was so glad to have a place to themselves. It had a bathroom, spotless clean, with towels, bars of fragrant soap & hot water—private—they didn't have to share with the whole floor. Far better than the Hotel Bristol where she lives back in the slums 20 blocks away.

Mickey strips off her boxers & T-shirt last, & they stand naked together, toes wiggling in the thick, warm carpet. Then Mickey pulls Alyson into her arms. Hungry, mouth to her mouth; they kiss, swirl their tongues around & around, wet. Alyson sighs & Mickey runs her hands over the girl's breasts, squeezes each nipple—and she moans. Her body is small and easily held, it grows hot fast. She's so eager, pulling Mickey tight.

Alyson is awkward and nervous in bed, but warm. Surprisingly warm—for an upper-class snob.

Snow piles up on the window ledge. Bustling city, traffic flowing down below; the black iron scaffolding of the El tracks winds thru the Loop. Skyscrapers loom, gray metal on gray-blue sky. A city in motion; pigeons fly thru the air; & people small as ants in distance, coming & going.

"I can do anything in bed." Alyson had said. "I know all kinds of techniques." Alyson had had five women lovers & was currently dating an older Lady Professor at the Institute. When she found out Mickey had a lover she lived with, Alyson seemed more eager to please. "Everybody in our little circle is taken. I've never had a lover all to myself. I'm so lonely. I see Professor Berger just one night a week. And she lives in terror somebody is going to find out & she'll get fired. Mickey, you're lucky everybody knows you're gay &

you've got nothing to hide. At least that part is easier for you."

Mick knelt on the sheets. Had the cock, was pulling short hairs off its base—Lucy's. Then stuck it in the metal ring attached to the harness, tightened the straps around her body, and they slipped back under the sheets. Alyson was wet and ready from having already cum. Mickey held the tool in her hand & stroked the dickhead carefully against the entrance to Alyson's hole. Pushed it in and banged her with slow, gentle thrusts of her body. "I bet yuh ain't seen action like this, huh? This is the real deal!"

"Professor Berger uses one, Mickey. In fact, she's a terror with it on—it's frightening. I think she lets all her inhibitions out when she finally gets to switch roles. You know, from being the sweet little gray-haired Professor in orthopedic shoes to a dildo-wielding lesbo from hell bubbling over."

And the butch socks it to her—BAM, BAM, BAM—bed squeaks; and emotionally, feeling a strange new cold reality; almost a form of spiritual death—that it's not Lucy.

Afterward, Alyson is nervous & guilty, and not sure if she should see Mickey again. Worried, knowing what her parents would do if they found out. And tells the butch, "I've only had five other women, but you're the best. You're gentle & strong too. And you go a long time…."

"Yeah. *But* you don't want to see me again."

"I don't know! You're so butch! If anybody who knows my parents ever sees us together, I'm ruined." Mickey thinks to herself dully: 'Shit. By the time she's made up her mind, I'll be gone. Out of this goddamn city. Anyway, I was just passing thru….'

They do meet again; same hotel. Alyson spends big $ money on the room & room service & they make love between the sheets all day. Money is like water thru her fingers. When they first walked into the lobby of the hotel downstairs, Mickey caught a glimpse of herself in the mirror. Very handsome. A masculine silver chain on her wrist; black hair slicked back flat plastered to the sides of her head. Slacks, jacket, man's shirt open at the collar, T-shirt. A transvestite female. Beside her is the perfectly-heterosexual-appearing Alyson. The contrast is a shock, glaring out of huge mahogany-framed gold-etched mirrors reflecting the couple back and forth over the red-carpeted lobby of the vintage hotel; and Mickey sees what she just look like—for just a second thru the eyes of this girl. And understands.

Alyson spends a lot of time wondering about what other people think of them. The judgments of society. Unlike nasty girls who live dirty lives & who've been turned out by some butch at an early age and have been involved in the sex industry, or drugs or jail life and have little to lose.

This rich girl believes in planning for her future. The two lay under the sheet and discuss different ways to disguise Mickey so Alyson can introduce her to her rich parents. "You'll have to dress different, and not be so mannish in the way you walk and talk." And Mickey feels the earth move under her feet. The sky, changing directions.

Yes. She, too, is drifting.

As usual, Alyson & Mickey expect to meet at the bar, she's not sure when—a fleeting instant in which the young heiress will whirl in out of the snow accompanied by her peers; and on the sly, tell Mickey her plans—what day & time they can rendezvous in the hotel.

Then the Syndicate closed the 169 Club. Because of too much police heat.

Mickey would never see Alyson again.

The Palm Gardens, that dive under the El tracks with its pimps & hookers, was all that was left.

CHAPTER FORTY

"Cum with me Lucy!"

"Yes Mickey."

Mickey's Royal Birthday Fuck. The bantam butch was 19.

The redhead was going to service Mickey sexually for her birthday. It was going to be a Big Bang.

3 hours in bed. Do all kinds of raunchy acts together. The femme was suppose to keep her butch aroused by every means possible for her to break her record: to cum 8 times.

They had not obtained release for 3 nights before; had saved themselves—so as to be ready.

And when they lay down, it would be intense.

Room was cozy tho snow piled on the window ledges; red sign blinked woozy pink color stains of light from the tavern underneath; the items the butch had bought from her paychecks—a heater, a hot pad had made their lives better. The rainbow-tie-dyed curtains decorated their space, as did the wooden crates of their belongings painted blue, red, green, yellow & purple.

The butch kneels on the sheets, picks short hairs off the dildo. Lucy sits up in bed in her slip; a dreamy far-off look in her eyes, a sexy smile on her wide lips. Suddenly her eyes open wide when she notices what Mickey is doing. Lucy knows she hadn't let Mickey use it for a while. Mad. The hair color is light, curly. "WHOSE HAIR IS THAT? IT'S NOT MINE!"

Mickey soothes Lucy: "Alyson don't know what to do. She put her finger on me a feeble little bit." Lying to her redhead lover. "She's just a kid who needs some experience. I did it to her out of *mercy.*"

Mickey lies & tells Lucy further—since she wanted to enjoy her Royal Birthday Fuck; has been saving sexual stamina for it—having denied herself several nights, hoping to break her grand record of consecutive cums—and is horny as hell: "It wasn't that bad, but no one can compare to you. I just did it because, you know, about them tricks & so-called friends of yours, & it was only fair that I have my chance to be a playboy, too, just like you got to be a fast lady all over town. And I know you say tricks are different, but don't get mad, Lucy, I know you are sorting your life out. I will be patient…" And knowing inside it's too much—the men, Phyllis, her drug house, the skid-row nights. And Lucy's not going to change—or so it seems to this 19-year-old. And she's disappointed. Lucy sobs. Has turned her pale back with its curvy hips and breasts; red hair splayed, head buried in the pillow; hurt. The explanation has not worked. Mickey lays there frustrated and pissed. She is not going to get her Royal Birthday Fuck. And throws the cock & harness hard against the side of the wall—where it bounces off, still hard & ready.

As their relationship weakened, the first thing that dissolved was Lucy's sex drive. The redhead would lay up in bed loaded, in a hazy, half-smile limbo. While Mickey confused, tossed & turned in the fire of unfulfilled desire. Lucy hadn't spread her thighs wiggling willingly for weeks—it was an obligation, at best. Mickey forced her. Got on her femme, body weight held her down, knees forced open, lay between Lucy's legs, pushed her thighs open & stuck two fingers into her hole. Firmly and resolutely. Lucy bites Mickey, who screams; but keeps on moving fingers in Lucy's wet cunt until the redhead finally surrenders and says she'll give up the rest of her body and her love—with the understanding—the forced promise elicited from a panting & horny Mickey that she will turn over the major part of her paycheck & Lucy will run the affairs of their house—meaning Lucy will take Mickey's paycheck to buy dope & sport Phyllis & her junkie sidekick Leah to a fix—in exchange for a high, & a studied gaze of hollow passion or a thrilling caress. So Mickey finally forces Lucy to do The Nightly Fuck, which was OK. But since Lucy had lost interest, there was little desire in it; Mickey had to do all the work. Lifts her legs up & pushes them back to get her cunt in the right place in Lucy's; & halfhearted oral sex. Sometimes Lucy would nod out in mid-lick. And penetration ceased. No more of Lucy's two short-nailed middle fingers to pound in her cunt. Or dildo, twisting, swirling, screwing with deep thrusts inside of her.

Sex life had died. Sex life—a thing that was most important to Mickey.

The potent and powerful Mickey:

Rode her women hard; sucked their clits & fucked their cunts; BANG! BANG! Stroked & caressed & plunged with finesse into their hot pussies, till women moaned & groaned in ecstasy, pulled Mickey's hair by the roots & shot their wad of discharge dripping down their thighs. "THANK YOU, MICKEY! OH! THANK YOU! I'VE NEVER HAD AN ORGASM LIKE THAT IN MY LIFE! OH, I THINK I CAME 3 TIMES. I JUST KEPT CUMMING AND CUM-

MING!" Could roll over & allow the femme to ride their hot clit on her muscular thigh; and Mickey would urge them: "RIDE IT, BABY! RIDE IT, COWGIRL! RIDE!" And could lay on her back & take it like a woman—10" of female cock up her cunt. And fisted her women, freaked out with them, and disciplined them as necessary.

The potent and powerful Mickey:

Had created an identity of herself as a lesbian butch stud.

Would go to some city with a better environment would try her identity out in California. Where there's no police raids, and prejudice, not so much religious hate focused from citadels of evil power—The Satanic Church of Jesus Christ.

The potent and powerful Mickey was a true, real in-the-flesh person representing gaiety in three-dimensional action; besides those brief museum-piece beings; or a paragraph about Sappho in a history book.

Lucy & Mickey had no images of themselves on TV or the media. This was just fine to the redhead, who could identify with Lucy on the TV series, but the butch was different.

Felt she was not a woman, not a man.

'I must be part of The Third Sex I read about in a paper-back book one of the gay kids bought in a drugstore and was passing it around…that's what I am.'

Sometimes the cold & judgmental society made her feel she was not part of the human race.

An outlaw, somewhere along the fringe; female in gym shoes, slacks, man's shirts, metal wristband, hair slicked back behind her ears, greasy with oil, flattened to the sides of her head; an odd character representing herself and herself alone. Because she was depicted nowhere else in any society across the face of the globe.

Cumming into the power of herself as a lesbian butch, thru adolescence, from her childhood as a tomboy; cumming into awareness. Not as a total male-imitation, but a hot-blooded lesbian butch—seeking to love lesbians.

An aggressive lesbian butch.

Who did not want to be a man, to have to play the games men must; to assume their role & inflexible stance; but with a hot, consuming desire to fuck a woman. To take her mate thoroughly. In the superior position.

To take a female. To stroke inside with herself. Some part of herself—fingers & tongue. With her butch spirit and persona. To enter them with female cock, & stimulate their G spot until the woman came all over herself & was satisfied.

Straight society had scorn for her lesbian identity. An essence too powerful for them to fathom.

Mickey, in butch strength, did forgive Lucy, & was sorry the femme was so weak, and was dragging her glorious plumage & feathers thru the muddy gutter while trying to make a decision.

And Mickey was moving on.

Each fuck might be their last. The promise of love had flown.

Oh, how she longed for Lucy—this one last time. So they had oral sex; her cunt in Lucy's mouth. The femme's fingers done with red-painted nails parted Mickey's curly black pubic hair. Stroking tongue flicks over her wet meat, mouth sucking her butch clit, pulling it, & licking it with her made-hard tongue & motions of her lips & mouth.

Until her pretty face grew wet; wisps of red hair flew over Mickey's strong thighs with the effort. Lucy sucks, swallows her lover's juice.

And afterward, looks up from her knees between Mickey's bare feet; hot, clutching her wet slippery body, face damp with Mickey's cuntjuice; and asks, "Did you have enough baby? Are you satisfied? Do you want more?"

Mickey wants to penetrate her hard core. Belts the 10" cock to her crotch—its shaft plummets out of her crotch nest of black fur into a shivering dickhead, simulated real; straps around each thigh. Lucy lays on her back, knees bent up; Mickey crouches over Lucy, holds the cock in one hand, runs its tip up and down over Lucy's pulsating pearl clit over & over turning up the flame of desire until Lucy gets sopping wet; then pushes the tip of the dick in her hole a few inches, pulls it back, almost out, then repeats this awhile, as Lucy's hole gets bigger & wetter and she's writhing on the sheets, begging to be fucked, well fucked; as Mickey holds the cock pushes it in/out, twirls it around & around, screwing it in; then lets go of the rubber rod, grips Lucy's shoulders tight and pushes her hips, thrusting the dick all the way deep into her, up to the hilt. "OOOOHHHHHHOOOOO!" Lucy moans as she feels hard dick enter her, screwing down! into the center of her womanhood.

Mickey charges like a bull, riding, humping lunging, driving the dick from her hips like a piston. After 15 minutes of frontal fuckplay, Mickey commands her mate to turn over & raise up on all fours and fucks her like a dog from behind. Sticks the dick in her cunt; 10" is a good length—extra inches are needed to get past Lucy's big, soft ass. Jams the cock in and out of her juicy cunt, while reaching around her waist, rubs her fingertips into the redhead's furry cunt, rubbing along the pussylips to her clit nestled there, while fucking her with rapid strokes of her rod. Rubs & fucks. Lucy rears her ass up in passion like a bitch in heat & begins humping Mickey's hand which is petting her clit. The butch jams her dickhead in, pulls out, then jams in long & deep piston strokes, rhythmical & rubs her pearl clit. Lucy hollers, rears up in heated desire. Wants to cum, but Mickey holds the power—she withdraws her hand. "Not yet, my pretty wench. Wait for my love. I want to shoot my wad, too." For the grand finale, stops, turns the redhead over on her back straddling her head with one knee at each side, and sticks the cock in her mouth. "SUCK MY COCK, WHORE!" Mickey commands & sticks the cock past her lips & down her throat. It's freakish watching her with the rubber cock in her mouth, dominant Lord & Master, & Lucy obeys. Finally Mickey withdraws her saliva-slick cockshaft from Lucy's mouth & sticks it back in her one last time—in the Missionary Position. Fucks hard so they slap bellies; beating her down on the bed with hard cockthrusts.

Working into a heated passion by her fucking, which rubs her own clit as well, Mickey rides her woman in a wild exhilarating ecstasy; the bedsprings squeak, squeak, squeak.

All this work, Lucy is filled & screwed. Played with, licked & sucked, and still doesn't have her release. Because Mean

Master Mickey is holding back—stopping short—which works Lucy into a frenzied heat of passion, her dripping cunt on fire to be satisfied.

"Beg me for it, bitch! Beg me to let you come!"

"Please, Mickey. Master Mickey, please let your slut cum. Please! My pussy is wet for you! My pussy is aching for your satisfaction! Please fuck your whore, please!"

Mickey wants to feel Lucy's pussy cum inside—its waves & contractions. Unbelts the toy, throws it on the bed where it bounces, forever stiff. Slides down Lucy's legs once again; runs her tongue over Lucy's pearl clit & enters her pussyhole with 4 fingers clenched together into an apex, screws the fingers in careful & hard. She means business. Thrusts back and forth between the length of her fingertips to the bridge of her knuckles—which is the widest part of her hand. Mickey bends down now to lick her clit. Thrusts & licks; licks hard. And the femme tosses her head back & forth from side to side on the sweat-drenched sheets, feeling it. The rapture made by the motion of Mickey's tongue tip on her clit fast, and the pumping of her hand steady shoving in her cunt "OH! OH! OH! OHHHHHHHH! YES! YES! *YES! YES!* YES! YES! *MICKEY! YES!!*" Then the redhead cums hard. Her cunt squeezes Mickey's fingers so tight she can't move them. BANG BANG! Like fireworks along the Midwestern sky.

So, she got to dominate her completely for the evening with no complaints.

Mickey turned 19 years old.

For her birthday got a new shirt—from the Thrift Store. A card. It said: "To My Butch With Everlasting Love, Your Lady Femme, Lucy. Happy 19th!"

Lucy held her own legs open by the ankles. Mickey lowers her body down between Lucy's outspread thighs. With two fingers spreads her pussylips for greater clit contact, presses her swollen womanhood against Lucy's cunt—her hard pearl clit buries itself in the femme's hot, wet meat & takes her pleasure one last time.

Rides up and down making friction & feels the coursing of lust pull her nervestrings tighter. Each thrust takes her higher;

the urging of her loins cumming to Lucy, cumming to her; "CUM! CUM! CUM!" Lucy says. Squeezes the hot meat of Mickey's back, embraces her ass with pressure drawing the butch deeper into her; humping her hips in rhythm to the butch's thrust; fast, faster. "CUM! CUM! CUM!"

In the final moments during, a long lasting plateau, Lucy wraps her bare legs around Mickey's ass & pulls her cunt tight into her for hard clit contact as she is multiple-orgasming.

Lay on top of her; feels her naked breasts, pinkish nipples. Feels her heart beat in unison to hers; as two once-caged birds having taken a flight to freedom together. And is drawn into Lucy's tenderness, which is almost as soothing as sex.

'It soothes this restlessness in me. I'm satisfied. I've cum… Yet…restlessness is just a breath away.'

After all we must travel on our long/short journeys. Earth's a transient place. We aren't here to stay but for a little while.

CHAPTER FORTY-ONE

Finally did it. Fists.

She had gone in with 4 fingers as usual; stopped by the bridge of her knuckles. This time, her hand slid in all the way, fingers straight ahead, turning over into a fist wrapped over her thumb & pushed into her cunt.

Lucy had been very relaxed that day; high on a pill & wine. They started with the 4 fingers which they'd worked up to over the months & her cunt accepted easily.

"Try. It's built to handle it." Mickey urged her. "Try."

"It hurts, Mickey!"

The butch lay over her on her knees, leaned on one elbow. Her gel-lubricated hand pushing, pushing up to its widest part at the lips of Lucy's pussy, framed by pubic hair. It didn't go. And she sucked Lucy's nipples alternately right, then left. Occasionally a kiss; tongue darting between Lucy's lips.

The two women used lots of gel—K-Y lubricant. "Lucy! It'll be OK! Just pretend like you're having a baby! A baby's a lot bigger than a fist!"

"HAVING A BABY! *GOD! OH!* IT HURTS, MICKEY! IT HURTS! STOP! STOP!" Lucy's fingers turned into claws that dug into Mickey's back; so she felt Lucy's pain, too, secondhand. They both wanted victory; the goal—to get Mickey's fist inside her vaginal chamber.

It hurt Lucy so bad, but she was trying to be a woman and take it—the wide part of Mickey's hand, across the four knuckles kept shoving. Knocking at her door. Lucy's face contorted in pain. Tears filled her eyes. Mickey pushes. Keeps pushing her hand, only stopping to pour lubricant on them. "STOP! MICKEY! I CAN'T TAKE IT!" Immediately the butch stopped pushing, but didn't pull out. Her wet, sticky fingers webbed with a milky white liquid mix of female discharge & lube. And it hurts bad. Lucy's temperature has risen; she's panting. Her whole body throbs. Lucy sweats. Red hair sticks to her face. She tries to accept the pain. Breathes deeply. Long, slow breaths to calm her rapid heartbeat. To relax. Takes the pain—for her butch's sake. For their love's sake. And because they've been trying so long & she really wants to—and this is their goal.

So Mickey changes tactics; slides down Lucy's torso and runs her tongue into her pussylips; and touches her clit which is red & swollen. Licks her tongue tip over & over Lucy's clit, making hard contact, so new streams of desire begin to course thru the femme like the pulling gravity of an underground river yearning to the ocean, to freedom; & simultaneously starts twisting her lube-greased hand around in Lucy's hole, pushing in again. Cuntjuice drips down the redhead's thighs; this feel of her lover's mouth hot on her clit—mixed with pain. Mickey makes her tongue hard, licks fast; each stroke makes waves of desire grow, intensely, & the pain, fierce, grows with it; giving pain & pleasure as Mickey pushes in, in; so Lucy can stand it. Hot sensation of pleasure, intensifying—and pain.

And then her hand pushes thru. Tight sphincter muscle gives, lets her in, into Lucy's soft, loose insides. As she came into her, she curved her fingers down, bent under, into a grip; thumb tucked under her fingers fisting inside Lucy's cunt. The redhead femme's insides were loose; she pushed slowly,

slowly up, till she was in halfway up her forearm. Victory! Lucy hugged onto Mickey, clutching fiercely. Sweat & tears roll down her cheeks. A small amount of blood colors the discharge and lube which streaks their thighs & the sheets beneath their bodies. The butch sweats; beads of salty water roll down her back. Lucy is in Mickey's control. Fist inside her body. The butch has made a fist—not a fighting weapon—but a Love Fucking Fist.

Their hearts beat together. And Lucy feels the fist slide up inside the smooth mucus-lined walls of her vagina, which sucks Mickey deep inside. Wet, slippery, rubbery; fist in up to its forearm; pounds Lucy gently for a while.

Came out of her slowly. Once outside in the cool air, out of the hot intensity of her woman's inner body, the fist unclenches; Mickey buries her face in Lucy's nest of pubic hair; her tongue licks & sucks hard, soon gives the femme an orgasm. Intense. A long cum in her wet lips. Lucy's body trembles after & down deep inside her soul has a sense of peace.

Lay around, watched TV, exhausted. Had very few words. Very tranquil. Well fucked. As discharge with some red blood leaks out.

Funny, because it hardly made any difference anymore.

As far as lovemaking.

And that was just about it for Mickey and Lucy.

…For now.

CHAPTER FORTY-TWO

Ancient brick building; Hotel Bristol. 5 story.

So Lucy had shot up their little extra money into her green-blue vein; Phyllis & Leah keeping her habit mercifully weak because they were such junk-hogs themselves, they consumed most of the drug in secret, giving Lucy only the boiled-down remnants & soaked cotton tastes. She got a high, and got to the erotic play of lesbianism, upstairs in that shooting gallery with red walls. Afterward, she'd stagger out, high & in bliss. The two dope fiends would cook up the big part of the hit and shoot themselves up heavy-duty.

Large area, some reconstruction being done. So there were many vacant lots, & blocks with no buildings & the wind swept over this plain with a constant roar.

It was winter—cold hung in the air, and the wind made them want to hurry; its long, bony fingers of poverty pressing their backs.

'I hate them, people with money—*hate* them.'

Because life seems more trouble than its worth.

Poor people were lined up in front of the food giveaway for two blocks. Conditions were really bad.

A woman passed out in front of them in line, & the line stepped around her & kept moving.

At the end of 2 hours, they got their food. 2 bundles. 4 cans of white beans, 4 of green beans. 2 sacks of flour, 2 blocks of butter, 5 pounds of cheese, & a loaf of bread.

The two had Lucy's food allotment, rent paid, plus $1.50 in bus tokens—good for 6 rides at 25¢ apiece—from Welfare. They had Mickey's $55-per-week check—and it still wasn't enough. Lucy's extra spending on drugs made them as poor as ever.

Mickey sat on the side of their bed; shivered in the cold. Nobody had turned their little heater on. Breakfast wasn't cooked. As usual, Lucy was zonked out unconscious these winter mornings; wrapped up in blankets, she slept. 'I added more hours on my job, and still we're hurting. It's a bottom-less pit. We can't get nowhere. Nor accomplish nothing.'

The butch slicked her hair back behind her ears with Vaseline, stepped into her trousers & buttoned up a shirt. Saw days loom against them—days of poverty until her pay.

Turned to gaze for an instant at the curvaceous redhead—a sleeping Princess under sheets.

At this sight, where before she'd have tender feelings of love, or horny anticipation of sex, now there was just anger.

Wind whistled against the broken windowpanes stuffed with rags—gray & rotten, most left by the tenants who'd stayed there years ago. And the tie-dyed curtains moved perceivably as they blocked the chill breeze. Cobwebs hung from the ceiling above the distance Lucy could reach—it was painted gay greens & blues with red/yellow up to this point— like an omen of disaster hovering just beyond their familiar circle of warmth.

Teeth chattered in the cold. Anger seethed in her veins. 'She blows our money on dope and rides in taxicabs to Phyllis's little Junk Palace! We'll be desperate for money again before my paycheck! I'm earning $40 per week more than Welfare used to pay me, and we're just as poor as before.'

These nagging worries were the tail end of each subject she'd think about.—It always returned to The Money.

'I'm angry! Because we're females, we can't even be masters of our own bodies.

'We live in this noisy neighborhood; it's not safe. Lucy sells her body because she's mentally weak—she ain't strong enough to starve, & don't want to go without her bottle; all because I earn only $1.50 per hour and men are earning $5.

'And she's asleep; but when Lucy's conscious, she's so confused being a part-Indian; and not the same as the full-blood squaws and braves in the B-29 Club. And confused about being a woman who was molested as a child. And now seeing she's a lesbian. She's not the same as Lucy & Desi on TV. She's a stranger, just like myself. And confused about all that garbage that happened to her when she was a kid. The State kidnapping her & her sisters & brothers away from her mother for being an unfit parent staying drunk all the time & nobody supervising their home, & the place full of garbage knee deep in all the rooms, so the sanitation department had to wade in in rubber suits & clean it all out when another tenant reported them & they finally discovered the problem. This hotel room looks like a slice of Paradise compared to the conditions how Lucy grew up; that's why she don't see nothing wrong about living on skid row. And she's still mad— really mad—about the man who was supposed to be her guardian in the foster home raping her, & mad—real angry mad—that his wife wouldn't do nothing to save her. And she feels like there's something wrong with her. Not just him, but with her. And the same thing happened to me, I got abused—by three people, but with women. So I know how it feels. MAD! And confused. And she's my woman... And she's still a little girl, living in the past, sucking on a cold baby bottle with sour milk and clinging to a torn blue blanket. And the lady in the foster home & the police letting the man rape her, & keep on fucking her & keep on, so everybody knows about it in the foster home, him & Lucy, & also some of the other little girl kids her age; & still nobody will step in & do nothing; she has to live with this memory forever, or go to a psychiatrist & get rid of that part of her brain somehow; which she can't afford to do financially. So she goes to Phyllis's Drug Palace to escape everything & that doped junkie bitch Phyllis is encouraging Lucy to come over by offering her little bits of sex. Little tastes of sex. Not the whole sex like we do together. Just cold kisses. A caress—which Lucy dreams about for days after—& Phyllis flirts & winks and opens up a button of her blouse to show Lucy & gets Lucy strung out on exotic mind-fuck-semi-sex which is actually never real sex hardly at all; & keeps her begging for more always, & keeps her high.

'THIS GODDAMN WORLD IS CROWDING IN AROUND ME! It's bad enough being a butch & cut off from everybody in society—including that nice girl I fucked, Alyson, who refused to be seen with me in public; now I'm even cut off from other butch dykes & the femmes who ain't afraid to be seen with butches—*real* femmes—because we ain't got a place to meet.

'And *now* I finally got my fist up Lucy, it's supposed to claim her as my woman, that she'd let me, & we were gonna cut our initials in each other's arms like Rusty & her Lady did, but suddenly there's no point in it anymore.'

The uncomfortableness of her life. The days of her oppression.

2 more days to go before Lucy's welfare check. 1 week before Mickey's pay. No food. The bundles of canned goods had

been devoured, & Mickey was forced to go out on the street. It was a shame. She had a job, new used clothes & was taking her first baby steps on the ladder of success & yet had to resort to stealing cans of food off shelves of grocery stores in the neighborhood like she'd done when she first got to Chicago 10 months ago. It was a terrible risk. Mickey hated to think about going back to jail.

Stole one can at a time, one each from a different store; and continued until there was 2 dinners. 4 cans of tuna fish. 4 cans of chili & beans. 2 cans of corned-beef hash.

Then Mickey walked to work. Would finish up at midnight. Broom in hand, rag full of grease from the nightly cleaning of the popcorn machine. Outside the yellow windows of the movie house, in the snow, are women hooking, a quarter-block down. Lights from the theater marquee makes their hair change colors as it flashes off & on. Turning their white faces green, blue, red, orange, yellow. Like the rainbow. Blue like the feeling. And green for the cash money they were bound to find.

Rushed home to be with Lucy—not sure if she'd be there, or at Phyllis's drug house, or on a safari thru the skid-row dives.

Spent gay time at Shrimpie's. By nickname. Sign hung outside left from better days: P.A.L.M. G.A.R.D.E.N.S. Flicked off and on, pushed color into spent shadows on the curb. The club touched a 3-corner base; gays, skid-row type, petty hustlers.

So, for a time, one could see a bleach-blond gay kid, a snaggletoothed derelict the ilk of Freddy or Duke, & a low-life prostie blotched with junk abscesses on her arms, and a black pimp sporting patent-leather shiny pompadour of processed hair wrapped in a red bandanna; all together on the premises.

Black wavy hair ripples thru her strong fingers in an unconscious gesture; in a suit & tie, drag, Mickey squints, looks out the barroom door. From a personal height, looking down at the other people surrounding her like ants. POWER is what she craves. 'Most of these people are beneath me. They will always sit on these bar stools forever. I'm moving on to a better place.' Only when sexing her woman was she on top of the world; &, posing in the gay club; where she & Lucy were idols to younger street kids & old ones, envious. POWER is what she needed. Felt so insignificant; that her life was barely worth the price of a can of beans in a grocery sack. A red-rusted iron crane taller than a house, reaching to 5 stories balanced in the distance, working in the lots of reconstruction. Progress was moving on. The world kept on turning. The world is for learning. It will not wait.

Rusty was one of the hard-core dykes who stayed on at the Palm Gardens. The two butches sat side by side on a bar stool. Rusty was bigger; sandy hair, coarse face, big hands. Rough; in blue jeans, boots, and a jacket.

"I fuck her with my pussy, I look down at her, I'm making her tits bounce around as I jam her, yuh know, it's so good to her. She cries: 'OH, MICKEY! OH, MICKEY!'" Mickey imitates in falsetto. "I'm dominant over her. Lucy is in my complete control. I got my fist up in her. She lays under me humping to my rhythm; we've got that worked out perfect. She is submissive to my every desire in bed. Since I've got my fist in her, I feel she's my total woman and I cum easy—just looking down at her. So now I'm gonna leave her. It don't make sense."

"Does she know yer gonna leave?"

"Yeah. And she still won't stop."

Secretly, the sandy-haired butch was glad to hear this; she had plans to try to talk to Lucy herself, after Mickey left town.

The stocky young butch continued mournfully: "I was suppose to carve my name in her to prove to everybody she's mine & show that she'll let me do anything to her; that she trusts me totally. And I'm suppose to cut her name in me, so that any other women know I belong to her. And put vinegar in the cuts so they turn to permanent scars. 'Mickey' has more letters than 'Lucy,' so we were thinking about carving 'Sweet Lucy' in my arm. But she's sleeping with this junkie broad & shooting dope & turning tricks! Turning fuckin' tricks! And everybody knows it!"

"Does she give you the money?" Rusty asked, matter-of-factly.

"Some of it."

"Well, she's whoring for you; that makes her even more your Lady. To sell her body & give you the money."

"No, it's not—not to me. I draw the line."

"To me there are no lines." Rusty says softly.

It was inevitable; Mickey found a strange rubber circle—it was Lucy's diaphragm. "YOU NEVER GOT RID OF IT! YOU LIAR! YOU PROMISED YOU WOULD! FOR *US!*"

"IT COST ME $30, MICKEY! I'M NOT GOING TO GET RID OF IT! IT'S JUST FOR EMERGENCIES!"

"YOU FUCKING WHORE! THERE AIN'T NO EMERGENCIES THAT REQUIRE FUCKING! YOU AIN'T MY BITCH! YOU'RE *EVERYBODY'S* BITCH!"

So finally Mickey told Lucy, "If you're gonna walk, if you're gonna do it, at least let me walk behind you to see you don't get hurt."

Not caring anymore. Yes. Still caring.

Mickey's at the bar, drinks beer tho having promised to stay sober. "I can't keep nothing. I blew my women in New York, & Miami. And now here in your old Chi-town, a redhead is slipping thru my fingers." Beer suds spill on the bar from the bottle; foam over her lips. Surrounded by a crowd of butches, eager—hot in their pants, waiting to get to Lucy next, when Mickey is gone.

In these Last Days, the black-haired butch struggles to keep Lucy from her petty prostitution.

It's a schizophrenia. One face pleads, "PLEASE DON'T FUCK HIM, LUCY!" And the other face is stoic: its hand reaches out & grabs the money and spends it when she does.

So they go down to The Palm Gardens, Lucy turns a date out of there—no more than one per week. And Mickey rushes to drink it up & buy drinks for her pals, & go to the gay restaurant which is no longer so gay because of the dwindling of troops—due to the raids—fewer left to pile in there at closing; and take cabs; and Lucy drinks up the rest, a lush, and goes over to Phyllis's house for the junkie semi-lezzes to handle her with their cold pale fish hands and shoot her with their magic needle.

That's when, for a price, which they could now afford, Mickey got this stolen ID, saying "Nicki Varner. Age 25," instead of 19. And claimed she was the daughter of the captain of the Vice cops—by the same name—for that precinct. A stroke of luck. A fluke.

After their wild nights of carousing & cabbing thru town, back in their rainbow room, Mickey undressed under a bulb draped with tie-dyed purple. Man's suit coat flung into a chair, stood in her wool stocking feet; distraught; rumpled hair, shirttail untucked; unzipped trousers sliding down her pale ass: "YER THE BOSS, LUCY! NOT ME! CONGRATU-LATIONS! I'M YOUR MAN! I LOVE YOUR BODY EACH NIGHT! I'M STRONGER THAN YOU! I GOT MY WHOLE FIST UP INSIDE YOU LUCY AND YOU LOVED IT! BUT YER THE BOSS—NOT ME! AND I KNOW IT! AIN'T NO USE FOOLING MYSELF! THERE'S NOTHING I CAN DO! I CAN'T TIE YOU UP TO MAKE YOU STAY AT HOME—NOT FOREVER!! I'D HAVE TO LET YOU GO SOMETIME! I CAN'T BEAT YOU UP—I WON'T BEAT YOU! YOUR MIND IS YOUR DECISION! I'M FUCKIN' AT THE END OF MY ROPE, WOMAN! DO YOU WANT ME OR NOT!" Mickey's down on one knee, pleading, hands held out, a tear in her trousers, sweat mixing with slick Vaseline in her black hair & beading her white pockmarked face. "I EVEN PUT ON SNEAKERS AND GOT OUT OF DRAG TO GET US A JOB! TO CARE FOR US AND OUR HOME!" And Lucy hugged Mickey ferociously. Pulled the butch back on the bed on top of her, moaned, "Oh, Mickey, oh Mickey... My baby Mickey, it's killing me, too."

Gray nights & days. A slushy snow, blackened with carbon-monoxide exhaust from millions of cars, buses, & trucks in this huge metropolis.

'Finally got my fist in her. Finally got her big enough, stretched her cunt, and got in, up to my forearm, and now

I'm leaving. Huh. Have to find a new woman out in California. A nice woman. And start stretching her all over again. And I'm gonna carve my name in her flesh, & hers in mine —in big letters, right away, while we're fresh & still have a chance to be happy together and live happily ever after! *We have the right!*'

Sleet drove down gray slush streets in icy days, & snow-misted nights. Mick felt childlike—ready to let go of it all, mop the floors of the theater until her next paycheck & go. A kid with wanderlust.

Mickey was a strong lesbian butch. Soon her thighs would be wet from loving of another woman.

Maybe—just maybe—in some far star-crossed act of God, she'd meet Lucy again, and pick up where they'd left off...but for now...wanderlust... To leave Lucy & let her decide between her bottle & living life. Between her drugs & Mickey's teenage love for her.

When Mickey told Lucy she was going to leave, there was a fiery outbreak.

Redhead screamed: "I TRIED TO MAKE IT WORK! I'M NOT A LESBIAN! NOT LIKE YOU ARE! I GAVE YOU EVERYTHING! I DIDN'T DENY YOU YOUR PLEASURE ANYTIME OR DAY OR NIGHT! I LEARNED TO MAKE LOVE WITH YOU LIKE YOU LESBIANS DO IT! I TRIED TO DO EVERYTHING I WAS SUPPOSE TO DO TO BE YOUR GODDAMN WIFE AND EVERYTHING! AND THAT DON'T MAKE ANY GODDAMN DIFFERENCE; YOU'RE GONNA LEAVE ME ANYWAY! YOU GODDAMN FUCKING DYKE! YOU'VE RUINED MY LIFE! WELL, GET OUT, THEN! *GO!* YOU GODDAMN FUCKING BULLDYKE BITCH! I *HATE* YOU!"

"You can come, Lucy, if you want. In California life's suppose to be better. I'll get a job, and maybe I'll make more than $1.50 an hour. At least $1.75 an hour, like you earned in the office. And I'll go to school in my spare time & get somewhere in life."

"I'M NOT GOING NOWHERE! I'M STAYING RIGHT HERE! I HATE YOU! I'M NOT GOING TO BE A

LESBIAN ANYMORE! AND NOT WITH YOU! NEVER AGAIN WITH YOU!"

"YOU CAN'T DECIDE WHAT YOU WANT, LUCY! I'M NOT SHARING MY WOMAN WITH EVERYBODY! SHE'S NOT GONNA SLEEP WITH TRICKS FOR MONEY! SHE AIN'T GONNA FREAK OFF WITH NO JUNKIE BROAD PHYLLIS FOR DRUGS!"

"I FREAK OFF WITH PHYLLIS FOR *LOVE!* LOVE!— THAT SHOWS HOW MUCH YOU KNOW ABOUT IT!"

"I GUESS YOU'RE NOT A DYKE WHEN YOU LAY DOWN AND FUCK WITH PHYLLIS! I GUESS SINCE IT'S JUST TWO BROADS FUCKING, THEN THEY'RE NOT DYKES, HUH!"

"PHYLLIS IS NOT A LESBIAN! SHE HAS LOVE! SHE IS A SOUL WITH A LOT OF LOVE THAT SHE GIVES TO ALL HER FRIENDS—INCLUDING ME! THAT DON'T MAKE HER A LESBIAN LIKE YOU ARE! THAT JUST SHOWS HOW MUCH LOVE SHE HAS! AND IT JUST SHOWS HOW MUCH YOU KNOW ABOUT IT— *MISTER!*"

Later Lucy crawled into bed next to Mickey like a sorry child. Red hair falling from its regal crown, wild, over her pale shoulders; her mascara running from their evening of nightclubs. "Don't say that I chose anybody over you, Mickey. I'm just using them—even Phyllis.... Mickey, try to understand.... The kind of home I came from, my mother was an Indian woman, full-blood, who was whipped, just totally defeated from the beginning. She took to drink.... We never had a home like you; your mother making you go to school and study, & driving you crazy by cleaning everything, & wanting everything perfect. Mine was the opposite. Everything always fell apart. Like our lives. We never had clean clothes. Our clothes were in a big pile shoved to the side of a wall, always dirty & smelly in school. We didn't have beds, or any set place to sleep; we just lay down and fell asleep anywhere we were— on a pile of dirty sheets somewhere in the house. I just stopped trying, like she had; but not as bad. And when I was

14, the man who was suppose to be my guardian—before he actually raped me, I saw it coming for months. I kept asking for help. The lady, his wife who owned the place, the police; nobody would help me, Mickey. Nobody ever helps me or does anything for me. So I decided just not to take life serious! I've hated myself for too long! Hated myself in school because I was dirty and dressed funny & not white—and because my mother and sisters & brothers were Indians, but I was different even then, so kids made fun of me. Hated myself for my so-called guardian assaulting me, thinking I must have done something wrong.... Well, I see now, none of it means anything. Only the guilt I attach to it, and I want to let go of that. That's what Phyllis keeps telling me to do! Let go of it! All the shit! Let go of it! Drop out of the rat race & not take life so serious! Mickey, you think I love Phyllis. I do love her, but not like I love you! I'm *in* love with you! I *love* her. She is part of the universal love of all beings on earth, and that's how Phyllis & Leah and I all love each other, together. Not like a man and a woman—you and me! I don't love her like that! Hold me, Mickey! Hold me in your arms! Just try to understand! I need Phyllis in a way it's hard to explain. I'm using Phyllis because I can lay down with her and she doesn't want anything from me. I can lay there naked and she won't touch me! If anybody does anything, it's me! It's good to be the aggressor for a change! And not have somebody pawing over me! She knows what I need! Time and space to think and figure out why in hell I'm on this earth! Phyllis is *old*, Mickey! She's 35 years old! She sees things we don't! She's a beatnik— they see things! She reads a lot when she's high! I'm learning from her!"

"You got a yen, Lucy. *That's* what you got from her! It's a little baby habit for drugs, it ain't grown up to a full-blown monkey on your back; not yet. It's a yen for Phyllis. You got a crush on that pockmarked bitch. And she don't want your body at all! Not like me! I *want* you! The whole you! You think she's this big spiritual lover and wise and too spiritually advanced to want sex, & she just lays there and lets you make love to her first, because she's just a spirit with no body. She's a drug ghost; ghosts don't have sex. She's a career junkie—for 20 years! She wants you to like her—yeah, she's getting you strung out on her, on her emotionally, like bait on a fish-hook—so she can use you, for your money to get her fucking heroin fix."

"NO! That's not true! I'd expect you'd think something like that! That's just what it looks like to you because that's the level your mind is on! You're preoccupied with sex and being jealous! You're always jealous of the people I love!"

"She wants you around for money to buy her drugs. Yes! She's a hustler & a thief!"

'Mickey don't understand....' The redhead's wide narrow lips pursed in a crooked line as she choked down a reply. 'Even if she's right...I still need Phyllis, bad.... I'm so fucking confused. I just need a way out of my problems.' And the butch was taking Lucy in her muscular arms; feeling her big tits with her strong fingers; mouth pressed down on Lucy's, silencing the conversation, pressing her back down on the bed, working her trouser-covered thigh between Lucy's thighs & her ass humped, rubbed her clit up and down on Lucy's leg—so the femme could feel the wet place soaking thru the fabric of her toreador pants to her skin. Lucy thought, 'She's gonna take me. Gonna make love to me, like my first girl in Foster Care. Like James does. Like everybody wants to. Even if Phyllis is a drugged junkie, I need somebody cold—to hold off. To keep away, yet want me around. To hold me at arm's length, but not let me go. To give me breathing room—so I can think. I need a woman to hold me in her arms and wait and be patient. I need a time & place for LUCY. I need some-body to just be there, and not want to take anything.'

CHAPTER FORTY-THREE

'Nobody talked on the long flight down to Miami. Four souls propelled forward, each only toward her thoughts. Four souls pushed inside time & space; then we came down to earth, took a taxicab to our hotel; and they were more talkative & animated.'

'Oh, I can walk for miles. I can walk and walk, and see the sun set down, a red pancake on the horizon covering the end of the city with red syrup; and walk and see the sun come up again, yellow & blazing holy guns of light. When I ran away from home over & over, starting when I was 12, that's what I did—walk—because I didn't have anything else to do, and no place to go.

'Night had fallen well. Black. Hot Miami rain. Each car's headlights that came around the bend of the highway along the ocean shattered the empty void; then left us alone, in passing.'

The women were questioning their toy—their baby butch Top; and Mickey, resplendent in glorious new clothes, flashing showy rings basked in the attention. The yearnings of her heart were being fulfilled. "And then they caught you and locked you up in juvenile detention?" A sudden bolt of lightning lit the sky & courses thru the building tops & clouds.

"It was hell," Mickey said.

They all made little noises like laughing or grunting in agreement. As she sat in the backseat of the cab, handsome in a tweed jacket with suede lapels, leather boots, tweed trousers & cap to match; Mickey's harsh laugher as she remembered, was a true sound of hell itself.

"Yeah." Mickey picked her teeth; gold rings flash on her fingers. "I spent many a year in and out of there…when I was a kid growing up." Her black eyes focused out the window thru the rain; clouds form ominously against black night. "The place was built like a brick shithouse. Every door was locked. When I reached 12, nobody could keep me at my mother's house no more…and no relatives would have me…and nobody else could adopt me…so between running away & sleeping in doorways down in the Village, I was locked up in some facility."

"In jail," mutters Valorie.

"Jail. Sure was. My only crime at that time was my mother attacking me. It's worse than being an orphan—having your own flesh-&-blood mother try to destroy you—physically and mentally."

"A kid in jail," says Gloria, pensive.

"Oh, I was a rough kid.... Those old bitches came in the dayroom, they'd say, 'What is this kid doing here? She's just a runaway.' There's girls in there for forgery, murder, adult crap. And they'd sit around complaining they had nothing to do, like they were already old broads, all worn out. So I'd step on the shower drain with my feet, stop it up you know; so the guard says, 'OK now you got something to do—Mop It Up!' And I use to sell my soda and my milk, sell it for cigarettes when I smoked then, and did my push-ups and my sit-ups. Actually, I wasn't a mean kid, just lonely and desperate and uptight."

Then, as the cab hurtled thru black space of the highway dividing ocean and land with a beam of light, the butch leaned back; her coiffed black-haired head against the cab seat, dreaming; feeling very nostalgic....

'We made the rounds of bars, gay ones & hustler dives, which Scheherazade knew, & Gloria. Laughing, shouting over all the other noises, the way you do when the muscles & veins stand out in your neck. Hit all the bars on the main drag; then some joint on Biscayne Boulevard, among the crowds, running blind drunk in well-heeled boots; madcap, making our own party & disturbing the phony straight couples sitting at tables in front of us; making more noise than the floor show & my girls spending Big Money, our last, left from New York scores; & aiming to make more. Valorie was bellowing at the top of her lungs, swaying to the music—all eyes riveted on the singer, a Drag Queen in her rhinestones. A spoiled-boy faggot beside us said something catty. "I'M JUST AS GAY AS YOU ARE!" Valorie told him. "I *MEAN*, JUST 'CAUSE I'M WEARING A DRESS & HIGH HEELS! DON'T LET IT FOOL YUH! I LIKE PUSSY!" The sullen child-fag turns back to face the stage of which he had a ringside view. He was alone and sorry. We were together & merry, enjoying our days of wine & roses as best we could.'

Mickey thought back: 'At our hotel, I was a pet butch. Sometimes they tormented me like a fish in a glass bowl, or a bird in a cage! They had all the money, & I only had what they gave me! I felt better when my wallet was full—then I spent it all back on them. We whipped each other with the girls' rhinestone-studded belts, and I turned each over my knee—as Pappa—and paddled their behinds until their cheeks turned rosy red. We laughed. We fought. We hurt each other with words in fierce arguments. Until time to go to work when evening fell, they lounged around in slips and panties & bras, blew smoke rings and ate from plastic containers of food I brought up. Mostly the orders were wrong. Eggs sunny-side up instead of fried; waffles which should have been pancakes. They drove me crazy with their demanding. I did things for them. Errands, massaged their legs—weary from standing & walking. The women were entirely self-centered, egotistical—to hide their terrible inner hurts—and acted their usual selfish selves. Then I would love them. Unfasten their garter belts & remove their stockings. Work my hands up, massaging from their toes up their shaved legs, lean pale thighs to their furry cunts. Probe thru pink pussylips to find the pearl—her clit—& massage each girl there, & her nipples at the same time; their silk bras & panties tossed aside. Scheherazade was so curious to watch—she hadn't been a lesbian before, like the others; and Gloria moans, it's her turn; pulls off her lacy G-string panties so I can enter her hole with my fingers; and suck her tits and we're flesh to flesh. She says, "I'm so glad I found my true self and went back to girls."

'Maybe I'll go to California,' young Mickey thinks. 'She'll come out there...but I'll have to send her the money... Maybe she's too smart to go...and won't take the risk...' And kept this worried train of thought for awhile. Then, a smile of relief; accepting her decision—regardless of its consequences. 'I *have* to go, even if it kills me.'

24 hours. I haven't seen Valorie. People ask about her, but I don't know.

When I went to the phone booth to call about Valorie, I didn't have to ask for the name of the women's jail, it was already written on the wall by the phone; MUNICIPAL HALL OF

JUSTICE—212–6002. And CITY CORRECTION—266–1000. Also was written; LOVE SICK. I WANT YOU HONEY, PLEASE BELIEVE ME HONEY I WANT YOU SO. Words of someone whose mate was locked up & whose head was turning around with sadness. I only had one broad then—her. I called City Correction, Women's Jail, but she wasn't there under either of her names.

Where was Valorie Patterson?

In the street, walking, a girl in tight hip-hugging knit skirt—just covering her pubic fur it's so short—a halter top over buxom tits; and high-heeled pumps; a plastic raincoat over this—open to reveal what she's selling; this girl recognizes me; it's Gloria, who will be my 2nd lady, and Valorie's stable sister soon. She recognizes me and stops. She's with a colored woman wearing a bronze wig, who is her current stable sister. "Have you seen my woman?" I ask.

"Have you got any money?" says the black woman.

"No, I haven't."

"I want to see her, too," says Gloria. "I've got $100 right here in the toe of my stocking. Have you got a pencil? Write down my hotel room number. I might choose you." Gloria says this, adding, "And I don't care who knows it." And casts a long look at the bronze whore.

"What should I do with this number? Call up or come by? Is it safe? Is your man up there?"

"What do you want to do with it?" asks the black whore.

"I'm looking for Valorie, too," says Gloria. "Everybody's looking for her!"

"She's probably holed up someplace shooting...whoever she is," says the black woman.

"We were all suppose to meet her last night," says Gloria. "All us girls; we have our little ho cluster down by the after-hours club."

"I'm really worried." Mickey is frantic.

"Since you don't have any money, give me that watch," says the black woman.

"I was thinkin,' after the way I treated her yesterday, I didn't mean to be so rank...but Christ, we're getting evicted because of her!"

"What are you gonna do with that watch? It's a nice watch. Expensive."

"Sell it, if I can't find my woman."

"She pay you good, Daddy?" says the black woman.

"OK," Mickey grumbles. "Sell it? I'm gonna EAT it, if Valorie don't show up! I'm broke! I haven't seen her in 24 hours! I'm worried!"

"I haven't seen her in 5 days."

"Give me that watch! GIVE ME THAT WATCH!"

"Fuck it!" says Mickey.

So Gloria comes with Mickey, pays her $100, and deserts her current pimp & stable sister; and they can keep Mickey's hotel room & eat take-out food and make love, hot & passionate, wet & sexual on the hotel sheets in the sultry August of 1958;—sheets with monograms on them, and on the pillowcases & towels. Make love; thus cement their business arrangements, sex roles, & friendship all at once. 'These two days I've worried about Valorie. I have exchanged information with people but nobody knows where she is, and we've called the jail, the hospital, & the morgue. My mind is blown open, after this new lovemaking; we lay on the bed seeing each other's bodies; too hot for the sheets; and Gloria tells me, "Ohhhh…Mickey, I like this … Your back is so hard. You've built up your muscles." Now we must discuss the business aspect—the tricks. And I must manage them, or they'll lay up in bed, munch on take-out food, smoke reefers, watch the TV that we rent by the day, and fuck with my body & never earn a cent & we'll get evicted like what almost happened with Valorie and me. So I set Gloria out on the curb to hunt for quick meat; with the $100 she has given me to choose me—for my services—I take care of our immediate future. Pay up rent, get her sexy whore clothes & fancy outfits dry-cleaned, pay for the TV another week, pay up the credit the lady at the restaurant had extended us, etc.'

Getting-down time comes & goes; Gloria has got out on the streets early & thus has plenty of money. Now it's time to close her plastic see-thru raincoat and saunter home.

Two figures stand in their hotel room. It's 4 A.M. They

embrace. Boots rise up into black trousers, into a black butch's leather jacket. Next to Mickey, Gloria in her very short skirt, bare pussy in Mickey's hand because she don't wear underwear. Hot, stinky cunt, turning juicy under the steady feels of the butch's touch. The femme unfastens her halter top so her big boobs bounce free. Her fingers tug at Mickey's belt, unfastening the buckle. Gloria kicks off her high heels & is barefoot. Mickey paws her tits, slides her hands down Gloria's sweaty body.

Lights from the street illuminate them.

These two lesbians set upon a journey from out of a burning past, with no future.

Gloria is pushed against the wall of the hotel room by a masterful butch stud; she feels her naked legs being pressed open by a trousered leg; feels fingers inside her cunt. She stretches her body, luxuriating, wiggles her ass, puts one bare foot up on Mickey's shoe.

RULES FOR BEING MICKEY'S LADIES is pasted on the bathroom mirror where the girls are sure to find it.

1. You may fuck bitches but only in my presence.

2. No dyke, woman, man, or any child, animal, or living creature comes before me in attention.

3. You must be obedient, or else you go.

4. You must do what I say always, & obey these rules.

5. You may fuck men, but only for money, not to freak off—that's what I'm for.

6. If you fuck a bitch in my presence, I must get some of her, too.

7. When you make money, I must get most of it for our needs & you better not fuck off the money on drugs & in the bar.

8. You must stand up for me and be loyal! For I am willing to stand up for you with my life. If a pimp or a trick pulls a gun on us, I will stand in front of you and protect you. If he shoots me he must pay for this and get some years in jail so we must press charges & testify if I get shot!—even tho we are dykes & hustlers we gotta have rights! If I must steal or rob to

help get us thru an emergency if we have no money, you must testify I was nowhere near the scene of the crime! That you say nothing—even if you did.

9. You must not get into fights while working! Run from troublemaking bitches! Do not start yelling back at them!

10. If any of us gets in trouble with the law, you are expected to remain calm and lie to save our skin. Give an alibi. Do not lose your cool!

IF YOU CAN FOLLOW THESE RULES YOU WILL BE A REAL WOMAN.

When Valorie returns home, dragging her soiled satin dress & carrying her high-heeled shoes, in the skin on top of her hand are six needle pricks.

"Speed?"

"No. H."

Heroin. The painkiller.

"You ever use it Mickey?" Pastywhite face smiles sickeningly; chipped front tooth, face not nearly as pretty as her voluptuous womanly body.

"Hell, yeah, I tried it! But I don't like it!"

"Why?"

"I'm afraid to get addicted! I can't enjoy the high because I'm too afraid I'll turn into a dope fiend! But it is good."

"Yeah. Well, I ain't afraid."

"Well, I am! Because I've fucked myself up so bad before—I thought I was going to die!"

The backs of her white hand over the veins have holes, and there are bruises in the surrounding skin.

Mickey recalled those New York nights, a full year ago, when she and Valorie & Gloria had got closer to each other. Lesbian hookers with their lesbian pimp—a stone butch, in fine clothes, silks & wools & tweeds with pairs of leather boots & a leather belt to beat their round white butts, and a leather cap to match, that Valorie had paid for at the clothes shop in time installments.

For a while they tried working by day after the trouble started, to avoid harassment from evil pimps who wanted the women to work for them & put the money in their pockets. Gloria's ex-man was raging to find he'd lost his money-making whore and got some of his brother pimps together to gang up on them, making their lives miserable. They could do more evil under cover of darkness, with no witnesses. When they did manage to work nights, days they'd do educational activities. Mickey, having spent years behind bars where all she could do was walk from one locked door to the next, at the ends of her ward, wanted to be free. So they went walking at will. In the sand at the Atlantic Ocean. Rockaway Beach. They went to the museums. Did things like go to Coney Island, ride on the roller coaster & eat clams on the hard-shell at Nathan's—like they were all going steady together & were on a date. A three-person affair. Tripping together in wonder & joy. Going to the movies, which was Valorie's favorite pastime. She loved to get high, then step into a fantasy world thru TV and movies. "If you had as many needles sticking out of you as you've stuck in you, you'd look like a porcupine." Mickey admonishes. "Look at rule number 7 in the bathroom."

Because they worked hard, ladies hustling, Mick running around doing errands & arguing & discussing in order to iron out their personalities and keep a smooth-flowing household; mostly they had no energy left afterward, but to lay all three in bed, eat cheeseburgers and turkey dinners & fried chicken from plastic & cardboard take-out containers, smoke cigarettes & freak out sexually with Mickey as the star.

"I got a girl named Gloria Deloria, and she's a Whoria for everybody but me!" moans Mickey, morosely; lying on the sheet in her boxer shorts & T-shirt.

"Oh that song!" Gloria cries. Claps her painted nailed hands over her ears, then ducks under the sheet. "Oh I wish I was dead! I hate that song! DEAD! I wish I was! I got nothing to live for!"

"She was a whore for you last night; yuh really freaked with each other!"

"Night before."

"I HATE THAT SONG! AND I HATE YOU, MICKEY!"

"GLORIA, GET DOWN!"

"She wants a piece of your ass!"

"Well, she ain't gettin' it. She ain't turned over her money!"

"If I do turn over my money, I'll have a piece of *your* ass!"

"Help yourself! What's your pleasure? Ass, cunt, tits, or clit?"

"ALL OF IT, MOTHERFUCKER!"

The hotel room is hot from the August heat. They have a fan blowing. The little family argues playfully. "It's like the giant and the little kid in the fairy tale? Ain't that what they say?" Valorie says, dreamily, like she's gone and swallowed a pill on the sly. "FEE-FI-FO-FUM! IF YOU CLIMB THAT BEANSTALK, I'LL HAVE YOUR ASS!" And Gloria gives in, goes to a hiding place she's burrowed deep in a drawer under her clothes, and produces her nightly earnings. And Mickey takes the roll of green cash; twenties, tens, and fives, tucks it away in her boot; then bounds naked, back to the bed. Gloria pats her hair in place, lays on her back, spreads her knees, holds them back with her hands offering an open view of her furry sex, so Mickey can get on her and fuck cunt to cunt, lesbian style. Valorie watches & fingers her own pussy, and gets hot. Soon enough, the bed's banging against the wall. 'Dick and dope, Mickey.' Lou the reformatory matron had told the young butch. 'Dick & dope is what these young girls want. And *you're* the dick—don't forget. It's you who's got to keep them in line! Use your dick and keep 'em off the dope and you'll have a good life; even here in this world behind bars.'

CHAPTER FORTY-FOUR

'When I finally saw the act, at first I thought Lisa was awful.... From the balcony; she was doing a foolish little stunt dance....' Mickey turned her face away in embarrassment. 'I was afraid to look back.' The butch left the balcony, tried to dismiss the scene from her mind. But later, at work, cleaning up the box office, she heard Al and Red backstage call up the girl's dressing room about the act. Mickey was supposed to connect the call and hang up, but instead she listened; thinking they were talking about how bad Lisa was.

"Who're yuh talking about, Al? Who was so bad?" Mickey asks later, shyly.

"Aw, one of the girls doing floor work; she better clean her act up.... The Vice Cops been crawling over this place for a couple of days. She's good, tho. Damn, she's good!"

So Mickey goes and asks Red, "Which girl? Who did the floor work?"

"Your girl Lisa."

'So Lisa is good, they think....' This encouraged Mickey. 'Well, if she's fooling us all and can't really dance, I'll be too embarrassed to watch. She's got one more show tonight at twelve. I'll be off work.' So she went past the straggling male customers, thru the worn doors into the dimness of the theater to catch The Midnight Shambles.

There, from the ground level of the theater Lisa came out, stunning in her sequined costume.

'She starts with very little on.'

She begins to move to the rhythm. The butch is slouched in her theater chair, afraid. Suddenly she sits up. Lisa's shedding clothes, but it's not the nudity that wows her, she's enticed by form and muscle working together to create art. 'Damn it, she's good!' Mickey's on the edge of her chair waiting for the spell to end, for the figure on stage to goof up, stumble, trip, or make a joke out of it; but she doesn't. 'Damn, it is good!'

'I came out into the lobby exhilarated. Lisa was really great. And compare her to the Star Billing girl, Miss Paula Picasso, who had years of experience; but Lisa has something that is fresh. And I like it. When she dances, she's saying something.'

From the box-office phone, she calls upstairs to the owner's office. "Red? Busy? This is Mickey! I got news! She— Lisa—is a hit! The audience loves her." The next 3 shows the following day there was an ovation during the interlude music after the first stripper had gone on, they were calling for Lisa!

She was wild! I got up backstage to tell her, and she ran back out—"GIVE A HAND FOR LISA LAMOUR!" —And they're clappin' like crazy.

Those days Mickey didn't have a home, just before she started being Lisa's lover. Didn't earn enough money to afford a room. Came to sleep in the theater office some nights, if the fag manager would risk letting her in; otherwise had to risk crossing town back & forth all night in a fitful guarded rest, on the subway that became elevated, its tracks weaving on stilts across the smokestack slums; or sleep in an all-night theater.

Shift over, dancers gone home. Manager has padlocked the door and left. Mickey sits in an Ale House across the street from the theater, which will close several hours later at 2 A.M. She sits in yellow light that filters onto the curb; then, it too goes off, as it closes for the night, and Lowell puts the chairs up on the tables, and the bar stools up on the bar to sweep & mop; and now, she's outside in the open air of night, where just a minute ago she sat behind the window looking; now she's walking. Beatniks and artists leave the padlocked bar, go singing down the street, swinging six-packs of beer.

So, the last light of the circle of civilization has pushed Mickey out into the shadows—in the city turf, under looming black buildings; to fend for herself.

It is the sense of your own wild freedom to go anywhere. To be wild.

You see the Outer Drive, the line of the lake's edge; you see the perpendicular waves, frozen. Out in the middle no ice has formed, the tide's still splashing. The El tracks cut the city apart. At one end a traveler will see the ghetto of African people spilling. Looking down between the ribs & beams of fire-burned buildings and sordid rooftops of tenements where the pied piper of drugs walks majestically thru mist bringing all power in a cellulose packet. "Don't you believe in this? It's magic," he says. Mickey thinks: 'Walking on air, under a blue haze.... When I get back up north, get off the train, & instead of ride, walk under the elevated structure of crisscross iron, on foot, down on ground level.'

Mickey came running up the subway exit, thru its huge dirty white porcelain bowels. Out panhandling under the stars.

Night. Womanly figure disguised as a boy, looked around her. North Avenue exit, where all derelicts hang out. White, black and Hispanic brawling with a drunken lisp. Puerto Ricans drag by in old ragged cars; oil burners exhausting blue fumes into the gutters. Tramps under neon advertisements flash turn from green to pink to orange beside the drugstore, where the fleeting figure of Phyllis & her junk rummies bought the legal cough syrup made with paregoric, an opium-based derivative to ease dope sickness; and Duke and Freddy bought nasal inhalers, broke the plastic containers, cut up the core insert, cooked up the pieces & shot it into their veins, and dropped amphetamine and diet-pill prescriptions from the Toe Doctor, to speed. The place of pain & heights. Of people who have struggled to get up & out, but their struggles push them down deeper. Phyllis is at home entombed in her cool coffin smiling the contented dope fiend's crooked knowing smile; buried deep under the refuse and twisted integuments of things. The junkyard. And those old battered El cars wheel on.

Now, Mickey was on the block under the El tracks—it's Shrimpie's bar.

Red inside, figures lounge like a huge dance hall. If nothing was here—no gay kids—deserted, the butch would subway back to Clark & Division for a quarter.

Curved train tracks lay between indigo points, which cut diagonally thru the city underground with only an occasional air vent on the surface—a grille in the sidewalk—that gives a rush of hot steam as the train pistons thru the tunnel forcing the stale underground air up in a gusher appearing thru the vent like hell's smoke.

Subway subterranean walls, curved, made of white tile. Trains moan, shudder the rails, the vibrations grow stronger; clanking to the station thundering yellow-eyed iron beasts, then slip away down the track into stillness.

Division Street, is not as dangerous as it seems to be out

here on the wild Northwest, where the land is being cleared; high cranes loom.

Past the now-vacant site of The 169 Club & the grand-mother of them all—the ancient Beach Ball Club—long gone, owned by the twin brothers, a Mafia front, who owned gay clubs for the last decade in this town; any dyke who goes to gaybars in Chicago knows them.

Clark Street's mouth. The artist/beatnik bars. Gold Coast. Hellish dives... On the map forms a particular box around a parody—named after the expanse where money begins—officially, just two blocks east, The Gold Coast; fancy apartments, and people alike, their noses in the air; bluebloods, by the lake. The $200,000-a-year people. The tycoons...and unofficial long Cadillacs that cruise the slums; the johns and occasional janes looking for a piece of tail that poor folks service.

Mickey hopped down the street. Sang a little song Gloria had taught her which she'd learned from her black stable sister. "TRAVELIN' HO! TRAVELIN' HO! AIN'T GOT NO MONEY! AIN'T GOT NO CLOTHES!"

No wonder Gloria had cut that pimp & his dizzy ladies loose & come to be with Mickey & Valorie. And they made good money. No wonder.

Farther east toward the lake, the rich climbed to their fortunes, some, to the exclusion of love. Some because they couldn't love. Maybe there was no one to love. So they take what's available. Now, silently, they buy their love and take their prescription dope & quietly commit slow suicide.

They took a cab to the theater.

Lisa & Mickey. Sat up in the balcony where they could, in the shadows of the grand old columns & dusty velvet drapes tied by golden rope, secretly feel each other's tits & hot pussies thru the fabric of their clothes. Lisa keeps looking back with arched penciled eyebrows at the projection room with its bullet-chipped glass; this window faces the giant screen directly, casting a flickering current of yellow light.

Both women were too paranoid to really get involved sexually in public. They pet for a moment. Keep floating in a delirious kind of joy with time suspended; senses wrapped in each other—Lisa's femme perfume scent and Mickey's men's cologne; within a curtain of hazy light projection of the fine lines and colors of each instant of the film.

Then Lisa picks up her traveling case, puts her little pink G-string inside with her makeup. It's time for the last act. Mickey reaches in the case, grabs the G-string which holds the odor of Lisa's pussy & sweat, puts it to her nose & sniffs.

"My butch bought me diamond rings, my butch bought me furs, my butch this, my butch that! We've all had a *past!*" I told her. "I don't want to hear about yours!"

"You'll hear about it if I want you to, Motherfucker! Nobody tells me what to say!"

"Lisa, you're just a regular woman, in a regular woman's body; but you have something special. Something great. Whether or not you lose it, or it stays with you and you develop it, is up to you. But you could be a star. A top-notch dance artist."

Broke my lecture off. Lisa is not listening, goes her way, looks under things for her costumes. She can't hear anyhow, she is a child—more so than Mickey in some respects, tho more worldwise in others. She had been on the fast-lane strippers' circuit since age 16. Yet still not wise. She don't even know what her own reflection in the mirror of her mind means!

You see women reduced to slums inside. Shambles. And you want to touch the child inside them and bring them out into the light. A feeling passes over you, you see, lurking in the dark windows of their soul a feeling of great beauty trapped; of sorrow. Of want unfulfilled. Of a woman who can rise to love you, or to bite and tear at you & destroy you like she's been destroyed.

Met Lisa October, Friday 13th weekend.

It was Sunday night. Mickey had worked matinee at the Annex Theatre (from 3:30 to 6 P.M.)—not long at all. Not long enough to afford to live. Angrily, she had demanded to work at the other theater, the Rialto. Red, the head manager there, arranged for her to work the candy counter, cashier & do janitorial for the evening shift.

The manager gave Mickey cab fare. It was raining, but she took a bus and saved $1.70. Started work at the Rialto. Began to talk to Ralph, the night manager. Ralph says: "Negroes are the only people in this country who got any human feelings left. Their the only race that has got any of it. The most sorry thing I see is to see the Negro go the way of the white man. With all these goddamn middle-class values; hypocrisy."

"Yeah, I know what hypocrisy is," Mickey agrees. "My goddamn mother is one. I never really knew what she was before. I mean, man, she can be waging a war on me! Cursing me out about the garbage on the porch, and in the same breath, the bitch asks me in this sweet voice: 'Oh, Mickey I'm sorry your dog isn't doing well. I'm sorry she's sick.' I don't even speak to her! She's so two-faced. A split personality. I think she's a schizophrenic."

"It use to be Negroes treated you as people. They had a natural personality.... They knew what it meant to live or die," Ralph said simply. "They were living in peril. They didn't have control over their lives. So they created kindness in their world. And religious belie...love of their family. Little things that money doesn't buy. They lived in each moment. Not in a bank account.

"They get equal rights, a few cars and television sets, and pretty soon they've become middle-classed assholes like the rest."

Ralph is a huge, stocky man; 300 lbs of muscle. And a fag. Sandy hair, blue eyes, and a sardonic smile of seeing reality under the accepted norm.

"People only know what they're taught. Let me tell you something. All these middle-class punks come in here, they're gonna watch a broad take off her clothes. 'OHHHH!' Then they go out of here so goddamn righteous! Oh, they didn't see a thing! Oh, that nasty old broad up there! The world —they're just out to fuck each other. People haven't got sense enough to know what moral *is*. That takes brains!"

"Well, actually Ralph, I'm sick of this world myself," Mickey says. "I've been planning to get away for a long time. I'm going to San Francisco. It's more free even than New York, I hear.... The eastern states are getting uptight. Police pressure...yeah, I'm heading out to California, tho it's two thousand miles away."

Ralph leans inside the cashier's booth; he, too, looks out into the creepy night.

"You know, people are afraid to think," says Ralph. "They'd rather light a cigarette then think. They'd rather take a drink than think! Well, all right, then some politicians got to do their thinking for them! And outsmart them!"

Thoughts drifted back to Mickey; remembrances of a dream-like state parade before her, evoking both sorrow and a sense of victory. She stood in the doorway of Shrimpie's; behind her, the near-deserted bar, floor stretching uneven into purple shadows; outside, the endless night....

'The Chicago night is wild. It's as if we will find some answer in it. Except that I haven't come to that point. I go out, driven to the edge of drunken sleeplessness.

'It was cold in Chicago that winter. I began to realize that if there's something I need, I must Take It.

'When you deal with people with fucked-up minds, who don't know what they want or who they are, like Lucy you have to make a decision for them. So I must convince her that she loves me somehow. I wish I had a better technique, like Phyllis. But of course she is so effective because she don't NEED IT. She don't need Lucy! She is the master schemer.'

"It takes brains to be moral," Ralph says. Disgusted, he whirls on his heel with a flounce and walks away across the carpeted theater to vanish into the darkened hall, following some man to the toilets. Mickey looks out on the street, taps her fingers. There she waits, wanting to find The One willing....

It was 4 P.M., and here's a stagehand teaching the new girl a step.

The new girl's illuminated by a spotlight 30 feet above the floor thru a maze of pipes and the repair lighting effect.

We unlock the dark theater. There are rooms in the back, dressing rooms converted into living quarters. Each one has a mattress, but no front door—just a curtain pulled across. The stocky butch grabs a broom; her gym-shoed feet squish across the cold cement floor; a sour expression on her face. Mickey felt vaguely mad, envisioning the probability of her new lover Lisa winding up on her back while the owner of the theater fucks her. It is a hassle the girls have to put up with; there's no end to the stories of this. The stagehand and one of the girls; a couple of other characters associated with the theater and the Main Attraction; the whole bunch of males, except for Ralph, hustling the women in vague opportunistic ways.

Opened the doors to see the show from behind the stage. Way, way down in a pinpoint of sudsy light, stomping onstage, a nearly naked woman is doing floor work in only a pair of glittery turquoise high-heel pumps; writhing; her back on the wooden boards of the stage. A very critical man is giving orders. "NO! NO!" He is very exacting. He cries and she starts again. "NO! THAT WILL GET THE PLACE CLOSED DOWN!" Catching his breath.

The women take a cab home; both wondering how long Lisa will be able to keep on dancing at the Rialto—for she's refused to sleep with the owner. All the other girls billed on the marquee have, but not her.

That night Mickey took her in bed, Lisa shuddered under the touch of strong fingers in her cunt. Lisa says, "I like the way you cum." There is an element of life even Lisa can use—adult experience. She has been fucking tricks since age 15. High rollers with big spending money. And fighting off the men backstage because they have no money. From the East Coast, thru three states into the Midwest & returning, on burlesque theater circuit. Life has taught her a few crude facts—but not everything. She don't seem to realize if you're fuckin' men, you're going to get pregnant. "Yer gonna take

birth control if I have to kick the pill down your motherfuckin' teeth!"

"I won't need it now I'm with you."

"You're with me and me alone? Is that a promise?"

There was a five-dollar draw signed by Lisa Lamour in the
cash drawer of the Rialto Theatre box office. Howls of the
Vice Cops going down North Avenue—plainclothes in an
unmarked car. (A give-away clue is the UAF police-band
super-large radio aerial.)

Electronic, freaky music; legs strut in time to black
rhythms. COME ON OVER, JIM DANDY! howls the jukebox, glowering in deep reds & purple from its weight of five
hundred pounds.

Mickey's figure danced alone in the bar; eyes closed. She
popped her fingers in the stream of jazzy images. And thinks:
'All Lisa's rhythm is an illusion. Underneath, inside her mind,
she is a frigid, self-conscious young woman.'

WE'LL LAUGH IN THE SUNLIGHT, HONEY!
WE'LL CRY IN THE RAIN!

Mickey listened to the jukebox, she looked across North
Avenue at the burlesque theater—she was due to go on as
cashier tonight at 8 P.M. The barroom clock said 7:15. Nearly
45 minutes! Mickey did a little dance in her men's lace-up
shoes. Love had made her get here early. Mannish, morose
eyed, but with a sly smile...she danced around the jukebox,
thought of her new lover: 'she's a stripper who's just begun
working there...I'm lucky...

'I have her jacket, her hotel key. I wear her ring. A fastidi-
ous pearl-studded ring....'

Mickey was a flamboyant soul who could cry, & laugh! As
she, too, stepped down life's corridors to the thud of bass
drums, visions of nude strippers in her eyes, stripping down
to their G-strings.

"Fifty dollars short!" cries the manager, Red. "Fifty dollars! I
can't have this! This is a theater, not a loan company! The owner
will blow his stack! Where's Mickey! She should be here!"

"Well, I don't know," Ralph says. "She says she's leavin' for California, didn't she?"

The owner is on the telephone now: "Hello? It's you? Good! Good! Well, I don't know. She signed the contract for this week—sure, then she skips town. I said *skips town!* Or as girls are known to do in this business... 'Oh, I'll be in tomorrow'—she said it herself—'I'm laid up in the hospital today!' Some hospital! Well, we need a girl...billing tomorrow!"

"Sure, you can work, my dear... Talk to Mr. B. *Mr. B.* The Big B. I'll talk to him for you. You can work, dear.... You have your slip?"

'I'm tired of whores' threats and men's assumptions! All right, Doctors! Psychoanalysts! Don't want none of your clean white answers! My heart has a pain which is growing like cancer.'

Mickey was bitter and morose.

Under high-powered amphetamines, lights and colors kaleidoscope; it is the highway; traveling again. Mickey pounds the barroom table. Dull winds of bad dreams. Shakes her unconscious like a bowl of jelly. She moves the mug of 7UP on the table, tracing wet patterns. Her mouth moves inside thoughts to form a silent prayer: 'Virgin Mary, Mother of God.... Blessed are You among women...' She could see women—from the rows of ghetto buildings down at the end of North Avenue to the west, all the way to the lake, where rich women in high-rise multimillionaire apartments are—they are connected. She sees a woman's mouth, like an animal, move. She is crying. Arguing. Soothing. Mickey thought of women.

Lisa! One minute she was a little child: "HA HA HA! HA HA!" Running about, an evil smirk of cunning; it was eerie that her face could grow so cold immediately. Lisa, the wicked child. Onstage, a bawdy, earthy woman. All woman, even tho she was only 16. Shaking her bare tits and her bare ass, and rolling her pussy at the audience; in her tiny pink G-string— small enough to show More Pussy! Saying, "SUFFER SUCKERS!" Moving her finger around the thread of the G-string,

& sticking it up into her pussy onstage, pulling it out, and licking it. Rolling her hot stuff at them. Giving them the finger and strutting offstage in her high-heel backless jeweled pumps—strutting offstage, twirling her scarf.

The audience stretched out in a long, dark, shadowed anonymous face. Men clapping for "LISA!" And the backstage music prerecorded tape droned it out.

Lisa, a stripper. Well built. Pretty. Small—petite. 5'2", 115 pounds. Slender legs, shapely thighs, tiny feet. A nice bust. A fair-skinned Negro; her racial heritage is not visible any farther offstage than the front row. Tan skin, green eyes, a valentine-shaped head; her eyes bare a hint of a constantly critical look, wrinkling her forehead in an angry squint.

After a while, you'll find out that shit and pussy and sweat smell the same. Only pussy is one degree stronger than sweat; and shit is a lot of degrees stronger than pussy.

Lisa takes off her pants. The meat of her young body flowed out. In the dim light of the closet, Lisa hangs up her clothes. Mickey rolled over in the hotel's double bed and awoke out of a dismal shallow sleep.

Drowsy figure in the bed looks up to see that Lisa has returned. BANG! Closet door slams. "I did floor work tonight!" Lisa said triumphantly. "I was DIRTY! I did everything! I got down and rolled like a dog! They loved me! HA! HA! HA! HA! They were jerking off so hard in the front row, foam was flying!"

Lisa and Mickey in bed doing it. Mickey got on top; their thighs locked to each other; wet, moist from discharge between their legs, excited, sex moving on each other, locked in a sweaty embrace. Their tongues sought each other's. The sheet's over Mickey's broad back; handsome, moving like an animal. Steady, humping. Occasionally one of Mickey's hands reaches down to Lisa's breasts, to squeeze their ripe fruit, and slips down farther now between the woman's thighs to stimulate her that sex-pulse, her clit, probing thru the wet moist nest filled with short kinky hairs. Lisa's green-painted eyes are closed. She exudes little-girl-sounding sighs.

They work together; probing with her index middle fingers

in unison into Lisa's hole, while working up a wet area from her own cunt all over Lisa's leg. And the bed's jiggling. Fast, faster; rocking. Felt herself about to cum... So then Mickey pants, "Do you love me?"

"You ignorant motherfucker! Get Off Of Me! Right *Now!* Don't talk to me like that, Bitch!" And she humps her body in an arch, which sends Mickey flying over to the side of the bed. Lisa, the bucking bronco. Mickey cries. Tears roll from her youthful eyes. Touches her lover with her square hands, beseeches Lisa to tell her what she has done wrong.

Lisa whirls around in bed, wrapping herself up like a corpse in the sheet—the mummy of Cleopatra, in curves. She was in A Pose—as Mickey would sorrowfully come to know—one of her many Instant Rejections.

'If love is a reversal of hate, then what are we? What is the basic ingredient in us? Because some say that love is an illusion. It dies again and again ... Is this hate our love? Is this why it always comes down to this? These bitter words, and slaps and leaving for the open road once more?'

After Lisa, Mickey came into the theater with that misty look in her eyes (and musty smell) of having loved a woman all night; for two nights.

'We leaped out of the cab that morning.' Mickey's hair wet with sweat from where she'd pumped away on top of Lisa all morning. "SHE'S THE JANITOR!—I'M THE STAR!" Lisa's green eyes flash in what is usually anger, but today is happy amusement as she gives the cabbie his money.

Mickey had gone in—they're both late to work. Will, the stagehand, greets her across the candy counter, blowing a kiss. "I know where you've been," he says. "You look all nice...all fixed up...a new jacket, Mickey.... Somebody must be in love!"

'It is the jacket and ring Lisa has given me. "All the butches in San Francisco wear jackets like this!" Lisa told me. "I want you to have it...you need it. Look at that rag you're wearing. Throw it away!"'

'I walked across the street to wait for the 7:30 show. "You be right over!" Lisa said. 45 minutes to kill... Tapping fingers on a table in a booth, to the beat of the jukebox.... Lisa would change clothes and come out.... I thought, 'Someone to appreciate me, to fix the clothes I wear, and be proud of me....

'Of course there were problems... I mean, when you start becoming yourself, a growing teen, emerging out of that chrysalis of jailbait at 15, now 16 going on 17; a shell-protective personality that is made of how you have reacted to people, to the world, and also made of what you yourself dare to be....

'Many stinging phrases echo.... In other words, I am sick & tired of my own illusions about myself.... Damn it! I don't want to live up to anybody else's righteousness—& I am a Homosexual...and all the world's illusions and motherfuckers are putting me in prison. And in their smiling, selfish zealous righteousness they are my prison guards.' Young Mickey assembled the enemy in her mind: 'Those Who Mean Well: parents, employers, friends, some weird, scared part of myself. I am a butch. A cutout doll from some comic book the world has seldom seen. A pasted-up man's figure made of men's 2nd-hand clothes from all the thrift shops; from all the frustrated generations of dykes before me—lesbians tethered inside a nun's gown; spinsters starving in attics; old maids; virgins veiled behind their self-denial; and gays who pretend not to be gay, laughing at Sister George.... I feel like a segmented cesspool.'

Mickey sat at the restaurant counter. The jukebox played songs that spoke in riddles. A pair of Vice Cops was lunching at the counter too, wearing expensive $200 suits—vicuna vines; glittering men's diamond rings; they pulled out their shiny alligator wallets. 'You can always spot the law; they would win the Academy Awards for acting.... I think the law must be a game. It is so far from humane laws.'

Mickey wore a brown leather jacket tonight. A gift from her lady. She was waiting for Lisa—spending some of the showgirl's easy money on coffee and a cheeseburger. Her brown leather jacket appears gold in the sunlight, which it seldom sees. The glistening leather sets off her face as she chews red, steaming hamburger; eyes closed in enjoyment.

'We had a double date on one of my few last nights in this town—on the North Side. Way up, near Wilson Avenue. We hit a straight bar.' Mickey butch and passing in very mannish clothes. Lisa, and a femme twin to her, some stripper from the Rialto, and one large, stocky 300-pound man in drab brown pants, a nondescript shirt—the manager of the theater—gay old Ralph. "Look at those two!" exclaims Lisa mischievously, referring to Mick & Ralph. "They're WOMEN! Aren't they—I mean, they're men...but they're WOMEN! Look, they ARE!" Lisa cries, pinching one of Mickey's tits; she knew exactly where to find the little nipple hidden away under Mickey's binder, and shirt, & sweater vest; under all her layers of clothes.

"I mean, this one's a MAN! But he's got tits! And that one —she's wearing a man's suit, but she's a WOMAN!— Ralphette! Ralphina! RAFAELLA! *RAFAELLA!*" she shrieked in one of her rare moments of pure joy.

'When we got too wild for the squares, we went to a boys' place. We walked in the gaybar, four of us—Ladies went in first—the two strippers & Ralph, who by now was flouncing and switching his large bulk and maneuvering thru the crowd like a slim girl, oohing, and aahhing & wiggling with a motion of someone squeezing into a girdle. Having longer legs & being more aggressive, Rafaella appeared, sitting at the bar first. "EQUALITY FOR MEN!" she cries, yanking a stool out for Mickey & put it in the center, so as a group the women sat around.

'"SAY, THAT'S RIGHT! WE'RE ALL WOMEN!— THREE WOMEN, ONE MAN!" The bartender, slender, short, a healthy-looking fairy came to take our orders. He smiles...he, too, was a woman.

'"I nearly fainted!"

'"So did I!"

'As the shock of recognition hit our brains—"The Men are Women! The Women are Men!"

' "How gay we are! HA!"

'Suddenly we saw there were no straight people left in the universe, and we had the world to ourselves.'

The empty barroom. Looming. Large. So big that even a few stars are included in it from the sky above. Cut in, from part of the atmosphere that twinkles way above the ceiling. A fag sounded like a baby crying; weeping in his beer. Mickey put her hand on his shoulder; "Be quiet! Listen to the music!" Mickey whispered, as to a child at its mothers breast. "TAKE YOUR PLACE ON…THE GREAT MANDALA…."

He's depressed because fags & dykes don't have a place to meet. One by one the bars are being raided, so we have to go to artists' hangouts, and beatnik places which have a semi-gay strain running thru them, and maybe, by chance, we'll meet up with one another.

The figure sitting at the bar crying in his beer didn't seem to be listening to the music, for its words didn't signal anything. TAKE YOUR PLACE ON…THE GREAT MANDALA…AND IF YOU LOSE, YOU'RE ONLY LOSING YOUR LIFE…

Stored emotions, tumbled out. She too had been locked up; then she began to feel again… This thing the words said…powerful & meaning-filled. And was touched by its power—which ignited the flame of hope inside her; as she was laughing, talking to the gay brother, tho he could barely hear—the meaning was 'Yes, it's time to begin moving again! Don't die on Me! Don't give up on Me! Don't surrender your life to the conditions of this world! There is a way! A way out of no way! Come On! Follow!'—This thing that would take her to a dozen cities, back and forth across the American continent; and thru dozens of women's lives.

"Music means so much…it means so many things," Mickey muses.

"It don't mean a damn thing!" says Lisa. She was foul. She had to degrade herself to music. Rolling like a dog at private stag parties & showing her intimate sexual organs; & bumping and grinding on stage for a bunch of sleazoids to jerk off to in the front row. She was beginning to hate everything.

And down, surfacing away from the threat of sex-communicable disease; mayhem; misunderstanding; melodies splotch on the rim of a color wheel in the Milky Way—which artists, stoned on chemicals, see. And wanderers stumble on. As green seaweed at the beach; growing, reaching out of the ocean from a new dimension. It was music in Mickey's soul. A super-modern spirit.

'Here is Buddha. God. Our Lady. The Great Something. Gray crowds lean under the El tracks; cries, stifled. Even like the rain. They can't move out of the pain inside themselves…

'These days of depression—just before I leave the city of Chicago…the way I will have to leave Lucy… All I have to do now is kill time. I ride thru the neighborhoods on the train; it inspires me with sudden pain of a different kind; snow covers the ghetto, there are others suffering beside myself. I see the momentous effort that needs to be done….'

'"LIVE FOR NOW!" is the beatnik philosophy. It was hell only one day after I met her.' Now Mickey sat in the cashier's booth and looked out.

Honky-tonk music flirted out into the street on a exiting patron's coattails, before the glass door closed with a whoosh; from some girls' show. Rain fell over it all, making the streets a mirror. Mickey's face behind the glass waiting for customers by her cash register full of numbers; and to press buttons connecting the telephone; two receivers hanging by both sides of her head at the ears; solemn face looks out; her hands toy with a tray of quarters…. WHY DID YOU TREAT ME BABY, TREAT ME SO GOOD?… NOW YOU DON'T LOVE ME BABY, LOVE ME LIKE YOU SHOULD. It cuts away thru her soul. Snarl of electric guitars.

Red came around the candy counter at a fast trot for an old man. He's been bustling around all day; he flings his jacket over his arm, prissy mouth, clamps a hat on his head. " 'Bye, my dear! I'll be seeing you!"

"Bye, Red." Mickey waves.

The door closes into the street. Red stands outside under the blinking marquee talking to her thru the hole in the glass ticket booth; his wrinkled pink face moves. Mickey strains, ear up to the hole to catch his words: "Well, it's the last show, thank God. Two girls don't show. That's how it goes. Well, they found something they like, they run after it, and PFFFFF! No girls, no show. Just like that! Oh, they'll be back after their *fling!*" His fingers tap on the glass. Mickey nods silently, clears her throat.

Now the street is deserted. She consults the clock. 2 more hours to go.

'As I busted my nuts in her mouth,' (thighs spread, cuntlips apart; center of her sex—the pearl in Lisa's lips, and tongue firmly probing, making it hotter; moist flesh hot. Hot.) 'As I busted my nuts in her mouth, the sun broke in my head. Atlas, God, and me were one. We covered the earth. We were young. Sin and the Devil. Legs trembled, broken-down, melting into the earth of her mouth. Now we were dissolving back into Mother Earth.'

Mickey thought about the lonesome road. 'When we need help, when we need each other, we are only like a city, each one of us, on a journey; and each person is an all-night way station for the next.'

As she rode between points with no destination on the Elevated/subway, in the dead of night, frightened because gangsters lurk here (a man had been beaten nearly to death, kicked in the head viciously earning a column in the paper last night—his widow, or wife—for he was still not officially dead, was suing the city for her husband's loss of about 50 IQ points, he had become and idiot; $10,000 per point)—Mickey walked down the gray stone stairs, hand on her knife handle—glistening 5" blade, ready to come out fighting in self defense; trembled at a loud noise (a false alarm) like many citizens, especially small female ones—and trains whoosh thru the pneumatic tube.

The world twists us. Sticks pins in us. Twists us into grotesque forms. Monsters who can still walk, but crippled.

We are injured further by each passing day.

Ghosts walk here now, burnt out. Dead wicks. Time has burnt us down with its repetition. And its inconsistency. Life as undependable as junkie Phyllis; a ghost dissolving and running off thru your fingers, and yet as steady. As junkie Phyllis burns down the drugstore hitting scab marks in her arm with her needle. Phyllis went back to that drugstore on North Avenue and Halsted Street, hitting it for more dope to feed her increasing habit; more and more dope—until the lady behind the counter and the white-lab-coated pharmacist snap their faces shut and tell Phyllis: "NO MORE!" And what is it all about? The inconsistency? The flake outs & disappointments?—and the killing, droning sameness day upon day?—That people are in NEED!

Then night comes to think your troubles away.... Once you were too lonely and sad to imagine there was a path out...to think up a solution...but now...an idea has lit your mind like a yellow light bulb....

They want you to stay. They demand that you stay the same.

They say that so much freedom has made us weak! To choose to go off and get lost in the night....

Endless highways of America, moving, moving....

CHAPTER FORTY-FIVE

"Hey, girls!" a black man calls. And lucky Lisa and Mickey didn't start any fights with him. Mickey should have been the one to speak: "FUCK OFF, CHUMP!" Protecting her girlfriend in the feminine role, in her low-neck dress. She, in disguise of a man; a butch lezzie. And they walked past the car—which was in reality Vice Cops parked in an alley. They are getting rough, looking for their prey. They instigate a situation, and when the criminal takes the bait, they blossom forth with silver police stars & official badges and handcuffs—they snatch her off the street—and off to jail.

"FUCK OFF! GO BEAT YERSELF OFF PUNK!" howls the dancer in her silver shoes; in a loud, stern voice. She meant business.

The two lezzies proceed on. "I hear they pose as Revolutionaries, like that group that blew up the Statue of Liberty? The cops suggested it. The cops got the dynamite and everything; then when the gang was ready to go thru with it, the cops turn them in! Cops will do anything!" A white man calls from a car: "PSSSSSSTTT!"

"Don't turn around...that's the heat over there..." We walked on, calm. We walk under city monolith buildings, NYC brownstones, SF muddy Tenderloin afternoons; Chi-town avenues of Division, North, Diversey—facing the setting sun. We walk, arm in arm...lesbian females, warriors, in the heat of the night, in the hurricane's eye.

It's Chicago again, for a second. A Drag Queen saunters past us. "ARE YOU GIRLS GOING TO THE UNDER-GROUND? IT'S FULL OF COPS, AND PLAINCLOTHES HEAT! COPS AND PLAINCLOTHES. OHHHH, MARY! IT'S SO GHASTLY! THE HEAT'S ON TONIGHT!" And his white made-up face on a spindly body sails off into darkness.

The muddy Times Square afternoon milling with freaks, lonely dykes (a few), hustlers, pimps, tricks, working girls (a lot) all the lonely people and never the twain shall meet where do they all come from? And Vice Cops, which follows as a bloodhound after The Scene.

Heat cruises the street. 100 police in plainclothes, or blue uniforms in squad cars, concentrated here; enforcing a dead moral code at the taxpayers' expense. We went down cement steps into basements of several after-hours clubs, looking for gay action. Nothing.

I lay in her hotel room, the Regency Hotel, alone in the sheets; big double bed, hands behind my head, naked. And the view of the building across the way, high up in space, strung with a million lights....

Lisa appeared about 12:45 A.M. Burst into the room after her last show of the night; with her green eyeshadow running, and her talented body wrapped in a coat. She now undressed for me, by stripping; in a Private Show. The body of Lisa Lamour lies beside me. The star at 1 A.M.

'If hate is a reaction against Love...and we hate what we

are…then what hope have we?' The ocean of my own thoughts roaring in my head. It is from this ocean I draw my nets.

"I'm not a woman." said Lisa, the only stripper among the pack of older hoofers who still has a childlike humor.

"I think you're a beautiful woman Lisa." The stripper does a backbend. "BEAT YOUR MEAT, SIR? BEAT YOUR MEAT?" Her head upside down looking between her legs.

"I lived in the subway before I met you, Lisa. I don't have a home. The street is violent. You see someone in pain who's hurt, you try to ease it. A girl or somebody, try to talk to them, and tell em 'Shuddup! It's gonna be OK! Just don't give up! Keep pushing!' You see a pigeon that's crippled— you'd like to uncripple it, so you get it some water in a cup, and a crust of bread. I always feel for beings in pain. But you gotta watch out because somebody is liable to hit you on the head while you're stopping to help somebody, take what little you got."

2 things Mickey learned from Lisa Lamour; was to wear deodorant and to clean the nipples of her titties off. And one thing she taught Lisa: to say, "I LOVE YOU, MICKEY!" While Mickey made her cum, or was in the throes of cumming herself. "Say it, Lisa! I'm gonna cum!" the butch would pant, on top of her.

"I LOVE YOU, MICKEY!"

"I'm always sitting with my ass hiked up on a sink in some lousy flophouse room, trying to piss. Lisa, now, you got a real nice hotel room—with its own bath."

In the heat of the night…beats an empty heart. Time howls in a vacuum…newspapers whirl along the gutters blown by wind. Symphony upwards, rustling… El trains cracking lights and sparks above…. As she lounged in the doorway of The Palm Gardens, killing time, these were Mickey's memories:

An evil eye, a staring sun up thru midnight, is the brain on alcohol. Hot, humming, wired, speeding… 'She had said she didn't want to fuck.' "Neither do I," answered Mickey. But the moment they got home, what did they do? Pull off each other's pants and focus in on each other's cunt.

As Mickey came to accept the harsh realities of life, she wore the mask more and more. The same trouble. The same enemies. It was making her angry and she was young. Men. No money. The police. The Mafia. The society that scorned gay people and created an atmosphere for all the other evil elements to be able to attack them.

Every now and then, a furrow would cross her brow; and she'd be thinking—hard. She'd be going away inside her mind to enforce her own identity as a lesbian butch. Remembering who and what she was. As if standing in the mirror in a pair of man's slacks, a suit jacket and hat wasn't enough proof. Times when men came on to her; when bill-board ads and TV and magazines of Amerikkka proclaimed she was Dead!—that lezzies did not exist! And these thoughts made her face different, harsh, from the young smooth-skinned Mickey. Smooth at that time in the end of the decade of the 1950s, from adolescence, unwrinkled; tho by now prematurely worried. And perpetually as a flame, both invisible, in spirit, and obvious; that one strong queer look about her.

Lobby of the Rialto Theatre. Lisa Lamour, using her normal voice; and her "stage voice" which is an Eartha Kitt-Yiddish combo—a sharp, foreign-type talk. And Ralph the fag night manager, and Mickey cashier/janitor. And Tony, the movie projectionist.

Tony has black hair the duplicate of Mickey; he also is Italian. Tony mimics a female, in falsetto, one of the dancers: "I can't dance when it's hot! 'Cause my feet stink, and then I can't dance!"

Lisa breezes thru the door from backstage; comes up to Tony, flirts with him wickedly: "BEAT YOUR MEAT, SIR? BEAT YOUR MEAT?"

"CUT THAT OUT WILL YOU? ACT LIKE A WOMAN!" Ralph yells.

"Yeah, Lisa, do like the nice man tells you."

"I'm not a woman!"

"You're not? Then what are these things? Huh?" Tony reaches out, his hairy hand, touching one of Lisa's tits.

"HANDS OFF, BUSTER! NOBODY PUTS THEIR HANDS ON ME UNLESS I SAY SO!"

"Well, I'll be seeing everybody.... Guess I'm just not wanted." Tony exits.

"To say the *least!*" Lisa yells.

"See there? That's all they want! One thing! I'm telling you!" says fag Ralph. A big queen—big as a football player in a drab plaid shirt and baggy trousers. His voice is excited; he's furious at the injustice of it all.

Mickey stares at them moodily; this is only the second time she's seen the new dancer up close. She kind of fidgets around in the background, by the candy counter.

"Men!" Lisa exclaims. Hands on her hips, still pissed.

"What do you want with a man, Lisa? They're fuckin' jack-offs." Ralph adds, in his baritone-but-nelly voice.

"Ralph, you're too serious! Whadda yuh mean, what do I want with a man!" Lisa glares, penciled eyebrows arched in a mixture of irritation & curiosity.

From the candy counter a few feet away, over a red-carpet stretch of lobby floor, Mickey has hungrily observed the sweet-scented, shapely vision of a showgirl, painted toes of her naked feet perched on a pair of gold high heels. Boldly she interjects: "Well...there's always something for every-body...somewhere...I guess.... But I haven't got *mine* yet...." Mickey is moody. Stands with her broom & dustpan & clean-ing supplies.

"Ah, you'll get what you want. It's possible...even in this life."

"RALPH!" Lisa cries in her little-girl voice. "Nobody *loves* me!"

"Maybe she likes you." Ralph says quietly and nods his head, indicating Mickey.

"He...wouldn't like me, because...I'm—I'm *one.*" Lisa confesses, distraught.

Mickey fairly drops her dustpan and yells: "WOW! *ONE WHAT!?* I'M ONE, TOO! I'M GAY! MAYBE WE COULD HELP EACH OTHER OUT!"

"I thought you were a man!" Lisa cries in surprise, in a bit of indignation.

"I'm a butch!"

"Well, there, Lisa. There you are!" says Ralph, having the last word. Simultaneously a man walks out of the darkened theater thru the doors into the lobby and heads down the steps to the washrooms. Exit Ralph off in the man's direction.

Butch Mickey approaches the glamorous Star: "Lisa, do you swing? Go both ways?"

"Yeah."

"I like women," Mickey declares. Has leaned her broom against the candy counter, and stands, hands hung at her sides, eyes dark, looking into Lisa's pretty face.

"Why don't you come up to my hotel after the show..."

"I'd like to! Where is it?"

Lisa writes her address on a matchbook cover; Ralph comes back upstairs. "Men! The jackoffs! You ought to see him down there! He's tryin to piss, he's got himself covered so I can't see it. Men! They don't want anybody looking at them! That's how their mothers teach them to be ashamed of what they got! It's all so phony! Middle-class bullshit!"

The man comes upstairs from the restrooms, red-faced with embarrassment; a newspaper under his arm. Avoids looking at them.

"BEAT YOUR MEAT, SIR?" Lisa yells after him.

"JACKOFF!"

"Moron! They come in here, 'DUHHH WHERE'S THE GIRLS? I PAID $3 AND I DIDN'T EVEN GET LAID! DUHHH! I WANT MY MONEY BACK!'" says fag Ralph.

"What's he gonna do with the newspaper? Put it on his lap? They use hats and coats, everything. I seen 'em."

"And beat off." says Lisa, disgusted.

"JACKOFFS!" Ralph hollers, slams his beefy fist down on the candy counter.

"Maybe he's a Vice cop. Be quiet, man!" says Mickey.

"VICE! VICE! The real vice goes on in there! Right in there!" Ralph points in the direction of the closed theater doors and the audience. "Damn middle-class jackoffs!" Pauses. "Oh, Lisa!" Sympathetically, and holds her hand.

"Oh, Ralphy!"

"SAY! WHAT *IS* THIS?" Mickey is jealous.

"Beat your meat? Beat your meat?"

"Oh, Lisa, you're a very beautiful woman."

"I'm not a woman, Ralph."

"Yes, you are very beautiful...." A man comes out into the lobby, goes downstairs toward the men's washroom. Exit Ralph down the stairs to watch him piss.

This leaves Lisa and the butch alone, for a few precious moments.

"Lisa... Gee...you know what you said about...swinging both ways? Gee, that's nice. I'm so glad you're not straight, like most of these girls. But you don't seem interested in me! You're talking to Ralph all the time, and *I'm* right here! *I* wanna hold your hand!"

"I *am*. Come up to my hotel, Mickey. Here's my key." Lisa fumbles in her purse for her key ring. "Wait for me, after the show."

"WOW! I'm ready to go! Do you really mean it?"

"Yes. Here's my key, Mickey. Now you *have* to wait for me! I'll be out here after the show. We'll go to my hotel. I'll do whatever you want me to do!"

Lisa. Her tinkling gay child's laughter: "HA! HA! HA! HA! HA! WHOOOOO!" Suddenly contorts her face with a nasty look. "WHOOO, MOTHERFUCKER!"

Soon there she was. A fluff. Mickey was standing by the red vinyl padded & gold trim doors in the lobby, alone. A few other men had gone out. Lisa came down to the front in backless high-heel pumps, a funny-looking hat on her head, all big. A hat that looked precious to Mickey. Lisa looked this butch person up and down. Mickey looked strange to her, and a little scary. "Hi. Coming?" She asked shyly. And they caught a cab.

Get to the hotel, Mickey lies down on the bed, which is the only furniture to sit on except for one chair. Lisa takes her clothes off and lies down, nude.

Golden light of the hotel room, fancy; the butch excitedly breathes the perfumed scent of this young woman. Mickey is eager; wild emotions race up and down her spine, as strong as the fiery desire in her loins.

All the hair was shaved off her cunt. Her pussylips showed. She prances up: "I'M GONNA TAKE A DOUCHE!"

"You don't need to," says Mickey.

"I'm *dirty!* That's why! I douche 2, 3 times a day.... My pussy stinks! That's why!"

"It's *suppose* to stink. I like it like that, anyhow."

"Nobody has ever told me that before!"

"Did you ever have a woman before?"

"Of course!" Lisa says defensively. "I've had lots of women—and butches! I went with one 3 years!" Later Mickey finds out this is a lie. "She died in an auto accident."

They lay on the bed together. They begin to caress. Mickey undressed down to shirt and boxer shorts. Lisa is buck naked. Lisa pulls the butch's shirt off and sees the binder, and together they take it off; white & tan fingers intermeshed. "LOOK AT THEM TITTIES! LOOK AT THEM TITTIES YOU GOT! WITH THOSE TITTIES I COULD MAKE $400 A WEEK! You got a body! Where did you get it? With that body I could make...$500 a week!"

"It's from exercises. All exercises." Mickey flexes her muscles.

"LOOK AT THOSE MUSCLES! DO THAT TO YOUR STOMACH AGAIN! DAMN! WHERE DID YOU LEARN THAT?"

"It's all muscle control!"

"Goddamn, Mickey! I'm a stripper and I can't even do that with my stomach! If I could, I'd make $500—no $600 a week!"

"I work out a lot. Lift heavy objects whenever I see something. Do all my sit-ups and push-ups & leg raises."

"Well, you could make some money with those titties, and rolling your stomach! I ought to have your body!"

"Well, exercises—that's all."

"I don't want the rest of those muscles, tho!"

"Just exercises your stomach then."

"I get plenty of exercises. 5 shows a night! 6 nights a week! Plenty!... Sure you don't want to be a stripper, honey? You could make some money!"

"Lisa, I'm turning off the light."

"Finish taking off your clothes."

"Listen…I'm on my period."

"Well, I'm no bloodhound!"

"Yeah. Well, I didn't expect you would."

"OH, SHUT UP! I'll eat you even if you are on your goddamn period! Take your pants off, bitch!"

"WOW! It feels funny! How come it's all shaved? I've never touched one without hair before." Mickey plays with her pussy in wonder.

"You can show more pussy that way…. No, I don't take my G-string off, I'd get the place busted! No, you can just show more pussy when it's shaved—and with them red lights shining on it, it looks just like a pussy without a G-string. Take your Tampax out. I'll do it! Let me do it! Relax! Breathe thru your mouth! It relaxes you! The doctor told me that when I was having my miscarriage…. Breathe out thru your mouth! And they plugged up my nostrils, there wasn't anything else I could do *but* breathe thru my mouth. This is nothing! A Tampax! HA! I can blow Ping-Pong balls out of my pussy! Sure! It's all muscular control! See! I've got muscles in my pussy! All that *body*—all those muscles you got on the *outside*, but you ain't got none inside. Hell, I use my pussy! I blow Ping-Pong balls out in my stag act! Oh! Oh, Mickey! Come on, butch! Get on top of me! Oh!"

"OHH! UH UH UH! OHHHHH LISA!"

"Oh, Mickey! Help me to be a woman! Help me to be a woman! Oh, love me! *Love Me! LOVE ME!*"

CHAPTER FORTY-SIX

Mickey spent a lot of time in the hotel after they got together; and in the hotel restaurant, by the jukebox waiting for their orders of take-out food.

Feeds quarters into the box. Taps her toe in time to the music. Mickey wears a brown suede jacket, men's; brown slacks and brown shoes, men's; and the pearl ring. Her body scented of Lisa's perfume, which rubs off from their constant embraces. Lisa has outfitted her lover in a new wardrobe.

1 A.M. Lisa returns from the theater via cab. Black net dress, sophisticated, high-heel pumps, mascara. Stands in the open door, yells: "THIS PLACE SMELLS LIKE PUSSY!"

Cold cream on her face, the glamorous femme reaches for the douche bag.

"LISA! Don't! You'll douche it all up! I want to taste you like you are!"

"Mickey, wait till I wash it! My pussy's all stinky!"

"I *want* it to stink! I *like* it dirty! That's because it's YOU!"

"IT'S NOT DIRTY, MICKEY! Honest it's not! It's just sweat from all that dancing... I'm tired... I did floor work. Yeah, I got down there, did the splits...rolled on my back, spread my legs and popped my G-string.... Sure, it's against the law! So what? I know that! Everybody knows that! Now LEAVE ME ALONE! I'VE GOT TO DOUCHE!"

Next afternoon: "I've got to go!" Enraged, Lisa bolts upright in the bed, a mummy wrapped in a sheet becoming untombed.

"What is the time please?" A groggy Mickey asks the hotel desk clerk, telephone receiver in her ear. "12:40? Thank you. Lisa! It's 12:40!"

"I HEARD YOU! THAT BITCH! SHE FORGOT TO GIVE ME MY WAKE-UP CALL! MY 12 O'CLOCK CALL! I HAVE TO BE AT THE THEATER AT 1! I've got to go! Get out of my way! JUST GET OUT OF MY WAY! Where is my boots? Where is my dress! OH, GET AWAY! WHAT USE ARE YOU? YOU DIDN'T MAKE ME CUM LAST NIGHT! AND NOW I'M GONNA BE LATE! ON ACCOUNT OF YOU FUCKING ME ALL NIGHT, MOTHERFUCKER! *AND THIS WHOLE ROOM SMELLS LIKE PUSSY!*— YOUR GODDAMN PUSSY! JUST SHUT UP AND COME ON! THAT'S ONE THING I NEVER DO! I'VE NEVER BEEN FIRED FROM A JOB! I'VE NEVER MISSED A DATE! WHERE'S MY STOCKINGS! FIND MY STOCK-INGS! JUST DO IT! AND SHUT UP! If you can't make me cum, I'll do it myself motherfucker! I've got work to do! I'll cum with my vibrator! It's faster than you are! I can't lay around all night trying to cum! I can't lay around all morning like you! Motherfucker, where are my earrings? My earrings! OH, NO! Not these! These don't have any wires!"

"Lisa, listen! Calm down, baby! You've got 45 minutes. You don't go on until 1:30. I'll go get a cab!"

"NO, BITCH! I HAVE TO PUT ON MY MAKEUP! IT TAKES ME 30 MINUTES TO PUT ON MY MAKEUP HONEY! TAKE MY TIME! Oh, goddamn, where are my rings? What time is it now? WHAT TIME IS IT NOW? ANSWER ME!"

That evening, near 1 A.M., Mickey gathers Lisa into her butch arms. And loves her in several positions. "OW! Lisa! Stop clawing my back!"

"OH! Help me to be a woman! Oh, Mickey! Mickey, let me eat you, too! Let me eat you! Come on!"

20 minutes pass, of pleasure to the butch.

"Did you cum?"

"No."

"You didn't? Why not? I told you to! Oh, goddamn it!"

"You didn't cum did you? I don't want to unless you do!"

"ARE YOU *KIDDING!* I HAVEN'T CUM SINCE I KNOWN YOU!"

"HAVE YOU EVER CUM WITH A WOMAN & NOT A VIBRATOR?"

"NO!... Yes!... I don't know! Oh...sometimes you feel so good, Mickey..."

"Then why do you stop it, Lisa? Why do you pull away!"

"I don't know...it gets so good, I can't take it anymore!"

"Let yourself go! You're holding back!"

"I can't! It feels like I'm about to pee or something."

"Well, go ahead and pee! Let yourself go! It don't bother me, even if you piss on me. I want to see you cum & be happy. You peed in the bed the other night and it didn't bother me! You got to relax, Lisa! Come on, baby! I want you to cum!"

"Love me! Love me!"

"Cum, baby. Let me love you."

"Oh go away!"

"What's wrong? Let me!"

"NO! 'CAUSE YOU WOULDN'T LET ME MAKE YOU CUM! SO FUCK YOU! I'M GONNA BEAT MY MEAT! THAT'S THE ONLY WAY I CUM, ANYHOW! I GOT A VIBRATOR TO DO IT! WHERE IS IT? THAT MAID! *SHE'S* BEEN HERE! OH! OH! Here it is, under the bed. I've got this! With this who needs anything else? Women, men, butches? *Anything!* OH! OH! There! AHHH! This is Cici! I put her between my legs! Lie down! Lie down, Mickey! Here! Put your hand on my pussy! Next to the vibrator! OH! OH! It feels good! OH! OH! I'M GONNA CUM! OH! OH! *OH!* Why don't you get on top of me, put your pussy on her. Go on! She'll make you cum, too!"

"Oh, hell, Lisa! Hell! Let me do you! Get rid of that thing!"

"NO! NO! Don't touch her! Leave Cici ALONE! Good old Cici! Ha!"

"Let me do it! You're gonna fix it so you can't ever cum with nobody!"

"OH, GET AWAY! GET AWAY, MICKEY! I know guys who give better head than you!"

"Well, fuck you!"

"SHUT UP! Come on, Mickey! Hold me! I'm gonna cum! Hold me, Mickey! Love Me! Oh! I'm cumming! OH OH OH OOOOOOOOOOOOOOOHHHHHHHH!... I shot a big wad that time. I laid a big load that time!"

"You came so fast!"

"Of course! What do you think? It's Cici! OH...Oh, that felt good!... Now I'm all right. Mickey! I think I'll make a telephone call! I'll call my mother! Don't go! Suck my pussy while I talk! Go on! Do it!"

"Lisa! Let me make love to you!"

"NO! NO! LEAVE ME ALONE! GO AWAY! I TOLD YOU! NOBODY CAN MAKE ME CUM BUT MYSELF!"

"I can! All you need is patience! I'll take time with you! I been trying hard every night! Take Time & go all night!"

"You take too much damn time! That's your problem!

YEAH! You can't fuck! You can't eat pussy! I'm more man than you are! Shit! How long have you been gay? Six months?"

"I been gay since I was 13."

"How old are you now? 14?"

"I'm 15!"

"Well, you act like it! Do they know you're 15 down at the theater?"

"They think I'm 17. Baby! Come on! Come on honey, I want to make love to you!"

"NO! It's surprising you get any women the way you come whining around me. UH… AH… UH…. Can I suck your pussy Lisa? UH…UH!"

"You're not as butch as you look! Where have you been all your life! Nowhere? Well, I've been places, baby! I get what I want when I want it! Right Now! Like this! SNAP! UNDERSTAND? Now, if I want to cum now, I cum now!"

"Yeah. OK."

"Mickey… The doctor says I'll never cum if I keep doing it myself."

"There's nothing I can give you, Lisa!"

"DON'T SAY THERE'S NOTHING YOU CAN GIVE ME! SHUT UP! JUST SHUT UP! YOU TALK TOO MUCH, MICKEY!"

"There's nothing I can do for you, Lisa."

"Just shut up!"

"Are we gonna be together tonight, Lisa?"

"Yes."

"Then stop yelling at me!"

"NO! I don't like the way you do it! You can't fuck! You're not butch! You fuck, then expect me to fuck you! I've had butches, baby! went with a bulldyke! I mean, you're the type that looks like a man, that goes like a man in public! But my bulldyke, I'm not expected to fuck her! She fucks *me*! That's how it is! I'm ashamed of you! In those secondhand pants and dingy old man's coat! When I met you, I didn't want to be seen with you! My other bulldyke, I was never ashamed of her! She dressed like a lady! She knew how to dress!... WHERE DO YOU THINK YOU'RE GOING, MICKEY! YOU'RE NOT GOING ANYPLACE! DON'T GO NEAR THAT DOOR! JUST GET AWAY FROM IT!...

"NO! YOU JUST SIT DOWN! YOU TAKE IT! I'LL TELL YOU A FEW THINGS ABOUT YOURSELF! YOU MAY THINK YOU'RE A BUTCH, BUT YOU'RE NOT! YOU'RE A LOUSY BUTCH! YOU'RE A NOTHING! YOU'RE SICK AND YOU DON'T KNOW IT! WHY DO YOU LIKE WOMEN, ANYWAY?"

"Goddamn you, Lisa!"

"I'M LONELY—THAT'S WHY I PICKED YOU UP, GODDAMN IT! I'M NOT A LESBIAN! I SWING BOTH WAYS! I WAS JUST LONELY! I WAS JUST HUNGRY FOR SOMEBODY! THAT'S ALL! STOP CRYING, MICKEY! SHUT UP! STOP IT! YOU AREN'T A BUTCH! THIS *PROVES* IT! BUTCHES ARE SUPPOSED TO BE MEN! MEN DON'T CRY! *I* DON'T EVEN CRY! WHERE ARE YOU GOING? ALL RIGHT, THEN! GET OUT! GET OUT! JUST GET ON OUT! YOU BETTER NOT LET ME SEE YOU AGAIN! YOU BETTER NOT SHOW YOUR FACE IN THAT THEATER AS LONG AS I'M WORKING THERE! GET OUT! GO ON!"

"GOD HAVE MERCY ON YOUR SOUL, LISA!"

"I DON'T BELIEVE IN GOD, ANYWAY! I DON'T NEED NOBODY! *NOBODY!* Mickey! Don't go! Please don't leave me!"

"Lisa! Don't touch me! You're hurting me! Stop making all that noise yelling at me! Or I *will* leave!"

"Go on and leave! I'm tired of you, Mickey!"

"I loved you, Lisa."

"CUNT! BITCH! WHORE! GO ON! I can't get any sleep with you in here! I can't sleep all night with you fucking me! I'll grab your snatch! I'll yank it out! I'll grab your cunt! I'll reach up inside your cunt and hurt you! Just give me a chance! You don't believe me! Wait and see! I hate you! Stop looking at me like that, Mickey! Motherfucker! Just get your ass out! Right now! Out! Get out!"

"You bitch. You nigger bitch!"

"I don't care what you call me, cunt! And take that jacket off before you leave! Cunt! I'll pull the hair right out of your cunt! You don't believe I will? Get out! Just Go And Leave Me That Jacket! I'm taking it back! You don't think I'm strong enough to do it? Well I will! I'll rip this whole jacket off of you! Don't you go out of here with that jacket! I'll have you hunted! You'll never work in that theater again! 'cause a girl did that to me! And I had her hunted! Yes, ma'am! I'm busy! Don't you get the message? You're not needed anymore! Get out! Get out of my life so I don't hurt you!"

So Mickey got out and wandered the streets a few days, not speaking to Lisa in the theater. And then Lisa breaks down and begs the butch to come live with her again at the hotel. And they spend a night of loving, warm, and wet sex, and emotional relief. Mickey cums and cums, riding Lisa, but doesn't dare ever again ask to use her mouth & tongue. And loves Lisa in every way. Morning light streaks their bed: "Oh, Mickey...you're still here! Oh! Umm! I feel so good! If I can wake up every morning like this, with you, I'd be happy!"

"Say, Lisa, you peed in the bed."

"I *WHAT*?"

"You peed in the bed...a little bit."

"YOU'RE LYING, BITCH! I DID NOT! WHERE? SHOW ME!"

"Here, right under this towel!"

"Oh, well, I *did*! I peed in the bed! How about that! I haven't done that for a long time! Just since I met you! Make sure they send the maid up! Find out what time it is! IF THE BITCH FORGOT TO CALL ME I'LL KILL HER! WEAR YOUR JACKET, MICKEY! THE ONE I BOUGHT YOU! IT'S MORE BUTCH! ALL THE BUTCHES ARE WEARING THEM OUT ON THE WEST COAST! WHAT KIND OF BUTCH ARE YOU! YOU LOOK LIKE A BUTCH *BUM!* FROM THE 2ND-HAND STORE! *HERE!* WEAR IT! WEAR IT! HOW LONG HAVE YOU BEEN GAY? ABOUT 3 MONTHS? NOW, MOVE! GET OUT OF MY WAY! DON'T GET IN MY PATH AGAIN!

"WHAT'S IN THAT CASE?"

"My underwear."

"It figures. Well, you carry that around, they'll think you're a stripper."

"CAB! CAB!"

"Hurry, driver! I have to make the one o'clock show! Say, you ought to come and see the show sometime—it's good."

"You're in it?"

"I'm in the features—he's the janitor!"

The moon passes thru clouds into Virgo. Mickey tells Ralph: "She's clawed me too many times. And I'm not wanted much anymore." Thinks privately as she wipes down the candy counter with a rag & starts up the popcorn machine: 'I swallowed so much of Lisa's cumjuice, I thought it would keep us together forever. If she'd had any shorthairs, they would have got stuck in my throat & my teeth. I wore out my clit on her pussy, to try to make her cum. And worked my fingers to the bone. And I can't love her enough to do it. But she plugs the vibrator in & cums in a minute. So she don't give me credit for being a butch.'

"I thought you two'd be good for each other."

"NO! She's got too many problems!"

"Well, so do you!"

"Yeah, but mine are...controlled. Yeah... Anyway, I'm going to California. That's my goal. One day. I love Lisa, Ralph; I'm in deep. I hate to think what will happen to her if I leave... It will be hell for me—she's been buying me stuff, and paying for our room & food. But she's violent. And we fight—physical fights. And she's older than I am, but she acts like a baby throwing tantrums."

So, the final ending. Their long/short relationship is over. It's the end of the song. Passage... Last trills of a seagull over the sky & then the waves wash in, cleaning the sand.

Ralph sees Lisa looking morose. "Go onstage. Do a good job! Bring the house down! I mean bring the house down, but don't get the place busted!"

CHAPTER FORTY-SEVEN

Mickey traveled the circuit with Lisa, from New York, to Cincinnati, St. Louis, Kansas City, Chicago, back to New York & they split up. Mickey turned 16 and was put back in jail by her mother.

'The very highest of drag is reserved for NYC. San Francisco is Western, casual. Newark, New Jersey; my parents grew up there, and old school friends. It's hard to be yourself with them around. But the isle of Manhattan....

'Ever go to a strange city, so you could do anything you felt like? Ever yearn to go because the walls of familiarity kept you in restraint? And still you weren't getting enough rewards for all the good you tried to do? No. So you had to flee, and go somewhere where you can be bad. And get all the things that you never had.

'Nobody knows me. I can go in drag. Rant and rave like a mad artist or a free gay person. Walk in the park. Talk to girls in gay bars, and nobody knows me, and I can do all the things I need to do to change my life.

'No reputation to uphold.

'I had left the city. The city holds my mother's voice. It is too close.'

Although by ordinary standards Mickey was a stranger, he had no friends—to his own mind. Yet he was known. Thus trapped in a paradox of conflict—being hemmed in, observed and gossiped about—critically, by a pack of uncaring acquaintances.... These people—former teachers, schoolmates, churchgoers, neighbors—recognized his figure and face. They knew what was passing as a short, small man in a 2nd-hand sports coat on the street was in reality, as a debutante, or a rose unfolding its petals; a butch come out.

I met Valorie while sitting in a gaybar in lower Manhattan. Had just turned 18; been released from jail, so Welfare paid for a room in a low-income hotel.

For a while I thought Valorie was on heroin. I knew she was a user and would come home with arms full of needle holes and blown blue bruised spots on her pale skin; but she was not an addict. It was a momentary impulse thing—a joypopper. Tho her state of mind seemed like an addict for days afterward.

She'd be a long time submerged down deep in herself. And from this position became a game player. Toying with us. Laughing snidely behind the back of her hand. Looking at the world out of a short-distance telescope; which means she is not really far away, but almost completely out of touch. Her body in its 2-day-old dress, stinks; quite real. And she sits there, drugged, picking her toes with relish. But, she is not quite in life either, but separated from Gloria & me. Toying with us. Looking at life, and smiling.

"Do you want to know where they live?" says Gloria's former stable sister, the sassy black whore, speaking to her pimp. "Over there, on the 14th floor of the Henry Hudson Hotel." There, stretching into hazy blue sky, rooftops with green foliage penthouse gardens, suites for presidents and little old gray-haired lady shareholders who've squirreled away blue-chip stocks & bonds.

The jungle didn't make Mickey sophisticated, just sad. Felt mean & lost. And the outer world—the good people—they walked by this drag butch; and shut her out, so that there was nowhere but the streets to be. 'Feel I'm inside a blizzard. Crying, with a perpetual cold; and uncomfortable inside my skin—which I can't escape.

'I had a job, but lost it when I went traveling on the circuit with Lisa. I'm 18! Now I'm a free adult! So things have changed—that's good. But also I see all my youth is wasting away! I'm attracted by girls who are flashy & pretty & sexy and whorish sluts. Different from the kind of girl I use to dream about—My Little Girl—my fantasy. My sweet woman, who is nice, who doesn't hang out at curbside. And the few nice girls I meet don't want anything to do with me because I'm in drag, and have been in jail and don't work or go to school either. They're afraid. They live with their parents in

Brooklyn or Long Island; in the same sterile white order with roles and laws like where I grew up until I couldn't stomach it no more and ran away. Now, I am among the poor going on 5 years—far from the way our father had intended us to be It is different from what I've known, what our mother taught us. We worshiped in church. Now I spit when I pass a church. I have fallen from Grace. I didn't know being gay—just loving a woman sincerely, from my emotions of all my heart and wanting her tenderness & excitement with all my body—would change my whole life—forever. But everywhere I turn, everywhere I go, everything I try to do, I keep bumping my head up against the STONEWALL. Being gay has put a circle around me—my life; that changes everything.'

Mickey moved. A piston in his nerves drove him. A clamoring testimony to the power of Being. Slept little. Hung out with Greenwich Village dykes & faygele boys. Ran the streets after different women; dressed in a sports jacket, tie—loosely knotted, shirt open at the collar showing a sturdy neck and T-shirt; creased trousers with pockets full of stuff—men's wallet on a chain, keys, knife, etc.—men's lace-up shoes & super-short hair; always hollering, joking & starving. No money. Just his good looks.

On the dance floor of a Mafia bar by night, deep throbbing of a lesbian song—The Supremes—we have claimed it for our own. Mickey & a girl hesitate on a beat. The party lights. The pounding sound vibrates as they rub their clits against each other's thigh. This might be the last night in a chain of wild weekends. Then the girl goes off, on the subway—back to Long Island—or she goes down, because she's stayed too long. Down. Busted for shoplifting in frantic attempt to get party money, money to eat, money to be free and keep living a gay life which is nowhere but here, in the street. Slammed down behind bars in the Women's House of D. (Detention.) Death, actually. Leaving Mickey to stand, breathless at the final lyric of the song. Alone.

Mickey thinks: 'Bleakness. I remember how my girl & her parents entrapped me. The lopsided shadows from the chimneys, the bricks crumbling cement; the slant of rooftops upon which I scuttled, jumping from the tops of apartment buildings to apartment buildings high above the city as people below watch. Wish I could take a pigeon flight; get out like a jet plane.'

Green treetops below. With pale hands the drag boy/girl clutches the fortress at its edge, to lower herself down a 15-foot drop to the next building. 'The sky above; I am in its full arms' embrace. The curvature of sky above me... Dark smoke blowing... I was out! Escaped! Free! With wild hair! Half of my clothes still back in her room & she's embarrassed, explaining it all to the authorities in uniform and police stars & her stern-faced parents locked in a yellow-windowed flat stories above the earth... I had grabbed a red scarf on my way out when we first heard adult mutterings in the hall—hers; of no use but to wave it like a flag!'

This had been the image of her Martyrdom at 16. When she was underage and still legal chattel—enslaved to the State, or to custody of a guardian. Now, of age, Mickey was more mature, had a stockier build, had a woman, Valorie to brush his black wavy hair with her gentle touch. Like the stars out in the night he was free; didn't have to run no more. And all the gay women were full of dope. Full of wine and singing, heads tipped to the sky. Romantic. Youth. Aimless.

The days of Wine & Roses.

Mickey would spend his state-allotted hotel-room money on Women's pleasure (drinks, treats at a restaurant, perfume, cigarettes) to keep them laughing & smiling; then have to sneak out with his one suitcaseful of men's clothes, check it in the bus terminal storage at Times Square & sleep on the subways, knife clutched under his coat, lying vertically on the hard seats as the iron beast roared, jolted and clanked down the tubes, if he couldn't find a woman to go home with and romance after the bars closed. Usually some drunken girl wanted him, held him close, wanting him for his hot furry cunt wet in his trousers, which the girl knew, craved herself; stroking his butch head with a red-nailed hand & pressing it to her tits. Mickey had good, hot sex, plus a place to lie down that night & shower & be clean for the next morning.

There was a new bar, a gay joint on the hustling strip in Times Square. Drag Queens flitted in and out, and a new variety of perverts, semi-straight could be found getting sex there. The Underworld ran the place. Hookers stopped off there to rest their feet & sip a drink.

Valorie and handsome butch Mickey; short dress & men's suit, became a couple in this dive, after becoming acquainted in a girls' bar down in the Village.

Valorie came in and out from the littered sidewalks of her work; like a genie of smoke out of a subway grille. Love was the force of a holocaust; as Mickey turned her face thru the smoky bar, dark eyes appraising her bare legs in high heels; a tiny purse at her side & leather coat to hide in over one arm. One by one, out of the cold came a parade of girls' figures bringing smells of tobacco and cool air wrapped up in their coats that disguise nakedness, sitting on a bar stool peevishly, rocking one leg crossed over the other so hard they wear grooves from their garter belts in the hot, damp plastic under their bottoms. The Vice is outside, making it difficult to work. Electric static runs thru the club. A buzz of whispered conversations among the fish-eyed made-up Drag Queens in big wigs & big bosoms, and the smaller females. They have to spend money on drinks as they sit and wait, fingers of hands tapping with impatience; clustered along the bar together.

Valorie & her butch Mickey are happy to be a couple. Touch thighs under the counter of the bar. Secretly glad she isn't working. It's more fun.

Mickey thinks: 'I remember carrying my suitcase so weighted I could barely hold it in my arms after the 8th block...numb...going from hotel to hotel, ran from friend to friend...room to room...struggling. I remember the Bleakness. My alcoholism. Sleeping (when not in the subways) in the empty all-night movie houses, walking in the wind. Past food smells from bars & grills I can't afford.'

This New York summer of 1958.

Suddenly, with a whisk of her full-length leather coat, Valorie has moved Mickey uptown. The two females find their way to the subway. A rumble starts. A tremor in the walls of the station, & the BMT COMES. Steam like fog, and it is very cold. Soon they are transported, are among high gothic spires, a sweep of an apparently rich, expensive neighborhood.

Angular, tall, unfathomable, austere. White. Steel and glass & metal. Super-high-rise apartment buildings that touch billowy clouds above. Mickey thinks as a child he came from a life of clean buildings like this; of clearer visions and a school which inspired her young head. Not as did the inmates of darkness; of her friends now; of the low miasma of stick-&-board slums. Not like Valorie.

This was their world. A nice hotel room mornings, peaceful, safe. Evenings in Times Square & nights in Village hustling grounds off 5th Avenue and bopping over to join the party lights with gay kids; clink of glasses & flitting drag butches, hair slicked back, peroxide blond; cigarette smoke & laughter.

This was her world: suit coat, hard face, rings on his fingers tapping on the bar, 7UP on the counter trying to stay sober, men's shoes on a bar-stool rung; a spoiled kept butch marking time; Mickey looks out at it...thru passing moods.... Smiled in the sunlight & laughed in the rain.

Mickey, Gloria & Valorie stand in line with other customers at a food joint soon after Gloria decides she likes butch cock in preference to men, and has joined their family. Waits for fish & chips; when a black pimp, well dressed in flashy threads, a snarl permanently etched on his face comes up to them: "ALL RIGHT, YO' TWO FREAKS! DIS SHIT IS OVER! LET'S GO! DIS IS MY LADY!" he proclaims to the crowd. He whirls about, coattails flying, brandishing the gun first at Valorie, then Mickey. It's broad daylight, the line of customers is in shock; Mickey and his ladies stand there saying nothing.) Gloria trembles but remains rooted to the spot, beside Mickey, unmoving; and the pimp snarls, whirling his long coat & exits. "It was a threat. Don't pay any attention. If he was going to do anything he would have then, while he had a chance." Mickey says, & knows under his bravado her knees are trembling, and he doesn't have the heart to go up against pimps guns & police & freakish, insane tricks & jealous rival girls of the hustling life. Where was the nice girl? Where was the promise of clean, safe love?

Mickey's ladies are humping, clipping wallets, boosting clothes from Department Stores—Macy's & Gimbel's, & bringing in a lot of cash. At night they lay down, three of them naked and freak off with cunt, good & hot. Cunt, cum & tits & ass; loving each other. It's so good. The threat diminishes into a dark cloud settling in the back of the butch's mind.

Then the pimp jams Mickey in the street alone.

Gun to her head; a silver-plated .22 caliber automatic. "YO' BE SUCKING MY DICK, BITCH, AND LIKE IT BEFO' I'M FINISHED!"

POW! Throws a punch into her face, as Mickey ducks, it makes a grazing contact; she slides back. POP! POP! POP! Three firecracker-sounding shots fire at her. All three intend to miss. Gunpowder hangs in the air. Mickey's on the ground, terror in her young eyes.

Afterward, he walks down the street full of rage, knees knocking; in enough fear to turn him back into a square. 'None of this pimping was my idea, it was theirs! I could get a job again! They could quit working the streets and get little jobs somewhere, like clerk or waitress! But they'd never accept that! They'd laugh at me! They make more in a day than I do in 2 weeks.' Pounds a perfumed fist into his ringed hand.

Later, inside the safety of their uptown room, Mickey blurts out what happened: "What is he? A nigger or a human being—or does he think he's God?"

"He's just a pimp and you've fucked up his money. We chose your dick over his, and he's mad and broke, and that sassy brown whore he has left can't bring money in like Gloria could. Gloria is white and can go anywhere to work, plus command a higher price. Gloria was with him because he's a freak & always knew she liked pussy & he's fine with that—as long as she remains in his stable. But she's sucking Mickey's clit now, and pimps don't respect a female pimp unless, Mickey, you want to get out there with a gun yourself & teach him some respect, but you don't have it in you. We know that. So don't worry, you're our man. Maybe we'll start working days, or out of a nightclub uptown and stay out of the streets; or maybe we'll get a gun—us ladies—& jam him up! But Gloria has another idea: she wants to leave town for the winter. It's getting cold; icy & snowy. Go to Miami—that'll solve everything."

Mickey was high from contact with the marijuana they smoked in the room. Evening, she watches her ladies leave to go out to work the bars; wishes them safe passage thru the fog.

CHAPTER FORTY-EIGHT

Valorie stuck her head in the hotel door. Her man Mickey was watching television. Across the room out the window, down, could be seen the green park, leafy trees—a classy location. Over the sound of the box, Val yells; standing there jeweled, in a long coat, hair down to her shoulders. Her butch replies some curse mumbled in Italian.

"THAT'S ALL RIGHT! WE'LL DO IT OURSELVES, THEN, MICKEY!"

"You girls are the Devil!"

"Thank you, sir!" Valorie says brightly.

Valorie exits with a cigarette. Mickey and Gloria follow. Elevator to the lobby. Bitch Number One and Bitch Number Two: that's what they call themselves; laughing, sharing a cigarette with red lipstick on its gold filter, pulling Mickey by her suit coat that has a new jeweled pin—an M—her initial, on the lapel.

The girls carry a portable radio thru the streets, turn it up and walk along with the beat in a dance step. Footsteps melt into distance away from the hotel. The expensive area is murky, reduced into nothing.... Gloria slows, conscious of a car that has rolled to a stop. Valorie keeps walking fast, yanks Mickey along: "COME ON, GLORIA! IT'S THE VICE!" Gloria walks. The car roars away.

"Are you sure, Valorie?" Gloria puffs, out of breath; "You might have made me miss some money!"

"I can spot vice!"

They sing, play the radio, smoke, laugh and come to a bar, set down into a lower basement level. The three turn into its entrance, descending; grope in darkness in the sudden switch from day as they enter a new atmosphere that they weren't familiar with. There's men in the bar in suits & ties, who turn to look. And a few women. The nice kind that work in offices on Madison Avenue as legal secretaries and managers & executives; dressed in business suits, who turn and give them a cold stare. When Mickey and her bejeweled, feathered ladies in their short skirts & bare legs stroll in and sit down at the bar, the bartender comes over and flatly refuses to serve them, asks them to leave. "There's no hustling in here, girls. There's the door." Chagrined, their little plan to work the bars is killed dead in its tracks. Outside the cops sit. Light on inside, over the dashboard writing on a sheaf of papers in a clipboard. Lying in wait. A businesswoman gets into a cab; then it pulls off. Dejected, the three head down the avenue, back to their familiar turf.

'...Steeltown... Dingy skid-row haunts...we had been there, past the people that you meet....'

"THERE'S COMPTONS!" All the sissies and Drag Queens and whores in big gaudy coats, sunglasses; 12 P.M. midnight. Valorie's radio is tuned way up! We float down the avenue bringing sound!

The curb littered, but vacant. All the working girls & drags are inside, where they sip coffee. "Uh-uh, girl. No, not me. I ain't goin' back out there because tonight's hot. It's bad business. And it's hot in here, too. Too many pills and drugs & stuff."

So, they go to party in a gaybar. Go have fun and put off working till later. On the way the three of them pick up an old alcoholic, half-carry him to his hotel, mercifully—and there go thru the pockets of his clothes hanging in the closet and get $2. Not Mickey—she hung back; she was afraid of sin & hell-fire. Valorie stands there and yells, "You are a fool!" at Mickey.

"Don't let her disrespect you like that, Mickey!" Gloria says.

"SHUT UP, BITCH, AND GO TO HELL! GIVE ME

THE MONEY!" Mickey hardens, hand outstretched. The alcoholic blinks at the ceiling, passed out in his bed. During the cab ride the rest of the way, on the $2, a long argument ensues.

"Mickey, if you're going to be our man you have to live the fast life. You have to have The Game. You can't be a nice little Catholic butch with snotty ideas about whose wallet to clip and whose wallet not to clip! Don't feel sorry for them! If that man hadda been sober he would have tried to kill you for wearing drag & being our man! Get them before they get you!"

Nighttime is the right time.

The radio is on. BREAKING UP WITH YOU! Song of the streets, those NYC nights; every night is so beautiful.

Gloria is out the door again, to hustle 5th Avenue and 12th. Got up off her bar stool and left without saying a word. "I don't like her working. Because of that pimp. I worry about her."

"You want to walk her to work, Daddy?" Val says coyly. They laugh. "Do you want to work the streets, Mickey? Then she won't have to work alone."

"Fat chance!" growls the butch.

Valorie is stone gay. Never had a male pimp. Would rather party tonight in the gay club & be poor. Flips her long brown hair, feet ready to dance; glad the butch is all hers.

Later, back at the hotel, Valorie is flattened on the bed, exhausted & sleeping. Gloria, stately, arrives, unwraps her coat. Has made $100. Gives it to Mickey, then pulls off her shoes, throws down the coat, and lays on the floor. "Come on, baby, don't wake her up! Get down here with me!" Gloria pulls her dress off; naked; braceleted arms, & legs fine downed with hair on her white skin. Tuft of pubic hair; pink nipples hard. "I've done my job, but I saved my kinkiest for you, Daddy. Is your tongue hard?" Gloria snaps her garter belt & wiggles her pussy. Puts two red-nailed fingers in her mouth, wets them & rubs over her cunt, draws the lips back. "Do me, Mickey!" Butch moans, hot desire inflames her body, beginning in her sex organs. Embraces this female who writhes on the floor; buries her head in the crook of Gloria's neck, forces two fingers into her by slowly probing, wiggling them, gains entrance to her smooth, wet chamber & makes short jabs, till Gloria's hole opens wider, then thrusts deep, repeatedly & licks down her body, head hovering over her tits, her stomach, pink tongue strokes, to her cunt. Jabs her fingers in her wet hole & licks her clit in synchrony; & Gloria arches her back to meet Mickey's thrust, her hands grab her own tits, red-nailed fingers squeezing the nipples. Butch's head is burrowed in the nest of Gloria's pubic hair working fast, hand jamming in also, pistonlike, bam, bam, bam: "OH, MY GOD! OH, MY *GOD!* OH, MICKEY!" WHAM BAM! Gloria orgasms, cunt tightens on Mickey's fingers, slippery cunt riding up and down Mickey's mouth & nose to sublime satisfaction.

Starlight filters over the bed where Valorie sleeps, drips down to the floor in a pool of silver, where Gloria & Mickey rock in each other's arms. Gloria, lean nude body in only a garter belt has serviced her butch who came hard. They talk afterward. "Val frightens me," Mickey says.

"Frightens you? How?"

"Scares me for her sake. Not mine. Because I see her going down a road she can't get off of. And Gloria, I see you so easily there too…. And myself… Yuh know… I'm the type I never use narcotics. I mean the hard stuff…. I've had morphine & heroin, but I stopped, because it's the most beautiful feeling on earth, and I knew if I kept on I wouldn't ever stop. And I'm afraid for us! If I ever did it again, as heavy-duty as it is, & me liking it so much, I could never again stop! Do you know?"

The three lesbians were due to be kicked out of the hotel because of unpaid rent. So they threw Mickey a birthday party & invited gay kids from the Village. Mickey wore a second-hand tuxedo purchased at a price from a dealer—black with satin lapels & satin stripes down the trousers. Mickey wore his strap-on cock down the left side of his crotch—an object of OHH! and AHH! by both fags & dykes. Mickey was a perfect host, greeting their guests with Italian warmth—handshake clasped with both her hands, or a kiss. His mother would have been proud. Opens beer bottles, directs kids to sit on the bed, or finds them a spot on blankets on the floor. Turns up the music box; passes around a bag of rolled-up joints of marijuana.

In the wee small hours at 5 A.M., red party light floods down on shambles. Piles of cigarette butts overflowing ashtrays; paper cups & empty bottles strewn about. A few dykes left; crashed out, sleeping against the wall.

Gloria & Valorie start the sex party. "We have an audience." They giggle, casting a mischievous look at the sleepers. Pull off each other's dresses. Butch feels hands all over her; pull off her boxers, her T-shirt; hears giggles, eager breath panting in her ear; fumbling nail-polished femme fingers—off comes the binder; the butch is nude; stands there in harness; the rubber cock pointing out of the curly pubic hair of her crotch to a length of 7". All three females are the same height, so when they hug, their fuzzy cunthair entwines —plus the rubber dick. They laugh and pull Mickey down on the bed. Perfume aroma. Nude women all over; hands slide in the wet sweat over her back. Feels their wet pussies rub against her thighs, her ass. Gloria wiggles down between Mickey's legs, holds one tit in her hand and strokes the butch's clit with the hard nipple. Red-polished fingertips & mouths stimulate her erogenous zones. The audience of sleepy-eyed, tousle-head dykes come awake & watch. Mickey feels two hot pussies ride her: Gloria at one end, Valorie on the other. A hand grabs her rubber cock, pulls, pushes, banging the end against her clit. They get Mickey to bend over on all fours and Gloria, naked but for her garter belt, parts the two moons of Mickey's ass and sticks her tongue into the butch's nasty asshole. Licks her crack, probes a finger into her pink ass & licks her butt. And Valorie wiggles underneath between her arms & legs which support her and demands, "Fuck me with your cock, Mickey!" Mickey holds her cock, lowers her hips down towards the opened thighs, aims the cock with one hand into her pink wispy-haired cunt and pushes its rubbery length into her. While Gloria's on her ass, has a finger stuck up her butthole and the other hand reaches around her waist, slips between the harness & Mickey's bare flesh, works into the wet nest of fur & pussylips to rub the pearly clit while Mickey plunges her dick in and out of Valorie, who reaches up underneath to feel Mickey's titties, large which hang over her, butch tits, bouncing with ringed fingers squeezing her nipples. Excited, Mickey was fucking hard and fast. Gloria rubs her clit frantically. "OH! OH! OH!" Valorie hollers. "FUCK ME WITH YOUR HARD COCK!"

"FUCK YOUR BRAINS OUT, BUTCH!" Gloria coaches. "GIVE IT TO HER! FUCK HER NASTY, SLUTTY HOLE! FUCK HER FASTER! *FASTER!*" Valorie's hips thrust up, slapping her belly against Mickey's; her hands leave the butch's dangling tits to clutch her manly shoulders as Mickey strains above her propped up on two hands, one on either side of Val's voluptuous body; Caresses her strong back while she pumps, driving bolts of white-hot lightning lust into her womanhood; & Gloria sends jolts of pleasure up Mickey's asshole with her inserted finger; while still rubbing her fire-hot clit under the rubber cock. All three females pant and moan and HOLLER. Gloria's probing into Mickey's cunt now with fingers, and working her swollen clit; Mickey's banging into Valorie, who thrusts her hips underneath in a steady beat. An orgy of sweat and cunt discharge; BANG! BANG! BANG! Mickey cums hard. Drops down over Valorie, like a workhorse cum to rest.

"HAPPY BIRTHDAY, BABY!" Valorie whispers, blows into Mickey's ear.

"I felt my baby's pussy clamp down on my fingers when she came!" Gloria declares proudly. 'They're making my job easier,' Mickey thinks, tired, as she rests, cuddled between her two women. 'I wonder—do all the lesbian hookers and their butch pimps do this at night?'

Midway into winter, random events hit them like wild cars out of control. A collision. Fate knocks them this way & that. Lost their hotel, had to move to a fleabag room just above Washington Square Park the Village. Hostile pimps muscled in whenever the girls tried to work. High life turns into death.

Walls go up. Girls working along the strip are afraid to be seen near them because Val and Glo' have got the reputation of being trouble. Give them the cold shoulder. No money. Valorie goes crazy, borrows a C-note from a Mafia loanshark to cop drugs to sell down on Sixth—Avenue of the Americas—to gay kids and turn it into $500, and then, foolishly goes to jail in a bust for solicitation for prostitution.

Winter winds blew mercilessly in the cracks of windows of their poverty room. Gloria is mad, paces like a cat back & forth. Mickey gets on Welfare so they can eat & pawns all but a few pieces of jewelry. Goes to visit Valorie faithfully each day.

The jail has no exits. Its waiting room door—a heavy iron slab—has no handles on the inside once it's shut. An escapee might try to pry the heavy door open with her fingernails. This room is an antechamber between iron walls; open to the elements on one side—a balcony which lets in rain & snow. A view down over a metal railing of a six story drop.

A crowd of people push to the closed iron door, which a policewoman will open. Soon Mickey and Valorie sit across a divider—brick wall with individual glass windows & an intercom—for a 15-minute visit. "I want a piece of your pussy every night, Valorie—that's all I ever wanted. And your emotional love. You don't have to do anything else! Just sometimes maybe clip a wallet or something. Let me get a job, and we can all live a simple life together. I'll give you two all the money I earn. If you girls even got just a little job, just part time, waitress or something, we could live OK! We wouldn't have to go thru this!" Waved her hand at the gray cement walls of the jail visiting hall. Mickey bent low, mouth close to the telephone mouthpiece, which communicated thru the glass to the prisoner who sat in a sorrowful dirty dress on the other side; fervently expressing her inner soul. "I'm a lover, not a criminal! I've just been going along with your girls because you're so good to me. I'm spoiled, too, but it ain't too late! I don't mind getting a regular job! I'll even sell my rings!"

"I FIGURED YOU'D START TALKING CRAZY THE MINUTE I'M STUCK BEHIND BARS! I HOPE GLORIA

AIN'T SOFTHEADED ENOUGH TO FALL FOR THAT BULLSHIT!" Valorie's pasty face sparks behind the double glass.

"Let's lay it on the line! Why am I visiting you, then? It's not for my health! It ain't for the money—you can't give me no money!"

"Yeah, well why?"

"Because…you mean something to me."

"When I get out, I want a regular place; a nice hotel with a bathroom! NO, I WON'T SQUARE UP AND BE POOR!"

"You can go back to dancing and forget the other stuff!"

"I'm out of shape! I have to get my weight down! I can't fit into my costumes!" Valorie was defeated.

People print notes, hold them up to the glass, talking silently in sign language because the two-way phones between prisoner and visitor are monitored by the guards. Mickey contorts her face, vehemently delivering a lecture on the evils of prostitution & why Valorie needs to stop, square up, be a dancer or a waitress. All the visitors were dressed in bright colors. Life went on as usual. Jail was a kind of sorority they went thru. On the other side of the glass two girls sat, one in a leopard coat; short black hair, acting coy. Other a redhead in sunglasses. A white pimp and a Negro; males, sat in front of the girls respectively; thick thighs pressing the swivel stools; big hammy hands holding on to the phone receivers… Loud talk, lightning fast, hard and to the point to these girls: "YOU BITCH! YOU *BETTER!*" "AW, HONEY!" Both girls received a brown envelope, which was money. Valorie was taking draws on the $100 she was arrested with. Valorie lounged behind the glass, pulled her pink-&-white-striped candy-cane-colored coat over her shoulders; it was cold inside the big concrete jail. Mickey thinks: 'I got this girl thinking I come here just to see her, but I come here to make sure she comes back to me when she gets out so I can get some pussy. I like the way Valorie makes love. She is very passive, lets me do what I like. And I don't feel it's a test to her because she really don't care, she don't get disappointed; not like Lisa, who nobody could satisfy. I want her sex. And, because I would be lonely without her love.' Valorie appraises Mickey thru the double glass. 'Mickey & Gloria are laying up in the hotel fucking their brains out. Gloria will lose her drive to get out there & make money and Mickey will encourage it. When I get out, I may not even have a pillow to lay my head on. Those two may have gone to living in a doorway.' Valorie was pretty nice behind bars; like a child one wants to do favors for. Mickey knows that once she's back outside, she'll be headstrong, back to her old ways.

"I keep trying to tell you you're a good dancer & you'd make a very good waitress." Mickey says aloud, while inner thoughts trouble her. 'I can't tell her nothing.... My words don't get thru to her. All she's concerned about is getting rich and buying a Cadillac car.'

Her costumes for her strip act are in a metal trunk, put aside; her daily clothes—nice ones—hang in the closet, scented with perfume from much use & the perfume she sprays on her body. Late in memory, this will seem like a dream; it's such a different way of life.... At the point Mickey enters her life, Val does a lot of sighing, fidgeting her hands in her lap, and playacting, and operating thru pills & wine into which she may disappear when she comes home at the end of night.... In a gauzy pink veil...a long red cape which flashes turquoise lining when opened, and needs laundering, mending, pressing & some tight knit outfit which is too small.

"You don't *have* to be a prostitute!" Mickey beseeches ardently. Valorie's eyes flash. She straightens up in her chair, motions the butch to "SHUT UP!—THE PHONES ARE BUGGED! One of the guards might have heard you!" 'She's lazy, that's why. It's easy money. Easier & bigger than dancing.'

"You just bark at the moon and eat shit, Mickey!"

"I'm no sucker Valorie!"

"I don't want to be a waitress!"

"I want to be your boyfriend, I don't want to be a pimp! I'll get a job! I swear! We won't have to worry about all this other crap! We can lift our heads up among women!"

"You just want some pussy. That's all you think about! I'm thinking about our future! I'm older than you! I understand what life's all about! Where are we gonna stay, and what're we gonna eat! Only a fool hollers at the moon and settles for shit to eat! I want caviar to eat! I want a new leather coat! I want to stay in a nice hotel like where we were!"

"Well, when you get out of this goddamn jail, there's gonna be some changes! We've got to do something! Gloria can't work—it's too rough! Back on Welfare again! You'll be getting out in 25 days, I hope you aren't planning to run off & make a sucker out of me!"

They strained thru the glass; emotion in their faces; Mickey kept trying to blurt out things, & Valorie motioned her to SHHH! because of the guards listening in on the line. It was as loud as a party in the visitors' hall. And then their time was up.

Mickey thinks: 'When I see a jail, it's a feeling which is hard to explain. Because I was locked in one long enough. It's not the walls, it's something spiritual.'

"Are you gonna wait till your lady gets out of jail, or can we fly straight down to Miami now? She's your woman, not mine." Gloria informs Mickey.

"Yeah, we'll wait. We'll go together."

Gloria is on top of her. "UH! UH! UH! OHHH!" Mickey stares at the ceiling nonchalantly, feels Gloria's heavy weight; her pumping clit rubs up & down on Mickey's thigh. Then, sensing she's ready to bust a nut; runs one ringed hand over her back & begins to jiggle her leg: "OH! UH! UH! UH! AH! AH!" Gloria bounces fast on top of Mickey's leg, huffs & puffs in an explosive orgasm.

Scheherazade joins the no-luck whores & their butch because she has a crush on handsome Mickey, who she's seen under purple lights down the line of bar patrons in the Mafia dives; & the other girls have told her it's a treat to be with a lesbian. She's never done it before. Just a few fake shows at stag parties. Also she admires the sophisticated Gloria who picks her up in a straight bar; and even by her young age of 20 is totally sick & tired of male pimps with their superior strength bossing her and stealing her money.

They move off welfare row & back uptown.

Valorie gets out, and it's some heavy drama. Mickey tells

her, "You promised me you'd go back to dancing! It's been two weeks and you ain't gone to a single audition!"

"So, you picked the wrong lady! You knew what I did before we began! You told me you loved me anyway! I'm out there sellin' it in the motherfuckin' streets, I want some respect, not a lecture from you! You get all the money, don't you! You're the boss! *I'm not going to dance anymore! I can't fit in my costumes, Mickey! I don't even want to talk about it!*"

Today, with her ill-gotten gains, she buys a leather coat.

"I promised myself I never would get a leather coat. Every whore in Times Square has a leather coat."

"They have *leopard* coats."

"They have *leather* coats!"

Leopard coats, leather coats, striped coats, fur coats, coats that shout red. Valorie, Gloria & Scheherazade had one of each between them. Mickey had a black leather three-quarters coat and men's heavy gold jewelry.

When they left that night to work, Mickey stole down to the Village to meet a girl she wanted to sleep with; a nice girl she'd met at a gay club when her ladies were busy, gabbing, partying, their heads turned.

Girl floated by in a brown leather jacket; short blond hair in a femme ducktail that came to a little point which arrows down her back. Earrings dangle with miniature bells. Tight-fitting blue jeans; tiny elevated heels.

The girl showed only briefly. They talked, nervous, standing by the area around the entrance. She was totally gay. A student and cafeteria worker at Columbia University. The girl was Mickey's dream. But after the conversation & sizing up the gold jewelry and noting the fact that Mickey didn't work, the girl got cold feet and didn't want to go make love. And in the future, when Mickey was out with her ladies, she hastily avoided the butch; swiveling around on a bar stool, showing only the back of her blonde-gold hair.

Mickey had to work a long time before she got her clit hard —that is, so hot she could fuck & enjoy it immensely with each stroke & be riding in power; knowing she could then cum at any point. Like water slow to turn from cold to warm, she had to struggle with Scheherazade, Gloria, & Valorie, and the bedsheets showed it. Wild matted hair, makeup smeared; sheets hot, wet from female discharge and twisted when they were thru. "I don't know why my dick ain't working tonight ladies."

"You thinking about some other broad that's not here, that's why!" Gloria snaps. "Your heart ain't in it, Daddy!" The tension in the young butch's body was visible; moving in vain, struggling; then finally busts loose. After she did have her orgasm, she felt so sad, so hollow. It was not love...not like romancing with that girl had been. A young, fresh, innocent thrilling love. Mickey was right. This hard life wasn't going to work for her—'Where is the life that will?'

They copulate, cum, & tired, fall asleep. Leave Mickey, bewildered, to think about the future.

She feels death—a short black unknown tunnel ending abruptly with no exit. Fear prickles her skin. And a new sweat breaks out. 'This is my punishment for being with girls faster than me. Valorie is 24. Gloria's 26. Even 'Zade is 20. Guess that's why that nice girl seemed so sweet—she's not fast one bit. She's just 18.'

Squeezes her body from between two of the women and goes to the bureau to the radio & tunes up music & her soul floats free. Escape! Like a bird that flies outside the window! As a child flies in a dream; slow, steady, elevating up over the building tops where consciousness lies sleeping. Rising out of the night, majestically, unobserved by human beings, in free-dom. 10 miles down, is cement and tops of buildings below, small as child's play blocks. The isle of Manhattan is covered by snow.

Dressed in fine coats, the four stroll thru midtown. They make snowballs & have a battle. Three women under her control, proud as a peacock, she struts. Parties. Laughs. And inside is happy.

So, Mickey decides, 'Dreams don't come true. I can't change. Nah, I won't even think about it. I'll just enjoy my luck.' Has three companions to pass thru these days, and the women all like each other.

Tho it is impermanent, every day facing threats of police, pimps, & poverty's red eyes & gnashing rat teeth devouring them the minute the girls are unable to go out and hustle; despite the fear of death's dead end. And no future.

They make love in a 4-way. They go to the movies. Eat popcorn & drink sodas and sit in a row in the metal-&-cloth padded theater seats. How many more days they would be there in New York are numbered. 'My love affair with Scheherazade begins. She is a virgin to lesbianism. We do it a bit at a time.

Lick her; steady strokes making my tongue thick so it covers her pearly clit licking over and over. We French kiss & I pet her naked tits while watching TV for an hour; then go deep into her pussy with my fingers. Finally get to ride her— her legs apart, me between, going up and down, clit in her cunt while Valorie & Gloria cheer me on: "GO, MICKEY! GO, MICKEY!" Scheherazade holds me and humps and is happy, free & wild. I cum & she clutches my trembling body. She is young and not as worldwise as the others & we get a crush on each other. I am after her all the time; go for her nude wet body in the shower. Chase her to the closet when she tries to get dressed & she runs wildly screaming in excitement daring me to catch her and when I do I hold her & she holds me, & I work my fingers in her cunt, then jam them in and out in love & send thrills down her spine, while French kissing her deep. Our family's spiral out of poverty is complete with the addition of Scheherazade. She boosts clothes, jewelry, & we are well-heeled soon. She takes the subway to different boroughs and hits a new area every day of the week in a rotating fashion. We're flying high. I block out any dark thoughts of the future from my soul. We eat take-out food: I get down on my knees and lick my ladies submissively—all three of them in a row—till they cum. Gloria in her garter belt, tits hanging out over her bra; one high-heeled pump standing on each side of me; thrusting her wet gash in my face; tosses her head, wild, clit rides my tongue & seriously I perform. "FUCK IT, BABY MICKEY! FUCK YOU, BABY MICKEY! SUCK MY CUNT, BITCH! SUCK IT! *SUCK! SUCK! SUCK!*"

I lay on my back—as a butch bottom, spread my thighs to give up my furry cunt. "RIDE IT, GLORIA! RIDE IT, HONEY!" Scheherazade & Valorie cheer. "GO ON, HONEY! FUCK HIM! FUCK HIM! FUCK HIM GOOD!"

Fog & snow, like seeing thru a tunnel.

In the street, we see a Drag. A pair of turquoise toreador pants loosely hung over her narrow shanks; her thick bull neck, Adam's apple, ghastly pale white face dotted with beard stubble & huge hands reveal she is a man. Down on her luck. Scars of acne on her young face—she is my age, just in her teens. She faints. Crumples & falls in the snow. 'I don't want it to turn out like that for my Ladies & me.'

Walking one night, checking up on her women, Mick sees Valorie standing alone against a wall, then suddenly dive back into the vestibule of a building.

A pimp car screeches by, recklessly, snow flies off its tires. It's gone. Mickey grimaces; shoves her fists down into the leather coat pockets. 'All the fucking pimps & pushers in this neighborhood roll around on Cadillac wheels; dealing directly into our lives.'

Pay the loanshark back $200. They have $400 saved. Try to get an apartment but can't. Are going to end up spending it all.

Yellow light beams onto a snowy windowsill. Radiator sizzles heat; TV blares & music plays from the radio. The four sit on the double bed & play Bridge & other card games. Femmes in silk slips, panties & bra; butch in T-shirt & boxers. After 3 or 4 hours of munching take out food in plastic containers, and drinking wine & dancing to music; being gay, they come to conclusions: "I'd blow up every bank in America if I could!" Mickey snarls. "They lock up all the money! People who keep their money inside banks are so smug! It's a whole system they got, and they won't let me into it! I'll blow them all up off their foundations! I'll do something big!"

"This goddamn city is getting to my head," says Gloria. Everybody mutters "Yeah." Agrees. "These pimps are ruthless. They all want to get their hand in my purse."

Pussy & money. That's what they talk about, & inside

Mickey is hungry for peace. Yearns for peace. Not sure what she needs. Secretly each woman looks at the others, feeling she is less popular than her sisters. Is jealous of Mickey's attentions—and feels less sure of herself. As they slap the cards down on the bed, blithely blowing cigarette smoke, each woman has self-doubts: 'Why is it I have to share my man with two other bitches? Why am I doing this? Mickey don't love me enough? I had to share my last man with other women. Is it that I'm such a sorry bitch I don't deserve more? I'm a failure. Not able to find true love.' But they don't discuss this. Cover up their true emotions bragging & laughing.

There's police riding, making arrests. Pimps scowl, stay on their tail with strong-arm goon tactics. The girls can't work freely. Locked up in their hotel room, & in a feeling of gray boredom. Wanting big money. Yet wanting to stay alive & out of jail & not run the risk of mayhem & murder.

Scheherazade hits the snowy streets; goes down to where all the pretty girls work; as she saunters by a gray snowbank someone breathes a hurried proposition out of a car. $20 is all they earn that day. Gloria & Valorie sit up in a straight bar; admirers buy them drinks, & they come home drunk & still broke.

A few days later, a pimp puts a gun to Mickey's head.

They decide they'll pack their bags; and the next night take a flight down to Miami.

Their last night of hot sex in New York, the isle of Manhattan is strung with snowy green, red & yellow Christmas lights.

"They get 20 minutes, you get all night!"

"We'll make it freakish for you, honey!"

"Nasty and freakish and make our Baby Mickey cum, cum, cum! We like to watch you cum, honey! You cum so nasty and good!"

"You shoot a big load, butchy!"

"Mickey comes so hot!"

"His little ass goes up and down!"

The girls ran their fingers thru Mickey's ducktail hairdo. Valorie lay back, thighs spread, a moan on her lips. "SHE

REALLY NEEDS IT—GIVE IT TO HER!" Gloria cries in delight, claps her hands. A dildo is a shape defined by a vagina. Valorie craved to have hers filled. Hot dogs & cucumbers are passé. They have the strap-on dick. Fingers do a lot of tricks cocks can't. Mickey used everything. Loosened her woman up, fingers go round and round; then works the tool by hand; slides its rubber tip over and over her stinky cuntlips from clit to hole, then to her ass, pink & puckered, & back; then shoves it in her hole an inch, pulls out, then in, deeper, out, making her hot, ready, then plunges in up to the hilt. "AAAAAH-HHHHHUUUUUHHH!" Valorie cries, responding in ecstasy. Scheherazade holds Mick's sturdy white butt firmly in red-nailed fingers, sticks her tongue in Mickey's asshole, licks with fat, juicy strokes. Gloria lays at the top of the bed alternately sucking Valorie's tits, her head with flowing hair on Val's chest; and reaching up to milk Mickey's butch tits as they hang down over Valorie as she fucks her. "STICK YOUR FINGERS IN HER PUSSY!" Gloria hollers. Scheherazade pushes two fingers into Mickey's cunt, and her other hand rubs the butches fur & clit, making orgiastic sparks of hot desire. Mickey thrust her cock down deep into Valorie's voluptuous vagina and works it with short humps of hip action, herself hovering on the threshold of delight from what the girls are doing to her. Valorie humps up underneath, writhing and straining for clit contact. "Do me with your fingers, Glo!" She begs, breathless; but Gloria has other plans. Slides her butt down under Mickey, who is raised up on both hands, fucking, and gets her cunt over Valorie's mouth, and commands: "SUCK ME, BITCH! *SUCK ME!*"

As one huge animal with many pairs of arms & legs; having four steaming hot cunts, they work each other over, with a beat of amazing rhythm, bouncing the bed bang bang bang bang bang bang bang bang! against the wall. Lusty loins covered with sweat, spit & cuntjuice. Scheherazade rolls to the side, & humps her powerful clit against one of Mickey's legs, while she keeps filling the butch's cunt with fingers and jacking her clit under the harness; while simultaneously Mickey slams the rubber dick down deep into Valorie. "OH, FUCK

ME! FUCK ME WITH YOUR CUNT!" Mickey yells to Scheherazade, feeling her wet clit rub excitedly against her naked leg. "OH, DADDY, YOUR COCK IS SO HOT! DRIVE YOUR HARD DICK IN HER, DADDY! GIVE IT TO HER!" Scheherazade screams. And Valorie splutters—her mouth is full of Gloria's pussy. Humps frantically, needing release bad.

Mickey sees Gloria's ass quiver below her—cumming in Valorie's mouth. It lays still. Then, slowly she crawls up over Valorie's head, reaches her hand down under Mickey, who thrusts in & out, and works the pearl of Val's clit with her fingertips for a surefire BANG. They're all humping, and Mickey cums fast & fine in a glorious, smooth climax, but doesn't stop. Then Scheherazade makes it; and finally, Valorie, trembling, her stomach rippling, lets go with a terrific scream as she orgasms on the rubber dick and Gloria's hand: "AAAHHH!"

After, they embrace. Four pairs of arms; kiss, and lay panting on wet sheets, legs draped over each other. Pussy permeates the room, & sweat.

Different techniques for each girl. All shared their butch.

Mickey performed stud service for each in her turn.

Liked to fuck cunt to cunt as a routine; twice daily.

Entered them from behind with cock or fingers. Did a daisy chain—each cunt in someone's mouth—in a circle.

Saw what 4 women could do together.

CHAPTER FORTY-NINE

A new club had been born out of their oppression.

Out of Vice scowling down, the Mafia & its payoff-graft taverns & musclemen goons. For the gay kids had a new place owned by a gay man; decked out in purple streamers.

Excited fairies, young 15- & 16-year olds bearing false IDs that said they were 21 and legal, raced in, began dancing in gym shoes on the tiny dance floor; each gesture & mimic lit by blue & red & green lights. FUN!

A lot of nice gay kids came back—students, young women & men who worked honest jobs.

Femme Judy already was there; in a black cocktail dress, hair high on her head, sparkling rings & bracelets; in high heel pumps; fur coat draped over a bar stool, escorted by her handsome fag friend who her parents thought was her fiancé; who was off dishing with the gayboys.

Again, the club was under surveillance by slime, bearing the silver star saying Chicago Police Force.

Mickey hurried home thru the snowy boulevard from her job; slid on sheets of ice with glee in gym shoes; eager to press Lucy down on her back, spread her legs, and take her in the dominant position.

Tonight was not just the anticipation of sex; but eager wonder—about the place she knew they would go.

Psychedelics had just come about, an invention in a chemical lab—a mind-altering drug. Wired-up beatniks went barefoot, even in icy snow & in disregard for broken glass.

Minds discussed the Buddha & the end of material possession.

There was a fire inside Mickey she didn't know she had.

So Mickey still wouldn't have left town, but Lucy's fierce need to escape reality, her drug yen, pushed the issue. Mickey bitterly pounded her fist in her hand. Lucy had shot up more of their money. Had snuck out to Phyllis's and had returned pleasantly high; prepared dinner & then lay back obediently & did it—gave the butch her nightly fuck. An odd half-smile, like a mad Mona Lisa on her lips as she drifted in and out of conscious.

Cracks ran on the walls overhead; holes in the plaster where Lucy's gay purple & red & yellow, & green tie-dye hadn't covered.

'I can't get a job that pays enough.' Mickey was morose. So there was nothing she could do, but rob & kill and go to jail; so she had accepted Lucy's trick money and this was the beginning of the end. Hated Lucy for that.

Then another girl disappeared off a bar stool—in jail for murdering a man.

And it was one of the nice girls, who worked an honest job. A nondescript female with acne on her face, of legal age—

22. A former boyfriend before she'd turned gay had followed her around for a year, threatening her, assaulting her using the advantage of his greater size & strength. Finally she picked up an equalizer and shot him dead.

Mickey's untouched tears weren't enough. 'The world don't have Lucy, and I don't have Lucy.'

A few more lines would harden in their faces.

Bragged to Rusty & Gerry about her men's suits & rings & heavy gold jewelry—that she'd sold. Lots of expensive men's after-shave and cologne. Lounging on a bar stool, legs spread, a sneer on her face; examining her fingernails with a masculine gesture she boosted her ego: "I was their pampered pet. Two girls used to undress me every night. And the third rubbed my neck muscles where tension gathers. They'd suck each other's tits, and fought over who would grab my ears and pull me down between her legs and be first for me to dive into her cunt. I lay with 3 whores in Florida. Valorie was my favorite at first, but then I liked little Scheherazade. We had sex in every position over & over. I chose to bang Sche-herazade's pussy with my clit—she rolled it the best & had plump and juicy cuntlips. And Valorie serviced me orally like a champ. We held each other's hands while someone else fucked—to show love—and squeezed their hands at their supreme moment of passion. They loved to make me cum & they said my clit was sweet. They wore their lipstick off on my cunt night & day."

So this was the history of those years when they were young & straining to be free.

Mickey craving love from a mother she'd never had; for erotica from a woman. For lusty sex between a female's legs; and peace & a home with a woman.

Although Lucy was the love of her life, realized she'd have to move on.

'Time to get out of Dodge.'

Since unconsciously having arrived at a decision, which was now apparent, Mickey felt like she'd come out of a long sickness with Lucy and the drugs and the tricks & drink.

Crossed bitter snow-run streets where that first time she & Lucy had been introduced; that crossing of Clark & Division where the Cadillac had sailed by in early summer, in the heat of sex; of the weather; & of her soul. Where she'd stood, like an unlit match waiting to be struck; waiting for some force of the universe to urge her—where, she didn't know.

Just felt an itching in her soul.

Yellow lights of foggy taverns; it's the Career Club that hates gays. The SM motorcycle bar for men only. Snowy night. You have to smear the windowpane with your hand to see out. And traffic slips on the ice & it's beginning to snow again.

The lines were drawn. A narrow cross-over point as the ice breaks apart & continents divide.

It was warm at home because of the heater Mickey had bought; & rags stopped up the broken window panes; heavy tie-dyed curtains over those.

With all the love in the universe, Mickey began to love Lucy one last time. For all the tears shed, for all the gay girls that she'd known. For the carnal. For the spiritual. For the remembrance. For her initiation as a 13-year-old tomboy to sex. What it had been like laying on her cot, staring up at the jowled face of the matron; looking out of the barred horizons of her jail home; raising from that which is base, to the highest bodily emotion in minutes. For the trips across The Cities of the Plain. From the tips of her toes to the ends of her fingers. With all the layered years of existence, learning, teaching, touching; finding a better way, and then a better way still to satisfy a woman; Mickey came to her beloved one last time....

"In Florida, Scheherazade used to lick my ass, Lucy."

So the redhead licks Mickey's ass, sucks her asshole, slides her pink tongue along the rim with thick, fat strokes and sticks it in.

"And Valorie used to lick my feet."

And Lucy kneels, takes one foot between her hands, plants kisses on it, caresses; looks up at Mickey, who's lying back on the sheets; then her tongue works between each toe, loving her butch's feet. Minutes of pleasure drift by as Mickey felt the warm damp hands of the redhead femme adoring her feet, and careful saliva wet licks & kisses bathing her. Finally, after the greater part of an hour, when she's had her fill, Mickey pulls a weary Lucy to her. Strands of red hair fall over the femme's face; her eyes, deep pools of emotion, search her butch's face, seeking a response; and Mickey kisses her on the mouth. She could taste herself on Lucy's breath.

Tonight Lucy wanted something special. She knew Mickey was leaving, was not sure when; and wanted to do this—might not get a chance with another butch—most of them were so uptight about being men locked in womanly bodies; she strapped the harness around her own waist & thighs, cock pointing out of her own brown pubic hair.

Lucy lay down on top of Mickey; shy half-smile of now-blurred pink—once-red—lipstick, crooked on her lips; and the butch spread her knees for her, yielding, the expression on her mannish face was a mixture of humor & tingling expectation of the service she was about to receive. Lucy used her fingers to play in Mickey's cuntlips till they were wet; held the thick cock in her feminine hand—it made quite a sight, this hard organ apparently grown out of her very biologically female body—and she in earrings, painted fingers & toes—like a male transsexual. She pushed the dickhead into Mickey's hole a shallow distance, & jerked it in/out to warm him up, then drove the inches in deeper, the thick member accommodated by his expanding cunt. Deeper she thrusted. "COME ON, BABY!" Mickey exclaimed after a few minutes, panting, her butch strength could no longer be repressed; and holding Lucy firmly in a hug together the two rolled over so now Mickey's on top, Lucy under—wearing the cock. The butch's cunt is filled with Lucy's hard female dick, but now she's stroking it into herself her lean hips work with rapid piston pumps, pounding 10" inside her: as her cunt demanded more. Lucy humps underneath, too; the bed creaks up/down with springy squish-squish-squish sounds; the tingling of desire races along to satisfaction thru both females thru their clits & cunts out thru their nerves up the length of their bodies from toes to heads; the feeling so fine, she felt the top of her skull was about to blow off. Mickey lunges up and down fucking on top, pushing the dick into himself; and redhead Lucy wraps her hands around the butch's pale butt, which pounds fast; wham wham wham wham driving the base of the dick against Lucy's pearl clit in ecstasy to them both; Lucy humps fast; they're both giving it everything they've got; sweat rolls off their skin; pubic hairs intermeshed, wet; straight fucking —then the butch's legs start to shake; her flat stomach quivered, rippling on its surface; orgasm shot thru his cunt up to the highest height; cunt tightened, clenched, loosened; cumming, she was cumming.

Exhausted, they lay together, panting. "Aw, Lucy, you made me cum like a man and a woman at the same time!"

Seldom had Mickey had so fine an orgasm—a cum to remember in the days to come.

Sky is slate gray. Luminescent in patches of clouds behind which the sun still shines.

For a while skid row didn't see the redhead, strangely absent from her sin. Billows of frozen waves reaching a mile out—the beach saw the two as they wandered, hand & hand. A cold chill settled in Mickey's bones.

'The girl can't help it. The girl can't help it.'

Wind caught a newspaper & told it to Fly!

1959. Tail end of the decade. Lucy was docile now. She'd stopped fighting. Waiting until Mickey left town to abandon herself to the mental/physical pleasures of The House of Phyllis. That psycho-sex erotic drug yen.

Stopped fighting for love. Fighting for food, or for recognition of her sexual identity amid a world which tried to pull her both ways at once: straight, gay, each to its own opposite corner. The colorful boxes on the table remained empty of cans. If there was food, she'd eat. If not, fuck it. She forgot to care for her body, immersed herself in drug & drink.

Faces & facades.

Journey to the self, thru women & the night; and back again, healed, to a woman.

'What living's all about'—Mickey knew—'is to be simple & happy.' Her mouth was dry like cotton; a hangover from their night at the new gaybar.

Lucy & Mickey frequented this place with its purple

banners. The butch knew & tried to explain to the redhead: "It's hard to get the streets out of your system." Lucy was close to being hooked on it; & to those dilapidated buildings which begrudgingly had given them a transient home. Mickey wanted to escape.

Yellow light beaming down from a fallen gape-hole ceiling; musty odor of age & piss....

At a turn of the 2nd stair at the Hotel Bristol lay the evidence: wino drools at the mouth, shuffling nowhere; unable to make one word connect with the next. Can't make sentence of conversation that makes sense. Mind swimming in a haze of pea-green soup.

Couldn't the half-breed Indian woman see them? The end result in the last stop on the assembly line—instead of being put together—battered into bits & pieces? To heed the red light, a warning to STOP?

Late one night, Mickey heard it again. Coming from another room in their hotel, that music introducing the stage show at the Rialto Theatre—those trumpets, the inspired song.

'A lot of these girls that are down here, who spent the summer on this scene, by next season they've been blown away. Gone to Miami, or New York, Boston, or out to Frisco or L.A. Seeking new lives, fresh starts, new identities closer to the one they've always dreamed they were.'

CHAPTER FIFTY

So Mickey began running around Chi-town with her hot clit loose, after women, femmes, any female who would lie down.

Judy dressed up as if she was going to fancy straight night-clubs; regularly left her parents house in the Jewish sector with a fake boyfriend and came to the gay clubs—even that toilet 169 Club with holes in its floor; had been there wearing a black silk evening gown, pearls, high-heel pumps; fur wrap, a stunning tiara in hair cascading down over her shoulders.

Judy ached to try out the tough-looking stud Mickey. Stood in a slinky pose at the bar with her pretend boyfriend—they made such a good couple—adjusting the black strap of her gown.

Judy sent a note written in eyebrow pencil on the back of a bar napkin plus a drink to Mickey. Soon the two disappeared into the women's toilet together.

Tiny gray-painted cubicle containing a commode sink. Several gay girls waited outside impatient—to piss, but they had to wait.

They pressed full bodied against each other, clits against one another's thigh. Mickey felt the movement of Judy's leg grind urgently against her sex; soft hands caress her shoulders, down her back, to her ass, pulling her closer; felt her sex pulse pound in response.

Rhythm of music from the jukebox. Their tongue swirl in a delirious kiss.

Mickey was having sex with everybody.

Was torn by the imagination of what new loves she could have, & what love could have been.

Cold winter. Frozen. Ice. An older Mickey might one day remember this was a time when she was severely torn. Wanting her relationship to last, but having great needs to the contrary.

Two persons with different urgings drawing them separate ways.

Might remember that she'd wanted to go to Lake Michigan and jump into the deep blue water and drown.

It was the hardest decision she had to make in her life.

To fight like hell—by leaving.

Because she was weary of feeling powerless and wanted to feel like somebody. A courageous and handsome Mickey. Stuff happened to build her ego up, then send it crashing down into fragments. Several young girls hung around admiring, went to bed with Mickey, promised to show up again. And didn't.

It was the silent scream.

Vowed to change her luck. Rain of blows upon her conscious—invisible448 blows; none of the gay kids knew what was happening to them but that it was a struggle.

Mickey, in her course of 19 years on this planet earth had

learned to bow her head to larger males; to give society deference; to walk quietly, to step aside:

But to not lie down. To Be. In her burned a fierce resolve, stronger than before!

Mickey was very near the end of her stay in Chi-town; the rope was frayed; she was hanging on to it by her fingernails; by her money problems; her Lucy problems. A strain of anger torrents thru her days—had become a highway getting wider, pushing her out to the open road.

'Get out of Dodge... Get out of town....'

End: Tragicomic characters rise to Victory!

God Our Lady had created her butch; to be a lesbian/man; a being both visible & invisible. A face & body, a skin color wrapped over an erotic force, a character, a dream, & a desire webbed between skin & muscle & vein & bone.

They take everything you got down on skid row. Drink gets your job; then thieves steal your clothes, furnishings, home. Then they start on you. Nobody has any front teeth down on lower Clark Street. They take it all.

Your memories of the past.

Your hope for the future.

Soon spring would be around once more; the little lame balloonman whistling far & wee; to see who was left among the old troops.

A whole young crew of gay kids danced with frantic abandon as the ticking hourglass of time cast their shadows against the tavern wall by night; dancers like the trotters racing to the finish line.

Mickey felt older than the rest.

It had taken a long hard journey to get this far. Now, at last she could see thru the foggy glass of the unconscious—the door was half-open—a new summer was right outside; the Fledgling was going to fly on wings of opportunity!

She was going to shape up in California, definitely go to school with no doubt, get a career, & meet a nice lesbian girl. Keep doing her exercises and create her own destiny. That was what she had seen—for the future. That triumph was something possible to create, from within herself.

These were the kids. This was The Life. Late fifties, early sixties. A few went back to the straight side. More dykes and fags modified their behavior & appearance. A few—strong enough —survived as they were.

Mickey had fought the battle over a very long period of time & thru such great adversity.

Even Duke & Freddy split the scene, headed due southwest to pick strawberries in southern California; pick peas, lettuce & then move on.

"I hear there's people going around with bells on, long hair, who don't know who they are!... They wear sandals. And play guitars. All sorts of free freaks. So anyone there can be free. It's because of the climate—kind of like Florida, it's so hot. It makes all sorts of strange rapid growth of a tropic climate. It's like the same way the vegetation grows thicker— well, so do the people. They sleep on the beach. You don't have to sleep in the subway."

To cast her fate on the Great Mandala. That East Indian symbol of prosperity.

"Yeah, and there's a bunch of old dykes out there, 26 at least, and getting older; they decide to have children together and start getting pregnant! And they have their own Lady Doctors to help them do this!

"You can achieve things in California. If you're on the bottom of the ladder they treat you the same as the top. They accept you, whatever you are."

Lucy went to Phyllis for moral support. The redhead wore beautiful sea-green pants, a tropic turquoise-blue blouse, and a wispy pale yellow scarf under her big cloth winter coat; and rust-color boots for the snow; bought at the Thrift Shop on Mickey's paycheck.

The streets are alive with electrical sounds of the subway buried under asphalt. And that would carry Mickey to the train depot; and its rails pass out of state; past named cities & towns on a map which flee to history. Leave—the same way she had come in. Fancied what gay kids would be wearing out West— like Gaugin floral paintings; purples, yellows; fruit reds; as so were the styles of Miami of summer. California's warm, pleasant weather.

Was this life she'd entered into all a dream? The world she'd passed into and prepared to leave?

Would she ever be with Lucy again?

Had their love been just a charade? And in their embrace no compassion to rekindle?

Train will pass over the desert; just rolling on. Nothing but sand...once a great sea bottom. Sand, with a few tumble-weeds. Covered in patches by ten-inch-thick stubble of green vegetation... Tall thick cactus...like mutants on the moon. And that's all. The brown sand-land...sand colored by purple patches of strange flowers. Of topsoil earth; specks that have blown there from miles away and eons ago. Above, stratus of clouds moved by an occasional flapping bird uttering a shriek-ing cry.... And the conscious mind is a pinpoint of light. A raft supporting us over a great abyss.

View set against the momentous brown mountains that rise and fall hundreds, thousands of miles, that dwarf us; there we seem so much to be as a child's silver toy train made miniature in proportion, placed in the rise and scope of this land, opening into a scale model; and people are just pinup figurines, rigid, inside cellophane pasted-on windows in toy cars of alum-inum.... The train winds along a precipice where bramble falls away to an esca-lating drop of 100 city blocks.... We twist & turn serpentine. 8 silver train cars circumventing the mountains and in other places passing right thru them, via cast-iron tunnels bored thru the insides of rock to emerge on the other side, still winding.

Duke & Freddy said they were going to California. Where were they? Arrested for hitchhiking and possession of drugs; in the County Jail.

If someone looked back on it, they would say some of the gay humans were very brave.

To cross great contrasts of empty space, leaving their compact cities & their small worlds built inside. Some were sensitive & afraid—their journey was the hardest, but the best. Some were too afraid and didn't go. And there were those who felt nothing and went out & got little.

God gives us a body. We wear it until it gets old; then we throw it away.

So it is not the material things of this world that will pass into decay; possessions like TV sets, houses, property to be burnt up by the flames of time; but that which inflames the heart & soul of people—That's greater. To give up these material things for some greater vision. Something that lies beyond self and comfort; that touches the universe in totality of each person. So, also, it was a selfish act; each dyke & fag seated on a bar stool had picked up the lavender banner to carry it, thru the challenges, in the achievement of Outlaws; and run with it awhile—in the mainstream of all gay people.

After Mickey left town, Lucy became the town whore—for women only. Rusty came first, then Gerry; and other butches of the club. They lined up to be with her. The redhead did everything Mickey had taught her to do in bed to please a butch, except fist. That was for Mickey. But she couldn't hold on to any of them, & she in turn, ran thru their masculine square-tipped fingers like quicksilver. "She never goes steady with any butch. Lucy's waiting for Mickey to come back," says an old-timer who knows the scene.

Mickey awoke from a dream; didn't know if she'd been forward or backward in time.

—So all she could do was awake and strain to see beyond the veil of consciousness.

She was somewhere, in a world rife with danger.

There was no peace on earth; only restlessness.

Long stretches of highways marked by lights.

'Maybe I will find a place someday, somewhere a place... And maybe have a woman like Lucy waiting for me, but clean & sober, and not laying down for anyone but me.'

So these are the exploits of the bold & brave Mickey.

An aggressive lesbian butch.

She had races to run, & she stood the test of time.

There were other broads to bang. A few days, and horniness set in. No woman's cunt to ride, nor arms embracing her in love; legs spread as she takes her.

Would meet a new lover, fuck her cunt, suck; and get her fill.

She was out on the streets again!

ROSEBUD BOOKS

THE ROSEBUD READER

Rosebud Books—the hottest-selling line of lesbian erotica available—here collects the very best of the best. Rosebud has contributed greatly to the burgeoning genre of lesbian erotica—to the point that authors like Lindsay Welsh, Aarona Griffin and Valentina Cilescu are among the hottest and most closely watched names in lesbian and gay publishing. Here are the finest moments from Rosebud's contemporary classics. $5.95/319-8

ELIZABETH OLIVER

PAGAN DREAMS

Cassidy and Samantha plan a vacation at a secluded bed-and-breakfast, hoping for a little personal time alone. Their hostess, however, has different plans. The lovers are plunged into a world of dungeons and pagan rites, as the merciless Anastasia steals Samantha for her own. B&B—B&D-style! $5.95/295-7

SUSAN ANDERS

PINK CHAMPAGNE

Tasty, torrid tales of butch/femme couplings—from a writer more than capable of describing the special fire ignited when opposites collide. Tough as nails or soft as silk, these women seek out their antitheses, intent on working out the details of their own personal theory of difference. $5.95/282-5

LAVENDER ROSE

Anonymous

A classic collection of lesbian literature: From the writings of Sappho, Queen of the island Lesbos, to the turn-of-the-century *Black Book of Lesbianism*; from *Tips to Maidens* to *Crimson Hairs*, a recent lesbian saga—here are the great but little-known lesbian writings and revelations. $4.95/208-6

EDITED BY LAURA ANTONIOU

LEATHERWOMEN II

A follow-up volume to the popular and controversial *Leatherwomen*. Laura Antoniou turns an editor's discerning eye to the writing of women on the edge—resulting in a collection sure to ignite libidinal flames. Leave taboos behind—because these Leatherwomen know no limits.... $4.95/229-9

LEATHERWOMEN

These fantasies, from the pens of new or emerging authors, break every rule imposed on women's fantasies. The hottest stories from some of today's newest and most outrageous writers make this an unforgettable exploration of the female libido. $4.95/3095-4

LESLIE CAMERON

THE WHISPER OF FANS

"Just looking into her eyes, she felt that she knew a lot about this woman. She could see strength, boldness, a fresh sense of aliveness that rocked her to the core. In turn she felt open, revealed under the woman's gaze—all her secrets already told. No need of shame or artifice...." $5.95/259-0

AARONA GRIFFIN

PASSAGE AND OTHER STORIES

An S/M romance. Lovely Nina is frightened by her lesbian passions until she finds herself infatuated with a woman she spots at a local café. One night Nina follows her and finds herself enmeshed in an endless maze leading to a mysterious world where women test the edges of sexuality and power. $4.95/3057-1

ROSEBUD BOOKS

VALENTINA CILESCU

THE ROSEBUD SUTRA

"Women are hardly ever known in their true light, though they may love others, or become indifferent towards them, may give them delight, or abandon them, or may extract from them all the wealth that they possess." So says *The Rosebud Sutra*—a volume promising women's inner secrets. One woman learns to use these secrets in a quest for pleasure with a succession of lady loves.... $4.95/242-6

THE HAVEN

The shocking story of a dangerous woman on the run—and the innocents she takes with her on a trip to Hell. J craves domination, and her perverse appetites lead her to the Haven: the isolated sanctuary Ros and Annie call home. Soon J forces her way into the couple's world, bringing unspeakable lust and cruelty into their lives. The Dominatrix Who Came to Dinner! $4.95/165-9

MISTRESS MINE

Sophia Cranleigh sits in prison, accused of authoring the "obscene" *Mistress Mine*. For Sophia has led no ordinary life, but has slaved and suffered—deliciously—under the hand of the notorious Mistress Malin. How long had she languished under the dominance of this incredible beauty? $4.95/109-8

LINDSAY WELSH

PROVINCETOWN SUMMER

This completely original collection is devoted exclusively to white-hot desire between women. From the casual encounters of women on the prowl to the enduring erotic bonds between old lovers, the women of *Provincetown Summer* will set your senses on fire! A nationally best-selling title. $5.95/362-7

NECESSARY EVIL

What's a girl to do? When her Mistress proves too systematic, too by-the-book, one lovely submissive takes the ultimate chance—choosing and creating a Mistress who'll fulfill her heart's desire. Little did she know how difficult it would be—and, in the end, rewarding.... $5.95/277-9

A VICTORIAN ROMANCE

Lust-letters from the road. A young Englishwoman realizes her dream—a trip abroad under the guidance of her eccentric maiden aunt. Soon the young but blossoming Elaine comes to discover her own sexual talents, as a hot-blooded Parisian named Madelaine takes her Sapphic education in hand. $5.95/365-1

A CIRCLE OF FRIENDS

The author of the nationally best-selling *Provincetown Summer* returns with the story of a remarkable group of women. Slowly, the women pair off to explore all the possibilities of lesbian passion, until finally it seems that there is nothing—and no one—they have not dabbled in. $4.95/250-7

PRIVATE LESSONS

A high voltage tale of life at The Whitfield Academy for Young Women—where cruel headmistress Devon Whitfield presides over the in-depth education of only the most talented and delicious of maidens. Elizabeth Dunn arrives at the Academy, where it becomes clear that she has much to learn—to the delight of Devon Whitfield and her randy staff of Mistresses! $4.95/116-0

BAD HABITS

What does one do with a poorly trained slave? Break her of her bad habits, of course! The story of te ultimate finishing school, *Bad Habits* was an immediate favorite with women nationwide. "Talk about passing the wet test!... If you like hot, lesbian erotica, run—don't walk...and pick up a copy of *Bad Habits*."—*Lambda Book Report* $4.95/3068-7

ROSEBUD BOOKS

ANNABELLE BARKER

MOROCCO

A luscious young woman stands to inherit a fortune—if she can only withstand the ministrations of her cruel guardian until her twentieth birthday. With two months left, Lila makes a bold bid for freedom, only to find that liberty has its own excruciating and delicious price.... $4.95/148-9

A.L. REINE

DISTANT LOVE & OTHER STORIES

A book of seductive tales. In the title story, Leah Michaels and her lover Ranelle have had four years of blissful, smoldering passion together. One night, when Ranelle is out of town, Leah records an audio "Valentine," a cassette filled with erotic reminiscences.... $4.95/3056-3

RHINOCEROS BOOKS

GARY BOWEN

DIARY OF A VAMPIRE

"Gifted with a darkly sensual vision and a fresh voice, [Bowen] is a writer to watch out for." —*Cecilia Tan*
The chilling, arousing, and ultimately moving memoirs of an undead—but all too human—soul. Johnson's Rafael, a red-blooded male with an insatiable hunger for same, is the perfect antidote to the effete malcontents haunting bookstores today. *Diary of a Vampire* marks the emergence of a bold and brilliant vision, firmly rooted in past *and* present. $6.95/331-7

ANONYMOUS

FLESHLY ATTRACTIONS

Lucien Hardanges was the son of the wantonly beautiful actress, Marie-Rose Hardanges. When she decides to let a "friend" introduce her son to the pleasures of love, Marie-Rose could not have foretold the erotic excesses that would eventually lead to her own ruin and that of her cherished son. A Victorian rarity, intact! $6.95/299-X

EDITED BY LAURA ANTONIOU

SOME WOMEN

Over forty essays written by women actively involved in consensual dominance and submission. Professional mistresses, lifestyle leatherdykes, whipmakers, titleholders—women from every conceivable walk of life lay bare their true feelings about about issues as explosive as feminism, abuse, pleasures and public image. $6.95/300-7

BY HER SUBDUED

Stories of women who get what they want. The tales in this collection all involve women in control—of their lives, their loves, their men. So much in control, in fact, that they can remorselessly break rules to become the powerful goddesses of the men who sacrifice all to worship at their feet. $6.95/281-7

JEAN STINE

SEASON OF THE WITCH

"A future in which it is technically possible to transfer the total mind... of a rapist killer into the brain dead but physically living body of his female victim. Remarkable for intense psychological technique. There is eroticism but it is necessary to mark the differences between the sexes and the subtle altering of a man into a woman." —*The Science Fiction Critic* $6.95/268-X

RHINOCEROS BOOKS

JOHN WARREN
THE LOVING DOMINANT

Everything you need to know about an infamous sexual variation—and an unspoken type of love. Mentor—a longtime player in the dominance/submission scene—guides readers through this world and reveals the too-often hidden basis of the D/S relationship: care, trust and love. $6.95/218-3

GRANT ANTREWS
SUBMISSIONS

Once again, Antrews portrays the very special elements of the dominant/submissive relationship...with restraint—this time with the story of a lonely man, a winning lottery ticket, and a demanding dominatrix. One of erotica's most discerning writers. $6.95/207-8

MY DARLING DOMINATRIX

When a man and a woman fall in love, it's supposed to be simple, uncomplicated, easy—unless that woman happens to be a dominatrix. Curiosity gives way to unblushing desire in this story of one man's awakening to the joys to be experienced as the willing slave of a powerful woman. A touching volume, devoid of sleaze or shame. $6.95/3055-5

LAURA ANTONIOU WRITING AS "SARA ADAMSON"
THE TRAINER

The long-awaited conclusion of Adamson's stunning Marketplace Trilogy! The ultimate underground sexual realm includes not only willing slaves, but the exquisite trainers who take submissives firmly in hand. And it is now the time for these mentors to divulge their own secrets—the desires that led them to become the ultimate figures of authority. Only Sara Adamson could conjure so bewitching a portrait of punishing pleasure. $6.95/249-3

THE SLAVE

The second volume in the "Marketplace" trilogy. *The Slave* covers the experience of one exceptionally talented submissive who longs to join the ranks of those who have proven themselves worthy of entry into the Marketplace. But the price, while delicious, is staggeringly high.... Adamson's plot thickens, as her trilogy moves to a conclusion in the forthcoming *The Trainer*. $6.95/173-X

THE MARKETPLACE

"Merchandise does not come easily to the Marketplace.... They haunt the clubs and the organizations.... Some of them are so ripe that they intimidate the poseurs, the weekend sadists and the furtive dilettantes who are so endemic to that world. And they never stop asking where we may be found...." $6.95/3096-2

THE CATALYST

After viewing a controversial, explicitly kinky film full of images of bondage and submission, several audience members find themselves deeply moved by the erotic suggestions they've seen on the screen. "Sara Adamson"'s sensational debut volume! $5.95/328-7

DAVID AARON CLARK
SISTER RADIANCE

From the author of the acclaimed *The Wet Forever*, comes a chronicle of obsession, rife with Clark's trademark vivisections of contemporary desires, sacred and profane. The vicissitudes of lust and romance are examined against a backdrop of urban decay and shallow fashionability in this testament to the allure—and inevitability—of the forbidden. $6.95/215-9

RHINOCEROS BOOKS

THE WET FOREVER

The story of Janus and Madchen, a small-time hood and a beautiful sex work-er, *The Wet Forever* examines themes of loyalty, sacrifice, redemption and obsession amidst Manhattan's sex parlors and underground S/M clubs. Its combination of sex and suspense led Terence Sellers to proclaim it "evoca-tive and poetic." $6.95/117-9

ALICE JOANOU

BLACK TONGUE

"Joanou has created a series of sumptuous, brooding, dark visions of sexual obsession and is undoubtedly a name to look out for in the future." —*Redeemer*

Another seductive book of dreams from the author of the acclaimed *Tourniquet*. Exploring lust at its most florid and unsparing, *Black Tongue* is a trove of baroque fantasies—each redolent of the forbidden and inexpressible. Joanou creates some of erotica's most unforgettable characters. $6.95/258-2

TOURNIQUET

A heady collection of stories and effusions from the pen of one our most daz-zling young writers. Strange tales abound, from the story of the mysterious and cruel Cybele, to an encounter with the sadistic entertainment of a bizarre after-hours cafe. A sumptuous feast for all the senses.. $6.95/3060-1

CANNIBAL FLOWER

"She is waiting in her darkened bedroom, as she has waited throughout histo-ry, to seduce the men who are foolish enough to be blinded by her irresistible charms....She is the goddess of sexuality, and *Cannibal Flower* is her haunt-ing siren song."—Michael Perkins $4.95/72-6

MICHAEL PERKINS

EVIL COMPANIONS

Set in New York City during the tumultuous waning years of the Sixties, *Evil Companions* has been hailed as "a frightening classic." A young couple explores the nether reaches of the erotic unconscious in a shocking confronta-tion with the extremes of passion. With a new introduction by science fiction legend Samuel R. Delany. $6.95/3067-9

AN ANTHOLOGY OF CLASSIC ANONYMOUS EROTIC WRITING

Michael Perkins, acclaimed authority on erotic literature, has collected the very best passages from the world's erotic writing—especially for Rhino*ceros* readers. "Anonymous" is one of the most infamous bylines in publishing his-tory—and these steamy excerpts show why! $6.95/140-3

THE SECRET RECORD: Modern Erotic Literature

Michael Perkins, a renowned author and critic of sexually explicit fic-tion, surveys the field with authority and unique insight. Updated and revised to include the latest trends, tastes, and developments in this misunderstood and maligned genre. An important volume for every erot-ic reader and fan of high quality adult fiction. $6.95/3039-3

HELEN HENLEY

ENTER WITH TRUMPETS

Helen Henley was told that woman just don't write about sex—much less the taboos she was so interested in exploring. So Henley did it alone, flying in the face of "tradition" by producing *Enter With Trumpets*, a touching tale of arousal and devotion in one couple's kinky relationship. $6.95/197-7

RHINOCEROS BOOKS

PHILIP JOSÉ FARMER

FLESH

Space Commander Stagg explored the galaxies for 800 years, and could only hope that he would be welcomed home by an adoring—or at least *appreciative*—public. Upon his return, the hero Stagg is made the centerpiece of an incredible public ritual—one that will repeatedly take him to the heights of ecstasy, and inexorably drag him toward the depths of hell. $6.95/303-1

A FEAST UNKNOWN

"Sprawling, brawling, shocking, suspenseful, hilarious…"—Theodore Sturgeon
Farmer's supreme anti-hero returns. *A Feast Unknown* begins in 1968, with Lord Grandrith's stunning statement: "I was conceived and born in 1888." Slowly, Lord Grandrith—armed with the belief that he is the son of Jack the Ripper—tells the story of his remarkable and unbridled life. Beginning with his discovery of the secret of immortality, Grandrith's tale proves him no raving lunatic—but something far more bizarre…. $6.95/276-0

THE IMAGE OF THE BEAST

Herald Childe has seen Hell, glimpsed its horror in an act of sexual mutilation. Childe must now find and destroy an inhuman predator through the streets of a polluted and decadent Los Angeles of the future. One clue after another leads Childe to an inescapable realization about the nature of sex and evil…. $6.95/166-7

SAMUEL R. DELANY

EQUINOX

The *Scorpion* has sailed the seas in a quest for every possible pleasure. Her crew is a collection of the young, the twisted, the insatiable. A drifter comes into their midst, and is taken on a fantastic journey to the darkest, most dangerous sexual extremes—until he is finally a victim to their boundless appetites. $6.95/157-8

ANDREI CODRESCU

THE REPENTANCE OF LORRAINE

"One of our most prodigiously talented and magical writers."

—**NYT Book Review**

An aspiring writer, a professor's wife, a secretary, gold anklets, Maoists, Roman harlots—and more—swirl through this spicy tale of a harried quest for a mythic artifact. Written when the author was a young man, this lusty yarn was inspired by the heady—and hot—days and nights of the Sixties. $6.95/329-5

DAVID MELTZER

ORF

He is the ultimate musician-hero—the idol of thousands, the fevered dream of many more. And like many musicians before him, he is misunderstood, misused—and totally out of control. Every last drop of feeling is squeezed from a modern-day troubadour and his lady love. $6.95/110-1

LEOPOLD VON SACHER-MASOCH

VENUS IN FURS

This classic 19th century novel is the first uncompromising exploration of the dominant/submissive relationship in literature. The alliance of Severin and Wanda epitomizes Sacher-Masoch's dark obsession with a cruel, controlling goddess and the urges that drive the man held in her thrall. The letters exchanged between Sacher-Masoch and an aspiring writer he sought as the avatar of his forbidden desires—are also included. $6.95/3089-X

RHINOCEROS BOOKS

SOPHIE GALLEYMORE BIRD

MANEATER

Through a bizarre act of creation, a man attains the "perfect" lover—by all appearances a beautiful, sensuous woman but in reality something far darker. Once brought to life she will accept no mate, seeking instead the prey that will sate her hunger for vengeance. A biting take on the war of the sexes, this debut goes for the jugular of the "perfect woman" myth. $6.95/103-9

TUPPY OWENS

SENSATIONS

A piece of porn history. Tuppy Owens tells the unexpurgated story of the making of *Sensations*—the first big-budget sex flick. Originally commissioned to appear in book form after the release of the film in 1975, *Sensations* is finally released under Masquerade's stylish Rhino*ceros* imprint. $6.95/3081-4

DANIEL VIAN

ILLUSIONS

Two disturbing tales of danger and desire in Berlin on the eve of WWII. From private homes to lurid cafés to decaying streets, passion is explored, exposed, and placed in stark contrast to the brutal violence of the time. A singularly arousing volume. $6.95/3074-1

PERSUASIONS

"The stockings are drawn tight by the suspender belt, tight enough to be stretched to the limit just above the middle part of her thighs..." A double novel, including the classics *Adagio* and *Gabriela and the General*, this volume traces desire around the globe. International lust! $6.95/183-7

LIESEL KULIG

LOVE IN WARTIME

An uncompromising look at the politics, perils and pleasures of sexual power. Madeleine knew that the handsome SS officer was a dangerous man. But she was just a cabaret singer in Nazi-occupied Paris, trying to survive in a perilous time. When Josef fell in love with her, he discovered that a beautiful and amoral woman can sometimes be wildly dangerous. $6.95/3044-X

FOR A FREE COPY OF THE COMPLETE MASQUERADE CATALOG,
MAIL THIS COUPON TO:
**MASQUERADE BOOKS/DEPT HC54KT
801 SECOND AVENUE, NEW YORK, NY 10017
OR FAX TO 212 986-7355**
All transactions are strictly confidential and we never sell, give or trade any customer's name.

NAME _____

ADDRESS _____

CITY _____ STATE _____ ZIP _____

RICHARD KASAK BOOKS

EURUDICE

F/32

F/32 has been called "the most controversial and dangerous novel ever written by a woman." With the story of Ela (whose name is a pseudonym for orgasm), Eurudice won the National Fiction competition sponsored by Fiction Collective Two and Illinois State University. A funny, disturbing quest for unity, *F/32* prompted Frederic Tuten to proclaim "almost any page ... redeems us from the anemic writing and banalities we have endured in the past decade of bloodless fiction." $11.95/350-3

LARRY TOWNSEND

ASK LARRY

Twelve years of Masterful advice from Larry Townsend (*Run, Little Leatherboy*, *Chains*), the leatherman's long-time confidant and adviser. Starting just before the onslaught of AIDS, Townsend wrote the "Leather Notebook" column for *Drummer* magazine, tackling subjects from sexual technique to safer sex, whips to welts, Daddies to dog collars. Now, with *Ask Larry*, readers can avail themselves of Townsend's collected wisdom as well as the author's contemporary commentary—a careful consideration of the way life has changed in the AIDS era, and the specific ways in which the disease has altered perceptions of once-simple problems. $12.95/289-2

RUSS KICK

OUTPOSTS:
A Catalog of Rare and Disturbing Alternative Information

A huge, authoritative guide to some of the most offbeat and bizarre publications available today! Rather than simply summarize the plethora of controversial opinions crowding the American scene, Russ Kick has tracked down the real McCoy and compiled over five hundred reviews of work penned by political extremists, conspiracy theorists, hallucinogenic pathfinders, sexual explorers, religious iconoclasts and social malcontents. Better yet, each review is followed by ordering information for the many readers sure to want these remarkable publications for themselves. $18.95/0202-8

WILLIAM CARNEY

THE REAL THING

Carney gives us a good look at the mores and lifestyle of the first generation of gay leathermen. A chilling mystery/romance novel as well. —Pat Califia

With a new Introduction by Michael Bronski. Out of print for years, *The Real Thing* has long served as a touchstone in any consideration of gay "edge fiction." First published in 1968, this uncompromising story of New York leathermen received instant acclaim.. Out of print for years, *The Real Thing* returns from exile, ready to thrill a new generation—and reacquaint itself with its original audience. $10.95/280-9

MICHAEL LASSELL

THE HARD WAY

Lassell is a master of the necessary word. In an age of tepid and whining verse, his bawdy and bittersweet songs are like a plunge in cold champagne. —Paul Monette

The first collection of renowned gay writer Michael Lassell's poetry, fiction and essays. Widely anthologized and a staple of gay literary and entertainment publications nationwide, Lassell is regarded as one of the most distinctive talents of his generation. As much a chronicle of post-Stonewall gay life as a compendium of a remarkable writer's work. $12.95/231-0

RICHARD KASAK BOOKS

LOOKING FOR MR. PRESTON

Edited by Laura Antoniou, *Looking for Mr. Preston* includes work by **Lars Eighner, Pat Califia, Michael Bronski, Felice Picano, Joan Nestle, Larry Townsend, Sasha Alyson, Andrew Holleran, Michael Lowenthal**, and others who contributed interviews, essays and personal reminiscences of John Preston—a man whose career spanned the industry from the early pages of the *Advocate* to various national bestseller lists. Preston was the author of over twenty books, including *Franny, the Queen of Provincetown*, and *Mr. Benson*. He also edited the noted *Flesh and the Word* erotic anthologies, *Personal Dispatches: Writers Confront AIDS*, and *Hometowns*,. More importantly, Preston became a personal inspiration, friend and mentor to many of today's gay and lesbian authors and editors. Ten percent of the proceeds from sale of the book will go to the AIDS Project of Southern Maine, for which Preston had served as President of the Board. $23.95/288-4

AMARANTHA KNIGHT, EDITOR
LOVE BITES

A volume of tales dedicated to legend's sexiest demon—the Vampire. Amarantha Knight, herself an author who has delved into vampire lore, has gathered the very best writers in the field to produce a collection of uncommon, and chilling, allure. Including such names as Ron Dee, Nancy A. Collins, Nancy Kilpatrick, Lois Tilton and David Aaron Clark, *Love Bites* is not only the finest collection of erotic horror available—but a virtual who's who of promising new talent. $12.95/234-5

MICHAEL LOWENTHAL, EDITOR
THE BEST OF THE BADBOYS

A collection of the best of Masquerade Books' phenomenally popular Badboy line of gay erotic writing. Badboy 's sizable roster includes many names that are legendary in gay circles. The very best of the leading Badboys is collected here, in this testament to the artistry that has catapulted these "outlaw" authors to bestselling status. John Preston, Aaron Travis, Larry Townsend, John Rowberry, Clay Caldwell and Lars Eighner are here represented by their most provocative writing. Michael Lowenthal both edited this remarkable collection and provides the Introduction. $12.95/233-7

GUILLERMO BOSCH
RAIN

An adult fairy tale, *Rain* takes place in a time when the mysteries of Eros are played out against a background of uncommon deprivation. The tale begins on the 1,537th day of drought—when one man comes to know the true depths of thirst. In a quest to sate his hunger for some knowledge of the wide world, he is taken through a series of extraordinary, unearthly encounters that promise to change not only his life, but the course of civilization around him. A remarkable debut novel. $12.95/232-9

LUCY TAYLOR
UNNATURAL ACTS

"A topnotch collection..." —Science Fiction Chronicle

A remarkable debut volume from a provocative writer. *Unnatural Acts* plunges deep into the dark side of the psyche, far past all pleasantries and prohibitions, and brings to life a disturbing vision of erotic horror. Unrelenting angels and hungry gods play with souls and bodies in Taylor's murky cosmos: where heaven and hell are merely differences of perspective; where redemption and damnation lie behind the same shocking acts. $12.95/181-0

ORDERING IS EASY!

MC/VISA orders can be placed by calling our toll-free number
PHONE 800-375-2356 / FAX 212 986-7355
or mail the coupon below to:
MASQUERADE BOOKS
DEPT. HC54AT, 801 2ND AVE., NY, NY 10017

BUY ANY FOUR BOOKS AND CHOOSE ONE ADDITIONAL BOOK, OF EQUAL OR LESSER VALUE, AS YOUR FREE GIFT.

QTY.	TITLE	NO.	PRICE
			FREE
			FREE

HC54AT

	SUBTOTAL
	POSTAGE and HANDLING
We Never Sell, Give or Trade Any Customer's Name.	**TOTAL**

In the U.S., please add $1.50 for the first book and 75¢ for each additional book; in Canada, add $2.00 for the first book and $1.25 for each additional book. Foreign countries: add $4.00 for the first book and $2.00 for each additional book. No C.O.D. orders. Please make all checks payable to Masquerade Books. Payable in U.S. currency only. New York state residents add 8¼% sales tax. Please allow 4-6 weeks delivery.

NAME _____

ADDRESS _____

CITY _____ STATE _____ ZIP _____

TEL ( ) _____

PAYMENT: ☐ CHECK ☐ MONEY ORDER ☐ VISA ☐ MC

CARD NO. _____ EXP. DATE _____